"MY FATHER FIGURES THERE'S SOME KIND OF ISSUE WITH SUCCESSION BACK ON THE HOME WORLD."

"How so?" White asked. "There were plenty of other children and grandchildren."

"When you left. Maybe not now." Martini managed a weak grin in my direction. "You wouldn't like the succession rules."

"Male lines, male children only, right?"

"Right."

"Similar to Earth, Jeff."

"Only, on Earth, if there is no male child, they'll allow a female to rule."

"Not so on the old home world?" I asked White.

"Not so far as we know."

"And since Christopher's male, there's a chance he could be involved in the succession issues." Martini was so upset he could barely talk. "So they're coming here. But it's not to attend the wedding, most likely. At least, that's not the main goal."

I got a funny feeling. "What are they coming for, then, Jeff?"

He looked straight at me, and I could tell how much he hated what he had to say to me. "To pass judgment on whether or not you're appropriate royal marriage material."

"This delightful romp has many interesting twists and turns as it glances at racism, politics, and religion en route. It will have fanciers of cinematic sf parodies referencing *Men in Black*, *Ghostbusters*, and *X-Men*."
—*Booklist* (starred review)

DAW Books Presents GINI KOCH's
Alien Novels:

TOUCHED BY AN ALIEN
ALIEN TANGO
ALIEN IN THE FAMILY
ALIEN PROLIFERATION
(*coming in December 2011*)

ALIEN
IN THE FAMILY
GINI KOCH

DAW BOOKS, INC.

DONALD A. WOLLHEIM, FOUNDER

375 Hudson Street, New York, NY 10014

**ELIZABETH R. WOLLHEIM
SHEILA E. GILBERT
PUBLISHERS**

http://www.dawbooks.com

First Printing, April 2011
1 2 3 4 5 6 7 8 9

To Mom & Dad and Mumsy & Daddy,
for proving there really are people out there
who mate for life; and to Steve, who made sure
there are two more of us who do.

ACKNOWLEDGMENTS

Thanks and many "I am not worthies" to Sheila Gilbert for always saying those magic words every author dreams of hearing from her editor and continuously helping make my writing stronger and better, and to Cherry Weiner for still being the best there is—agent, friend, sounding-board, and shoulder.

To Lisa Dovichi, Crit Partner Extraordinaire, and to Mary Fiore, Beta Reader to the Stars, I say what I've been saying all along: Still couldn't do it without you.

Many thanks to The Galaxy Express, the Science Fiction Romance Brigade, 1st Turning Point, and Desert Rose RWA for tons of support and promotion. Same again to everyone at Haggard Chiropractic, Hand & Stone Paradise Valley, and Innerlooks Salon for continuous support and promotion, even though books are not your businesses. Much love and many shout outs to the awesome book review bloggers out there—there's too many to list here (though you're all on my Blog Roll), but you all do more to keep books alive and going strong than any others, and you have the love and thanks of this grateful alien nation.

Extra shout outs to: Gabrielle Weber for being my biggest little fan; author Amber Scott for continuous cheering, support, and enthusiasm; artist Daniel Dos Santos whose brilliant, beautiful covers make my books come alive; and Danny and Akiko, for insisting I practice reading aloud to them before hitting the con circuit (and thereby saving me from sounding like a speed-reading squirrel on amphetamines).

Thanks again to everyone I thanked the last times, anyone I might have missed at any time, and everyone else added into the "family" and the Big Dawg Pack along the way, for all you do and keep on doing—you know who you are and why I love and appreciate you. (If you're saying, but does she mean *me*, the answer is yes, yes I do.)

Extra special thanks to Team Gini, all those on Hook Me Up!, and all Alien Collective Members in Very Good Standing around the globe—you're the best fans EVER and each and every one of you totally rock my world.

Finally, as before and always, the biggest thanks and all my love to Steve and Veronica—I couldn't have created a better husband and daughter than you are in real life.

IN SPRINGTIME A YOUNG ALIEN'S THOUGHTS turn to love. And marriage. And, as fast as possible, the baby carriage.

Dating anyone from a different culture can be hard. Try dating one from a different planet. Oh, and working with him, too. Every day. Every single day.

I like being a superbeing exterminator. The hours are kind of random, but the benefits are great, especially the benefit of getting to live and work with the most gorgeous people on Earth. Sure, they have two hearts, can run at hyperspeed, and actually come from Alpha Centauri. But, hey, they're just regular folks, for the most part.

On the other hand, planning a wedding with one of them is not the easiest fish to fry. Not, realistically, that frying fish is all that hard. Not that I would, personally, know, either, since I avoid active participation in all kitchens except under extreme duress. Okay, fish fry equals bad example.

But mixing wedding planning along with protecting the Earth from all the threats, internal and extremely external, that plague it on a daily freaking basis is not a piece of cake. Particularly when you already come from a religiously mixed family and are mixing in a third one. That you can't tell your family about. No worries, been lying to them about my career change for almost a year, not like telling the grandparents another whopper will kill them. Right?

I'll just keep them distracted with lots of doublespeak and focus their attention on things like flowers and seating arrangements. Before they know it, the wedding will be over, and they'll all go back to their lives, none the wiser.

Yeah, I know. It's one of my plans. It'll go all *Dog Day Afternoon* somewhere along the line. But a girl can dream, can't she?

CHAPTER 1

"**W**HY ARE WE WAITING OUT HERE** in the middle of the night?" Martini asked for what, by my count, was the tenth time in less than an hour.

"Because Chuckie said there was something here we needed to see, Jeff. You know, like I've said for the past, oh, hours?"

"Why do you insist on calling him Chuckie?" Martini was really in a mood. Possibly because we'd been interrupted in the middle of a very romantic dinner by Chuckie's phone call. To me, not to Martini.

"Because that's what I've called him since ninth grade, and calling him Mister Reynolds seems sort of stupid, calling him Charles sounds like I think he's my uncle, and if I'm going to call him Chuck, then I'm going to add on the 'e.'" Of course, I knew the real reason Martini wasn't happy. But I wasn't going to bring it up. We'd had the jealousy chat months ago, and he was supposed to be working on dealing with the fact that other men occasionally found me attractive and trying not to be a jerk about it. Tonight he wasn't doing so well.

"Jeff, you know you could go on back to the Science Center and let me and Kitty handle it." Reader winked at me where Martini couldn't see.

"Right, thanks for the offer, James. But just how would the two of you get out of here if there were any problems?"

Martini had a point. We were perched on the top of Animas Peak in New Mexico, staring at pretty much nothing. Reader and I, being human, would have a hard time getting anywhere fast if Martini or another Alpha Centaurion wasn't with us. On the other hand, we could drive and fly because our reflexes weren't so good that they destroyed Earth machinery. So we had that going for us.

On the other hand, we'd gotten to this point via a gate, which was alien technology that let you move hundreds or thousands of miles in seconds and had the added advantage of making you completely nauseated. On the other hand, because we weren't aliens, neither Reader nor I could actually see the gate that had deposited us here, on top of a really high mountain, in the middle of the night. (Yeah, I know, that's a lot of hands.) I thought about the drop and sidled a little closer to Martini.

My walkie chirped. "Kitty, you there?"

"Hi, Christopher. How goes it at your location?"

"Dull, dark, and boring. You sure the C.I.A.'s not trying to kill us or freeze us to death?"

"Somewhat positive. We're supposed to see something. Soon."

"I'm seeing my bed. It's nowhere near me, but I can see it."

"Hilarious. How's Tim doing?"

"He's as bored as I am. So's Paul, should you care to know. ACE, however, seems fascinated."

"Glad one of you, or at least part of one of you, isn't sitting around complaining like an old lady." ACE was a super-consciousness I'd managed to channel into Paul Gower a few months back so it couldn't accidentally destroy the entire world. ACE usually did its best to hang in the background, but whenever Paul was bored, it tended to show up a little more.

"At least it's stopped asking about our sex life," Reader muttered.

"ACE is just interested in things."

"Girlfriend, I don't even want to get into how totally unromantic you get when you have to clinically explain kissing, let alone any other sexual act, to an entity that didn't have a body for most of its existence."

I thought about it. "Um, ick."

"In a word, yeah." Reader had been the top international male supermodel for several years running. Then he'd joined up with the boys from Alpha Centauri, or A-Cs as they called themselves. He'd been an agent longer than I had, but he had somehow become my best friend in my new life. We had a lot in common, including being in love with an alien. Reader and Gower had been a couple longer than I'd known them, which was going on a year. In that time, they'd fought all of once. I'd been with Martini almost a year, and in that time we'd fought . . . a lot more than once.

I could tell Martini picked up my emotions, because he reached out and pulled me to him. As he was the most powerful empath on Earth, this wasn't a surprise. He didn't go insane from all the myriad emotions batting around everywhere and from everyone because of the blocks and other empathic-protection goodies the A-Cs knew how to install in their brains and use. Martini didn't have blocks up against my emotions. Sometimes I wondered if that was a wise choice on his part.

"Sorry," he said quietly. "I'm just tired and tired of waiting. And you're freezing."

"A little." Okay, a lot. I just didn't want to complain. I was in the standard-issue clothing for working female A-Cs—white Oxford button-down, black slim skirt, and a long, black trench coat, all Armani. I was also in Aerosole pumps because the A-Cs believed in looking good while feeling comfortable. But we were on top of a high mountain, and while the guys were in their standard black Armani suits with their white Armani shirts and their long black trench coats, they seemed to shove off the cold better, even the human guys.

Martini opened his coat, pulled me against him, and wrapped it around me. "Better?"

I snuggled up and leaned my head against his chest. "Mmmm, yeah." He was warm, and I always found his body heat and double heartbeats soothing.

"Baby? Wake up."

"I was awake."

"You don't snore when you're awake."

"I wasn't snoring!"

Reader coughed. "Um, yeah, yeah, you were."

Martini's walkie crackled. "Yeah, we could hear you snoring over here." I could tell Christopher was snickering.

"You played my snoring for them?"

Martini shrugged. "I wanted to make sure they were awake. Not my fault you were sort of loud. You coming down with a cold?"

"No, I am not. Though if we're here much longer, I might."

"Blame good ol' Conspiracy Chuck. I'm not the one who suggested a romantic rendezvous out here."

"You know I don't call him that. Only people who weren't his friends called him that."

"Which is why I feel *great* calling him that."

I let it pass. I mean, I didn't want to head into one of Martini's favorite complaints, which was that I was far too willing to take Chuckie's calls. "Besides, this isn't a date."

"I know. I'm really clear that this is not how I planned to end the evening."

I pulled my walkie out of my purse. "Jerry, you guys okay?"

"Yeah, but why is it we got stuck on the coldest ridge?" Jerry Tucker was one of the Navy Top Gun pilots assigned to Centaurion Division in general and to my Airborne team in specific. He was on Chiricahua Peak in Arizona. Christopher's team was on Big Hatchet in New Mexico. All high, all cold at this time of year, all lacking a C.I.A. operative.

"The lower-ranking officers get the cruddy locations," Reader answered into his walkie.

"Thanks. You know, Matt, Chip, and I all outrank you, James."

"Only in the Navy. Around here, experience and longevity count more." Reader was trying not to laugh.

"Then how is it Kitty's in charge of Airborne?" Tim Crawford, also part of my team, was laughing. Like Reader, Tim lived to be a smartass.

"Oh, shut up."

"It's worse over here," Christopher snapped. "We're on the edge of a knife. The rest of you at least have something to stand on."

"That's why it's two A-Cs to one human over there. Stop whining. Jerry, anything over there? At all?"

"No, but I'm really glad you guys let Michael come with us." Michael Gower was Paul's younger brother and was visiting us while on vacation from NASA. He was also an astronaut, but I doubted this was why Jerry was glad he was there. The idea of not having an A-C with you while on a scary high mountain had dawned on me already. "You know, Cochise's ghost is supposed to haunt these mountains."

"A ghost would at least be something interesting," Reader offered.

We waited a few more minutes, then I heard something different. It sounded as though a very muted sprinkler system had just started up. "Chuckie's here."

The sleek, black helicopter set down far enough away from us that we weren't too windblown. A tall man bundled up in a long overcoat got out and sauntered over to us. I attempted to move out of Martini's arms, but they were locked around me. I was cold enough I decided not to argue.

"Took you long enough, Reynolds," Martini snapped as Chuckie got near enough to hear him.

Chuckie shook his head. "Always a pleasure, Martini. Kitty, how're you doing?"

"Fine. Cold and bored, but fine."

Chuckie nodded his head toward Reader. "Good to see you."

"Damn, but you lie well," Reader said with a smile. No one but me seemed to like Chuckie. Oh, well. He didn't seem to mind.

"If you two could detach from each other for a moment? It'll make it easier to show you what's going on."

Martini let me go, slowly. I took his hand and gave it a squeeze. He relaxed a bit. "Chuckie, what *is* going on?"

He looked at his watch. "You'll see in ... oh ... about a minute and a half. Might want to let White and your other boys know it's almost showtime."

"Christopher, we're almost set."

"Yeah, the C.I.A. graciously joined us just now."

"Jerry, you have federal company yet?"

"Yes, ma'am, Commander. We are in position." Jerry and the rest of my flyboys always went into Supreme Military Mode whenever we were dealing with anyone outside Centaurion Division. No one in Centaurion liked having to deal with the C.I.A.'s ET Division. Except me. I didn't mind if we were dealing with Chuckie, but only if we were dealing with him.

Chuckie reached into his coat pocket and pulled out some goggles. "You might want to put these on." He handed them to me and tossed a pair each to Martini and Reader.

I put them on, which, of course, required me to let go of Martini's hand. Chuckie smoothly took the opportunity to take my arm as soon as the goggles were on. "You'll want to pay close attention, Kitty."

"Why me? I mean, over everyone else?" I was trying not to

give off any kind of emotion other than professional interest. Being betrothed to the most powerful empath on Earth had a lot of advantages. But Chuckie had become an in-person part of my life again on a much more consistent basis starting when Martini and I had been in a very rough patch. I define "rough patch" to mean he was drugged out of his mind by an alien-hating conspiracy, and said conspirators almost murdered me in a truly horrible way. We were supposedly past all that, but since Chuckie had proposed during this time, and I'd considered it, Martini was never happy when Chuckie was around.

Chuckie sighed. "You'll see."

Martini was on my other side and took my other hand. I held his hand tightly, but I could feel how angry he was. "Reynolds, you want to loosen your grip on her?"

"No. Though you should hold on tighter as well." Chuckie reached out, grabbed Reader's arm, and pulled him over. "Hang on."

"Um, why?"

No sooner were those words out of my mouth, than we found out why.

CHAPTER 2

THE SHOCK WAVES HIT, and the sky lit up. Animas, Hatchet, and Chiricahua Peaks formed a very shallow triangle in the southern parts of Arizona and New Mexico. But this area was a hotbed of alien activity—most landings happened here, both intentional and of the crash-landing kind. No one knew why. I just figured aliens were attracted to mountainous desert areas. Martini said they were attracted to me, but I didn't really believe him.

If the parasitic superbeings the A-Cs had originally been sent to Earth to deal with kept to this area, too, our lives would be a lot simpler. Sadly, they landed all over the world, but they still seemed to prefer the United States in terms of overall percentage of attacks. The U.S. was the immigration country of choice even for alien jellyfish things that turned humans into scary monsters. It made you proud, really.

But what we were seeing didn't resemble a parasite or a superbeing in any way. The lights were a bizarre pattern, but we were high enough up that we could see them clearly. Geometric shapes, interesting and different, but not Earthly. And yet, they were vaguely familiar.

Walkies were crackling. "Jeff, what do you see?" Christopher was shouting.

"Same as you, I'd bet," Martini said.

"Is Kitty okay? I can't raise her!" This from Tim.

"She's fine. Jeff's got one hand, Reynolds has the other," Reader replied.

"Nice," Jerry said sarcastically. "And thanks to the C.I.A. for the heads-up on this one."

"You all okay?" Martini asked, his voice crisp, annoyed, and all business. He went into Commander Mode a lot around Chuckie, but always when any of us were in real or perceived danger.

Everyone was confirmed to be still standing on terra firma and seeing a pretty laser light show. "All we need is Pink Floyd playing in the background."

"You've got it on your iPod, I'm sure," Chuckie said. "You have everything."

"True." Chuckie did know me very well. Martini hated that, as well.

"How often is this happening?" Martini asked.

"It's a pattern. It showed up once last year. We investigated—nothing. Would have pulled Centaurion in, but you were dealing with the Mephistopheles situation." Or, as I called it, my introduction to my new life, since this was how I'd joined up as a Centaurion agent. I also called it Operation Fugly, which caused universal wincing whenever I said it aloud. No idea why—my names for things were always a lot more realistic than those the various government divisions came up with.

"You could have mentioned it when that was over," Martini said, sarcasm heading to full.

"We could have, but we had other pressing issues. It manifested again six months later." He let that one hang while we did the math. Six months later was right about when I was flying a stolen Mazda3 through the desert with a scary sociopath who also happened to be a politician chasing me. Though from what my mother and Chuckie both said, that description was redundant. Operation Drug Addict gave me nightmares only a few times a month now. Martini, who could pick up emotions even when others were sleeping, was possibly happier about that than I was.

"How soon after?" Martini asked, his voice clipped.

"The next night. Then it happened again, three months later. To the day."

I thought about it. "Um . . . you mean on my birthday?"

"Yes."

"Oh, I don't like where this is going," Reader said.

"Neither do we," Chuckie continued. "It showed up again six weeks later. Then one month later. Then three weeks later. Then two weeks. Then one."

"What's it on today?" My stomach felt as queasy as if I'd just walked through a gate from Arizona to Moscow.

"It's been daily for the past week." Chuckie sighed. "Anyone besides me find the light pattern somewhat familiar?"

"In a way," I admitted. "But I can't place it."

"Same here," Reader said.

Confirmation of familiar but not recognizable came from everyone but Martini. His grip on my hand was tighter, though.

Chuckie looked over at him. "Martini? Surely you recognize it?"

"Why the hell didn't you bring us in on this sooner?" Martini growled.

"We had to verify where it was coming from."

"That's bullshit." Martini sounded ready to get into a physical fight with Chuckie, and I started to get really worried.

Chuckie sighed. "True. We wanted to be sure it wasn't something your people were doing intentionally. Point of fact, something you, personally, weren't doing intentionally."

"You have some goddamned nerve," Martini snarled.

"It's my job. Surprising as that may be to you after working together for the past three years."

"We don't work together," Martini said through gritted teeth.

"Not so much, but we will be. You'll find the orders when you get back. Until we have determined whether this is benign or a dangerous threat, Centaurion Division, Alpha Team in particular, will be reporting in to me. Oh," he added, "and don't try calling in the P.T.C.U. on this. Angela's as worried about it as the rest of us are, and she already gave the final authorization."

"Why did you call my mother in for whatever this is?" For some people, this would have been an odd question, all things considered. And a year ago, for me, it would have been. A year ago, I'd thought my mother was a consultant, my father was a history professor at A.S.U., and my best guy friend was merely a brilliant, globe-trotting multimillionaire.

Discovering aliens walked among us had opened up a whole new world at home for me. Turned out my mother was the only non-Israeli, non-Jew ever in the Mossad, albeit retired now, so to speak. In between directing grad students and writing papers, my father moonlighted as an active member of NASA's ET cryptology division. And Chuckie was seeing the world because he was not only in the C.I.A. but was the guy in charge of dealing with Centaurion Division. Discovering that my mother had suggested him for the job was merely icing on the liar's cake my nearest and dearest had been feeding me for my entire life.

My mother was now the head of the Presidential Terrorism Control Unit, a federal agency most regular folks didn't know existed. Of course, they didn't know the C.I.A. and NASA both had Extraterrestrial divisions, nor did they know we had a full-on, ninety percent alien-staffed division called Centaurion, either. Most people probably slept better because of this ignorance.

"Because it clearly affects her daughter." Chuckie sounded angry, just a little, and I didn't think he was angry with me.

"Jeff? What's going on?"

Martini didn't answer. Chuckie sighed. "Kitty? What are you wearing around your neck?"

"The Unity Necklace Jeff gave me. Why?" By Alpha Centauri custom, this meant Martini and I were engaged to be married and both off the market. Which was great in terms of any and all A-Cs. But I didn't have an engagement ring, so the majority of the humans I knew didn't believe we were getting married.

"Oh . . . hell." Reader sounded freaked. "What's after her now?"

"Why is anything after me?"

"Kitty, look at the lights again. Look at them carefully." Chuckie sounded amused.

"What's so funny about this?" I was staring at them. They still seemed really familiar.

"Imagine the pattern as smaller. And hanging around your neck."

I did. "Oh. Well, you didn't say tilt it."

"Right, I realize that makes all the difference." Chuckie was definitely amused. But that humor left his voice when he spoke to Martini again. "I'd like to know what's going on, Martini. And I'd like to know now. Or you'll be explaining this at C.I.A. headquarters. In a private room."

Martini was still speaking through clenched teeth. "I have no idea."

I was moving from worried to scared, and I could see terrified waving at me from just around the next bend in the road.

"Guys? Does anyone else realize the peak we're on corresponds to the jewel in the necklace?"

"Yes," Chuckie said. "I do. I'm guessing I'm the only one other than your fiancé, but I'm very clear on it."

"Is that why we're standing here?"

"Yes. What's significant about this peak, Martini?"

"I have no idea."

"Come on, you gave her the necklace."

"It's from our home world. It's been in our family for centuries."

"So your family has been planning to invade Earth for centuries?"

"We're all here," Christopher's voice snarled from the walkie. "You, of all people, should know that."

Something tickled in my brain. Maybe it was because I'd been focused the past few weeks on wedding invitations and seating arrangements and all the horrors that go along with a wedding. "Um . . ."

"I'm fully aware of it," Chuckie said, calmly but with more anger in his tone. "I'm also aware you all brought the parasites with you."

"Um . . ."

"No they didn't and you know it," Reader snarled. "They're the only people stopping the parasites."

"Um . . ."

"Which have slowed down since Kitty joined up." Chuckie's voice was starting to rise, too.

"Um . . ."

"They haven't stopped, and they won't stop, as far as we can tell," Christopher snarled through the walkie.

"Um . . ."

"True. We're expecting a whole slew of them now," Chuckie said with a mirthless laugh.

"Um . . ."

"Look, we are not calling anyone here!" Martini was close to bellowing, but not quite there.

"Um . . ."

The walkie crackled. "ACE would like to mention that Kitty wishes to say something." It was Gower's voice, just slightly different, which meant ACE was in charge of their main consciousness.

The men with me all stopped bickering and looked at me.

I could feel everyone else on the walkies listening. "Thanks, ACE."

"ACE is happy to help."

"Hold onto that thought." I took a deep breath. "Jeff, when did you decide you wanted to marry me? I mean for real, not joking around."

Martini gave an exasperated growl. "Why are you asking me that, when you know the answer? The day we met, okay? Is there a problem?"

"Yeah, but not with that." I gulped. "Christopher's actually not quite right."

"What is that supposed to mean?" he snarked at me through the walkie.

"Well, I can't speak for the other A-Cs, but the two of you actually don't have all your families here on Earth."

"Come again?" Martini asked, sounding confused and a little hurt and angry.

"Your dad and Christopher's mother married into the family, they weren't part of the original families who were exiled here." The A-Cs on Earth were religious exiles from their home world, and they didn't like to talk about it much.

"So?"

"You told me the necklace travels through the male line, right?"

"Right. Again, so? My father gave it to me to give to you."

"That's sweet. Who gave it to him?"

"His father." Martini didn't say "duh," but I could feel him thinking it.

"Right. And you have no brothers, only sisters."

"Right again. And, again, so?"

"Meaning you're the last male in your family line."

"Yes. And, again, what does that have to do with anything?"

Reader started to laugh. "Oh, my God. This is going to bring a whole new meaning to the term 'reception from hell.'"

"What are you talking about?" Martini sounded angry and confused, and I could tell the hurt was still there.

"Are you sure?" Chuckie asked me.

"Pretty darned."

"WHAT?" Martini bellowed. It was always impressive—no one had his bellowing ability. On the top of a mountain it was massive.

"Oh, hell!" Christopher sounded freaked. "I think Jeff just started an avalanche over here!"

"Get off," Chuckie said calmly. "You've seen enough. Get into the chopper; we'll meet back at Caliente Base. Same for the boys on Chiricahua."

"No problem, the echo is still bouncing here. Tucker out." Jerry signed off, and the walkies went quiet.

"What is going on?" Martini asked quietly.

The light show was fading. Chuckie let go of my arm, and I turned to Martini. "Jeff, baby? I think it's a message."

"From whom, to whom, about what?" He pulled me to him, and I could feel he was tense and shaking, and his hearts were pounding.

"From your relatives on Alpha Centauri. I think they're coming for our wedding."

CHAPTER 3

CALIENTE BASE WAS THE SMALLEST of all the U.S. Centaurion strongholds. Located just outside Pueblo Caliente, Arizona, it was originally supposed to merely provide a safe access for Centaurion personnel into Arizona, which had a lot of activity.

Until about six months prior, when I'd sort of led a second generation A-C uprising, declared the younger A-Cs who were of age to be political refugees, and had the U.S. government annex Caliente Base as the home base for our refugees. My way with people is legendary.

This had worked out better than it sounds, since Christopher's father, Richard White, the A-C Sovereign Pontifex and therefore reigning religious leader of their large and extended clan, had, it turned out, been looking for a smooth political way to allow interspecies marriages, based on my firmly held belief that it was going to be better for both humans and A-Cs in the short and the long run.

Most of us had lived at the Dulce Science Center prior to this, and Martini and I continued to keep quarters there, in what I called his Human Lair. But we spent at least half the time in Caliente Base as well, since the younger generation were still considered refugees by the American government.

We were in the main conference room in Caliente Base, which was on the tenth floor of the complex. A-C complexes went down, not up, so we were well underground. But A-C technology was quite advanced, and the lighting made you think you were seeing the sun. Well, in the day. In the current wee hours of the morning, all the lighting did was make you tired.

We had all of Alpha and Airborne teams with us, as well as Kevin Lewis, who was my mom's right-hand man in the P.T.C.U. and assigned to a permanent position within Centaurion Division. He was a gorgeous black guy who looked as though he'd been a professional athlete. He had a great smile that included incredible teeth, and he was loaded with bags of charisma. He was also happily married, but that didn't mean I wasn't allowed to look at him. Sometimes I could do it without drooling, too.

With Kevin's addition, it meant there were three women and just an entire roomful of hunky men with us. I loved briefings.

"Can't you people do something about the lighting?" Chuckie asked. We were sitting in the romantic glow I loved when Martini and I were in the midst of an all-night sexathon. Trying to have a meeting like this was, at best, difficult.

"No." Christopher's snark was on high. "As we've already said, Caliente isn't as sophisticated a base as Dulce."

"Define sophisticated," Chuckie muttered.

"Look, it doesn't matter." My necklace was off my neck and sitting in the middle of the conference table, which I knew upset Martini emotionally, even though he understood the need logically. "We can all see it. It's pretty much an exact match for the light show from earlier tonight."

"So, you really think this means we have visitors coming?" Kevin didn't sound as freaked out as everyone else. Maybe it was because he was already married.

"Yeah, I really think so. The timing works out."

"Very much so," Chuckie agreed. "We just need to know if they're friendly or hostile." I got the distinct impression he didn't believe Martini had no conscious knowledge of what was going on or how this was being accomplished.

"Well, they're from Alpha Centauri, and they exiled us here. I'm betting on hostile." Gower sounded upset, just like everyone else.

"But why?" This question was from Lorraine, one of our only two other female agents. She was a bit younger than me and had gotten involved during my first outing with the A-Cs, aka Operation Fugly. Like all A-C women, whom I thought of as the Dazzlers, she was beyond gorgeous. She was also beyond nice and one of my two best girlfriends in the A-C community.

"I'm with Lorraine. I don't see why it's a negative." Claudia was my other A-C female operative and friend. She was about my age, winsome and brunette to Lorraine's buxom blonde, just as nice. They were both also scientifically brilliant and excellent medical technicians. I could sprint and hurdle and do some Kung Fu. Somehow, they reported to me. And didn't mind.

"Why so?" Kevin asked. He was taking over, subtly, which was okay with everyone in the room except Chuckie. Technically, the C.I.A. reported dotted line into the P.T.C.U., and we all liked the P.T.C.U. a lot better.

Lorraine shrugged. "So they want to come out for Jeff's wedding. I think it's nice. About time they acknowledged that we're all here and alive and doing the work they should be helping us with."

"They put up the PPB net to keep us from leaving the solar system, hell, to keep us from leaving the inner planets." Martini sounded as angry as he looked. "These people aren't our friends, they're our enemies. It's about time we accepted that."

"Paul? What does ACE think? This is really a time when we need his expertise."

Gower nodded, twitched a bit, and the ACE voice came out of his mouth. "Jeff is right. But Lorraine is right, too."

Silence. We all looked at each other.

"Um, ACE? That's it?"

"Yes." Gower twitched and blinked. "One day, supposedly the palsy will go away. Anyway, I think ACE is confused, Kitty. He can't imagine anyone not wanting to meet you."

"Oh, the superconsciousness hero worship," Christopher said as he rolled his eyes. "Can you get through to him that some people don't think Kitty walks on water?"

"Not really. ACE, ah, doesn't like that kind of discussion." Gower looked uncomfortable.

Reader laughed. "Be happy Kitty uses ACE's powers for good. Remember, ACE thinks Kitty thinks right."

There was a lot of good-natured laughing and kidding about this, but I knew it to be true. When ACE had come to Earth, I was the only one who'd understood what was going on. So I tried to think as ACE would and figure out why anyone would be coming out from Alpha Centauri for this wedding. I came up with nothing other than an idea of who might know.

"Jeff, is it normal morning in Florida?"

Martini sighed. "Yes, baby, it is." He pulled out his cell phone and dialed. "Hi, Dad, good morning. No, not yet. Yes, glad you liked the invitations, it took us three weeks to choose them. No, no, I didn't. Because I hate them. No, I'm not joking. I hate, no, make that despise them. You have got to be kidding. Mom has no right to invite anyone to our wedding, let alone them. Argh! Okay, fine! Look, that's not why I'm calling."

He looked over at me and covered the phone. "Against all logic and common sense, my mother invited Barbara and her husband to our wedding."

"Is she high?" Barbara had tried to force Martini to marry her daughter, Doreen. In fact, it was this incident that had caused the younger generation's revolt and mass exodus to Caliente Base.

"Who knows?" Martini went back to the phone. "Thanks for the update. Glad to know everyone's healthy, and I could not have lived without the newest babies' pooping, eating, crawling, and walking reports. Now, can we get to the reason I called, since we're about to go to a state of national emergency?"

Apparently not. Martini leaned on the conference table, his head on his free hand, without speaking. He grunted occasionally.

"Is every call to them like this?" Chuckie asked me quietly.

"Pretty much."

"No wonder he's always in a bad mood."

Lorraine was on her phone, undoubtedly warning Doreen that her parents were going to be coming to our wedding. She looked at me. "Doreen says she and Irving will be happy to physically prevent her parents from entering."

I managed a laugh. "Tell her thanks and I'll keep it in mind." Irving was a human science geek, meaning he was what every Dazzler under thirty was hoping to bag. Dazzlers really went for brains. If the packaging was decent to look at, that was a bonus, but it wasn't what mattered. Once we were all relocated to Caliente Base, I'd had to pass a law that they were not allowed to try to meet Stephen Hawking—they would have killed him with love, and I figured we still needed his brain.

Martini was finally getting a word in edgewise. "Great,

Mom. Thanks. Can I please talk to Dad again? National emergency and all that. Yes, I really do think it's more important than the seating arrangements. Yes, more important than the two families meeting. Trust me, that's going to seem like nothing shortly."

We were trying to figure out just how to have our families meet. My parents and my Uncle Mort, the career, high-ranking Marine, all knew the truth about Centaurion Division. And they were the only ones in my entire extended family who did. Since my mother was a former Catholic and my father was Jewish, we were already getting the whole mass versus temple questions coming. I hadn't figured out how to explain that we were going to end up doing neither. I'd done a ton of research into Earth religions to find the one with the closest ceremony to what our A-Cs performed. So far, not a lot of luck.

It appeared Martini had his father on the phone again. "Dad, cutting to the chase here. Do we still have relatives alive on the home world and would they actually think about coming to my wedding?"

He sat up, then he sat back, then he stood up and stepped away from the table. This was never a good sign. I looked at Christopher. He pulled out his phone and dialed. "Dad? Sorry, but we need you here, right now. Thanks." He nodded to me. "He'll be here shortly, just needs to dress and get to a gate."

Martini was still on the phone, and I could see his whole body was tensed. Chuckie could, too. "Okay," he said quietly. "I'm willing to buy that Martini had no idea of what giving you that thing would do."

I felt myself relax a bit. "He wouldn't do something to put me in danger, let alone the entire world. He's spent his whole life protecting it."

Chuckie patted my hand. "I know. But I had to be sure."

"You don't think he's faking it?"

"I see his sarcastic ways are rubbing off on you." Chuckie leaned next to me and spoke softly in my ear, so no one else could hear. "I know they can't lie. I've seen him angry before, more than you, probably. I've also seen him scared. And he's both."

I gave him a dirty look and leaned next to his ear. "You make it sound as though Jeff wets himself or something. He's not scared often, if at all."

Chuckie laughed, then did the ear thing again. "I love this, but you're going to get in trouble when he's off the phone. And I didn't mean it as an insult. Like most of us, he gets scared. But he shows it like, well, I show it, or White shows it— by getting angry, going into an authority mode, and so on." He laughed softly again. "I'm not insinuating your man's a wimp, Kitty. If he were, I'd be running Centaurion already."

I was going to ask him what that meant when Richard White entered the room. He'd used hyperspeed to get dressed and over here, which was sort of a relief. He took a look around. "What's going on?"

Martini looked at me over his shoulder. "Tell him." Then he went back to his phone call.

I took a deep breath. "We have unexpected company coming."

White looked at the necklace. "Oh, my God."

CHAPTER 4

WHEN THE HEAD OF AN ENTIRE religious organization says that, any calm left in the room goes running to hide under the covers.

White sat down in the only open chair, which happened to be the one Martini had vacated. It didn't appear to be an issue—Martini was still on the phone with his father, and I got the impression it was going from bad to worse.

"You want to explain this? Keeping in mind we have both the C.I.A. and the P.T.C.U. represented in the room?" White looked shaken enough I felt it necessary to remind him he wasn't with family only.

He shook his head. "I can't believe it."

"Neither can we. Not that we know what 'it' is, but we're willing to bet we won't believe it, either."

White looked at Chuckie. "Were there lights somewhere?"

"Funny you should ask." Chuckie explained the light patterns, both physical and timewise, and where they were located. "What about those mountain ranges is significant?"

"Nothing, they're just close and in the right formation." White had his head leaning in one hand. I was prepared for every A-C to do this shortly.

"So that message could have been sent in to any region?" Chuckie was being polite, but I could tell he was getting tired of one-sentence answers.

"No. It went to the nearest formation by the active piece." White indicated the necklace. "How did you realize what it was?"

Chuckie shrugged. "I'm observant, more than most people." This I knew to be true. "I've seen that thing around Kitty's neck any time I've seen her for the last six months. It was easy to recognize. Six months ago, the second time I saw it," he added.

"Why didn't you bring this to our attention sooner?" White sounded angry.

Chuckie let the knife show, just a bit. "Because we had to make sure this wasn't some kind of dangerous power play by Centaurion personnel." He pointedly looked over at Martini.

"Jeffrey has nothing to do with this," White said, eyes narrowed.

"Bullshit. He has everything to do with it. However, I'm willing to accept that he had no idea what giving that necklace to Kitty was going to trigger."

"Richard, it's sort of creepier than that. The first light manifestation appeared during Operation Fugly." On cue, White winced. "Um, I mean, during the Big Takedown. Or whatever you call it." I never paid attention to their names for offensives—they were always official and boring.

"When Jeff knew he wanted to marry her," Christopher added quietly. "As near as Reynolds has told us, pretty much the same night."

White nodded. "They are tuned to the family, and Jeffrey's the last in Alfred's line." He closed his eyes. "This will happen with you, too, Son."

"What?" Christopher looked shocked. "I'm not getting married. And I'm part of your male line."

"Yes, but it's different for you because of your mother. And I know you've not declared for anyone yet, but when you do . . ." White's voice trailed off and he looked at me. "Oh, dear."

"This just went to DEFCON Worse, didn't it?"

"Oh, hell." Reader had his head in his hands. It *was* catching.

"What? James, what?"

He looked around. "Oh, well. Not like it's a secret to anyone in this room." He sighed. "Kitty, Jeff wasn't the only one who, ah . . ." His voice trailed off, and he shot an uncomfortable look toward Christopher.

Who went pale. "Oh, you've got to be kidding! We're past that!" He shot a look at Martini. "Really, we're past that." What we were past was the fact Christopher had also wanted me when we'd first met, and we'd had a brief, wild moment in

an elevator. Martini had had a hard enough time letting the
incident go, but Christopher and I had been very careful since
then and hadn't done anything remotely romantic; in fact, we
acted like opposing magnets when something potentially romantic loomed.

"Yeah, yeah, doesn't matter," Martini shot back. "Reynolds
is going to be a bigger problem."

"Me? Why?" Chuckie sounded confused for the first time.

Martini spun around. "Because you still want to marry her
if you can. It's complex, and it's not pretty, and I need to get
the rest of the details." He looked at Gower. "We need everyone on high alert. Everyone's going to have to be briefed,
in shifts, key personnel first. But down to the youngest child
who's of age to know why we're all really here. Oh, and all of
my family, and I do mean all, down to the youngest kids who
can communicate verbally or mentally." He went back to his
corner.

We all looked at each other. "Richard, you mind telling us
what's going on? I mean, it's that, or we all just go running off
screaming into the streets."

White took a deep breath and let it out slowly. "Alfred and
my late wife were cousins, not as close as Christopher and Jeffrey are, but about as close as Jeffrey and Paul and Michael,
are."

Interesting, hadn't known that. "Okay . . . so, cousins married a brother and sister. Not totally unusual."

"No, not at all, on either one of our worlds." White didn't
want to go on, it was obvious.

Michael, who'd been uncharacteristically quiet this entire
time, spoke up. "You want me to explain it?" He was a smaller
version of his older brother—big, black, bald, and gorgeous.
He was also a major womanizer, but I doubted that had rel-
evance here.

"How do you know?" White sounded shocked. Gower
looked as shocked as White sounded.

Michael shrugged. "My mother told me about it. She
was . . . concerned I would use our Unity Necklace . . . inap-
propriately." Oh, wow, so him being a womanizer *was* relevant.
Doubly interesting.

"What did she tell you?" White sounded guarded.

"That we were close enough from a blood standpoint that
it could affect us."

"What could affect you?" I figured the rest of us were getting as impatient as I was.

Michael gave me a wry smile. "Jeff and Christopher are part of the Alpha Centaurion royal family."

I sat there. This didn't compute. At all. "Come again?"

"Royal family. You're marrying into it." Michael seemed to find this funny.

I looked at White. "He's kidding, right?"

"No, he's not." White looked as though this was a conversation he'd never wanted to engage in. "Alfred and Theresa were the grandchildren of the reigning monarch when we all left."

"They exiled their own grandkids?" Oh, I did not want to meet this part of Martini's family at all.

"No. Alfred and Theresa made the choice to come with us to Earth."

"Hang on. Paul and Michael aren't that close to this bloodline, from what you all told me. You and Lucinda have another sister, and their father is her husband's brother. So, what's the connection?"

"Our other sister also married into the royal family," White admitted.

"Farther away from the monarchy," Michael added. "More like a distant cousin of the reigning monarch's, versus his direct grandchildren."

"Is your home world a lot less populated than ours?"

"No, more populated, at least it was when we left," White replied. "Why?"

"It's a little odd to have this many people married into the monarchy, at least around here."

"America doesn't have a monarchy," Michael reminded me.

"England does," Chuckie said. "Were you all in someplace smaller like that?"

"I suppose, maybe smaller. Think of it more like living in Washington, D.C. Our families were politically involved, after all."

I turned to Christopher. He looked as shocked as I felt. "You didn't know?"

"Not really. My mother never talked about her family. She only spoke about the family here on Earth—she told me and Jeff they were the only A-Cs who mattered."

"I can understand why." I looked back to Michael. "So, what else?"

He shrugged. "My mother was worried this sort of thing would happen. When a member of the royal family declares for someone, it's a huge political deal. It's never done lightly."

"Your mother's an Earth woman. How did she know this?"

Michael laughed. "How to put it? She's a lot like you. She badgered our dad until he gave her all the history." I resolved to meet Mrs. Gower sooner as opposed to later.

I thought about the one image of Terry that Christopher had created for me in the air. She was in a tiara. For whatever reason, that hadn't seemed odd to me at the time, possibly because I was half-dressed and trying to figure out how to hide what had happened from Martini and marveling over Christopher's imageering talent. Christopher had called me princess, too—I'd never made the connection that his mother had been one.

Christopher hadn't, either, if his reactions were any clue. "Dad, why didn't you tell us?"

White sighed. "It just didn't seem . . . relevant. You boys had so many other pressures. Why tell you that in addition to everything else, you were related by blood to the monarchy? What good would it have done?"

"Did they put the PPB net up to keep humanity in, or to keep Martini and White on Earth?" Chuckie had recovered the quickest, and I could hear the conspiracy theories whirling through his brain.

"Both," Martini snapped from his corner. "Almost done here."

"So, I'm just spitballing here, Richard, but I'd have to guess Terry's family were no more thrilled with you marrying her than your father was."

"Less, if you can believe it."

"How excited were they that Alfred married Lucinda?"

"Much less so. They married well before Theresa and I did. Alfred was disowned, it was a huge controversy." White shook his head. "They did offer to let Alfred and Theresa rejoin the family if they renounced their marriages to us and remained on our home world while the rest of us went to Earth."

"So, since they both passed on that offer, why would they care about whatever Jeff's doing now?"

"I have no idea," White admitted.

Martini slammed his phone closed and turned around. "I do. And it sucks."

CHAPTER 5

MARTINI RAN HIS HAND THROUGH HIS HAIR and leaned against the wall. "My father figures there's some kind of issue with succession back on the home world."

"How so?" White asked. "There were plenty of other children and grandchildren."

"When you left. Maybe not now." Martini managed a weak grin in my direction. "You wouldn't like the succession rules."

"Male lines, male children only, right?"

"Right."

"Similar to Earth, Jeff."

"Only, on Earth, if there is no male child, they'll allow a female to rule."

"Not so on the old home world?" I asked White.

"Not so far as we know."

"And since Christopher's male, there's a chance he could be involved in the succession issues." Martini was so upset he could barely talk. "So they're coming here. But it's not to attend the wedding, most likely. At least, that's not the main goal."

I got a funny feeling. "What are they coming for, then, Jeff?"

He looked straight at me, and I could tell how much he hated what he had to say to me. "To pass judgment on whether or not you're appropriate royal marriage material."

The room went quiet. Then Reader laughed. "So what? You're not going back there, what do you care what they think of Kitty?"

I looked at the A-Cs and thought about the PPB net. "They wanted you kept here, to the point they put up the barrier. We have no idea of how closely they're monitoring us. Could be minor, or we could be scrutinized under an A-C microscope daily; again, we don't know. So that means we don't know if they can or can't force Jeff, or Christopher, to do whatever they want."

Martini nodded. "That's what my father's afraid of."

Chuckie cleared his throat. "Okay, then that makes it official. I'm in charge of Centaurion Division until further notice. Alpha Team will be reporting directly to me, and all activities will have to be approved by me before being put into action."

A-Cs normally went very quiet when they were thinking. But when they were upset . . . not so much. The room erupted. Everyone was shouting, snarling, arguing. Chuckie ignored it. He leaned over to me. "You want to get them under control? Before I lock them up?"

I looked at Martini and caught his eye. He stopped in mid-argument with White. I raised my eyebrow. "SHUT UP!" Ah, the Martini bellow—perfect for stopping hysterics, starting avalanches, and causing windows within a mile radius to rattle.

"Thanks," Chuckie said. "Let me make this clear. You didn't have a choice in the first place. As the C.I.A. feared, we have hostile visitors from space coming. As the C.I.A. is relieved to learn, our own aliens did not intentionally call them over for a visit. As I see I will have to explain, the best thing in the world for Centaurion Division right now is for all of you lovely people who are unable to lie to be able to admit, truthfully, that you are not the ones giving the orders."

He and Martini were having a staring contest. They both looked angry, and they both looked as if they weren't going to back down for hours, if ever.

"Jeff, he's right."

Martini didn't blink or look away from Chuckie. "How so?"

"You *can't* lie. We're about to be invaded, and you, Christopher, Richard, probably Paul, all your families, are all going to be put into compromising positions. We don't know if this is a legitimate visit or an excuse for invasion. And if you're put into a position where someone from the home world gives you an order they expect you to take to the rest of the A-C population, the only thing you may be able to use to refuse is the fact that you don't make the final decisions."

Chuckie was also still staring Martini down, and he shrugged. "She's right. You don't have to like it. But by the original agreements your people signed when the United States government agreed to house you here as displaced refugees, you have to agree, or you have to vacate."

"We're not in a state of emergency."

Chuckie barked a laugh. "Like hell. You said it earlier and even if you hadn't, it's obvious. Best case scenario is they come and approve Kitty, and we have to do a massive cover-up. That would make our lives hell, and that would be the easy scenario. But let's be honest—no one thinks that's what's going to happen, least of all you."

Martini deflated a bit. "Fine. However, once the state of emergency abates, sovereignty reverts back to the Pontifex."

"Yes."

"Define, clearly, when the C.I.A. will consider the state of emergency abated." I wasn't C.I.A., but I'd been a marketing manager before I'd joined Centaurion, and I knew the dangers of doublespeak better than most.

Chuckie looked away from Martini and grinned at me. "Once all the hostile aliens have left or been subdued."

"I want it in writing, and I'll be going over it for loopholes."

He laughed. "Not a problem." He looked back at Martini. "Okay?"

"No, but we'll deal with it. Officially, Centaurion unwillingly concedes the C.I.A.'s limited authority during a time of interworld crisis."

"And unofficially?" Chuckie sounded supportive, not challenging.

Martini closed his eyes. "Unofficially," he opened his eyes, "help us. Please."

Chuckie nodded and stood up. "Unofficially, I may want to marry her, but she wants to marry you. So, yeah, let's get that taken care of." He walked over to where Martini was standing. Christopher joined them.

It was always interesting to me to do a physical comparison. Martini was big, well over six feet, broad-shouldered, built like a brick house, rippling muscles without being overdone like a bodybuilder. Of course, I couldn't see all that right now, but I had his naked body happily memorized. His hair was dark and wavy and his eyes were light brown.

Christopher was a head shorter, smaller all the way around,

the lean and wiry kind. Straight, lighter brown hair and green eyes. As Chuckie had mentioned at our high school reunion, Christopher was actually more the type I'd always gone for in school.

Chuckie was like a blend of the two of them. Tall like Martini, but more along Christopher's build, sinewy and smooth. He moved casually but had the reflexes to make you think he could be part A-C. Dirty blond hair, which would have a bit of a wave in it if he'd let it grow long, and blue eyes.

All of them were good-looking, but though Chuckie was handsome by human standards, only Reader and a couple of other human agents had a shot of passing as an A-C in the looks department, after all.

Normally I enjoyed looking at any of them, Martini in particular. But tonight I got a bad feeling, seeing them standing there together. Martini caught it and looked at me. "What's wrong?"

I shook my head. "I don't know. But I think we'd better be prepared for the worst. Whatever that's going to end up being."

Before we'd met ACE, Martini had implanted a portion of Christopher's mother's consciousness into me. It was only a trace, but I'd liked having it there, liked being able to connect to Terry in times of trouble. ACE had removed it, telling me it was better this way. That bit of Terry was now a part of ACE—but I never got to connect with it any more. I wanted to now, more than ever.

If Terry had still been inside my mind, I'd assume the nameless dread I was feeling was coming from her. Since that couldn't be, I had to assume what Martini called my feminine intuition was picking up something. Either that or I just needed a nap.

Reader got up and went over to the other three. "Look, how do you want us to get things rolling? Sitting around isn't getting the troops prepared."

Same size as Christopher, pretty much. Most gorgeous human I'd ever laid eyes on in the flesh. Our joke was that if he were straight, we'd run off, get married, and forget there were aliens on the Earth.

It occurred to me that I was looking at four men who'd achieved the top levels early in life. Martini was the strongest empath on Earth, and Christopher was the best imageer; Chuckie was the smartest guy in any room, and Reader had been the top international male model for years. There was a lot of drive and talent there, and the rest of us weren't slouches, either. I relaxed, feeling confident we'd be able to handle whatever was coming.

The dread hit me, harder. I looked over at Paul. He looked sort of glazed. I tried thinking in my mind, the way I had with ACE in the past. ACE, are you there?

Yes, Kitty, ACE is here.

What's wrong?

Terry wishes ACE to warn Kitty. His mental voice sounded upset. ACE's prime directive was to protect, but he also knew doing everything for us would destroy us and turn him into a despot. Which meant I had to help him settle this in his consciousness, or he was going to short out and take Paul with him.

ACE, are the A-Cs coming more powerful than you are?

ACE is . . . not sure.

They created you, or at least okayed your creation, didn't they?

Terry confirms this as so.

Then, that means maybe they are more powerful than you. Or will know weaknesses you have that we don't know about.

I could feel ACE considering this. That would mean it would be . . . correct . . . for ACE to protect . . . ACE?

Yes, I think so. We should see what's coming, but I think we all need to be prepared. They're far more powerful than any of us on Earth.

Yes. Terry says Kitty must be prepared. The test is not for Jeff, it is for Kitty. And Terry knows the royal family will want Kitty to fail.

Great. Okay, thanks, ACE. I'll do my best. I didn't want to push ACE for more. It was better to save that for when we might really need it.

ACE knows Kitty will be able to triumph. Kitty thinks right. I saw Paul's expression shift, and he shuddered a bit.

Martini came over to me. "Are you okay?" he asked quietly.

"For now, yeah." The dread had subsided, and I was suddenly exhausted. "Jeff, I want to go to the Lair, okay?"

"Okay. Right now?"

"Yeah. Chuckie's in charge; let him deal with this." I picked up the Unity Necklace. The dread came back along with a sharp pain. "OUCH!" I dropped it back on the table. Dread disappeared, pain stuck around. Well, one out of two wasn't bad.

"What?" Martini asked as everyone else spun toward me.

"The stone . . . it burned me." I showed him my palm. I had a burn mark in the rounded shape of the jewel.

Lorraine came over and pulled a tube out of the small med case she carried with her at all times now. She put something on the burn, and the pain stopped.

"How did it get hot?" Christopher asked.

Michael leaned forward and put his hand on it. "It's cool to the touch."

I put my hand toward it again. "I can feel the heat from here." My hand was a good six inches away. I left it there as the others put their hands on the necklace. It was cool for everyone else, including Martini.

"What in hell is going on?" Martini asked finally.

"I don't think whoever's coming likes me."

CHAPTER 6

WE WERE BACK AT THE LAIR. It was on the fifteenth floor of the Dulce Science Center, and no one went there but Martini and me. Other than what I now called the A-C Elves. I had no idea if there really were elves about, but someone or something did the housekeeping, ensured that the right clothes were there for you, no matter when you showed up or what room you showed up in, and snatched your dirty laundry in the night. I assumed the same elves provided the drinks that appeared in the variety I wanted, anywhere, any time, as long as it was in a fridge of some kind. As of yet, Martini hadn't shared how this was done. I got the impression he enjoyed the fact I really wanted to know.

I would have loved something stronger than Cherry Coke, but A-Cs were deadly allergic to alcohol, and the last thing I wanted to do was either kill Martini because there was too much alcohol residue in my mouth or have him unable to kiss me.

My hand didn't hurt much any more, but I was staring at it. I knew better than to tell Martini that his aunt's consciousness was in ACE. Neither he nor Christopher were really over the trauma of losing her, and that had happened almost twenty-one years ago.

I was cuddled in Martini's lap, and we had the TV on, watching *Love Boat* reruns. He loved all the cheesy old shows, and I just wanted to have something on I could pretend to pay attention to. This was the most human room of any A-C location I'd ever seen, and right now it was overwhelmingly comforting.

"Baby, it'll be okay." He'd said this about a hundred times. I still didn't believe it, or believe that he believed it.

"Why did you tell Chuckie he was more of a problem than Christopher?"

"Because he's a viable alternative who's already proposed to you, hasn't married anyone else in the meantime, and isn't in our bloodline," Martini growled. "And since he's ostensibly my superior, it makes him a better catch for you, at least the way the home world hierarchy apparently thinks. According to my father, that actually makes it easier for the royal family to insist that you can't marry me. I won't be leaving you at the altar—I'll merely step aside and let a more appropriate man have you."

How Emily Post of them. I had no comment to this that wasn't going to start us off into some kind of fight over things we weren't going to allow to happen. Besides, I was more stuck on something else. "Royal family?"

"I didn't know!"

"I know." I had a thought. "I wonder if Barbara knows."

"I'm sure she does."

"No wonder she wanted Doreen to marry you."

"Like Doreen would enjoy having her hand burned any more than you would?"

I managed to laugh. "No, but I'm sure Barbara wasn't thinking about anything other than making a great match for her daughter."

He stroked the back of my neck. "You think I'm a good catch?" I could hear the fear lurking there, just hidden beneath the surface.

I leaned my head against his. "Yes, Jeff. And not because you're some royal scion or prodigal son or whatever. And not because you're the head of Centaurion Field and pretty much run everything, either."

"Why then?"

I nuzzled his ear. "Because you're gorgeous, you're smart, you're funny, you're built, and you're a god in bed. And you're mine."

He turned and kissed me. It was deep and strong, and his mouth controlled mine just like always. I felt worry slip away. I didn't care about anything when he was kissing me other than hoping it wouldn't stop and that we'd move to making love as fast as possible.

On cue my phone rang. I sighed and dug through my purse to find it. "Hi, Mom, you're up early."

"Your only child being the target for unfriendly alien attacks normally warrants rising before dawn." My mother's sarcasm knob went well past eleven, and it was on high already.

"How'd you know?"

"Charles called me." I picked up the unstated comment that Mom wasn't happy that Chuckie had called instead of me.

"I was waiting for it to be a decent hour," I lied quickly.

Mom sighed. "Kitten, this isn't something that we can afford to wait on. You can't treat an alien invasion the way you're treating your wedding."

"What is that supposed to mean?"

She heaved an even bigger sigh. "Everything's taking you and Jeff forever. At this point, I counsel running off to Vegas."

"I wouldn't have thought you'd approve of that."

"Would have approved when Charles suggested it all those years ago, would approve at this moment because it's getting ridiculous." Chuckie had actually proposed to me twice in my life. I'd just been far too dense to realize it the first time. My density was becoming legendary. The worst part was that I still couldn't catch when I was being dense, and my nearest and dearest still insisted on not sharing until it was far too late. "You haven't even confirmed your bridesmaids yet."

"Um, I'm working on it." I was. I wanted Amy and Sheila, my best girlfriends from high school, and Caroline, my sorority roommate, and Lorraine and Claudia. The issues were that three of them didn't know I was marrying an alien, and I had no idea who should be the maid of honor. So I'd stalled the lying and that uncomfortable decision off by having them all sort of on hold. Pathetic, but a great example of my wedding planning skills so far. Growing up I'd spent a lot more time reading *Ms.* magazine than *Modern Bride*.

"Work faster."

"Noted. Mom, our wedding plans aren't really the issue of the hour. Okay, I mean, they are, but we have bigger issues."

"Like Jeff being a member of the royal family? Which means we have an entire contingent of exiled royalty here, which bloodline you happen to be marrying into. Your father's thrilled, by the way."

I managed not to share that, so far as I could tell, he was the only one. "Other issues." I was reaching, but I wanted off the wedding and royal family conversation train.

"Like Reynolds being in charge," Martini muttered.

I leaped on that one. "Yeah, Mom, why did you put Chuckie in charge of Centaurion?"

She barked a laugh. "Because I want the only C.I.A. big shot I can trust in charge. It helps that he's brilliant, understands you intimately, and also understands the A-Cs perfectly."

I wondered if Martini could pick up emotions through the phone, and I also wondered what my mother's were at this time. My parents loved Martini and felt he was a good match for me. But Mom had shoved me at Christopher and apparently was still holding a torch for the idea of me and Chuckie as a couple. It wasn't really like her to keep on once my decision had been firmly made. I got the impression Mom really wanted me to be positive I wanted to marry Martini because she was worried about more than whether I'd really picked the guy who was right for the long haul.

Of course, Chuckie's family were humans who adored me. Though Martini's parents seemed to sort of like or at least tolerate me. Now. Chuckie's family also weren't invading from another planet to pass judgment on me. Maybe Mom had a point. Maybe the invading aliens had a point—I wasn't exactly Princess Diana material. I did my best to think about flowers so I didn't give Martini any emotional signals.

"Okay, fine. What are we supposed to do, though?"

"Do? Figure out what's coming and how to stop it while listening to Charles and not getting yourselves killed." Mom didn't add the "duh" in there, but it was clear that she'd just exercised impressive self-restraint.

"Duly noted. We have to listen to Chuckie?" I wasn't the one who had problems listening to Chuckie, of course, but I felt I had to represent Martini's interests here.

"Yes. Unless you resign and all the A-Cs leave the planet. Let me mention that I don't think that's a viable option for anyone, nor is it the option I, personally, think anyone should exercise."

"Good to know. Any other words of wisdom?"

"Please God find a decent wedding dress soon, so the rest of us can figure out what we're going to be wearing."

"Thanks for focusing on the big picture, Mom."

"Any time, kitten. Love you and love to Jeff."

"Love you, too, Mom, and same to Dad." We hung up, and I felt exhausted again. "Normally talking to my mother doesn't make me want to sleep for a week."

"Your body's responding to stress," Martini said, as he stood us up, still holding me, in one fluid motion. A-Cs were super strong as well as super fast. He carried me into the bedroom. "You want to talk about the situation, plan the wedding, or go to bed?"

I didn't have to give this one much consideration. "Bed."

Martini chuckled. "I meant to sleep." Martini's other super skills were empathic and bedroom. He said lust was an easy emotion to pick up, particularly mine. Then again, it was an easy guess, because I was always lusting after him.

"Oh, so did I. You know . . . after."

Martini grinned. "I love how you focus on the priorities."

CHAPTER 7

AFTER AN IMPRESSIVE SEXUAL DISPLAY for a normal human, but what was bedroom business as usual for Martini, we fell asleep. I woke up hours later, his arms tight around me. I nuzzled into his chest, and he gave a sleepy growl.

I estimated we'd fallen asleep an hour or so after dawn. It was still daylight—the internal lighting was on full. But I had no guess as to what time it really might be.

Before either one of us was fully awake, a voice came through the intercom. "Commanders Martini and Katt, Supreme Commander Reynolds requests your presence at a briefing."

"Supreme Commander?" Martini sounded wide awake. "Gladys, what the hell?"

"He knows you well. Mister Reynolds said that would probably wake you. And to tell you he's kidding, about the title, not the briefing."

"Hilarious guy. Remind me to punch him when we get to the briefing. Fine, Gladys, please tell Mister Power Mad we'll be there as soon as possible."

"An hour," I shouted. "At least an hour."

"I'll pass that along, Commander Katt."

"Thanks, Gladys." The com went dead.

"You know, I hated Reynolds enough before I found out he was interested in marrying you. This is going to be sheer hell, having to take orders from him."

"He's just got an interesting sense of humor." I sat up and stretched.

"Mmmm, do that some more." Martini stroked my breasts.

"Oh . . . Jeff . . . we have to . . . get dressed . . ." My voice trailed off as he moved his mouth to help his hands with the work of sending me to orgasm heaven.

In light of our upcoming briefing session, he used the speedy approach. I was yowling like a cat in heat, my standard reaction, within a minute and climaxing within the usual two. Martini looked extremely pleased with himself as he got out of bed, picked me up, and headed us into the shower.

I was always in the Happy Place if we were showering together. Somehow, we managed to fit in another couple of screaming orgasms before we cleaned up and got out. Royal family be damned—they were not going to prevent me from showering with Martini on an at least once-daily basis, certainly not without a huge fight from me.

I decided not to put on the Armani fatigues today. I chose a pair of jeans, my Converse, and, in light of the impending state of emergency, the Aerosmith shirt I'd worn during Operation Fugly. I figured a little nostalgia couldn't hurt.

Martini was in, of course, the standard Armani issue. In the year we'd been together I'd gotten him into something else only a few times. He'd been willing to be casual during the day when we'd gone to Cabo—of course, most of the days in Cabo we'd been in swimsuits or naked in our private cabana. But at night he'd adapted the suit to wherever we were going.

Otherwise, I'd gotten him into a pair of jeans and a T-shirt exactly twice since then. I'd almost given up—A-Cs really loved their formality and their Armani. I'd resorted to haunting the Armani website to see if there might be anything in upcoming collections Martini would consent to wear. As of yet, no luck, but I'd certainly learned more about fashion trends and gotten some great ideas for my wedding dress, which was, as my mother had so nicely pointed out, as of yet, neither picked out nor ordered. We were six weeks away from our wedding, but I wasn't worried. I was panicked. But something, like horrible space visitors, always kept popping up.

We left the Lair and got into the elevator. The one incident with Christopher in here had pretty much been wiped out of my clear memory by Martini's ravaging me in it shortly afterward. I normally loved being in an elevator with him—it was always a toss-up as to whether he'd stop it and we'd see how often I could climax, or he'd at least ravage my mouth to the point where a climax was a strong possibility.

We went with the latter today. I hated having to be someplace on time, it took away so many potential orgasms.

We reached the launch area, which was the top of the Science Center. There were the usual personnel milling about doing things I still, after a year, didn't understand or try to learn about. I was dedicated that way.

All of Airborne was waiting for us. Tim, who was our official driver, my five Top Gun pilots—Jerry, Hughes, Walker, Joe Billings, and Randy Muir—and Claudia and Lorraine, our medical. Randy and Joe were their boyfriends, and the four of them looked particularly worried. I could understand that. Martini and I were pretty much going to be the test case for interspecies marriages. It was how White had gotten around the older A-Cs totally freaking out. If all went well for the two of us, then more couples would be allowed to do their counseling with the Pontifex and, of all people, my mother, then walk on down the aisle to wedded bliss.

Tim was the only one of our team not dating an A-C. He was dating Alicia, whom we'd met during the fun trip where we'd all almost died about ten times, good old Operation Drug Addict. She worked for the airlines and thought we were all part of the P.T.C.U. She was doing great with keeping that a secret, and we figured one day we might be able to tell her the truth. Jerry, Hughes, and Walker were playing the A-C field—there were so many Dazzlers to choose from, and my flyboys were the ultimate combo—all great looking by human standards and all really, really smart.

"Everyone ready?" Martini asked. "Wouldn't want to keep Mister C.I.A. waiting." The guys all grimaced. Claudia and Lorraine just rolled their eyes.

Something I hadn't considered for a while occurred to me, but now wasn't the time to ask the girls why Chuckie—who was tall, handsome, rich, human, and beyond brilliant—wasn't right after Hawking on the Dazzler Wish List.

"We really have to take direction from Reynolds?" Tim asked.

"Presumably," Martini growled, and I flipped my mind onto flowers while I tried to determine if he was growling because of the mere mention of Chuckie's name or if Martini had picked up that I was thinking nice things about Chuckie. Then again, he was an empath, not a mind reader. I relaxed.

"Chuckie's not that bad. And we need his help right now. So, yeah."

"Kitty won't," Jerry said with a grin. "She'll pretend to, but she'll do what she wants."

The entire team nodded. I felt a little embarrassed.

Martini laughed. "Too true."

"Chuckie knows me pretty well," I muttered.

"Yeah? Then how'd he let you shove him through the gate when Reid had you two cornered?"

He had a point. And Chuckie wasn't empathic. Okay, we were good.

My cell phone rang, and I dug it out of my purse. "Hi, Christopher, what's up?"

"Oh, we're just wondering when Airborne's going to grace us with their presence. And Jeff. The rest of Alpha's sitting here, taking bets on when Reynolds loses his cool and starts screaming about how late you are."

"Chuckie doesn't lose his cool." This was true. He'd had a lot of reasons to in high school, when he'd been short, ravaged by acne, and a total geek-nerd combo. He'd never lost it when people had picked on him, though I had. He'd always told me success was the best revenge. Becoming a multimillionaire twice over before he was twenty-five and now running the C.I.A.'s ET Division qualified as overwhelmingly successful in my book. I was, as always, so proud of him.

"I hate it when you think about him," Martini muttered to me.

Focused on the stupid flowers again. They didn't seem to be working. Maybe I should try trees. "Be there as soon as we get through the gate. By the way, where is 'there,' exactly?"

Christopher sighed. "You don't know?"

"No. See, if I knew, I wouldn't have asked. It's my crazy little way."

"Crazy is the accurate description for you. And, apparently, Reynolds. We're not in any of our bases."

"Um, why not?" I looked around. All of Airborne seemed confused. I looked up at Martini. "They're not at a base."

He raised his eyebrow. "Oh? Where the hell are we going, then?"

"Jeff has no clue either. Want to share, or do you secretly like hanging with Chuckie waiting for the rest of us?"

Christopher sighed. "We're in Las Vegas."

"Come again?"

"Vegas. We're in freaking Las Vegas. Reynolds is cracking up, by the way."

I was sure he was. Chuckie had a wicked sense of humor. And he and I had spent a wild week in Vegas when Circle-K had bought out his chain of convenience stores for the first of those multimillions. That was when he'd suggested we get married, the first time, but I'd thought he was kidding. He hadn't been, as I'd discovered six months ago, when he suggested it the second time. Before my week with Martini in Cabo, Vegas with Chuckie had been the best vacation, and sex, of my life. And Chuckie would enjoy tormenting Martini, and apparently Christopher, with this knowledge.

"Let me guess . . . you're in the Mandalay Bay somewhere."

"Oh, you're good. Yeah, top floor of THEhotel."

"Not the Four Seasons?" Which didn't surprise me at all that much. Chuckie preferred sleek to grandiose.

"Reynolds says he knows you'll like THEhotel better." I could hear how annoyed this was making Christopher.

"He's right. We'll be there as soon as the gate's calibrated. At least the Vegas bathrooms are clean."

"Yeah, wouldn't want anything to keep you from spending your money quicker."

"You don't like gambling?" I loved it.

"We gamble our lives every day. Gambling money seems anticlimactic." Christopher had a point.

"Well, whatever, be there shortly." I hung up. I looked around at the team. I couldn't help it—I was sort of excited.

"Well?" Martini asked. "Are we heading where it sounded like we're heading?"

"Oh, yeah. We're going to Vegas, baby!"

CHAPTER 8

MY TEAM HAD THE MOST HUMANS ON IT, and all of them looked pleased. Claudia and Lorraine looked confused. And Martini looked beyond annoyed. "Vegas. Great."

"Oh, come on, Jeff. It'll be fun."

"Right. We aren't going to be having fun. We're going to be figuring out how to stop my relatives from ruining our lives."

"True, but ... it's so cheap and tawdry and glittery and loud. And it never sleeps!" I loved Vegas, when you got right down to it.

Martini sighed. "Can't wait. Truly."

We walked to a gate and calibrated for the McCarran International Airport. Martini sent Tim first, then the rest of our team. He recalibrated quickly, his hand a blur. Then he swung me up into his arms.

I hated going through the gates. They still looked more like airport metal detectors than anything else to me, but they also brought new meaning to the term "sick to your stomach." About the only way I could get through one without wanting to barf my guts out was in Martini's arms, with my face buried in his neck. He stepped us through, and in a second we'd gone from the middle of the New Mexico desert to the middle of the Nevada desert.

McCarran was one of the few airports where a bunch of people coming out of a stall, three of them women, didn't cause too much notice. Anything went in Vegas. We lucked out in that there weren't any men in the bathroom, and our little parade coming out of the men's room didn't attract any looks—there were slot machines all over the airport, and people were paying a lot more attention to them than to us.

However, once we were in the area to get to a taxi stand, I noticed someone watching us. He was hard to miss—he had a camera the size of his head. And it was aimed at us.

I nudged Martini. "Why are we getting our pictures taken?"

He looked over and shrugged. "Guy likes to take pictures of pretty women."

"Um, Jeff, really? That's what you're picking up?"

He sighed. "Baby, we're in an airport. Loaded with people with their emotions going off the charts."

"Oh. You have all your blocks up on full."

"Right. He's not giving off any kind of threat emotions—those I can still feel. So what if he takes pictures of us? We're in a tourist spot, and Christopher's people will alter anything we don't like."

The man had snapped several shots while we were talking. He lowered the camera and grinned at me. He was under six feet, dressed in casual, baggy clothes, well worn but clean. I couldn't tell if the clothes were hiding muscles or a slight pudge. Black hair, beard, and, as he walked closer, I could see twinkling blue eyes. I couldn't tell his age— maybe 30s, maybe 40s, maybe not.

"How're you folks doing?" he asked. He had a slight twang in his voice, but I couldn't place it, other than to say I'd bet he was from the Southwest somewhere.

"Fine. We don't want our pictures taken."

His grin got wider. "Pity. You shouldn't be out of Home Base then, should you?"

Chuckie had trained me well. The only people who referred to Nellis Air Force Base or the Groom Lake portion of it as Home Base also called it Area 51. Based on how he looked, this man wasn't an A-C, and based on how he dressed and was acting, he wasn't a human agent, either.

"Just who are you?" I tried to ask nicely. His grin managed to get wider, indicating I'd failed.

"Mister Joel Oliver. *World Weekly News*." He put out the hand not holding his humongous camera.

None of us extended ours in return. "What does a rag photographer want with pictures of tourists?" Tim asked, more politely than I'd have managed.

Oliver shook his head as he retracted his hand. "You're not

tourists." He leaned closer. "I know who . . . and what . . . you are." He straightened up. "And I'd love to do an interview. I'm our top photojournalist."

"I'm sure that's impressive to someone, Oliver," Martini said casually. He seemed so calm and cool. Glad one of us was.

"*Mister Joel* Oliver, please. Full name."

"Why?"

Oliver shrugged. "Ensures my byline's always right, my sources are sure who they're talking to, and I like hearing the Mister."

"Like Mister T?"

"And for similar reasons." Oliver shook his head. "You'd be amazed at what names I get called."

"I'll bet you twenty dollars none of them would shock or surprise me."

He laughed. "I don't take sucker bets." Oliver looked straight at Martini. "I know your people alter my photos. But they can't alter what I write. You have powerful friends who do that, though. But it won't stop me."

Martini shook his head. "I have no idea what you're talking about. Now, if you'll excuse us, we have a meeting to attend." Martini jerked his head at us, indicating it was time to move on.

"With the head of the C.I.A.?" Oliver asked as we headed for the limo line.

Martini smiled. "Nope." He clearly wasn't lying and it was obvious Oliver could tell if the look of disappointment that flashed across his face was any indication.

Of course, that's because Oliver hadn't asked the question properly. Chuckie wasn't the head of the C.I.A., so Martini wasn't telling an untruth. He was avoiding telling the truth, which was about the only way the A-Cs could manage lying. It was nice of Oliver to have made it so easy. I didn't want to count on that happening again.

Oliver followed us to the limo stand. "So, Miss Katt, how have you recovered from your recent ordeal?"

"How do you know my name and what ordeal are you talking about?"

"You were pursued by crazed madmen through the Arizona desert not too long ago, weren't you? By Representative Leventhal Reid and an associate, I believe?"

"No idea what you're talking about," I said airily. I was

human, and lying was a natural extension of my former career as a marketing manager. "I think you have me confused with someone else. As I recall, that politician was high on meth and after some poor college co-eds."

"I doubt I'm confused. My sources say that Representative Reid was high on the idea of killing you. In a particularly gruesome way. You had a long call with Emergency Response during that time, too."

I did my best to think about flowers, not to hide anything from Martini but so that I wouldn't give anything away to Oliver. I'd thought that tape had been confiscated and the A-Cs had done some kind of memory alteration on the Emergency Response phone team. Guess something had slipped through. Or one of the military personnel called in had talked.

As I thought about it, there were a lot of ways this could have leaked. Then I thought some more. The only person who seemed to think we were a story was Mister Joel Oliver. Who worked for the biggest rag tabloid in existence. I stopped worrying.

"Whatever, dude. You believe what you need to believe to get you through the day."

Tim had two limos waiting for us now. We couldn't really use hyperspeed under the circumstances. Martini ushered the others into one, and he and I went into the other alone. As we drove off, I looked out the back window. Oliver was still there, snapping pictures. He waved at us just before we moved out of sight.

"Why, just out of curiosity, are you so tense?" I asked as we settled into the back, far away from the driver. "You worried about our new friend, the photojournalist?"

"Not too much. No, I know why Reynolds chose this location." Martini had his arm around me, but his body felt rigid.

"So what? Jeff, you're worried about nothing." I felt Oliver was a better thing to worry about, but I didn't want to bring it up. If Martini wasn't worried that we had our own paparazzo following us, I probably shouldn't be, either.

"Right. He's rich, he's successful, you've known him years longer than me, you love him almost as much as me, and we have a nightmare headed toward us."

I considered mentioning that I didn't love any man as much as I loved Martini, not even Chuckie, and having the jealousy chat with him again, but I'd accepted a long time ago that he was always going to be possessive and jealous. Besides, it was flattering, considering he could have landed any woman on Earth.

"I don't want any woman on Earth," he muttered. "I only want you."

"Good. Because I only want you." I pulled his head down to mine and kissed him until we were lying down on the seat and about to become part of a reality TV show.

"You folks need to sign the release form," the driver called to us.

Martini snarled, sat up, and pulled me up next to him. "Not just no, but hell no."

"Fine. The way you two were heading, you were gonna end up the top-rated segment." He sounded disappointed.

"Sorry, maybe next time." I straightened my top. "By the way, why are you taking the long way?"

"Because I thought you two were going for it."

"Get us there, now, or I'll sue your ass," Martini growled.

"Whatever." The driver turned off the main street, and we started moving faster. We pulled into the hotel's parking garage while I brushed my hair and straightened the rest of my clothes. "You're sure?" the driver asked me as Martini paid up.

"Positive. I charge a lot for visual proof."

"Ah, well, I can see why." The driver gave me a wide grin. "Here's my card. Call any time."

Martini took the card from him, tore it into little bits, and dropped them back into the driver's hand. "She's not a hooker, she's not a porn star, she's not on the market, and if you don't stop looking at her chest, I'm going to rip your throat out."

"Have a nice day!" I called to the driver as Martini dragged me into the hotel.

"Stop flirting."

"I'm not flirting. I'm being nice after you were rude." A man I'd never seen before who was really great looking held the door for us. "Thanks!" He gave me a big smile and an appraising look.

Martini growled and dragged me to the desk. "I hate it here already. Just so you know."

"Oh, Jeff, relax." Another good-looking guy came out of the elevator banks and gave me the big smile and obvious once-over. I loved Vegas.

"Right. Stop flirting with strangers. It's bad enough you flirt with Reynolds. Still. And James."

"Chuckie's clear on who I'm engaged to, and James is gay."

"Can't tell that it matters, to either one of them." Martini went to the front desk. "We're here to see Charles Reynolds. I think he's registered here."

"Yes, Mister Reynolds is on the top floor." The desk clerk pointed to the elevator banks. "You don't need a key to get up there. He's expecting you."

As we headed off, I spotted the two guys who'd checked me out. They were chatting at the main intersection between check-in, the elevators, the parking garage, and the exit to the casino. They were handsome enough to be A-Cs, but since they were both in jeans and casual shirts, it was a good bet they were just hunks. Both looked at me and gave me the big grins while they checked out my assets. I tried not to be flattered and failed utterly. I really loved Vegas.

"What part of stop flirting with strangers isn't coming through?" Martini groused as he dragged me into the elevator banks and out of view of my admiring public. I chose not to be annoyed. It wasn't as if I were here looking for someone to pick up, after all.

I caught movement out of the corner of my eye. Someone was in an alcove to the side of the elevator banks. I hadn't noticed anyone when we'd walked by. I nudged Martini, but before either one of us could move, a man walked briskly out of the alcove and away. "Mister Joel Oliver, what a surprise. How'd he find us here?"

"Listened to the directions we gave the limo driver, I'm sure."

"I guess. You didn't pick him up?"

Martini grunted. "No, though I can recognize his emotional feel now. But there's a lot of interference here, even more than at the airport." Made sense. Most emotions ran higher in Sin City, especially the closer you were to a casino, and we were very close. I decided not to worry about Oliver right now, especially since Martini still sounded annoyed.

"Think the rest of the team is here already?" I asked as we waited for the elevator to arrive.

"Unless they're filming an orgy, yeah. I assume Oliver followed them here, not us."

"Good point. I think Tim and the girls might be open to the orgy idea, though."

"Thankfully, I know without asking that the flyboys are not."

"Your Puritanical attitude is rubbing off on them, I see."

"Like you wanted to be filmed?" he asked as we got inside the elevator.

I shrugged. "Might be fun to watch." I didn't actually think so, but it was fun to needle him sometimes.

Martini grabbed my waist with both hands, lifted me up and put me against the side of the elevator. "How fun?"

I put my legs around his waist and pulled him into me. "Lots of fun."

We practiced for our next Vegas limo ride the entire way up. Fortunately, it was a high hotel. Unfortunately, we knew hitting the stop elevator button would cause alarms to go off. We compromised by making out wildly. I had to brush my hair again, and his, when the elevator stopped.

Clothes adjusted, hair faking it, we got out and walked down the hall. I could hear voices as we neared a large set of open double doors. The suite Chuckie was in took up at least half of the top floor. Martini was muttering under his breath again before we were through the doors.

Which was funny, considering his family was loaded and lived in a palatial estate in Florida. I hadn't realized until today that it must have seemed like home on Alpha Centauri to Martini's father. From what Christopher had said, they'd lived in a pretty palatial embassy when Terry was alive. Again, must have seemed normal to her. Chuckie's money started to seem a lot more natural. I was an American, after all—royalty was interesting, but I was a lot more comfortable with the idea of success through capitalism.

Everyone else from our team was there already, and so were Reader, Gower, and Christopher. The Pontifex, who also was considered a part of Alpha Team when it was convenient, was noticeably absent.

This was the most comfortable briefing room I'd ever seen. The suite had a conference table, but it was loaded with food and drink, none of it alcoholic, I noticed. All the chairs were sleek and comfortable looking, and there were settees where the couples were perched.

A can of Coke flew through the air. I caught it automatically. "Dude, you have got to stop that. I hate it when it sprays all over."

Chuckie laughed. "Sure you do." Martini's muttering got more intense.

"Nice spread. I didn't know we were moving in." The place was huge, and the view was incredible. I stared down the Strip and found myself hoping we'd be here when it got dark.

"Not at the moment." Chuckie indicated we should sit as he went and closed the double doors. I heard him lock them.

I decided not to rub it in and sat in a chair. Martini sat next to me and gave me a look. "His place, we play nicely," I said quietly.

"You're so damned willing to play nicely with him."

"Because she's smarter than you, Martini." Chuckie sounded amused. He made eye contact with me, and I recognized his expression—there was someone nearby he didn't like who didn't like us right back. "But I'm willing to make allowances for Centaurion to be . . . adjusting to the way things are now."

"For the time being," Martini corrected. I nudged him and tried to send an emotional "hush." I caught Reader's eye, he cocked his head, and I shook mine. He nodded and scooted his chair closer to Gower's. I saw him put his hand on Gower's wrist and assumed they were communicating in some way.

"For the time being," Chuckie said with a small smile. He seated himself in the chair on my other side. "How do you like the place?"

"It's okay. Is this room clean?"

"It's spotless. The maid service is impeccable." Chuckie looked at me, and pointed to the centerpiece on the table. It looked like a bizarre pineapple, only it was orange and purple and pretty freaking ugly.

Gower's eyes looked glazed. I assumed he was having ACE share with everyone that it was quiet time.

"Ah, good to know. I'd love to stay here, then." Great. Bugged. Presumably by the C.I.A. But I figured I'd better be sure. "How's things with your parents?" They were both in Temecula, California, where he'd moved them once he'd made his money. It had been their dream to retire there, he'd just moved them a lot sooner than they'd expected. And I knew how they were, because I kept in touch with them, just as he kept in touch with my parents.

"Oh, they're fine. I don't see them very often, but we talk all the time. They send their love." He shook his head.

Okay, it was an audio bug, not visual, thank God for small favors. And it wasn't from the C.I.A. So, why was Chuckie letting it sit there? "Your sisters and brothers?" Like me, he was an only child.

"Fine, you know, the usual." He shook his head again. Okay, so not an American agency. So, who?

"How's Australia been?"

"Great, you know how I love the travel." He shook his head again, harder.

Not foreign. Not national. So, who? I could only come up with one other idea. "I'll bet the view of the Luxor's pyramid laser light show must be awesome from up here."

"Best view you could hope for. Like being on top of a mountain watching it." He nodded, emphatically.

Bingo. But how?

CHAPTER 9

MARTINI GOT UP. "You mind if I have a bite to eat?"

"No, go ahead, that's what the food's for." Chuckie nodded and Martini shrugged.

"Christopher, you look a little pale. You might want to eat something too." Martini jerked his head, and Christopher got up.

They started talking about baseball while Chuckie and I continued to chat about family members who didn't exist. The others got the clue, and soon the whole room was filled with aimless chatter.

Martini picked up the centerpiece and examined it. He shot a look at Chuckie while discussing the merits of the Diamondbacks over the Dodgers. Chuckie shrugged and pulled a small, black, rectangular thing out of his pocket. He put it near me: nothing. He got up, wandered around the room, still talking about his nonexistent siblings, while he put it near the others in the room. When it was by humans, nothing happened. When it was by Gower it turned purple, and when it was by Martini, Christopher, or the girls, it turned green.

Chuckie waved the alien-detector near the centerpiece. It turned red. He then pulled the Unity Necklace out of his pocket—I hadn't realized he'd taken it, but then, I hadn't been thinking about wearing it after what had happened earlier. He put the box near the necklace, and it turned red.

Martini nodded, and he looked seriously pissed, but not at Chuckie for once. He and Christopher started to take the centerpiece apart, carefully. Inside the ugly pineapple thing they found an oddly shaped piece of metal. I could see it and, like the necklace, it didn't look human-made.

Martini put his hand out, and Chuckie gave him the Unity Necklace. Martini played around with it a bit, and all of a sudden the two pieces fit together. Martini looked angrier, and Christopher looked pretty pissed off, too.

His hands moved so fast I couldn't see them, and I had to look away or get sick. So I looked at his face. Hey, I didn't have to look far away. Martini finished whatever he was doing and held out the combined pieces of metal to Chuckie, who held the little black box near it. It still glowed red.

Martini grimaced and looked thoughtful for a few long moments. "Kitty, you need to fix your hair."

"I do?" Everyone gave me "duh" looks, even Chuckie. I pondered. "Oh. Right you are." I pulled out my hairspray and handed it to Martini. He sprayed the combined metal all over, then held it out to Chuckie again. The black box glowed a weaker red.

Martini continued spraying and Chuckie continued testing until the red glow dissipated. Once gone, Martini went into the bedroom, came back with a bath towel, and wrapped the metal up inside it.

Martini put the towel-wrapped package down on the table, then he, Chuckie, and Christopher sat down. I could tell Martini was furious, but he was controlling it well.

"You sure it's . . . clear?" Chuckie asked.

Martini nodded. "It's neutralized. I'd guess if we wash the hairspray off, it'll spring right back into action, but I don't think it can function right now."

"Makes sense," Chuckie said.

It did? "So, what's that black box thing, what was the metal thing inside that freaky fake pineapple, and what did you do?"

"This is an alien-detector," Chuckie answered. "Oh, and duh."

"Yeah, fine. I didn't know we had those."

"Well, 'we' don't," Martini snapped. "Apparently, however, the C.I.A. does."

Chuckie rolled his eyes. "As this incident has just proved, there are aliens we don't know about."

"That metal stuff is alive?" I'd been wearing a living thing? I felt freaked out.

Martini took my hand. "No, it's not alive."

"Just sentient," Chuckie added. "You didn't mention that when you gave it to her, of course."

"Because I didn't know," Martini snarled.

"Boys? Enough of the caveman stuff. What's going on?"

Christopher answered. "The necklace responded to the bug. It's not called a bug, but that's how it works."

"Wow, the words all make sense individually, and yet, when put together, not so much."

"ACE can explain for Kitty."

"Thanks, ACE, I'd appreciate it."

Gower nodded and spoke in the ACE-voice again. "Like with ACE, the A-Cs on home world can put talents into . . ." Gower twitched and I figured he was having to help ACE with the right words. "Into inanimate objects. Useful for many things."

"Like spying."

"Yes. A-Cs are most advanced of all species in their solar system."

"So, they used these things to spy on the other planets?" No wonder they'd been able to stop the warlike planets in their solar system from doing anything—they'd nipped them in the bud before they could be a problem. Logical and tidy, which were A-C traits. Vicious and nasty, which were also A-C traits, just not traits the Earth A-Cs had. Thank God.

"Yes. Have sent this here to spy on Kitty."

Something about that didn't make sense to me. "Um . . . how?"

"What do you mean, how?" Christopher asked. "Through a gate or something."

"So, this metal stuff can move on its own?"

"No," Martini said. "It can't move at all. It doesn't think, either, despite our Supreme Leader's comments to the contrary."

"It just transmits information, like a good bug," Chuckie said, and I could hear the knife in his voice.

"Guys? If it can't move via its own steam, then how the hell did it get into this room?"

There was dead silence. Aliens and humans trained to work with aliens think time.

ACE answered. "Someone must have put it in here. ACE does not understand why Kitty did not know that."

"The hero worship is particularly nauseating during intimate moments," Reader tossed out. "If I get one more 'would Kitty do that?' question—"

"He's kidding, ACE," I said quickly. Not that I thought he was, but I didn't want ACE to get its feelings hurt. "And, sometimes it helps to ask a question aloud, even if you think you know the answer."

"Ah, a human thing. ACE has data for that." ACE had the consciousness of any human who'd died in space joined to it. It sort of made them part of the God in the Machine, and I was happy they were there, since their presence had altered ACE's mind-set toward protecting the Earth from the other races, not the other way around.

"Jeff? What did you do with the necklace and the bug? And why did my hairspray neutralize it?"

"The hairspray was a guess. Since we're all allergic to alcohol and there's alcohol in it—and since hairspray worked so well against Mephistopheles, and this clearly comes from our home world—I figured it might work."

"Whoever wants us followed knows we're all here now, however," Chuckie mentioned.

"True." Martini sighed. "And as for what I was doing, it's a game my father taught us," he inclined his head toward Christopher. "We used to think it was fun. He'd give us different metals, and we had to make something new with them without hurting the original shapes. Most of the time, he had us play with the metals and the Unity Necklace, but not always. I didn't know it was anything but a child's game before. But I'd guess once I make another call, and, you know, get through all the haranguing from my mother, I'll find out this was commonly used by the royal family."

"To spy on their underlings," Christopher added with a snarl.

"Or their enemies." Chuckie let this one hang on the air for a bit. "I think we need to stop pretending the only issue will be Kitty passing whatever marriage test they're going to administer. We didn't send bugs or spies over to check out Charles marrying Camilla, so this isn't what I'd call standard royal wedding protocol."

"It's not, as far as we know," Claudia offered.

"You're confirming that?" Chuckie asked her.

"Sure." She shrugged. "Girls care more about this stuff than boys. My mother told me about how weddings on our home world were handled. Spying on the bride-to-be wasn't mentioned."

"My mother didn't say anything about this, either," Lorraine added. "And she told me all about the last royal wedding she'd seen, right before they left our home world." She shot a look at Christopher. "I think it was your parents'."

He looked shocked. "But they disowned my mother, that's what my father said."

Lorraine looked uncomfortable. "They probably did. My mother would know for sure. But, disowned or not, I think they still had a royal wedding."

"Maybe we should ask your father if they got bugged."

Christopher sighed and pulled out his phone.

While he was engaged, Chuckie leaned over to me and Martini. "Regardless of the Pontifex's answer, this creates some serious issues. So, Martini, before the rest of the C.I.A. starts demanding I allow them to move into every Centaurion stronghold, any idea of what's really coming?"

"Not really. We should pull my father in, sooner as opposed to later. He's the one with the information."

My brain kicked at me. "Uh, guys?"

"Yes," Chuckie agreed. "But I'd like you to ask him, if you don't mind. I don't want to give the impression we're demanding his cooperation."

"Guys?"

"Well, that's so nice of you," Martini said, sarcasm knob turned to full. "How is it my father rates consideration when our Sovereign Pontifex doesn't?"

"Guys."

"He rates consideration because he's the only one with any real idea of what's going on, and, just in case, the C.I.A. doesn't want to create an interstellar incident by upsetting a royal scion."

"Guys, oh, guys."

"I'm supposedly a scion and so's Christopher. You don't seem to mind upsetting us. In fact, near as I can tell, you live to do it."

"Guys? Really, need your attention."

"You really have a problem with authority, don't you, Martini?"

"Guys? Please, focus."

"I have no problem with my own authority, Reynolds. I have a big problem with yours, or what you think is yours."

"Guys, don't force me to get tough with you."

"Keep pushing it, Martini. I'll be glad to show you just how much authority I have over you and anything you want to do."

I stood up, turned my back to the rest of the room, and lifted my shirt up. Both of them stopped with their mouths open and turned to stare at my chest. I was in the A-C version of a WonderBra and the twins were looking particularly large and perky. The men looked like deer trapped in headlights. "Wow, now that I finally freaking have your attention, can the two of you stop fighting with each other and listen to me?"

"Gah," Martini said.

"Ummm . . ." Chuckie sounded no more coherent.

Martini recovered first. "Put your top down." He was trying to sound growly but it was coming off more like an embarrassed, possessive hiss.

"Ummm . . ." Chuckie hadn't seen the twins in a while, but I could tell he wanted to get back in touch with them.

"I want you two to listen to me, and listen carefully."

"Top . . . down . . . now."

"Ummm . . ."

"You both going to listen?"

"Down."

"Ummm . . ."

"Nod your heads if you're going to listen to me when I put my top down." Two heads nodded. Two pairs of eyes didn't move, however. I lowered and resisted the impulse to pull my shirt up and down for a bit. "Now, look at my face."

Both sets of eyes moved up to meet mine.

"Good. So proud." Martini opened his mouth, and I lifted my shirt over my stomach. He snapped his mouth shut. "Good boy, Jeff. Now, I'm going to say something, and I want the two of you to listen to my words. Okay?"

They both nodded, eyes still wide, expressions still shocked.

"If the metal cannot move on its own, and we can be fairly sure no one in this room brought in that horrid pseudo-pineapple centerpiece, then logic demands that we ask ourselves these very important questions. You ready?"

They both nodded again.

"Who bugged the room? And what planet do they call home?"

CHAPTER 10

MARTINI RECOVERED FIRST, if you could call it that. "Don't know. Don't do that again. Ever. Unless we're alone."

Chuckie was back to staring at my chest. "Love Aerosmith."

"Yes, I still do." I snapped my fingers in front of his face. "Come on back now."

Reader was next to me. "You know, that was possibly the most hilarious thing I've ever seen. Not your rack, girlfriend, but their reactions to it."

"I warned them I was going to use the big guns."

"They are big, I'll give you that."

"Stop looking at or talking about her chest, James." Martini was growling.

"Jeff? I'm gay, remember?"

"Don't care. Stop looking at them. Stop talking about them." Martini looked at Chuckie. "Look at her face or, better yet, look at me, or I'm going to kill you."

"I saw them first," Chuckie said. This was true.

Martini was about to lose it, I could tell. "Boys? You either focus on my questions and how we answer them, or . . ." I raised my shirt over my stomach again.

"I don't want to answer the questions," Chuckie said. "Punish me for it."

"That's it!" Martini leaped up.

I jumped in between them. "Jeff? If you grab him, I'll be sandwiched between the two of you. Is that what you want?"

Martini growled, loudly, but he backed off.

I kept eye contact with Martini. "Chuckie? Enough with the comedy jokes. Serious questions want serious answers."

"I really want to be punished for my disobedience," he said from behind me, and I could tell he was standing. "But okay." He leaned down and whispered in my ear. "He's fun to bait. But . . . damn, they're still magnificent . . . and mesmerizing. Seriously, my parents love you, so, you know, consider the benefits of human marriage."

"Flattery will only get you so far." I tried not to smile or blush. Martini's expression said I failed at both.

"I'll keep working at it, then." Chuckie stepped away from us, and Martini relaxed a tiny bit.

"So, back to my questions. Who bugged the room?"

"It wasn't a human," Reader said. At least someone was paying attention to the issues at hand.

I turned around to see Christopher, Tim, and my five pilots all staring at me in various stages of shock, as near as I could tell. Claudia had her face in her hands, and Lorraine appeared to be recovering from trying to laugh without making noise. Gower was shaking his head.

"What?"

Tim pointed behind me. I turned around. To see that the wall behind Martini, ergo, the wall I'd been facing, was a mirror.

"Oh." So I hadn't noticed that when we got in. So what? "Um . . ." Didn't quite know what to say. "Whoops" about covered it. But I didn't feel the need to admit it out loud.

Randy and Joe seemed to be recovering. After all, they had girls in the room who had racks at least as good as mine. Lorraine was still laughing silently, and Joe had her in his lap now. Randy was patting Claudia on the back—I realized she was laughing too, so hard that she was having trouble breathing. My friends, there for me when I needed them.

"The United States Navy is proud to serve under those, Commander," Jerry said finally. "In fact, I'd like a picture, in case we ever need to remind the rest of the troops what it is we fight for." Walker and Hughes nodded their agreement.

"Dudes, they're not that big." I mean, they weren't. I wasn't Pam Anderson material.

"As women love to tell men, it's not the size that matters, Commander," Walker said. "It's how they look in their packaging. Or something." He sounded dazed.

I looked at Christopher. "What did your dad have to say?"

"He's never mentioned your breasts!"

I took a deep breath. All the male eyes in the room followed my chest. Even Reader and Gower were looking now. "I meant what did he say about a royal wedding?"

"Huh?" Christopher seemed stunned.

"Jeez, it's a pair of boobs. Covered up, at least somewhat, in a bra and now, again, in a T-shirt, too. Surely all of you have seen something like them before."

"Never used as an interrogation device," Jerry said. "I'm with Reynolds. Punish me for my disobedience."

I could hear Martini's growl—it was on "rabid dog" and about to head to "enraged bear". I decided to try to get things back under control. "Sorry, they're Jeff's now. Okay?"

"Lucky bastard," Hughes and Walker said in unison.

"I'm beginning to see why Centaurion hired you on," Chuckie added. Martini's growl wasn't subsiding.

"Okay! So, we have an alien plot, possibly much more sinister than just asking me if I know which one is the fish fork and which is the butter knife. Can we focus? Either that, or I'm going down to the casino to play craps."

"Can you change into a low-cut top before you do that?" Jerry asked.

I looked at Reader. "A little help?"

"I saw a great low-cut top in the women's clothing store in that mall they have connected to the casino. It was glittery and see-through. Want me to go see if they have it in your size?"

I put my hand on Reader's forehead. "Are you okay?"

He shrugged. "Just trying to sound like one of the boys." He flashed me his cover-boy grin. "C'mon, you know it's fun to see Jeff almost pop a vessel."

I rolled my eyes. "Not helping." I looked back to Christopher. "Seriously, what did your dad have to say? About why you called him? His wedding? Royal? Bugged?"

Christopher was still staring at me. "I can't believe you pulled your top up in front of all of us."

I managed to refrain from mentioning that he'd seen the twins in all their glory a year ago. Apparently, he wasn't as past all that as he said he was. "Christopher. Info from your dad. Needed now."

Christopher handed me his phone. It was still open, and the call was still live.

"Mister White?" I figured formality might be a good idea.

"Here, Miss Katt. From what I picked up when Christopher stopped speaking to me midsentence, you've used the age-old technique of flashing to get the situation under control. Your ability to adapt on your feet remains impressive."

"Thanks. Anything for the cause. Speaking of which, we found some weird Alpha Centaurion bug that Jeff and Christopher seemed to have dismantled or at least subdued."

"Interesting. Alfred would know more about this than I, however."

"Yes, but I don't think I want to call Mister Martini at this exact moment."

"Because Jeffrey's ready to explode?"

"Wow, you do know him well."

"Very. How is Mister Reynolds dealing with this?"

"He found the bug. Apparently the C.I.A. has some alien-detector thing. Does nothing by a human, turns purple by a hybrid, green by a pure A-C. And red by the bug. It also turned red by the Unity Necklace."

"Interesting again. I truly would have expected the Unity Necklace to have become inactive. As we've seen, not the case."

"So, they're sentient? For real?"

"In a way. Call it smart metal. From our home world, obviously. We can't make metals here work in the same way."

"So, the bug, it would have had to have come from the home world?"

"Yes. However, all our families here have their Unity Necklaces. Any who might have been separated when we were exiled here would have made a new one before leaving."

"How do the bugs work?"

"They attract to a Unity Necklace." He said it like it was obvious.

"So, any bug can attach to any Unity Necklace?"

"No. Think of them less like a bug and more like a tracking device. These necklaces are hugely important in our culture. The loss of a necklace is devastating. In the past, we had several suicides over the accidental loss. Hence, the tracking devices were created."

Wow. People killed themselves over losing their necklace? I'd have felt like total crap if I'd lost it, but I didn't think I'd have gone suicidal. Then again, I wasn't an A-C.

"So, how does the tracking device work?"

"It's set to find its necklace. The ones Jeffrey and Christopher played with as children were the ones Alfred and I had for our necklaces. I would have thought they were the only ones in existence for those specific necklaces, but I believe my thinking is incorrect."

"So, the tracking device finds the necklace, and then what?"

"It transmits location to the owner, by means of another piece of the intelligent metal."

"Is that how they knew which mountain ranges to light up the night skies with?"

"No, that would have tracked based on Jeffrey."

"How so?"

White sighed. "It's more complex. If it's not relevant at this moment, it would be easier to explain it to you in person."

"There's not a bottom line I can give to Chuckie?" Who, I knew without asking, would want a better answer than "tell you later."

Another sigh. "I would be happy to share it with Mister Reynolds. He actually has the capacity to understand the explanation."

"I'll ignore that comment about my mental prowess." I handed the phone to Chuckie. "You get the scientific mumbo jumbo, but I want the Pontifex back."

Chuckie shrugged. "Hello, Pontifex White. No, I haven't demanded this answer yet. Yes, she's right, of course I'm about to." He was quiet for a couple of minutes while the rest of us basically watched him listen to the phone. It didn't seem to faze him, but I was used to that. "I understand. Yes, nothing we can do about it. Yes, that's a good idea, thank you. Here's Kitty."

Chuckie handed me the phone. "It's based on a process similar to how their Operations Team functions." Oh, right, the Elves had an official title. "High-level math, higher-level science. Trust me when I tell you that you don't want to know." He looked at Martini. "We'll be putting some people onto this—I don't think we want the heads of American Centaurion tracked like timber wolves, at least not by our enemies."

Martini snorted. "As if you're not tracking us."

Chuckie grinned. "Of course we are. But we're not your enemies."

"Right."

I decided going back to my call with White was the better part of valor. "Okay, happy to have let Chuckie do the heavy thinking. But I do have another question, Mister White."

"No insinuation that you're not able to think heavily intended, Miss Katt. I just know where your strengths lie. So, please, do go ahead."

"The night sky thing. Is that triggered from across space, or does it trigger closer to home?"

There was a pause. "The trigger would be Jeffrey, again, based on the complexities I shared with Mister Reynolds. However . . . I don't know about the relationship between physical location and original home world."

"You're saying you don't know if the light show went on at Alpha Centauri at the same time as here?"

"In a way. I'm saying I assumed all ties were severed when we came here. But if we were on our home world, the light show, as you call it, is an announcement that a royal match is beginning, the declaration made and accepted, and so forth. And at home it would be triggered by the agent of the royal family who was assigned to guard that particular member."

I looked at Martini. He still looked upset. But I could tell he was picking up my feelings, because he cocked his head and gave me a questioning look.

"So, Mister White—who's here, watching Jeff?"

CHAPTER 11

"NO IDEA, MISS KATT. I have to say I doubt it's any of our own people."

Made sense but could be wrong. "You'd have told me Beverly was trustworthy, too, though."

"Yes, good point. Bottom line is I have no idea." He coughed. "That's what Alpha Team is for."

"Oh, fine, got the hint. Thanks so much. If someone announces that he or she is the Royal Family Spy or something, you will manage to let me know?"

"With all haste, yes."

"Super. So, any other issues we should know about that I'm sure will make my eyes cross?"

"Not that I know of, but, again, I'll contact you if something occurs to me. Besides, if you're feeling stressed or confused by something I tell you, just pull your top up, and I'm sure we'll be even." He did have a sense of humor. He hid it, but it was there.

"Point taken. Talk to you soon, Mister White."

"I'm breathless with anticipation of the next call, Miss Katt."

We hung up, and I tossed the phone back to Christopher. "Okay, so there's someone here who's spying on Jeff and probably Christopher, too. Possibly all of the Martini family. The Pontifex has no guess as to who, and we have no guess as to how many. Could be Earth A-Cs who are still loyal to the home world, could be that the home world opened the door on their side and sent one or more spies here."

"I don't think it's anyone who calls Earth home," Gower said, in his own voice. "Beverly backing Yates, that was understandable. He *was* our religious leader before he'd been exiled. But we have no loyalties to the Alpha Centaurion throne."

"You know, the person I'd like to talk to about this is your mother."

Gower looked startled. "Why? She's an Earth woman."

"She warned Michael, so she's smarter than the rest of your family." And I had to figure she'd gone through what I was going to, at least in some way. I wanted to talk to her for more than this threat—I wanted to talk to her to find out if she regretted falling in love with an A-C.

"Call your mother and ask her if she'd prefer to come here or have us to go to her." Martini's voice made it clear this was an order.

"She'll want to come here." Gower grinned. "She loves Vegas, too."

I knew I'd be able to relate to her. "Great, let's ensure she gets here safely."

"I'll have my father come with her."

"Have them under guard." I looked to Chuckie and Martini. "Seriously. Human and A-C. I think Chuckie's right, and we should be considering this as an invasion of some kind. Which means I want to bring Kevin in, full-time, on this."

Everyone in the room but Chuckie nodded agreement. We'd all like Kevin around to give Chuckie someone to focus on other than Martini or Christopher.

Chuckie, however, gave me a slow smile. "Nice try. But no. I have Mister Lewis otherwise occupied."

"But he doesn't report to you."

"Oh, actually, he does. Since he's the assigned P.T.C.U. representative to Centaurion Division, and Centaurion currently reports in to me, so does Mister Lewis."

I tried not to grimace. "Okay."

Chuckie grinned. "I know you're all disappointed. However, I've stared down your mother, Kitty. Mister Lewis presents no challenges."

"Jerk."

He laughed. "It's my job. And I'm good at it." He looked around. "Okay, any ideas about who delivered the bug? And are there any more in the room?"

"I have a question first."

Chuckie rolled his eyes. "What a shock."

"Does the necklace transmit information like the bug did or does?"

Martini shrugged. "No idea. Didn't know they were sentient, bugging us, or tracking us until this hour."

"Let's assume it does, in some way. That means whoever's watching you has been watching for at least six months."

"Okay," Martini said, patience clearly being forced. "I can buy that. So what?"

"So, why now? I mean, why right now? It's six weeks before we're supposed to get married. I can understand that maybe they wanted to come out and give me whatever test it is that I'm undoubtedly going to fail, but why wait until now? Wouldn't it have made more sense to do it, say, before you officially proposed? Or right after I said yes?"

"No idea. I don't know these people, their archaic rituals, or why they're coming. I just know I hate them." Martini's teeth were clenched.

"She's got a point," Chuckie said, and I realized he was speaking in a soothing tone. "Look, I'm not accusing you, hell, anyone in this room, of some sort of subterfuge. It's pretty clear this is a surprise to all involved. Let's get Gower's mother and your father out here, and maybe we'll get some answers."

"He won't come without my mother," Martini said, sounding utterly depressed. "She gets upset if he comes out West without her."

"Why?" This sounded odd, since all their family, other than Martini himself, Christopher, and White, were back East.

He sighed and rubbed his forehead. "Like every other woman in my life, apparently, she loves Vegas."

"Great, road trip." I looked back to Chuckie. "Whoever's watching Jeff must be watching you."

"Why so?"

"You got the pineapple. You know, in the Mob, that means you're marked for death."

"It's not a pineapple. And we're not dealing with the Mob. Besides, that's F.B.I. territory."

"I just think they're after you, too."

"What are you suggesting? We all go underground into one of the Bases?"

I thought about it. "Actually, no. I think we all want to be really easy to find."

".What?" This was chorused by Martini, Chuckie, Christopher, and a few of the others.

Reader shrugged and leaned against the table next to me. "Girlfriend's right. Why make it hard for them? Hard means we have less maneuverability. Easy means they have more of a chance of making a mistake."

"How so?" Chuckie didn't sound convinced.

I sighed. "Look, someone's on Earth, someone I think it's safe to say we can all consider at least somewhat unfriendly. We haven't known about it, but they've been here at least six months. Maybe they didn't show up when Jeff made the decision he wanted to marry me, but I feel pretty sure they showed up as soon as I put on that Unity Necklace. So call it six months. We've been under observation, close observation, since then. And no one, including ACE, has spotted it."

Gower twitched. "ACE was not looking for this kind of threat."

"Can you look now? I mean, if it's not going to be a conscience issue."

Gower's head nodded. "ACE will look. ACE will tell if it will not go against how ACE must interact."

"That's great, ACE, and thanks."

Gower twitched again. "I don't mind ACE, but I hate the palsy that comes with him." He sighed. "You're right, though. I can tell when ACE knows something he desperately wants to tell me but feels he can't. He's as worried as the rest of us, but he has no idea of what's going on any more than we do." Gower looked directly at me. "No one in his consciousness is clear on what's going on, either."

Ah, I'd always known putting ACE into Gower was the right choice. So Terry had no idea of what was up, either. Then there was more going on than just the standard Royal Wedding crap. I considered that my thinking the word crap, let alone the rest of the way I spoke, thought, and acted, was probably going to guarantee that whoever was administering whatever test were going to flunk me. I wondered if Martini was going to have to listen to them and tried not to let the worry that he might get out of control.

A hand was on the back of my neck, massaging gently. He'd picked the worry up, of course. "It'll be fine, baby," Martini said softly.

"Let's hope so," Chuckie said, his voice crisp. "Because I

think Kitty has a point." He tossed the alien-detector to Tim. "Check out every single thing in this suite." He looked at my pilots. "There are a few more of them in the small black bag on my bed. Get them, and help him."

None of them moved. "Guys? We're answering to Chuckie right now, remember?" I got a couple of betrayed looks, but they all got up and did as requested. "Chuckie, you might want to remember that they haven't adjusted to the change in chain of command yet."

"And you might want to remember that they're all military or A-C trained, which means they adjusted to it the moment Martini said yes. As long as you, White, and Martini are fighting it, however, they're going to do their best to support insubordination." He wasn't smiling

"Don't talk to her in that tone of voice." Martini's voice was low and threatening.

Chuckie faced us, and I saw, clearly, how he'd risen in the C.I.A. so fast. He wasn't out of control, but his expression was icy, and the authority radiated off of him. "You all, *all*, report to me now. I'm being nice because I realize it's a shock and you're being attacked personally. But if you don't get it under control within the next five minutes, I'm putting C.I.A. into every Centaurion stronghold, and that includes your family's estate. We are in a state of international and interstellar emergency, and if you're not part of the solution, then you are automatically part of the problem. And, better than any human alive, I know how to solve alien problems."

CHAPTER 12

"BY KILLING US?" Martini's voice was calm, but I could tell he was ready to attack.

"No, Jeff. By outing you."

Chuckie nodded. "I'll do it, in a New York Minute. You'll be so busy dealing with the world governments and world-wide human reactions that you'll all be dead or leaving within a week."

"You're a piece of work." Martini didn't sound any more relaxed.

"No. He's a human. And he's C.I.A." I turned around and looked up at Martini. "Jeff, he doesn't want to. Don't you understand? He spent his whole life trying to prove you all were really here. Other than my mother and her team, he's the best friend we have in any government agency. I know you two butt heads, but that's because you're alpha males—you, Chuckie, and Christopher—and it's a natural thing. You and Christopher get along *only* because you're so close and closely related. But you conceding authority to Chuckie doesn't diminish yours."

Martini didn't look convinced. "Why do you trust him?"

"Because I've known him since I was thirteen."

"People change."

"Sure they do. And he has. He's become more like you. But what he hasn't become is someone I can't trust." I focused all my energy on trying to show Martini what I meant emotionally. I wasn't sure it was working—my emotions were getting jumbled for a variety of reasons.

Martini took a deep breath and let it out slowly. "Fine." He looked back at Chuckie. "We'll get it together and keep it together. Sir." There was no sarcasm in his tone, particularly on the last word.

"I don't need that. I don't want that. Kitty's right—I'm the best friend you have right now. I'm not trying to 'rule' Centaurion Division. I'm trying to keep out the people who want to take over and turn you into something none of you want to be."

Oh, I knew what that was. "The War Division."

"Right. How'd you know?" Chuckie didn't seem worried, just curious.

"Leventhal Reid couldn't have been the only politician out there who could see the advantages of turning the A-Cs into weapons. The parasites are slowing down, and the only thing stopping them from pushing for a change in A-C status is the fact that ACE is in Paul, and that means Centaurion can pull out the biggest gun this planet's ever seen." Of course, ACE wouldn't do it, and Paul wouldn't okay it, but that was, at least currently, our little secret.

Chuckie's expression told me he was in on the secret, however. I did know him well, and I could tell when he knew I wasn't telling him everything. I could also tell when he knew what it was I wasn't telling him. But he didn't argue, just nodded. "Right."

"So, what's the plan?" Martini asked. "And what do you want us to call you?"

"What you always have, but leave off the dirty words. However, when your distant relatives appear, figure you'd all better call me something that would indicate to them that you're not the one ultimately in charge."

"So I'm back to what we were trying to decide before you two got into your latest fight for dominance. I think we need to be really out in the open and easy to find."

"Why?" Martini didn't sound convinced, but he did sound as though he was calming down, which I felt was the more desirable outcome.

"Because—and I'll say this again since I know no one but James was listening to me—whoever's watching Jeff and presumably Christopher is also obviously watching Chuckie. I think it's safe to assume they know we saw the light show. They could be aware Chuckie's in charge of Alpha Team now, or just think he's working closely with us, but it's *his* room that was bugged."

"To me, that would indicate we should go into lockdown." Christopher didn't sound his usual snarky. I guessed he was still recovering from the twins' surprise appearance. I wondered how he'd handle a typical Vegas show.

"Not if we want to find them before whoever's coming arrives. Especially since it doesn't seem like they'll be coming via a gate." I looked around. Apparently I was the only one who'd had this thought.

"Why would you say that?" Lorraine asked slowly. "It's fast and safe."

"It's not grandiose and impressive. The peasants love a good show."

Chuckie and Reader laughed. "Yeah, girlfriend, they do that." Reader shoved off from the table. "I know where this is going. Or, rather, where we are."

"Where's that, James?" Martini didn't sound as though he had any idea.

Reader grinned. "We're gonna stay in Sin City. I'm going to order up clothing and necessities for the entire team for, how long do you think, girlfriend?"

"Week, week and a half. No A-C Elves here."

"Right. Sounds good. We can buy that top for you later." Reader pulled out his phone and wandered over to a far corner of the room.

"We're staying here?" Martini sounded mildly freaked.

"Yeah, I think that might be a good idea," Chuckie conceded. "They found me here without issue, might as well not make them work any harder."

"Why are we doing this, exactly?" Christopher asked. "I'm not wild about being out in the open where anyone can attack us."

"If they're Earth A-Cs, seeing them here will be sort of an alert, wouldn't you think?"

There was silence. I could hear Reader telling someone what to pack up for us.

"It's a big town, with a lot of people coming through," Gower said finally.

"It's a big town with a lot of security all through it. This is probably the most secure town in all of the United States.

Security we can tap into since we have the C.I.A. intimately involved."

"Fine. Then you're all moving into this hotel." Chuckie went to the room phone and dialed.

"While you're talking, see if they can tell you who cleaned your room and brought up the spread, particularly the pseudo-pineapple."

"Oh, yes, Miss I'll Take Charge." He grinned at me, though, so I knew he wasn't angry with me.

So did Martini. "I want to be on record that you and I are not staying on the same floor as him and you're not, under any circumstances, sleeping in here with him."

I looked up and over my shoulder at him. "Jeff, of course I'm not going to sleep in here with him. I'm with you, and I'll be sleeping wherever you're sleeping.

"Okay, Martini and Kitty, you're in the suite on the other half of this floor," Chuckie called, right on cue. "That keeps the floor secure. I have everyone one else on the floor directly under us. Includes room for Gower's parents and yours, too, Martini. I took all the others that were open, too; we'll probably need them for a variety of reasons. That fills up the floor, so we've got the top two. Means we have roof access without an issue as well."

Martini started to growl. I turned around again. "Jeff, it's a huge suite. He won't hear us."

"Right. I hate taking orders from him, you know."

"I know." I took his hand. "Tell you what. Later on? Why don't you give me some orders? And," I moved closer and dropped my voice, "I'll argue about taking them."

His eyes started to smolder. "God, I love how you think."

"Consider this, too—we won't be on the same floor as your parents."

"Hmmm, maybe Reynolds is my friend after all."

Chuckie hung up the phone. "They couldn't reach Catering. Someone's supposed to call me back. Housekeeping is the standard staff. But, realistically, I don't think it was them. The pineapple thing came with the food."

"Works for me. Jeff, you going to call your dad? And, Paul, you need to call your mom, too."

Gower nodded, pulled out his phone, and dialed. Martini grumbled. I decided to give him incentive and wandered over to Chuckie. "We need human as well as A-C guards on the Gowers and the Martinis. What do you suggest?" I heard more grumbling, but also heard Martini dial his phone. Good, he *had* picked up my annoyance.

Chuckie sighed. "I'll have Agent Lewis handle it."

"Where *is* Kevin, anyway?"

"Checking out some leads it makes more sense for a human Federal officer to check out." Chuckie grinned. "I'm not telling you, so don't try to get it out of me."

"I'm sure I could if I worked at it."

His grin got wider. "Not with Martini around."

The room phone rang before I could come up with a suitable retort, and he went to answer it. I was relieved and wistful both, which probably wasn't good.

It was shocking to me to realize I was finding it harder to be here with Chuckie than I'd expected. This part of the Mandalay Bay hadn't existed when we'd been here, but we'd stayed in the complex. The part of me that was thrilled to be staying here for a week or so was doing its best to ignore the other part that felt it wasn't a good idea to put myself into any kind of compromising position with a legitimate romantic option. Martini was too easily able to pick up when I was thinking things I shouldn't be.

Gower and Martini hung up about the same time. "My parents are all set," Gower said. "My mom's looking forward to it, my dad, not so much."

"Have Michael come out here to finish his vacation. We can use the help—we need to have help we know we can trust—and maybe your dad will have more fun if he's here, too."

Gower shrugged. "Good plan." He opened his phone again.

"My parents are coming," Martini said in a voice of doom. "My mother has a different impression of why we're here, though."

"Oh? What does she think we're doing?"

"Girl-time bonding." He looked as doom-filled as he sounded. "You might want to see if your parents can come out, too."

"I'll see if we have enough rooms."

Chuckie hung up before I could get my phone out. "Caterer's a jerk, but the food was catered from one of the restaurants in their version of a food court."

"Which one?"

"L'Avventura."

I shook my head. "There's no restaurant named that here."

"You're sure?"

"Yeah, I'm positive." The week with Chuckie wasn't the only time I'd spent in Vegas, and I lived to eat out at nice restaurants—at least, I had before I'd discovered sex with Martini. Fine dining had dropped a bit on my list since then. But not so much that I wasn't fully aware of every restaurant here.

I walked over to the huge television that dominated one wall in what I supposed was the living room. The hotel amenities book was there. I flipped through it. "No L'Avventura."

"Check the mall," Reader said as he finished his call. "Could be there."

I did. "No. Nothing like it."

Martini and Christopher looked at each other. "Be right back," Martini said. They both disappeared. I checked the double doors—they were unlocked.

"That has to be weird to live with," Chuckie said casually.

"You get used to it."

"Do you?"

I looked up at him. "Yeah. Thanks, by the way."

"For what?"

"For still being you."

He grinned. "Well, that's something."

"I'm going to fail the tests." I hadn't meant to blurt that out.

Chuckie reached out and stroked my cheek. "He doesn't care. It won't matter to him. Martini's not focused on regaining the throne—he's focused on protecting you, the Pontifex, and the rest of his people. Not going off to a world he's never seen to take care of it or solve its problems."

"You sure?"

"Yeah, I'm positive. I wish I weren't. I'd be happy if he disappeared and left you here. But he won't, not willingly."

"What if they force him to?"

Chuckie shrugged. "Then we'll do what we Americans do best."

"What's that?"

He grinned again, but this time it was feral. "We'll make them sorry they ever bothered us."

CHAPTER 13

MARTINI AND CHRISTOPHER WERE BACK, both looking angry. "Get your buddies in here, fast, and get the phones fixed," Martini said to Chuckie.

"Not that I mind, but why?"

"Catering never took an order from the front desk for anything to come up to this suite. Catering says their phones haven't been working all day—they've had to send a runner to the front desk on an hourly basis. Said runner also never took an order to or from the front desk for this suite. The desk clerk, however, is positive she gave your order to someone from her catering department."

Chuckie's eyes narrowed. "You're sure?"

"Haven't found a human yet who could lie to me," Martini snapped. "Oh, and we tell the humans from the A-Cs by the heartbeats. And A-Cs can't lie to me, either. So, yeah, humans down there, not A-Cs. Confused humans who haven't spoken to you, ever. Who also, let me mention, didn't send any food up to you."

"Stop eating or drinking," I barked. "Lorraine and Claudia, full medical scans on everybody, right now."

Reader opened his phone and made another call while the girls leaped into action. They scanned Martini, Christopher, me, Gower, and Chuckie first, then themselves and the rest of the team. "Our telephony team's on the way. More medical's coming, too," Reader told me. "Along with the rest of our supplies. And a ton of adrenaline. That we'll want to keep under lock and key."

He didn't need to tell me. Martini's empathic blocks and synapses burned out under too much stress and activity. Sleep was a regenerative, and so were some medical procedures, but he routinely reached a point where he had to go into an isolation chamber, and if he didn't get into one, he had to have adrenaline or die. Point of fact, I had to slam a huge hypodermic that resembled a harpoon far more than a sewing needle into his hearts. It was horrible, but it was a better option than letting him die. We'd had plenty of enemies use his adrenaline dependency against him, particularly during Operation Drug Addict, so there was no reason to think this time would be any different.

The girls were done. "Nobody has anything wrong that we can tell," Lorraine said with relief.

I looked at the table. "What, if anything, wasn't eaten by someone on the team?"

We all examined the offerings. "That," Chuckie pointed to a dish near the center. "I have no idea what it is, by the way, which is why I didn't touch it. But it's undisturbed from how it was when it arrived, so no one else had any either."

Reader and I looked at it. "No clue."

"Me either, girlfriend. Yo, Tim, flyboys, need you for a minute." The rest of the humans came over. Reader pointed. "Don't eat it or taste it, but do you have any idea of what it is?"

They all shook their heads. "Looks gross," Jerry said.

"Sort of like boiled okra," Joe offered.

"Only not like my mamma ever made," Randy added.

All the A-Cs were staring at it. "Familiar?" I asked Martini.

"No. I'm with the others, that looks disgusting."

I reached out and took the alien-detector out of Jerry's hand and held it toward the icky foodstuff. It glowed red.

"Sentient food? I mean, after it's been cooked?"

"They don't find sentience," Chuckie said. "They find something alien to Earth."

"Why the color spectrum, then?"

"Because we have DNA samples of what pure A-Cs and hybrid A-Cs are made of. So we can spot them. You know, so we know who the friendlies are?" Chuckie looked over to Martini. "Red means alien we don't know about."

Martini nodded. "That's why the necklace and the tracker showed red. They're metals from our home world, but not metals that are in our DNA. Baby, run it over everything else."

I did. Only the one dish glowed red. Tim checked out the minibar and all the stuff in the refrigerator—all clean. Something in my brain kicked. "You said the front desk clerk thought she'd given Chuckie's food order to the Catering department's runner, right?"

"Yes," Christopher confirmed. "And we're not quite as stupid as you always seem to think. Already checked out every person in the Catering department. No one's missing, no one's extra. Everyone who's supposed to be here today is, and no one has a day off today, either."

"So we have an extra body. That the front desk clerk thought was someone she knew."

"Right." Christopher shrugged. "No idea of what to do about it, though."

I hated to say this in front of Chuckie. "Okay, then the A-C we're looking for is an imageer."

"Come again?" Christopher sounded insulted. "What makes you say that?"

"Because you don't have shapeshifters." I looked around. Everyone else looked blank too. I had no idea why. It seemed obvious.

A-Cs with imageering talent were able to manipulate images, which was how the Imageering side of the Centaurion house kept the regular humans from realizing parasitic jellyfish things had splatted onto a human and turned said human into an alien superbeing monster.

In addition to manipulation, an imageer who'd touched the picture of a person would know everything about that person—Christopher had explained it as pictures taking a copy of the mind and soul as well as the body. The stronger the imageer, the more information he or she could glean from the touched image.

Christopher was the strongest imageer on the planet, and during Operation Fugly, he'd touched some of the pictures I'd had displayed in my apartment. This was why, during Operation Drug Addict, he'd recognized my old boyfriend from high school, Brian Dwyer, before I did. Well before, but hey, as I liked to remind everyone, I was the big picture girl. Details were for other people.

Chuckie almost never allowed his picture to be taken. I'd always figured it was because he didn't think he looked good when he was younger and was more comfortable out of the limelight as an adult. Now I wondered how long he'd known just what kinds of aliens were on Earth.

But it wasn't relevant to the current problem. Other imageering skills were. When we were recovering from that mad moment of not-too-wise passion in the elevator, Christopher had shown that imageers could also draw images using air molecules or some such. To me, this knowledge should have made what I was thinking obvious to all, but apparently the heavy thinking was somehow being left to me. Always the way.

"The fake runner shorted out the phones to Catering, probably after he or she heard Chuckie call for food. He or she overlaid an image of the real runner onto himself and took the order from the front desk clerk. Same faker delivered the food to Chuckie. No one's the wiser. They've tapped the phones, so it was simple to call Chuckie back, since they've kept the lines out to Catering. They made up a restaurant name, and Bob's your uncle."

"My uncle's name is Richard," Martini said. "But, okay, that makes sense."

"So they're on the premises somewhere," Chuckie said.

"One of them is, for sure. But A-Cs move so fast, it wouldn't need to be more than one."

Christopher closed his eyes and took a deep breath. Then he pulled out his phone. "This is Commander White. I want a full personnel status report for today. Every imageer, where they were, who they were with, every detail. And I want anyone who can't prove his or her whereabouts put under immediate house arrest. Yes, I'm serious. Yes, I want this done immediately. No, it's not a drill, it's real. No, this is me telling you, not the C.I.A. Look, you want me to come down there and explain it personally to you?" He was snarling. "Right. Faster than that. Yes, that's why I said immediately." He covered the phone and looked at Reader. "James, we need Security to main Imageer control stat—I don't think I'm talking to who I should be."

Reader nodded and dialed. I looked at Chuckie. "I am so sick of being infiltrated."

"Maybe they're just confused."

"Maybe." Martini had his Commander hat on, too. "But maybe not." He pulled out his phone. "We're on internal alert. Yes. Right. Imageering. No, I'm not kidding. No, not Christopher. Every other imageer, however. Right. Handle it fast, handle it right, because if I have to come down there and handle it for you . . . Right, good. I want to know the moment you find anything suspicious. Any kind of suspicious. Right. Good. Yeah, Christopher's very concerned. Yes, thanks for taking care of that already. Appreciate the help. Thanks, Gladys."

"Gladys? You called Gladys for this?"

He gave me a sideways look. "You'd be surprised at what Gladys' job title is."

I thought about it. "I supposed Center Operator isn't it."

"No."

I thought about it some more. "Why does the Head of Security run the intercom system?"

He grinned. "Because we don't want a peon disturbing our rest." He nodded to Christopher. "She's already got the Pontifex secured."

Christopher nodded back and mouthed, "Thanks."

"Yes, I really would like to know who's in there with you. Really? How interesting. Hello? Confirm, please. Okay, good. Take them all in. I want all of Imageering under the closest scrutiny. Looking for anything suspicious, particularly anything that relates to Commander Martini. Regular updates would be nice. Yes, with extreme prejudice." He hung up and rubbed his forehead. "This sucks, but good call, Kitty."

"You think your department's been infiltrated?"

"Well, the reaction time's not exactly what I'm used to when we're under alert, so yeah, I'm pretty sure we have a problem."

"Only one?"

"Hilarious." Christopher looked at Martini. "Jeff, if my department's infiltrated, what about yours?"

"If we have a rogue imageer out there, who knows?" Martini sighed. "At least it'll be fast."

"How so?" Chuckie asked.

"We move fast," Martini said. "And we move faster in these kinds of situations."

"How fast?"

Christopher and Martini's phones both rang. Martini grinned at me as he answered. "That fast."

CHAPTER 14

MARTINI AND CHRISTOPHER WERE BOTH DEEP in conversation when there was a knock. Chuckie pulled a gun out of his jacket and motioned for the rest of us to get away from the door. I dug my Glock out of my purse, and Reader and Gower pulled their guns out of their jackets as well. Nice to know the three of them were wearing shoulder holsters. Martini and Christopher still refused to, another thing I was working on.

Everyone else got out of the way. Four guns were probably good for one door, and that way, the others were in fallback position.

Chuckie opened the door so that he was to the side. And we were greeted by the threatening sight of Melanie and Emily, Lorraine and Claudia's mothers. "Nice welcome," Melanie said dryly. She looked a lot like Raquel Welch had when she was playing a cave girl.

Emily, who looked like a young Sophia Loren, shook her head. "Nice to see things are always tense for you guys."

We put the guns away. "Nice to see you. What're you two doing here?"

Melanie shrugged as they started dragging several fully loaded luggage carts into the room. "James felt having people you could trust deliver your supplies, particularly Jeff's adrenaline, would be a good idea."

I loved Reader. "Great idea."

"Plus, we wanted to have a good time, too." Emily laughed

at my expression. "Lucinda's coming, we got the word. You'll be happy we're here, trust me."

Lorraine and Claudia trotted over to help their mothers. "You're going to stay?" Lorraine asked.

"We won't cramp your style," Melanie said. "Promise."

"Sure, you say that now." Lorraine grinned. "It's great to have you here, Mom. Joe's being a stick-in-the-mud and doesn't want to let me gamble."

Melanie laughed. "We'll see about that." I'd never really questioned where Lorraine and Claudia got their personalities from. As mothers went, Melanie and Emily were my faves, right after my own and Chuckie's mom. I pushed the fact that I didn't really like Martini's mother, and she really didn't like me, as far down as possible.

"Are your husbands coming, too?"

Emily rolled her eyes. "No. They hate Vegas. Which is good, because that way we have contacts back at the Science Center we can trust. I can't believe Imageering's been infiltrated."

"How did you know about that?"

Melanie shrugged. "The Science Center's already been searched. We're all clean, but you never know."

"In five minutes?"

They exchanged glances. "Um, Kitty? Hyperspeed, remember?" Emily looked concerned. "Are you feeling okay?"

"Just overwhelmed." A thought occurred. "Hey, do you two happen to know what this is?" I pointed to the dish of creepy food. "Don't eat it, we think it's poisoned."

They stared at it. "It's familiar . . ." Melanie shook her head. "I think it's a dish from home."

"You think? You don't know for sure?"

"All of you always act like there are only two generations here," Emily answered. "But really, there are three or more. We're a lot younger than Jeff's parents, as an example. We don't count as the older generation, and since we have children in it, we don't count as the younger generation, either. Our parents came as operatives, too, but they were older, and many of them aren't with us any longer. We were little when we left the home world, but we remember it."

This made sense, it just hadn't really occurred to me. I felt unobservant, which was pretty much my par for any course.

Chuckie sauntered over. "Ladies, glad you could join us. Charles Reynolds." He put his hand out.

Melanie took it first. "Right, the new boss." She gave him an obvious up and down. "Hmmm. Well, I suppose if Jeff ever acts stupid again, you're not a bad option."

Chuckie managed to keep his jaw closed, but his eyes went wide. "Uh . . ." He offered his hand to Emily.

"Oh, Angela likes him," Emily said chidingly as she shook his hand. "I'm sure he's not as much of a jerk as the boys think he is. Nice grip." She turned his hand over. "No manicure? You're not the rich pompous ass they said. Interesting."

Chuckie looked at me. "Are they for real?"

"They're the heads of the Bluntness Division."

Chuckie started to laugh. "Would you two mind sharing a room? We're going to run out of space, I think."

"Sure, we'd rather, girl sleepover kind of thing," Melanie said. She gave him another close look. "Angela says we can trust you."

Chuckie shrugged. "She's known me half my life, and she recommended me for initial hire and promotions within the Agency. I'd assume she doesn't hate me."

"No, she doesn't." Emily was also giving Chuckie another once-over. "You sure this isn't some elaborate attempt to win Kitty back?"

"There is no 'back' in that sense." He didn't sound flippant, he sounded regretful. My throat got tight. This was not a conversation I wanted to hear, or have Martini hear. I busied myself with staring at the mystery food.

"Huh. That's not what my daughter said," Melanie replied. Oh, great, Lorraine had filled her mother in on my love life.

"Well, it was a long time ago." I recognized his tone of voice. Chuckie wasn't enjoying this conversation, either.

"Nice to see you both, glad you're staying, think you could stop torturing the two of them? And me?" Martini didn't sound angry, at least not with me or Chuckie.

"Just protecting your interests, Jeff," Emily said with a laugh.

"Right. Look, I hate him, he hates me, but even I'm sensitive enough to realize that standing here rubbing in who's got the girl isn't a great way to work together. And we have to work together." Martini put emphasis on the last sentence.

Dazzlers of all ages were two things—gorgeous and brilliant. Melanie and Emily were no exceptions. They got the point. "Fine, fine. Well, how do we get a room?" Melanie said with a sigh.

"Reader's probably got that covered," Chuckie said. Our latest female additions wandered off to find him. "Thanks, I think," he said to Martini.

"Don't mention it. Really, don't mention it. I hate having to remember you're not the antichrist."

"Yeah, I can relate. I hate having to remember that you're not a moron."

Play-nice time was over. Time to swallow the lump in my throat and keep things moving along smoothly. "Jeff, Emily and Melanie think this is a dish from your home world, but they're not sure." I was still staring at it. It was still unappetizing. It also hadn't moved, so I decided I could sleep again.

"We'll have my parents take a look when they get here." Martini came over to me and stroked the back of my neck. "I'm not upset," he said very softly.

I looked up at him. "Really?"

"Yeah. Any inroads he made were my fault. Hard to be upset with you about it."

"Jeff, that was six months ago."

"Seems like yesterday."

"Sometimes. Not always." I took a deep breath and tried to relax. "So, have we found out who infiltrated what?"

Martini grimaced. "In a way."

"In a way?"

He sighed. "It's both not as bad as we feared and worse."

"Oh, good. Routine."

CHAPTER 15

WE WERE ALL GROUPED AROUND the conference table again, Melanie and Emily included. The rest of Chuckie's suite had been declared clean of alien stuff, and Martini and Christopher had done some additional checks using hyperspeed, so we all felt there were no human bugs other than the ones Chuckie had removed before the rest of us had arrived.

"Okay, we have at least one rogue imageer," Christopher told us, and it was clear he was furious. "They're damned good, too. The reason my team was so slow and confused was because 'I' had just been there an hour or so prior and given them different directions."

"More than one rogue." Chuckie, Reader, and I said this in unison.

Christopher rolled his eyes. "Why?"

"You all move fast, but not that fast. What was going on here required someone in place to catch any phone calls you made that would have tipped you off. So whoever was impersonating Christopher in Nevada or New Mexico wasn't the same person."

"New York," Christopher said.

"Pardon?"

"Imageering bases out of New York and some out of Los Angeles. The media centers?" His snark was on full. "You know, you've worked with us for a year, you'd think you'd know that."

"But you base out of Area Fifty-One and Dulce."

"I'm on Alpha Team." He looked at Martini. "Can you explain it to her later?"

"Sure, but she's right. It's more than one." Martini sighed. "They imitated his voice, too, which is hard."

"Not really," Reader said thoughtfully.

"Why so? I sound that average?" Christopher clearly didn't find this amusing.

"No. But recording devices are easy to come by. And what orders did they give? Something you would normally?" Reader was playing with his phone.

"Apparently I said to pull all field imageers away from their empathic counterparts. I'd never give that order. I never *have* given that order."

Reader nodded. "But you've used all those words at one time or another. If girlfriend's right, and we all know she usually is, then whoever's doing this has been around for at least six months. Plenty of time to get everyone's voices recorded." He flipped open his phone and hit a button.

"Pull all field imageers away from their empathic counterparts." It was Christopher's voice, and not tinny at all.

Reader closed the phone. "The prosecution rests."

That sat on the air for a while. "Um, if that's the case, then they can impersonate any one of us."

"How long can a strong imageer keep up that kind of facade?" Chuckie asked.

"Depends." Christopher shook his head. "Not long enough to fool someone who knows the person well."

"What do you mean?" Chuckie's voice was getting the knife in it again. He didn't like the delays one-sentence answers provided.

Christopher sighed. "Okay. I'm the strongest imageer on the planet. Maybe whoever's infiltrated is stronger, but let's just go with the idea that they're not, at least for the moment." Everyone nodded. Christopher's eyes narrowed and all of a sudden, I saw Chuckie sitting there, next to himself.

"Wow, you've been practicing."

"Yeah." It was weird hearing Christopher's voice come out of Chuckie's mouth. "No one else on my team can do anything to this degree, but I figured if you could think of it, I should probably make sure I could do it well and that we knew how to counter. Imitation seemed like the obvious extension to drawing on the air."

"Thanks, I think. And, I have to say, it's kind of creepy."

"Glad you think so," Martini said quietly.

"I can't do Reynolds' voice," the Chuckie that was Christopher said. "But, okay, it looks like they're two of us here, right?"

"Right."

Christopher stood up. "Come with me for a minute," he said to Chuckie. They both got up and walked out of the room. A few seconds later they both walked in and stood in front of us.

I got up and walked to them, and Martini came with me. I pointed to the Chuckie on the left, Martini to the one on the right.

"This is the real Chuckie."

"Yep, because this is Christopher." Martini grinned. "The heartbeats are a giveaway."

"I'm more interested in how Kitty knew who was who visually," the real Chuckie said.

"Because he doesn't walk or stand like you. Close, but you saunter and Christopher doesn't, so he had to imitate your movements, and he was good but not quite right. Same with how you stand."

"Fine, but you've known me a long time."

"Yeah, but I think Christopher's point is made. I still had to study you two. If he'd just walked in as you, I wouldn't have questioned right away." I looked up at Martini. "But now the test is, how easy is it to tell two identical A-Cs apart?"

The image of Chuckie shimmered, and Christopher was there again. "Harder, because of heartbeat signature." All of a sudden, I was looking at another Martini. Christopher jerked his head, and the two of them disappeared into the bedroom.

"This'll be a fun test for you," Chuckie said under his breath.

I'd been thinking the same thing. "Yeah."

Two Martinis walked out. I had to remind myself that having a fantasy about this wasn't going to make the real Martini happy with me, since he knew who was impersonating him.

But it was harder. Christopher had spent his entire life with Martini. There were no differences in walk, stance, or even expression. They were both grinning at me, and they weren't speaking. "Wow, um . . . I hate this."

Chuckie put his arm around my waist. Both sets of Martini eyes narrowed. "Huh, that didn't work." He took his arm away.

"Oh. Duh." I went to the fridge and pulled out two sodas. I threw both of them at the heads. The Martini on the right dodged and caught the can. The one on the left just put up his hand and caught the can. "Jeff's on the right, Christopher's on the left."

The one on the left turned back into Christopher. "Good plan."

"Only works because I know you're shorter than Jeff. Look, what this is proving is that whoever's out there can imitate whoever the hell they want to, at least for a short while. And in a crisis situation, a short while will be all they need."

Christopher disappeared and Reader was there. "Yeah, but I can't sound like anyone else." It was Christopher's voice coming out of Reader's mouth.

"That is beyond freaky. Please stop now."

Christopher was back, grinning. "Okay. By the way, it's really draining. I'm pretty much ready for a nap now."

"Really?"

"Manipulating an existing image is one thing—I can do that for hours and not get tired. Drawing an image on the air is another. It's harder and requires total concentration to create and keep it there. Creating a three-dimensional image that has to move and function like a living being? That's hard as hell. I don't want to do it again today, for example. I could if our lives depended on it, but I don't want to discover what that adrenaline shot to the hearts feels like."

My stomach clenched. "It would make you that tired?"

The real Martini stepped in between Chuckie and me and started to massage my neck. "Relax. He's fine." I saw him shoot Christopher a look.

"Yeah, just being dramatic," Christopher said quickly, as his eyes looked anywhere but at mine.

Lorraine didn't buy it either. She came over, grabbed Christopher's arm, and dragged him off into Chuckie's bedroom. "Claudia, med kit, please." Claudia went in with her.

I could hear Christopher protesting that he was fine. "OUCH! Stop doing that!" He didn't like it, whatever it was.

"Think they're harpooning him?"

"No. He wouldn't be coherent." Martini sighed. "They're just giving him some rejuvenating fluids. They hurt, they're just not agonizing."

My throat felt tight again. I had to harpoon Martini on a

regular basis. I knew it was horrible, for him and for me, but I hated hearing that it was the agony I'd always suspected it was and that he remembered how much it hurt.

He hugged me. "Stop. I'd rather be alive."

"Me, too," Chuckie said. "And it's starting to sound like we may have a challenge achieving that."

"Good point. What was the goal of pulling Imageering away from Field?"

Martini shook his head. "No idea."

"Disruption. Ability to put rogue agents in place. Ability to murder Field agents or leave them exposed." Chuckie was saying these things as if he were making a shopping list. "Destabilizes existing structure. Creates lack of faith in leadership. I could go on, but I think you get the idea."

"So, what is it they want? I mean, is this going to turn out to be the usual, where there are at least two plans going on at the same time? You know, one where we have a psycho in charge and the other where we have a total megalomaniac running the show?"

"Could be," Martini said. "My vote's for megalomania, of course. You don't show up on another world by choice unless you have a reason. We're handling the good reason. That only leaves a bad reason for anyone else from the home world to make an appearance."

"Yeah, but why are they doing all this? Are they hoping to replace you or White with a double?" Chuckie had his conspiracy hat on, I could tell by his voice.

"I'd notice if someone impersonated Jeff."

"In time?" Chuckie shrugged. "Maybe. But in time for what? To not marry an imposter? To save his life?" He jerked his head toward Martini. "To save the world? Can't say. We don't know enough yet."

"Maybe we'll get more when my parents arrive," Martini said. "And, if not, we'll have the fun of my mother complaining about how far behind we are with the wedding preparations. So, you know, a good time should be had by all."

CHAPTER 16

ROOMS WERE ASSIGNED, luggage was handed out, and people settled in. Martini and I went to our side of the floor. It was pretty much a mirror image of Chuckie's suite, including the full wall mirror I'd missed before.

"See the big mirror?" Martini asked as he came up behind me. "We don't take our top off in front of the big mirror unless Jeff is the only other person in the room." He wrapped his arms around me and nuzzled my neck.

"Mmmmm, okay." He switched to nibbling my neck, which doubled as my main erogenous zone. "Whatever you want."

"Thought you were going to argue." His tongue was tracing a pattern.

"Uhhh . . . oh, God, Jeff . . . ohhh . . ." So much for arguing. Maybe later.

He spun me around and kissed me, and I melted against him. I was ready to go for it, but he pulled away after a few minutes. "I have to make sure the room's safe. And," he added morosely, "my parents will arrive any time."

"Okay." What good was a suite if we weren't going to get to have sex on every available surface? But I decided voicing that thought wouldn't be fair. He'd been as ready to go as I was.

Martini hypersped through the place and checked for bugs. We all had an alien-detector now, thanks to Chuckie. Nothing found, human or alien. I was shocked, but I figured the foray into Catering had alerted the rogue that we were onto him or her, so she or he was lying low. Or causing havoc elsewhere.

"So, what's your plan?" Martini asked me after we'd hung up our clothes in the walk-in closet that was part of the humongous master bedroom. This hotel room was larger than the Lair, let alone the apartment I'd lived in before I'd met Martini. Our meager assortment of clothing looked sad and lonely in the huge closet.

"I want to go shopping."

He laughed. "Why doesn't that surprise me?" He pulled out his wallet. "Uh . . . do I have to go?"

My turn to laugh. "No, not if you don't want to." He handed me a wad of cash. "Jeff, I have my own money."

"Right, and there's more of it in your hand. It's not cheap here from a cost standpoint." He looked worried. "Do you need more?" He opened his wallet again.

"I have no idea, but stop throwing money at me." I wondered how much of this was because Chuckie was right next door and figured a lot of it.

"Okay, you have the credit cards, right?"

"Yes, but I don't think I want to use them here, just in case." Just in case I'd have to look at the bills a month later and ask myself why I'd bought something I could only wear in one place and spent that much money for it. I'd been here a lot more than once, after all.

"Well, do if it's something you really want."

"I really want you in something other than a suit."

"I thought you liked how I looked in the suit." He sounded hurt.

"I do. I like how you look naked, too. I also liked how you looked all of the two times I could get you into jeans."

He shrugged. "I don't feel comfortable in them."

"Did you wear suits as kids, too?" I asked with a laugh.

Martini looked embarrassed. "Yeah, we did. We were at the Embassy a lot . . ." His voice trailed off and he looked miserable. "I'll wear whatever you want."

I hugged him and felt like a total jerk. "Oh, Jeff, I'm sorry. You look great in the suit, you know I think so. It's not like we're going to a playground or something."

"So, when we have kids, you won't want me in the suit at the park or anything?" He sounded panicked.

"Baby, stop. We'll worry about it when we have to." I felt like crap for making him feel like crap. This wasn't exactly going as planned, not that I'd had a plan. I nuzzled his chest. "I think you're just as handsome when you're dressed casually. But it doesn't really matter. It's not the end of the world. If you didn't want to wear a tux for our wedding, that would be a problem."

"No, I'm fine with a tux. White or black?"

"I don't know." The panic about my lack of a dress, or even the idea of a dress, hit me. "I sort of wanted to decide once I knew what I was wearing."

"Well, shop for that here, too."

"Huh?"

"It's Vegas. Lots of weddings. Lots of shops with dresses. Take the girls and go shopping."

A thought occurred. "I don't want the girls, actually." I dug out my phone. "James, you guys settled in?"

"Yeah, girlfriend. Nice digs. I'll give the C.I.A. this much—they live for the first-class treatment."

"I think it's Chuckie more than the agency."

"Maybe so. So, what's up?"

"You, um, indisposed right now?"

"No, we're not having sex. Paul's tired. ACE is really upset and it's worn Paul out. Why?"

"I want to go shopping, I want someone whose taste I can trust along with me, and Jeff doesn't want to go."

"Calling in Gay Fashion Support, are we?"

"You know it."

"It's one of the reasons I know you're smart. I'll come up. I don't want you wandering this place by yourself."

"You wandering is okay somehow?"

He laughed. "I'm a guy."

We hung up. "James will be here in a minute."

"Well, at least you won't be by yourself."

"You can come if you want to."

"Nah. I hate shopping."

"I know, you're male."

"James is male, too."

"James is a former fashion model. He understands clothes. And the need for clothes. And how to be sure what you buy looks good."

"Yeah, yeah, yeah. And if he were straight, you two would already be married. I'm real clear on that." He gave me a grin. "Happily, he's not straight."

"Or even bi."

"There is a God, and sometimes He likes me."

There was a knock on the door. Reader was there, not in the usual Armani issue. He was in more casual slacks and a buttoned shirt that was designed to be worn out, not tucked in. He looked great. "Ready, girlfriend?"

I pointed. "See? See this look? Imagine yourself in it."

Martini sighed. "I'm trying. It looks better on James."

Reader shrugged. "Jeff, you've got the body structure and the looks to pull off just about anything. Even a Speedo." Martini looked panicked.

"Um, no Speedo." He could indeed carry it off, but I didn't relish the idea of every straight woman and gay man within eyeshot leaping on him. He needed trunks. Long trunks. "I like my men in trunks." Although tight trunks weren't out of the question. My mind started having a field day.

Reader laughed. "Aww, come on, where's your sense of adventure?"

"No Speedo," Martini said emphatically. "But I like where your mind's gone," he added to me with a grin.

Reader shook his head. "Paul can carry it all off, too, not that you'll ever see it. It's a cultural thing, babe, so stop worrying about it."

I leaned up and gave Martini a kiss. "Okay, I'll stop. See you in a while. Call me if your parents show up and are upset I'm not here. Call me if anything's happening. Call me before you hit Chuckie for any reason whatsoever."

He laughed and kissed me again. "I'll call. But figure you have a few hours to kill. Have fun while you can, okay?"

I grabbed my purse, gave him one last kiss, and then we were out the door.

Got to the elevator and Reader put his arm around my shoulders. "Alone at last, lover."

CHAPTER 17

WE BOTH CRACKED UP. "Yeah, I feel so illicit." I put my arm around his waist.

"Too true. So, where're we headed?"

"Oh, show me the shop with that top in it. You never know, maybe I'll have the guts to wear it."

"Will do." He looked at me out of the corner of his eye. "Great bridal shops here."

"Yeah. And yeah. Help me."

Reader flashed his cover-boy grin. "Of course, what are friends for? I've been giving it thought already."

"You have?"

"I knew you weren't. Not enough, anyway."

"Teach me, oh very wise one." We arrived at lobby level and walked out of the elevator. I examined everyone we went past, but no one looked familiar or wrong, not that I had a lot of faith in how I'd determine wrong anyway.

"I don't want you in some billowy tent."

"What are you, my mother suddenly?"

"Nope. I'm your Fashion Adviser. And trust me, with your figure, we're looking for something that doesn't hide the fact you've got curves."

"I don't want to look fat."

"You're not fat. You're also not a stick. You look like a woman. We want to enhance that. Besides, you'd be amazed at what's out there. We do want a low neckline, of course."

"We do? I'm going to be in some sort of a church."

We were in the casino now. It was loud and flashy, bells

were ringing, people were making noise, the hustle and bustle
was at a decent hum. I smelled smoke and booze and money.
It was only Reader's grip on my shoulders that kept me
from wandering to an active craps table. The two guys who'd
checked me out earlier were at one and seemed to be winning.
One of them looked over his shoulder, spotted me, grinned,
winked, and nudged his buddy. Who also turned around and
gave me the grin-wink combo. I felt myself blush.

Reader sighed. "Focus, girlfriend, focus. We have a goal.
Gambling later. Wardrobe now. Flirting with guys not in our
expanded circle never."

"Okay. So, low neckline why?"

He laughed. "Because you have a great rack. And this is the
best time to show it off. Besides, it'll make Jeff happy."

"It will?"

"Trust me."

As we headed toward the side of the casino that connected
to the mall area I felt someone watching me. I looked over my
shoulder. There were a lot of people there, but no one really
stood out. I looked at the craps table. The two hunks weren't
there any more, so it wasn't them.

"I told you to stop flirting with strangers."

"I'm not. I felt someone watching me. Us, probably," I
added. After all, of the two of us, the one more likely to get
stared at was the former top male model. I looked around
again to see if someone was staring at Reader and just including me in the eyeballing. But again, no one stood out.

"You've just got pre-wedding jitters," Reader said as we
got to the escalators that took you out of the casino and to the
mall that connected the Mandalay Bay with the Luxor.

We got off the escalator, and the reason for my feeling we
were being watched appeared. "Nice to see you folks again,"
Mister Joel Oliver said cheerfully as he snapped a few shots
of us.

I wasn't quite sure what to do. Reader was. He stopped,
still holding onto me, and flashed the cover-boy grin. "Smile,
girlfriend."

"Why?" I asked as I did as I was told.

Oliver sighed and lowered the camera. "Because happy, smiling, and clearly *posing* people aren't interesting shots." He gave
Reader an impressed look. "I understand why you 'retired,' but
really, the fashion magazines of the world are missing you."

"I'm flattered," Reader said, still smiling the smile that put everyone else's to shame. "But leave us alone or I'll call Security on you. No cameras in the casinos."

Oliver shrugged. "We're not in the casino. Besides, you being here is gonna be great publicity soon. I can see the headlines: Alien Conspiracy Heats Up Vegas."

I was glad Reader had a firm grasp on me, because I wanted to tackle this guy to the ground. "You're high."

Oliver shook his head. "Nope. Keep fighting the good fight, though."

"What fight would that be?"

"Protecting the weak and the helpless from the evil from outer space. I mean, that's your group's stated mission, isn't it?"

I wondered where Chuckie, or my mother, might be and whether I could get them to arrest this man. Then again, I'd had a lot of training in how to treat someone who sounded like a loon. Just talk to him the way most of the people we'd gone to school with talked to Chuckie.

I laughed. "Dude, you're crazy. No wonder you work for the world's worst tabloid. You probably still live with your mother. In her basement." I nudged Reader. "Let's leave the conspiracy loon alone with his theories."

"Sounds good." Reader stopped smiling and hailed someone. Someone in a uniform that had Security in big yellow letters on it. "This man's accosting us, sir, I think to take pictures of your slot machines."

The security guard moved in, and Oliver moved on. "Good one," he called after us. "I'll see the two of you again. Soon."

"Well, that was fun. Maybe this was a bad idea."

"Nope. Tim gave us all the intel on that guy before you and Jeff got to the briefing. Reynolds is researching him. He'll be neutralized or defanged soon, I'm sure."

"Neutralized? As in killed?" My voice squeaked.

"I doubt it. Stop worrying. Let's shop and get your mind onto relaxing things, like spending Jeff's money."

I decided Reader was right and spent the walk to the shop he'd spotted trying to relax. I did this mostly by window-shopping, which Reader was happy to let me do. We strolled along, looking at all the glittery things that insinuated I should save them from a life of boredom in the shops and take them home to a life of adventure in my closet. Considering what seemed to go on in my closet, maybe I had an obligation to bring the Elves something from Vegas.

The only time I'd ever shopped in these stores was when I'd been here with Chuckie. Not all of them were high priced, but most were. However, I had tons of Martini's cash with me, and his charge cards, and by the time we'd wandered past about a third of the mall I was getting kind of excited.

Reader spent most of this slow walk discussing body types and why he wanted me to look at either cocktail length or mermaid-style dresses that were more on the minimalist side than poofy and overly adorned. I couldn't really argue. I wasn't tall, so something with a long train would look ridiculous. Something with too much foof on it was going to make me look like a doll. I had my doubts about mermaid, but I was willing to try anything at this point.

We finally reached the shop with the top in it. It was a really sexy top in a store full of really sexy clothing. "What were you doing in here?" I asked him while we looked for my size.

"Browsing." He grinned. "No, I don't cross-dress, and neither does Paul." He shrugged. "I like clothes. It's how I spent most of my former life, in and around clothing. And it's nice to see something else other than freaking black and white Armani all the damn time." He sounded like I felt.

"Yeah. You know it's bad when I'm in jeans and an Aerosmith T-shirt and I feel exotically dressed."

"Exactly. You wouldn't believe the whining I got from Paul when I bought what I'm wearing now."

"He's not cheap, is he?"

"Hardly. He just doesn't understand why I'm not thrilled to be in the suit twenty-four/seven. I'm not joking, it's cultural."

I found my size and thought about this. "James, do you think it's just them, just 'our' A-Cs, or do you think all of them on the home world are that way, too?"

"No idea. I've never given it any thought." He was quiet for a few moments while we looked for a skirt to go with this top and something to go under it—he hadn't been kidding, it was sexy, glittery, and extremely sheer. "You're thinking we could spot the enemy agents by how they don't alter what they wear?"

"Something like that. I'm freaked by the idea that I could go back to the room and it wouldn't really be Jeff up there."

"Yeah. This whole damn thing bothers me. I'm with you.

The timing's beyond strange. By the way, have you gotten your bridesmaids lined up?"

"Um, no. Why?"

Reader sighed. "I knew he hadn't told you yet. Jeff's already got his side asked."

"Who?"

"Christopher's best man."

"Naturally."

"Right. Jeff's also asked Paul, me, Tim, and Jerry."

"You and Paul I expected. But Tim and Jerry, too?" Not that I minded. After all, if I figured out how to hide that I was marrying an alien from Amy, Sheila, and Caroline, I'd have five girls. If all of them could make it, which hadn't been confirmed yet because I was so far behind.

"I stopped him before he asked the rest of the flyboys." I looked at Reader's expression. He was serious.

"Oh, my God. Is this normal for them?"

"I don't know. Paul and I aren't really married. Same reasons no one else is. He offered me the Unity Necklace, by the way, but we discussed it, and it just seemed as though we'd be creating problems. Either it would've started a lockdown on A-C and human relationships, or we'd have been okayed by Richard because we weren't going to have children, and that would have made things worse for everyone else. Jeff's sisters were all married before I joined up, and Paul's sisters are younger than Michael and, shocker alert, they want to marry humans. So I have no idea of what a typical A-C wedding looks like."

"No weddings have happened in the time you've been with Centaurion?" This seemed hard to swallow.

"They have, but none that I've been invited to."

"I might not have five girls." Wow, that made me sound like the most friendless soul in the universe. "I mean, I have five. I think." I had plenty of friends, just not that many I wanted in my wedding.

"Who besides Claudia and Lorraine?"

"My friends Amy, Sheila, and Caroline. Only . . . Amy's in Paris, Sheila's got three kids, and Caroline's in D.C." And Caroline would ask why I wasn't marrying Chuckie. Again. She apparently hadn't liked the reason I'd given her already. "And none of them know I'm marrying an alien."

I started running through my other sorority sisters—I

could ask them, but none of them had a clue what I did now, and none of them could be trusted with it, either. Also, like Caroline, the rest of the girls knew Chuckie and, unlike Amy and Sheila, they all liked him. I knew without asking that if I called to ask any of them to be in my wedding, the first question would be why wasn't I marrying Chuckie. It had been the first thing Caroline had asked, after all. And those kinds of conversations somehow always led to horrific fights with Martini.

This brought up another problem, which was how Martini was going to handle my sorority sisters' attendance at our wedding. Only some of the girls would go with the idea that Martini was so great looking that it was natural I'd said no to Chuckie. The rest of them would point to four years of him and me being inseparable and really question what the hell was wrong with me. Guilt—always ready to remind me that I'd been too dense to realize Chuckie had been serious when he'd proposed the first time, when he'd taken me to Vegas for a week—was joined by its new bestest bud, Stress.

"I'm so screwed."

"We'll figure something out," Reader said reassuringly. "If Tim, Jerry, and I have to be unasked, we'll all survive."

"I want you up there."

He stroked my face. "You don't have to be scared. I'll be there, whether I'm nearby on the altar or in the pews. I promise." He pulled me to him and hugged me. "Jeff's not picking up how frightened you are, is he?"

"I think he thinks I'm worried about other things, not the getting married part."

"You'll be good at it. Being married. I know you think you won't be, but you will."

"But I still like Chuckie. I . . . I'm afraid I might be in love with him, at least a little." I hadn't meant to blurt it out, hadn't planned to tell anyone, and I knew I'd done a pretty good job of hiding it because Martini wasn't on a rampage. But it was true.

I was relieved that I'd managed not to add the word "still" around the "be in love" part. The realization that I'd been waiting for Chuckie until Martini had shown up wasn't one I was proud of, even if said realization had come after Martini had proposed and I'd said yes. A part of me really regretted Chuckie proposing, clearly and comprehensibly to me, after

I'd already met and fallen in love with Martini. And all of me felt like a rotten person and a worse fiancée for thinking about any other man when I was engaged to the greatest man on the planet.

Reader kissed my forehead. "I know. It's obvious."

"Oh, great. So I'm hurting Jeff for sure?"

"No. It's not obvious to him, not even empathically, or if it is, he understands. I don't even think it's obvious to Reynolds. It's obvious to me."

"Why?"

He sighed. "Because the pressure you're under would make it incredibly appealing." He gave a bitter laugh. "My parents have no idea of what I do, they just hate the fact that I gave up a great career—a career I'd been working at since I was three years old, by the way—to do something vague with people they have nothing in common with. They don't understand what I see in Paul, other than the fact that he's great looking. But it wasn't as if I'd dated dogs before. They'd just managed to accept that I was gay when I ran into the A-Cs."

I hugged him tightly. "I'm sorry."

"It's okay. But I know what you're going through. I have a couple of old boyfriends I'm still sort of in touch with. And they're in touch with my parents. And there are days, hell, girl, there are weeks, when I wonder if it would be easier to just go back to my old life."

"Why don't you?"

"Same reason you haven't left yet. I love the man. I also know what we do is a lot more important than standing in front of a camera looking good and making clothes and accessories look good." He hugged me again. "And instead of getting to just fall in love with Jeff and deal with all the normal things a couple goes through, like I did with Paul, you two have been busy saving the world from bigger threats than Paul and I had to deal with during our first year together. Not to mention you have the fate of every A-C under thirty riding on your nuptials. Kind of a lot of pressure, at least from where I sit."

"His mother hates me, too."

"Well, maybe not hate, but I know what you mean. And I'll bet Reynolds' parents love you."

"They do. I've known them since we were thirteen." And I knew, without any doubt at all, that they'd make awesome in-laws, great grandparents, and they already got along fabulously with my parents.

"I'd guess they knew their son was in love with you, too, and were happy about it, or at least hoping you'd come around."

"I don't know. Probably. Everyone but me seemed to know." My heart felt tight. "I did so many things because of him, things I didn't even realize would be important when I was older. I never say the wrong thing to him, I never have to be something I'm not, no one's going to give me a test to see if I'm good enough to marry Chuckie. And I'm going to hurt him so much by marrying Jeff."

"Or hurt Jeff by marrying Reynolds. Yeah, that's the way it works. But," he leaned me away from him a bit so I could see his face, "I think you made the decision already. Before you knew you had the option. You've always had an option other than Jeff. More than one."

"Christopher."

"That's one. Or just leaving the whole business behind."

"I guess."

"Of course, I think if you did, he'd come after you."

"Yeah, Jeff does have a little bit of stalker boyfriend in him."

"You like that."

"I guess so."

"No, you do. I know you're not as confident as everyone else thinks you are. Hell, I'm not, either. We both know how to pretend effectively. So does Jeff. You think you'd have said yes to Reynolds if he'd proposed before you met Jeff, but my money says you would have said no."

"How so?" My money didn't say no, but maybe Reader was right.

Reader shrugged. "He's too laid back for you. That's a great trait in a close friend, and for some a great trait in a mate. But you're attracted to Jeff because he's intense. That happy, jokey, 'it's all good' attitude is a sham, and you know it. Reynolds never loses it—I'm sure he can, but I interacted with him when Reid was after you. He was as upset as the rest of us, more so, really, but he never lost his cool, never panicked. On the other hand, if Jeff had kept his cool you'd be dead."

"I suppose." It was something to think about, though I knew Chuckie better than anyone, and there was absolutely an intense side to him. I was just one of the few people who ever got to see it. Because Chuckie only let the people he really loved and trusted see that side, which was why Reader didn't think it was there.

Chuckie was indeed laid back, but he'd learned how to be, how to keep his cool when bullies wanted him to lose it so they could pound on him. The drive that made him constantly successful came from the intense part of him. I knew the intensity was there—I'd seen it up close, personal, and naked, after all.

Guilt, of course, chose to share that my being with Martini in front of him was probably trampling Chuckie's heart. Guilt also reminded me that, despite Reader's thoughts to the contrary, if I'd been even remotely clued in, I'd have married Chuckie and never have met Martini. Stress suggested it was only a matter of time before Martini figured this out, too.

Because Guilt was an Equal Opportunity Emotion and didn't like to pick sides, it shared that the moment Martini realized I might have even a shred of regret related to marrying him, his heart was going to be trampled, too. Stress also mentioned that there was no way Martini wasn't going to pick up that I'd been thinking about having had sex with Chuckie, and that he'd be less than thrilled that my thoughts about sex with Chuckie were and remained extremely positive.

"James, I'm honestly not feeling any better about this."

Reader hugged me yet again. "Someone always loses in a love triangle. That's the way it works out. You just have to be honest with yourself—who do you love more? Who do you want to spend the rest of your life with? Whose children do you want to have?"

"What if I say Chuckie?"

Reader was quiet for a moment. "If that's your real answer, I think my plan would be to get you and Reynolds as far away from Jeff as possible."

"I don't think Jeff would try to hurt either one of us." Because he'd be too hurt to do anything other than walk away. "Christopher might, of course."

"You trying to tell me I need to charter a jet? Or just grab the fastest car we can get our hands on?"

I looked down. No Unity Necklace. I'd gotten used to looking at it any time I'd felt romantically insecure in the past months. But it was now part of a metal ball of spying badness. I knew I'd never be putting it on again. I looked at my hands.

No ring, either. Nothing that said who I belonged to, or who wanted me to belong to him.

I looked at the picture on my chest. Steven, Joe, and the rest of my boys stared back at me. What would the guys in Aerosmith suggest at a time like this? The first song of theirs that popped to mind was "Love in an Elevator."

I laughed and looked up at Reader. "No. I do love Chuckie, and I always will. But . . . no one compares to Jeff."

Reader grinned. "Good to hear, girlfriend. I wasn't looking forward to that particular road trip. I'd have done it, mind you. Like I told you when we met, you're my girl, and I'll always be here to take care of you."

I hugged him as tightly as I could. "I love you, James. I don't know what I'd do without you, and I never want to find out."

"No worries, I promise you'll never have to." He patted my butt. "Now, go try on the clothes. You'll feel better, and then we can get out of this store and find your wedding dress."

CHAPTER 18

I WENT INTO THE DRESSING ROOM as suggested. There had been plenty of times during the past year when I'd thanked God Reader was around, but none more than right now.

I took a deep breath, then undressed. This was a no-bra outfit, but we'd managed to find an almost-as-sheer spaghetti tank to go under the main top. I was still basically naked with fabric, but it was a tad more subtle. The skirt was tight, short, and silky. I would need the right pair of hooker-heels, but I had to admit I looked hot in this outfit.

I wandered out of the dressing room to find Reader, since I wasn't buying a thing without his okay, but I didn't have to go far. He was waiting for me, about three steps away. "James, what do you think?"

He grinned, grabbed me, shoved me back into the dressing room, and kissed me. With tongue.

The mind can move fast, and while this was happening, mine was whirring at its version of hyperspeed. Two things screamed at me—Reader was gay, and he had to kiss better than this. He was really strong. I couldn't get away, so I slammed my knee into his groin. He pulled away, laughed, and kissed me again.

Kung fu time. I'd studied the art in my younger years and had taken it up again in earnest once I realized my life was going to involve a lot of scary things trying to kill me on a regular basis.

I dropped into a horse-stance, did an arrow point with one hand and slammed that into his throat and another arrow point into his side into a pressure point. He released a bit, and I grabbed his inner thigh and gave it a vicious pinch, while I did a palm-heel strike to his chin. Knocked him against the wall, and, happily, his head hit, hard.

I forced myself to focus on terror and Martini. I knew I needed backup.

Reader shook his head, and as he did, the image shifted. It wasn't Reader, but then I'd already figured that. It also wasn't a guy.

I'd also figured that, but it was still kind of icky. I had no issue with lesbians, but I didn't swing the bat that way, and I kind of resented getting molested. Willing experimentation was one thing, but attempted rape I had an issue with regardless of the sex of the attacker. "Listen, space bitch, keep your mitts and your lips off." I was in a squat on the ground and sent up a rising kick to her stomach, just in case she wasn't clear.

She took it like a champ, grinned again, and lunged at me.

And slammed back into the wall. Her nose looked broken, and she was out. I looked up to see Martini standing there, fist still out. "Good emotional signal. Potentially your best yet."

"Thanks, I've been practicing."

He put his hand down, I grabbed it, and he pulled me into his arms. "Did she hurt you?"

"She kissed me. I feel like I just went on stage with Madonna." I gagged a little but kept it together.

"How'd she get to you?"

"Oh, hell." I pulled out of his arms. "Stay here and keep her out. Call for backup. Pay them for whatever it is I'm wearing. She impersonated James." I grabbed my purse and took off.

"Kitty!" Martini was calling after me, but I didn't stop. Reader was nowhere in the shop.

"My boyfriend'll pay for this!" I shouted to the clerk.

"But he left," she said.

I stopped. "No, the guy in the dressing room is my boyfriend. The other guy is my friend. Where did he go?"

She gave me a look that said this wasn't the first time someone had said something as odd as this to her. It was

Vegas, after all. "Some black guy came in and he left with him."

"Big, bald, and totally hot?"

"Yeah."

"Oh, God. Look, the guy in the dressing room is my boyfriend. I was just attacked by some lunatic. Help him, and he'll pay for whatever it is I'm wearing." I ran out of the door. The store alarms went off immediately. Oh, yeah, I was wearing the antitheft tags. Well, hopefully I'd get them off legally later.

I didn't see anyone who looked like Reader or Gower. So I had to think, not just run. I assumed my attacker was here alone, because the other one was off causing havoc elsewhere. She was an A-C, based on strength and imageering ability. She was also rare, because I knew females didn't normally get empathic, imageering, or troubadour skills. So she was strong and fast and really well trained. But she'd had to get back in time for me to walk out of the dressing room and see her impersonating Reader there.

I started praying Reader was still alive and only knocked out somewhere. So if I were disposing of a body, please, God, an unconscious body, where would I stash it?

I looked around for the refuse. Saw a young, pretty cute, Hispanic maintenance guy pushing a trash cart and ran to him. "You got a body in there?"

"Um, no?" He looked at me like I was from another planet. If he only knew.

I looked in, no, no body. "Where are the big cans?"

He started to point, and I dug into my purse. My mother had given me a P.T.C.U. badge. I wasn't an agent, but as Reader and Christopher both said, if the head of the agency gives you one to have and to hold, feel free to use it. I opened it in front of him. "Federal officer. My partner's been kidnapped. I think they took him out and dumped him somewhere, and it has to be close. Take me to the closest dumpsters to that store," I pointed to where I'd just come from. "And make it fast, because if he's dead when we get there I've got the potential to take it out on you."

The maintenance guy nodded, and we took off at a dead run. Fortunately, he was in decent shape. "Why're you in those clothes if you're an officer?" he asked as we raced along.

"Undercover."

"Not really."

He had a point. "Look, can we just try to save my partner's life?"

"Sure, sure." We were behind the stores. Once you were away from the glitter, the backside of any mall was the same, apparently. He led me to a set of double doors, and we smashed through them. To see a lot of garbage cans and a big garbage truck.

"Oh, great." The truck had a can on its forklift. I knew how our team's luck ran. "STOP!" They didn't.

"They can't hear you!" the maintenance guy called. He ran toward the can and leaped. It was amazing—he was about my height but damn if he didn't catch the can and get up there. The drivers saw him and stopped.

I ran around to the side. "Federal officer! Stop and put that can down!"

The driver looked at me. "Are you kidding?"

I waved the badge. "Can down now! I've got an officer missing."

"He's in here!" the maintenance guy shouted.

"Put the damn thing down now, or I'll shoot you in the head!" I pulled out the Glock and aimed. I never remembered to set the safety, so that saved a step.

The driver lowered the can and put his hands up. "Don't shoot, lady. I got no money."

"What part of the term 'Federal officer' do you not understand? Get out of the damn truck." The maintenance guy jumped into the garbage. I saw him struggling. "Get in there and help him. Now!" I pointed the gun at the other guy in the garbage truck. "You, too." They both got out slowly. I could tell they wanted to run. "You run, I shoot you. It's that damn simple."

The maintenance guy started shouting to them in Spanish. They both started moving now and crawled up.

"Holy Jesus!" the driver shouted. "There's a man in here."

"No, duh. Get him *out*!"

They lifted the body up—it was Reader. My chest felt tight, and I was having trouble breathing. The maintenance guy looked at me. "He's hurt bad, but he's alive."

I burst into tears. "Get him out of there." I dropped the

Glock back into my purse and found my cell phone. "Jeff, are you okay?"

"Yeah, baby. We've got the agent tied up, literally. Where are you?"

"James is hurt." I was sobbing.

"Hang on." He hung up, and I went to help them get Reader's body down without hurting him more.

The maintenance man took a look. "Head trauma." Even I could have called that one—there was blood on Reader's forehead. He opened Reader's eyes and took his pulse. "I think he'll be okay."

"Um, don't take this the wrong way, but—"

"I'm a med student. This is my third job. I'm a bartender at night and I deal blackjack swing shift. Tito Hernandez, by the way."

"Kitty Katt. I'm not a stripper."

"Yeah, can't tell in that outfit, of course." Tito was checking Reader's neck and limbs. "You have a phone. Call an ambulance."

"How? I'm not from around here."

Tito rattled something off in Spanish. One of the trash men pulled out a cell phone and dialed.

I realized the trash truck guys were staring at my chest. "Um, I wasn't planning to wear this out in the day."

"Don't plan to wear it out without armed guards." He looked up at the trash guys and rattled something off in Spanish again. They nodded and backed away.

"What'd you tell them?"

"That you're a crazy hooker and this guy's your pimp."

"Seriously?"

"Yeah. It's more believable than you being a Federal officer." He took my arm and placed me. "Want you blocking the sun from him." My shadow fell across Reader's face.

"How'd you do that jump?"

"Training. I also cage fight."

"Jesus."

"I like to think of him as my copilot, yeah." He looked up at me. "You guys have some serious enemies here?"

"I think my boyfriend took out the enemy."

"He's not your boyfriend?"

"No . . . but she thought he was. Interesting."

"You want to explain that?"

I took a good long look at Tito. "Maybe so." I dug into my purse. "Mister White?"

"Yes, Miss Katt. Christopher called me somewhat hysterically. What's going on?"

"I want to hire someone."

CHAPTER 19

"COME AGAIN?" WHITE SOUNDED CONFUSED.
  "I want to hire someone onto the team. What's the standard procedure?"

Tito raised his eyebrow at me. Reader groaned, and Tito turned back to his patient. I took Reader's hand. Groaning meant coming back, I hoped.

"Normally they kill a superbeing."

"How about if they know how to react in a crisis, don't argue about things being dire, can leap twice their height to save one of our agents from being smooshed in a trash compactor, and are fluent in Spanish? And if they're," I let go of Reader's hand to feel Tito's bicep, "pretty damned buff, in med school, holding down three jobs, and also a cage fighter?"

"Who was almost smooshed?"

"James. He's alive, thanks to Tito much more than me." I took Reader's hand again. Tito had a great bicep, I had to admit.

"Tito is our new recruit?"

"If I get to ask him, yeah." The adrenaline was starting to wear off, and I was starting to shake.

"If Paul and Jeffrey approve."

"Paul's not going to be in any condition. James is *hurt*." My voice was moving up to the dog-only register.

"Ah. And this Tito is taking care of James?"

"Yes. Look, yes or no?"

"I'll trust your judgment. Please go ahead. Remember,

however, most people don't believe in aliens without seeing the proof."

"Chuckie did."

"Fine. Carry on, and please keep me posted on James' status."

"Will do." I hung up and wondered where Martini was. "Tito, got a proposition for you."

"Want to be a doctor, thanks. What the hell did they hit him with?"

"Want to train with doctors better than you're ever going to meet at med school? And, she hit him with, I'm guessing, her fist."

He looked at me. "There's a lot more to this, isn't there?"

"Yeah." I took a deep breath. "Look, they just tried to kill my best friend. You saved his life. And you did it by doing the things we have to do every day to stay alive."

"Who's we?"

"Centaurion Division." A man's shadow covered mine. "World government agency, United States based."

Tito looked up at Martini. "You her boyfriend?"

"Yeah."

"Good. Give her your jacket before the hombres decide they don't care if they get deported back across the border."

Martini did as requested. "We have her locked down. And I do mean down." His voice was a growl. "If James dies, I'm killing her."

"Let me."

"Okay."

Tito looked back. "Um, not really sure I'm for cold-blooded murder."

"The person who attacked your patient is an alien from the Alpha Centauri system. She's here to kill or at least severely bother the Alpha Centaurions who live here peacefully with us and help us protect the Earth." I heard sirens in the distance. They were getting closer.

"This a *Men in Black* joke?"

"No. Jeff, they called for an ambulance."

"Don't want one, but we'll take the gurney." He pulled out his phone. "Alpha Team has a man down. Need a floater, on my mark. Needs to take four and a gurney to human medical. I want that gate active in less than thirty seconds." He dialed again. "Christopher, you and Tim take the bitch to lockdown.

I want her miserable. James is down, and he looks bad. Yeah, I'll have the girls get Paul. You take Reynolds with you, too, have Melanie and Emily stay with the flyboys and do guard duty. Right."

Martini looked at me. "You want to bring this guy on why?"

I reiterated Tito's skills.

"I want to be a doctor. I don't want to get involved with a bunch of crazies, no insult intended."

"Oh, none freaking taken. Jeff, call the girls."

He nodded. "Lorraine, we're at Code Red, man down from Alpha Team. Yeah. Yeah, she's a mess. I want you and Claudia to get Paul and get him back to human medical. Keep him calm, don't let him know how bad it is." Martini eyed Reader. "It looks really bad from where I stand. Like brain gone bad."

I started to shake. Tito reached out and grabbed my arm. "He's not a doctor. I'm not either, but I'm closer. It's bad, but he's not brain-dead. There's optical activity."

"Is he paralyzed?"

Tito tightened his hold on my arm. "I don't know."

The ambulance arrived. Martini was suddenly standing there with the gurney. He bent down and lifted Reader easily. He put him carefully onto the gurney and strapped him in.

Tito stood up and looked at Martini suspiciously. "How'd you do that?"

Martini reached out, grabbed Tito's hand, and put it onto his chest. "She told you. You want to listen?"

"Holy Mary, mother of God!" Tito yanked his hand away. "You have two hearts!"

"Yeah, I'm an alien." Martini nodded his head toward a shimmering in the air. "I'm going through. Bring him." He shoved the gurney through the gate and disappeared.

Tito's jaw dropped. "Um . . ."

I grabbed his hand and pulled. "Come on." I didn't think about the ambulance drivers or trash guys. I didn't care about them or what they would or wouldn't tell anyone. I only cared about seeing if Reader was going to be okay.

It was the worst gate transfer of my life, though it felt like they all did. But it seemed like it took forever. My foot finally hit the ground, and Tito came through with me. We were in the med lab at Dulce, and Reader was already hooked up to a lot of scary-looking machines.

Dazzlers I didn't know were working on him, and they all

were moving fast and to a woman looked grim. Martini put his arm around me. "It'll be okay, baby." He didn't sound like he believed it.

Tito looked around. "Wow."

"Yeah." I was crying again.

Gower arrived, flanked by Lorraine and Claudia. "What happened?" he asked me softly.

"She must have thought he was Jeff. Or something." There was more to it, I knew that, but I was too upset to think about it. "Paul, I'm so sorry."

He pulled me away from Martini and hugged me tightly. "It's not your fault." He let go and got closer. One of the Dazzlers gently shoved him back. "Sorry, we can't have you close. Actually, you all need to get out."

Tito stepped closer. "Why are you doing that procedure? He's had double head trauma."

"Pardon me?" The woman spun on him. "Who are you?"

"Tito Hernandez. It looks like all the trauma's in the front, but I think he got slammed into a wall. The back of his head's a mess."

"Tito didn't tell me that," I said softly to Martini.

"Because he's good." Martini was watching Tito closely. "Clean him up, let him stay in here." It was an order.

"Jeff, that's not a good idea," the Dazzler who appeared to be in charge said.

"James is a human, he's a human doctor. Do it." Martini pulled the rest of us out.

We all stood in the hall, no one looking at anyone else. Martini's phone rang. He walked away from me to take the call. Gower reached out and pulled me to him. I buried my face in his chest and just let the tears come.

"Leave us alone . . . please," Gower said quietly. I heard footsteps fade away and could tell the others had given us some space. Gower's body twitched. "Kitty, ACE is afraid."

"Me too, ACE."

"James is going to die."

CHAPTER 20

I COULDN'T CRY MORE THAN I WAS. I couldn't stop, either.

"It's not fair."

"No, it is not."

"Why doesn't God ever come help us?" I didn't mean to say it out loud. ACE and I had had this conversation before, after all. I knew why—God wanted us to do it on our own. "Why can't he come and save James? Just this once, actually save the good person who doesn't deserve to die?"

"Why does Tito feel responsible?"

"What?" This seemed out of left field.

"Tito is in there with James. Tito feels if James dies it will be Tito's fault. Why? Tito did not harm James, Tito is not the one who caused the injuries."

"Oh. Tito's learning to be a doctor. He helped me find James. He tried to take care of him."

"Why would that make Tito responsible?"

"Doctors and nurses, paramedics, all the people who are trained to save lives—they sort of have to act like God, in that sense. They have to be good enough to save someone's life, to steal a life back from death, from God, if you will. That's a lot of pressure and responsibility. I think Tito feels responsible because, well, that's how most people who try to save someone feel—if they could have done one thing differently or better or faster, then they would have saved the person." Like me. If I hadn't wanted to go shopping, if I hadn't asked Reader to go with me, then he'd be okay.

"It is not Kitty's fault, either. Kitty is blaming Kitty. Paul is blaming Paul. The same with Jeff. Everyone feels responsible. Everyone but the one who hurt James. *She* feels happy." ACE sounded madder than I'd ever heard him.

"I'm going to kill her, ACE. In cold blood. I just want you to know that, so it won't be a shock to you when I do it."

"No, Kitty. Kitty must not become what she is."

"He's my best friend. I love him. He's the only person I can talk to sometimes who understands—me, this, everything we do. There's no justice on Earth that can make her suffer like Paul will suffer, like I'll suffer, if we lose James. And I'll be happily damned if that means she can't hurt someone else I love."

"Why didn't Kitty ask God to save Kitty before?"

"You mean when Reid was about to run me down in the desert with an Escalade and I was sure I was going to die?"

"Yes."

"Because I knew God wouldn't help me."

"Kitty did not ask ACE for help. Kitty asked ACE to join Kitty with ACE, but not to save Kitty. Why?"

"I didn't want to put you into a position where you'd have to say no."

"James asked ACE to save Kitty then."

I *could* cry harder. What a nice way to find out. "But you didn't." My brain kicked. He had—ACE had told Martini what to do in order to save me. "ACE, please, please, do something to save James, to bring him back the way he was."

"ACE cannot do that, Kitty." But the way he said it, I had a little bit of hope. Gower twitched and tightened his hold on me. "We're going to lose Jamie, aren't we?"

"I . . . don't know."

I heard a ruckus from the medical bay. Gower and I detached and took a look. There was a lot of running around, and someone was trying to hold Tito away from Reader. "Jeff! Help!"

Martini was right there. "What's wrong?"

"Tell them to let Tito do whatever he wants." I ran into the room. "Leave him alone, let him get to James!"

The woman in charge turned to me. "He wants to do something that's likely to kill the patient."

"The patient's dead if I don't," Tito said urgently. He looked at me. "I know what I'm supposed to do."

"Jeff . . . *please*."

Martini took my hand. "Let him do what he wants." It was an order.

The women backed away, unwillingly, but they did it. Tito started doing something that I couldn't watch. I turned my face into Martini's chest and I prayed. A lot. I heard Tito asking for things, giving orders, just generally sounding like a brain surgeon, at least from what I could figure out. I couldn't pay attention—I could only think about Reader being okay.

It took forever; at least that was how it felt. But finally, I could feel the tension in the room go down. I risked a look over my shoulder—everyone was just standing there. Gower was by the bed, and he was crying. "Oh, no. Please, no."

The Dazzler in charge looked at me. "I call it a miracle." Martini and I went over to the bed. Reader's breathing was normal. "Full brain function, all internal organs functioning properly, we've tested, no paralysis. He's going to have a hell of a headache when he comes to, but he should be back in action within a week or so." She turned to Tito. "I don't know how you did it, Doctor, but thank you."

Tito looked at me. "I'll take the job."

"Welcome to Alpha Team," Martini said. "I think I speak for all of us when I say we're really glad to have you on board."

I tried to talk in my head, in the way I had with ACE before. Thank you, so much. More than I can really express.

ACE just showed Tito what Tito already knew how to do, ACE said in my head. Tito is a good person. Kitty has chosen well again.

Never better than choosing you, ACE.

ACE is here to protect. *She* is not. I knew who he meant. They are coming, and they are evil. ACE will have to help Kitty to fight.

Thank you.

This is ACE's world, too. I felt warm and loved, which was ACE's way of hugging my mind, then he slipped away.

Gower started to laugh. "Oh, hell."

"Paul, are you okay?"

"He's going to be pissed when he wakes up." Gower was laughing as if there was really something funny going on.

Martini let go of me and put his arm around Gower. "It'll be fine. Come on, Paul, let's get you resting."

"Nah, I'm fine. Now." Gower looked up at us. "Jamie's really going to be pissed, though."

"Um, why? I think being alive is going to make up for a lot."

Gower grinned, still laughing. "He's bald."

I looked. Sure enough, they'd shaved his head. I'd been too upset to notice. "He's got a great head, I think, anyway. He'll look fine." It was Reader. There was pretty much no way he couldn't look awesome.

"He'll look hot," Gower said. "But he thinks two baldies in a relationship is . . ." he started to laugh again, ". . . really gay."

Tito and I looked at each other, and we both started to laugh, too. "I'm straight, for the record," Tito gasped out. "But my older brother's gay, and, you know, he's got the same opinion."

"What's your brother do?"

Tito grinned. "He's a cop."

"Protection runs in the family," Martini said. "Good to know."

"How long will James be out?" I asked when I finally stopped laughing.

"Less time than if he was in a human hospital," Martini replied. "We have things we can do that speed up human recovery. Not as fast as an A-C, but faster than normal."

"Good. We need to brief Tito and bring him up to speed on what's going on. And I need to go kick some serious ass."

"Already done." Chuckie's voice came from behind us. He looked deadly. "We have the information we need."

"How?"

Christopher came in. "The C.I.A. has different methods than we do." He didn't look upset about it.

Chuckie looked over at Reader. "Is he going to be okay?"

"Yeah. Luckily. Oh, Tito Hernandez, Charles Reynolds. He's the head of the C.I.A.'s ET Division. Tito helped me and saved James' life."

"He on the team now?" Chuckie managed a small smile.

"Yeah, he is."

"Good. We have a lot of pain heading toward us, and you'll be particularly gratified to know, Kitty, that, true to form, there's more than one plan active."

"Oh, good. Routine."

CHAPTER 21

GOWER AND I ACTUALLY DIDN'T WANT to leave Reader's room. The medical staff didn't want all of us in it. We compromised and stood in the hall.

"The assassin, and that's what she is, isn't with the Alpha Centaurion government," Chuckie said without preamble. "She thought she was killing Jeff, by the way, so she's not very bright."

"No, it's not that." I thought about it. "James and I looked like a couple."

"You want to explain that?" Martini asked.

I rolled my eyes. "Sure. He had his arm around my shoulders; I had mine around his waist. He held me, kissed my head, that sort of thing. We were talking about my wedding dress; he was picking out sexy clothes for me. I can see how she'd confuse it."

"You have something you two were going to tell me and Paul later?" Martini sounded jealous. He looked jealous, too.

"Oh, Jeff, for God's sake."

Lorraine cleared her throat. "Jeff, it's called pre-wedding jitters, okay?"

"What is?" He sounded confused.

"She's scared, you idiot," Claudia snapped. "And who can blame her? Your mother hates her, she's the poster girl for interspecies marriage, we have your distant relatives descending on us to give her some horrible test we know nothing about. And instead of getting to do normal wedding things, she's working on Alpha Team trying to save the world again. Of course James was holding her. He was probably keeping her from running screaming into the street."

Martini looked at me. "Oh. Right. Sorry." He looked embarrassed but no longer jealous, so I took that as a win.

"*So*," Chuckie said, "the assassin was able to mistake Reader for Martini."

"Which means bad briefing. James is a head shorter than Jeff. And human, though she might not have bothered to check his heartbeats." Another fact rose to the surface. "Hang on. She pretended to be Paul to lure James out of the shop, so she had to know he wasn't Jeff."

"How do you know?" Chuckie asked.

I related what the shop girl had said. "And why the hell did she kiss me?"

"She thinks you're hot would be my guess," Tito offered. Everyone looked at him. "What? I'm new, but Kitty didn't say I couldn't talk, and it seems really obvious."

"What assassin stops to have a tumble?"

"The overconfident kind," Chuckie replied.

"She's an imageer, and that's rare in A-C women," Gower said. "Maybe it's made her unstable."

My mind kicked. "Chuckie, how do you know she's from Alpha Centauri?"

"Double hearts, strong, fast, imageer. Seems like a match."

"Paul? Jeff? The other races in your home world system . . . what were they again?"

"Humanoid, reptilian, mammalian," Gower answered.

"The warlike planet, what were they?"

"Humanoid, close to us, close to Earth, too. Probably why they were warlike." Gower sighed. "They can't get off the planet, Kitty. The PPB net there would keep them in."

I looked at him. "Maybe their ACE got lonely, Paul. Or angry."

Gower twitched. "Yes, Kitty, ACE agrees. Angry. Planet was angry, so entity would be angry."

I thought about it. Earth was considered pretty warlike, but we were out in the middle of nowhere, spacewise, and we all knew it. So ACE took on our planetary lonclincss as its own. The warlike planet over in the A-C system, on the other hand, would know there was a lot of company nearby. Company that had taken great pains to keep them from ever leaving said planet.

"ACE, did the Ancients visit all the planets in the A-C system?"

"ACE does not know, Kitty. Paul might." Gower twitched again, and I restated the question. "We don't know. Might have."

I closed my eyes and relived my brief fight with the assassin in the dressing room. "Christopher, I hate to ask you to do this, but I need to test something."

"Sure, Kitty, what?"

"I want you to pretend to be a female, full-on body image. Then I want you to attack me."

"Uh, why?"

"Do it," Martini snapped. It was an order—he was in full Commander Mode.

Christopher shrugged and turned into Martini's mother. Then he lunged for me. I punched him as hard as possible in the solar plexus and desperately tried not to enjoy it. Failed. The image disappeared instantly as Chuckie caught Christopher. Felt bad now. Wondered if it counted. Figured it didn't.

"Nice punch." Chuckie looked at Martini. "You'd really better fix that relationship before the big day."

"Are you okay?" I asked Christopher.

"Yeah," he gasped out. "Why?"

"I hit that bitch a lot and a lot harder before she lost the image. So if the most powerful imageer on the planet can't hold the image when he's being attacked, that means she's not an imageer."

"What is she then?" Martini asked.

"She's a shapeshifter. And I'm going to go talk to her now and find out what's really going on."

"Not alone," Chuckie said.

"No problem. You, Christopher, Jeff, and Tito. Paul, you stay here."

"No. She tried to kill Jamie and I'm sure she'll try to kill you. I'm coming with you. He won't wake up for a while." Gower sounded as though he wasn't going to back down.

"We'll watch over James," Lorraine said. "Go ahead."

"Okay. Call Serene in while you're waiting for us."

"Why?" Lorraine was speaking for everyone, I could tell.

"Because we need someone who can see the real people, not what they appear to be. Serene might be the only one who can do that reliably. Get her here under guard."

"Okay. Brian will probably want to come along."

"Fine, we can use someone else we can trust who'll be in life-threatening danger."

Lorraine managed a laugh and pulled out her phone. She and Claudia went into the room with Reader.

The rest of us headed off. "Where is she?"

"Fifteenth floor," Christopher said. "Sorry, it's the only place we have for this kind of lockdown."

"Not a problem." I wasn't going to let her get out, let alone into the Lair.

"She thought she was killing your mate," Christopher said as we got into the elevator. "Believe me, Reynolds is C.I.A."

Chuckie smile a very wolfish smile. "She tried to kill someone on my team. We have protocols."

"My mate?" Reader and I called them mates, sometimes, but I'd never heard an A-C refer to a spouse this way.

Chuckie's eyes were closed and I could see the conspiracy wheels turning. "Why did you ask about the Ancients?"

"Because they were shapeshifters. I'm pretty sure they're our angels from Bible stories. We've figured they had trouble adapting to our bad air when they came back in recent times, since they died on the A-C home world." He opened his eyes. "No spacesuits."

He raised his eyebrow. "You're kidding."

"No. Anyway, according to ACE, our A-Cs are the most advanced of those races."

"But that doesn't mean the others weren't around when the Ancients first came by," Gower said. "But shapeshifting was an Ancient trait. They were trying to save the worlds, not destroy them."

I thought about Operation Fugly. "Why are we assuming that every one of the Ancients was good? I mean, Mephistopheles is proof the devil was around. Couldn't some missionary have gone bad?"

"They do all the time," Tito offered. "I know plenty of priests who didn't stay all that close to God. I mean, humans are fallible."

"The Ancients weren't human," Gower said.

"That doesn't mean they weren't fallible. Or that they didn't get tired and decide to settle down. Maybe they thought they'd help the warlike folks more by being there full time. There's a ton of possibilities. But I think we've got Ancient blood in the folks from the warlike planet."

Christopher nodded. "Okay, I'm good with the working hypothesis. Now what?" We got out of the elevator and, happily, went the opposite way from the Lair.

"Why the hell did she kiss me?" It still wasn't computing. It had given her away, and anyone with half a brain would have known it would. Someone could imitate how Martini looked, but if he didn't kiss the way he did, I'd know it wasn't him.

"She thought you looked hot," Martini offered. "Why does it matter? You didn't like it, did you?"

We reached the holding cell. She was in there, extremely well strapped down. I could see signs of torture. I didn't mind and figured I should. I saw her nose had been fixed, but it still had some tape on it. I took Martini's jacket off and handed it back to him. "No, Jeff, I didn't like it. You're a far better kisser."

"Why are you wearing security tags?" Chuckie asked.

"I sort of stole the clothes."

"Yeah, but I paid for them," Martini said. "Here, hang on." He fiddled with the tags. "Your other clothes and shoes are back in the suite in Vegas, by the way."

"Thanks, but, Jeff, the tags stain the clothes if you take them off wrong."

"Only if a human does it." He held out the tags. They looked opened properly. He'd also taken off the price tags. I took a look and quickly looked down. The scary expensive clothes weren't stained. "Thanks. And, um, thanks for not minding that I bought this."

"You look great. Maybe the outfit will last long enough to wear out to dinner, but I'm not betting on it."

"Me, either. So, Chuckie, do I want to know what you did to her?"

"Probably not."

"It was less than I was ready to do to her," Christopher said. I could tell he was serious. "The C.I.A. just has some techniques that are more quickly effective."

"Was she afraid of you?"

"Not really. She seemed contemptuous, honestly . . ."

Chuckie's voice trailed off. "You're not thinking what I think you're thinking?"

"Never piss off the comics geek-girl. Yeah, I'm thinking exactly that." I looked up at him. "Kill her if she gets loose, but otherwise, I'm gonna go have a girl chat with our shapeshifting Wonder Woman."

CHAPTER 22

THEY LET ME INTO THE CELL. It wasn't all that large, but it was big enough that I didn't have to be right on top of her. She had short blonde hair and was very muscular but in an attractive way. I almost laughed, though—she was clearly not from the A-C home world. Not that she was ugly, but she wasn't a stunning beauty, either. Her eyes also looked wrong—larger, more elongated, and they were dark purple. Her limbs were the same, elongated just a bit, but enough to look out of proportion for a human. A-Cs were in perfect proportion, I verified that every night.

She gave me a slow smile once the door closed. "Is he dead?"

"Who?"

"Your mate. The one I fooled."

"No, he's not dead. He's not my mate, either."

"He loves you. You love him." It was true, but not in the way I assumed she meant.

"What makes you say that?"

She laughed. "It was obvious."

"Why did you kiss me?"

Her eyelids lowered. "You are attractive."

"And you're so crappy an assassin that you stopped to grab some nookie before killing the target?"

"You are not my target."

"James was?"

"No. He was . . . annoying." Interesting. Reader hadn't been the target, and she'd known it from the get-go. So who was she really after if she wasn't after the guy she thought was my mate?

"Why?"

"He was pawing you. And you enjoyed it." Her eyes flashed. "You are a woman of power, yet you let them touch you. You show off your body for them." And the trash guys, but who was keeping score?

"We'd call you Amazons here. What do you call yourselves?"

"You cannot pronounce it."

"Yeah, we hear that a lot. Apparently double suns make you strong, speedy, and fast talkers. Pity none of you ever want to become an auctioneer or something equally benign. You're all really annoying, though, I can say that. You can speak our language, how?"

"Radio waves carry. Even through the net." Her eyes flashed again.

"No one on this planet put that net up. We have one around us, too."

"The ones who put it up are coming here. To crown a new king. And he will die before the crown reaches his head."

Great, they *were* after my mate, my real one. "No one here wants that crown."

"Liar. All men crave power."

"Sure, but there are different ways to get it. Besides, you're power-mad, too. So, what do you call yourselves that we can understand?"

"The Free."

"Hilarious. Since you're the least free people out there."

"Yes, we do understand the irony. We will be freed from the tyranny, and we will make all who bound us pay."

"You realize that most of the people you're going to exact your revenge against are innocent of the crimes?"

"No man is innocent."

"Oh, for God's sake. How do you all reproduce without men?"

She gave me another slow smile. "Come here and I will show you."

"Wow, you're so smooth. I don't want to have sex with you. You're not my type."

"Because I'm a woman?"

"Because you kiss like crap. I mean, I realize it was the start of a girl fight, but jeez, you sucked, and not in a good way."

"I can do things no man can or will."

"Wow, you all buying that on your planet? Sure, there are plenty of men who don't have a full range of moves. Mine doesn't happen to be one of them. Plus, if that kiss was your opening salvo, you just cured any bi-curiosity I might have had. Gag me, okay? I'm gonna assume, however, that Earth lesbians kiss better, because a girl should always keep her options open. Now, cut the crap. You didn't come across the galaxy to hit on me, and I think you're a psycho bitch, so I'm not fixing you up with my single lesbian girlfriends, either. The love connection's out, so why the hell are you here?"

"To destroy the royal family's hopes of succession." She looked out the door. "I see them. Know they will die."

"Everybody dies. But I'm not going to let you kill them."

"Why not?"

"Because I don't like your style."

She shifted, and Reader was staring at me. "You would prefer his style?"

"Oh, yeah, totally. Of course, he's in love with someone else. Another man, to be exact. He's one of my best friends, not my lover."

"Men and women cannot be friends."

"Well, sure, not all the time. Like, two of the guys outside the door are friends of mine, but between you, me, and the straps, they'd both do me in a New York Minute if they could. Of course, they won't because they know I'm not in love with them, and, unlike you, they don't force themselves on women who aren't willing." Of course, Christopher sort of had, but I hadn't been all that unwilling.

Train of thought change time—I knew Martini was focusing his full empathic skills on me right now. "But James is my friend, only. And unless he stops being gay, which seems unlikely, he'll only be my friend. Which is too bad, really, especially since I'm damned sure he kisses better than you."

She glared at me. "And the other three?"

"Well, the totally hot black guy is my friend's boyfriend. Be glad I'm the one in here, not him. It's a toss-up between which one of us hates you more."

"So, your lover is still alive?"

"If you mean the guy you're pretending to be right now, yeah. He's still alive, no thanks to you."

She laughed. "He will be nothing. I smashed his brain. On purpose."

I decided Chuckie hadn't tortured her enough. "Pity for you. Because he's going to be fine."

"Impossible." She shifted back to herself.

"Nope, quite possible. He's going to be fine. Without hair for a little while, but he's so damn good looking that it won't matter. Oh, and yeah, I can see why you like shifting into him; he's beyond hotter looking than you."

"And the others?"

"One of them's a new recruit and the guy who saved my friend's life. And the other one actually is my mate. See if you can guess who's who. I gave you the easy one." The one she already knew.

I knew she was fully aware that Reader wasn't my man—she wouldn't have used Gower's image to lure him if she hadn't been. She hadn't made a mistake attacking Reader so much as a choice to up the body count. Attacking him had given her away and ended in her capture, but she didn't seem worried, more like she was playing a game. And that meant I had to figure out what game it was and what she thought she was achieving before she got a chance to hurt anybody else. Specifically Martini, because I wasn't buying that she didn't know which one he was any more than I was buying her pickup lines.

"We will kill them all. That way, there is no confusion."

"Who's 'we'? I'm supposed to believe there's more of you whacked out bitches on my planet?" I knew there was at least one other, but I was hoping we'd catch a break.

"My mate is here. She will ensure my freedom and the death of your beloved men," she spat the word, "and your enslavement."

"Oh, it's always the enslavement with you people. Never the playing nicely with others. And I'm supposed to believe there are only two of you here? What a lame-ass invasion. Two insane Amazons against an entire planet? No wonder you all were locked onto your home world—who'd want to let the lot of you out?"

"We are all that will be needed."

There was something in the way she said it. Or rather, in the way her eyes didn't meet mine. Wow, no one from their entire solar system could lie. Amazing. "You're not actually emissaries from your government, are you?"

She looked at me and her eyes were wide. "What do you mean?"

"What's your name?"

"Why?"

"I figure I'd rather call you by your name than Whacked Out Psycho Space Bitch, which is what I'm leaning toward. Oh, and, yeah, yeah, yeah, I'm sure I can't pronounce your freaking name in my language. You're a chick, fake it."

I half expected her to say Diana. "You may call me Moira." Oh, well, she was too militant and anti-Earth to be the real Wonder Woman, after all. On the other hand, I figured she'd picked the name for a reason—Moirae was what the Greeks called the Fates. And the A-C solar system had been around and active when all the Earth races were still babies.

"Great. So, Moira, what's your mate's name?"

"She is not captured, I will not betray her."

"Fine. So, when did you two decide on this plan of conquest, before or after you got exiled?"

Her jaw dropped. "Wha . . . what do you mean?"

I leaned against the wall. "I'm just spitballing here, but I'm guessing that your world leaders wouldn't be wasting their time coming to Earth. I don't care who you think's here, it's too damned far away. Especially since the planets that made the decision to lock you guys down are all a lot closer to home."

I shifted. Martini made leaning against walls look a lot more comfortable than it was. "Now, the royal family is sending someone out here, ostensibly to give me the royal marriage test that I'm going to flunk impressively, but no one in the entire universe can convince me that the head royal honcho or honcha is going to be arriving on our unwelcoming shores. Only the completely moronic would do that, and they may be many things, but stupid surely isn't one of them. So they're sending a representative, or several. Then they'll enact their little plan of world domination or world extermination on us. But your people wouldn't care about that. They want to deal with the folks nearby, to make them pay for what they did. And I can understand that. But you can't, can you?"

"No blood from that line should remain!"

"So, did they rape and kill your family members or something?"

"No. They enslaved our entire race."

"Yes, yes, enslaved, big net, got it. I'm asking you if they did something else to make you suffer."

She looked as though she didn't understand the question. "They denied us our place in the stars. That is sin enough."

Great. She and presumably her mate were fanatics. Wonderful. "So, the two of you decided, what? That you were going to take care of any remnant bloodlines?"

"We were sent here by the Grace of God to enact vengeance."

"Oh, right. Um, I don't think that's God's plan."

"Of course it is. Why else would She have allowed us to escape?"

CHAPTER 23

"ESCAPE FROM WHERE?" I wasn't surprised Moira was calling her God a female. It would have been a lot weirder if she'd thought God was male.

Moira didn't answer. She just gave me a dirty look, then checked out my chest. I had a feeling she was doing it to make me uncomfortable. Didn't work, especially since I'd just flashed the twins at all my guys a few hours earlier.

"So, you two were under arrest, weren't you?"

She looked away from me. "No."

"Who arrested you? Your own government?"

She kept on not looking at me. I moved into her line of sight. She turned her head to the other side. I had the feeling she was going to try this child's move all day. Another thought rose up.

"How old are you?"

"We don't count age like you do."

"I'm sure. How old are you in the way you *do* count?"

"I am of age."

Aha. She was a kid, by their standards, anyway. Only kids made sure you knew they were old enough to do what they were in trouble for doing. A fanatical kid. But a kid. And kids had fears and usually not a lot of defenses against them. "So, Moira, just want to tell you something."

"What?" She turned back to look at me.

I got up closer to her, but not so close she could head butt me. "When I find your mate, and I will, I'm going to make sure I destroy her in the most evil, painful way possible. I'll make sure to smash her brain in and do other horrible things to her. And I'm going to make you watch. You'll get to see her suffer, and then you'll get to see her die. How does that sound?"

Moira didn't look as confident. "You will never be able to catch her."

"Caught you."

"Only because you had help."

"I've got a lot of help. And your mate doesn't, does she? She had you, but you're not going anywhere. In fact, I'm going to shoot you full of drugs, so you can't escape even if you manage to get out of the restraints. They might kill you, but I'm willing to take that risk."

"She is more experienced than me. You won't catch her."

I did my best to give her my mother's most intimidating smile. It worked, if the look in Moira's eyes was any indication. "Of course I will. She's going to come to try to rescue you. And I'll be waiting. I'll have so many traps waiting for her that even if most don't work, one will. Then you'll get to see her suffer and die. So you can feel what it's like when you hurt a person someone else loves."

"Why would you do that?"

"Because you not only hurt someone I love, you gloated about it. You were happy to hurt him, and you had no reason to do it other than pure viciousness. On this world, we have an old saying: an eye for an eye, a tooth for a tooth. My father's people wrote that, millennia ago. It's still apt. I'm going to make sure you suffer like you made me and my friends suffer. Only worse."

She swallowed. "You won't succeed."

"Sure I will. I'll bet you've missed check-in time with your mate. She'll be looking for you, realize we've got you. There's only a few places we'd take you. She'll be here, soon. And I'll be ready."

I dug into my purse and pulled my phone out. "Chuckie."

"Yeah. Why are you calling me?" I looked out of the corner of my eye and saw him walk away from the window. I went farther away from Moira, so she couldn't hear him, at least, I hoped.

"I want all manner of security put on the Center. Make them evil, make them nasty. Do your worst, and do a lot of it. Space Bitch's girlfriend's going to be coming to save her, and I want our little friend here to see her gal suffer and die. Got that?"

"Um, yeah. I assume this is all for show? Since Reader's alive and going to be well, I mean."

"You got it. Make it vicious. Oh, and I want Space Bitch here to be drugged out of her man-hating mind. So she can't do anything. Oh! Quick thought. Do we still have all that truth serum?"

Chuckie started to laugh. "God, you crack me up."

"Great! Bring it. I want her full of it. No, I don't care if it'll cause her brain to stop functioning if we give her too much. Good. Yeah, of course we'll toss her to the troops once we're done with her. Right. Of course to rape her in all possible ways. Why would you even need to ask? Maybe we'll let her mate live long enough to watch."

"Martini is indicating that our prisoner is starting to cry. Wow, you're nasty."

"Yes, I know. She's a threat to our world security, and her partner will be more of one. I want them both treated like the animals they are."

"You know, I was a lot nicer than this."

"I'll bet. Yeah, that sounds great. I want the one who's still loose to suffer. A lot. Yeah, of course you can break, shoot, or cut off things that aren't necessary to survival."

"Okay. I think she's broken, or at least close to. Should I put on security for real, however?"

"Yes, make it so."

"Oh, over and out, Captain Not Quite Picard."

We hung up, and I turned back to Moira. "You could have cooperated. Pity for you, nice for me. I'll have some men along shortly to drug you and do horrible things you'll hate to you. You won't be able to fight back. I may film it, just for the pure entertainment."

She was really crying. "Why would you do that? The men I can understand. But you, you should be joining us."

"You attacked my best friend and tried to kill him. You were proud of yourself for attacking an innocent person whose only goal for the past few years has been to protect other people on this planet from harm. I would never join someone like you. You stand for everything I despise."

"You don't understand . . . they have to die." Moira was still crying.

"Why? You give me a reason I can believe in."

She shook her head. "They're men. Men are evil by nature;

they can never become good. They're the reason our world was locked away and kept from the stars, because of the men. We destroyed ours, and we must destroy all the others, to purify the universe."

My father had given me a lifetime course in comparative religions. He'd spent a lot of time focused on how to spot a fanatic and how little you were likely to be able to do to alter said fanatic's viewpoint. Logic didn't work on most in-the-bone fanatics; neither did kindness or any rational idea. The best you could do was understand how their minds worked, then stop them from harming others, as humanely as possible. Sometimes, however, you couldn't be humane.

I had a fanatic in front of me and probably a more intense fanatic out there, since Moira's mate was probably older if I took the term more experienced at face value. And I had no way of knowing if they were the only ones here or if more were coming.

A part of me felt pity for Moira. To hate half of the population of most worlds so much, with so little reason. To have dedicated her life to what she saw as right and I saw as pure evil. But she was evil, just as ACE had said. Not evil because of who or what she was, but evil because of how she thought and what she was willing to do, and took joy in doing, without any provocation or cause.

All Reader had done was be loving to me, and she'd done her best to kill him for that—because he was a man, because she'd identified him as one of the overall targets—because she could. And she'd gloated about it. I'd killed several people by now, for what they'd done and wanted to do to Martini and to me and to the people we cared about, but I'd never gloated about it.

"I'm sick and tired of hearing about purity of the race, the world, or the universe. I've never heard that argument come from anyone who was sane, or decent, or close to a loving God. If your God truly tells you to do this, then She's evil and doesn't deserve anyone's worship or obedience."

"Our God is right, and She will help us to smite you and all who stand against us."

I got right in her face. "Moira? I've got one thing to say to you. Bring it, bitch." Then I reared back and punched her right in the mouth. "That's for James. Be happy he's the kind of person who wouldn't tell me to rip out your throat for what you did to him."

It was a good hit. My hand hurt a little, but I didn't massage it. I was ready to hit her again. She licked at the blood running down the side of her mouth. "Nice. Take the straps off me and do that."

I was about to when the door opened. "All done." Martini walked in with a needle and pulled me away from Moira. He grabbed her wrist and shoved the needle in. "Time for the crazy chick to go night-night."

Moira's eyes got fuzzy, then closed. Her head fell to the side.

Martini kept a hold of me and walked us out of the room. "Love the nasty side of you. You can't possibly take her, and she was hoping you'd let her out of the restraints so she could kill you. Just in case you were wondering."

"Oh, okay, fine. Wow, but I hate her, and I think I'm going to hate her mate even more."

"I'd guess so, yeah. She was scared and upset by what you said, but, honestly, anyone with a penis should be terrified of these women. And there's a whole planet full of them? No wonder someone put a net up."

"I think the net turned them into this. I don't care right now. I want to see James." And shower. I felt kind of dirty.

Christopher locked the door. "We have guards on all levels." I saw several of the big Security A-Cs in the hallway.

"Make sure we have someone guarding the pipe. Inside only, though. I don't want any of our guys exposed outside, just in case."

"Good point." Christopher made a call.

I looked around. "Where are Paul and Tito?"

Martini put his arm around me and hugged me to him. "James is awake. They went to see him." I opened my mouth, and he shut it, gently. "Yes, we're heading there now." He bent and kissed my forehead. "You're quite the little tiger, aren't you?"

I didn't feel tigerish all of a sudden. Martini picked it up and picked me up as well. I wrapped myself around him and didn't worry that Chuckie and Christopher were right there. I just wanted to feel safe.

Martini kissed the side of my head. "It's okay now, baby."

"Not yet. But I'm going to make sure that it will be."

He chuckled. "That's my girl."

CHAPTER 24

WE GOT UPSTAIRS TO THE MEDICAL BAY. Tito and Gower were in the room with Reader, and there were Security guards all over the place. "Figure James is too vulnerable to leave without guard," Martini said. I agreed and was glad he'd thought of it already. Of course, that was pretty much his life's work, protecting people.

He put me down, and we went into the room. Tito stepped aside so I could get near Reader's head. He looked like he was in a lot of pain, but his eyes looked the way they always had.

"Hey," he said.

I grabbed his free hand; Gower had the other. "Hey yourself. How're you feeling?"

He managed a weak chuckle. "Like I was hit by a Mac truck. Love that outfit on you. Try to not wreck it."

"Probably too late for that."

"Yeah." Reader looked at Gower.

"Be right back, Jamie," Gower said quietly. Reader nodded, just a tiny bit. Gower gave me a small smile, then he and Tito left. I realized Martini wasn't in the room, either.

"James, I'm so sorry." I felt like I was going to start bawling.

"For what, girlfriend? Saving my life?"

"I'm the reason you got hurt."

"Hardly. That crazy chick was the reason." He closed his eyes.

"I'm sorry." I bent and kissed his cheek. "I'll get Paul back in here."

Reader tightened his hold on my hand. "No. Just you right now. I . . . need to tell you something."

My throat got tight. "Okay."

He opened his eyes and managed about half of his standard cover-boy grin. It was still great. "I was dead, you know."

"No, you were close."

"No. I was dead. I saw the light, I heard . . . voices. And I heard you, you and ACE. Then I heard ACE tell Tito what to do to bring me back." He swallowed. "I know you think, and ACE thinks, that it was what ACE told Tito to do that saved me. It helped, of course, but . . . I was already dead."

"I don't understand."

He reached his other hand up to my face. "God decided you needed to have someone around you could talk to."

The tears rolled down my face. "He chose well."

Reader tugged at my hand. "Come here, you need to rest."

I figured the medical team would throw a fit, but I'd handle that when they came in screaming at me. I crawled onto the bed next to him. It was an A-C facility so the bed, like everything else, was top of the line, and it was large for a hospital bed, easily fitting two on it.

Reader put his arm around me and gently put my head onto his chest. "Relax. Nothing hurts but my head."

I managed a laugh, though I was still crying. "Jeff and Paul are going to wonder about this."

"They wonder about us already." He stroked my arm. "I wouldn't have wanted you to kill her."

"I know. But I would have anyway."

"Yeah, I know. I shouldn't complain, I think it's why I'm back, so to speak."

"Why?" I closed my eyes. I wasn't used to leaning on a chest with a single heartbeat in it anymore, but it always felt good when Reader held me.

"One act can change someone. If you'd killed her, or any of the others had done it, it would have made you what she is, just like ACE was afraid of." He hugged me. "We're here for a reason. It's not always a clear reason, and we're never going to win every time, but our reason is to stop evil, not become just like it."

"She's still alive and wants to kill every man in the universe. And she's not alone."

"Not saying evil's got a pass, girlfriend. Just saying I don't want you to go to that side of the house."

"Good thing you're still alive and functioning then."

"Like I said." He hugged me again. "You know, it was interesting."

"Being dead, or almost dead?"

"Yeah. I saw a lot of things."

"Like what?"

"Can't remember them all—they're fading more the longer I'm conscious. I think I'll forget this, what I've been telling you, soon. Maybe not the light, but most of the rest. You might forget it, too. Consciously. But I think it'll always be inside us."

"Okay. Do you remember anything else?"

"Yeah." He laughed softly. "I saw a lot of universes . . . I saw myself reflected in a lot of them."

"What were you like?"

"Pretty much me." He hugged me tighter. "You were in all of them. We were always together, in some way."

"Good."

"We were married in about half of them."

"Yeah?"

"Yeah. Happily, too."

"I don't think we want to share that with Jeff *or* Paul."

"Nope. I just want you to know, though . . . if something happens to me here, and I'm not with you, I'll be with you in all those other universes."

"I love you, James."

"I love you, too, Kitty."

We lay there together, and I let the hatred for Moira and what she'd done subside and ebb away. It was hard to hold onto the hatred, lying here, next to Reader, knowing he was alive and going to be okay. I started to get sleepy. "James?"

"Yeah, babe?" He sounded as drowsy as I felt.

"I'm not buying my wedding dress without you."

He chuckled. "Good. I want you looking like the hottest thing on two legs. No one I trust with that job besides myself, other than Jeff, and he's not supposed to see the dress beforehand. A-Cs have the custom just like we do."

"You really think mermaid style would look okay?"

"I think you'll look beyond beautiful. Just like always."

"Coming from the best-looking human in the world, that means a lot."

"Good. Go to sleep now, you need the rest."

"You too, but . . . I don't want to. I don't want to forget."

"Me either. But, it won't change anything between us, even if we do."

"You sure?"

"I'm positive." He hugged me. "I saw it. Always together, one way or another."

"That's all right, then."

"Yeah, that's my opinion, too." He yawned. "Go to sleep, Kitty. Big days coming. We need to be ready."

"They'll differ from our other days how?"

"The prosecution rests."

CHAPTER 25

I FELT SOMEONE LIFT ME UP. "What's going on?"

Martini cradled me in his arms. "You were asleep on the bed with James. I'll discuss how cozy you two looked later. You okay?"

"Yeah." My mind felt fuzzy. "We were . . . talking about important stuff."

"Well, he's asleep, which is good, and you obviously need a longer nap."

I wanted to remember something. "James is alive."

"Yes, he is. Miraculously."

There was something about that word I wanted to remember, or comment on, or something. But I couldn't grasp it.

"Where're we going?"

"Well, Paul's going to stay with James tonight. Tito's going to stay with them. Paul will use the time when James is asleep and they're awake to bring Tito up to speed on what being an agent is like."

"He already has a good idea."

"Yeah, he's bright. I think he's as smart as you and James."

"Good. What about everyone else?"

"Reynolds and Christopher are back in Vegas with the rest of the team. Reachable via phone if we need them, the usual."

"Where are we going?"

"To the Lair. If you can handle being on the same floor as whatshername."

"Moira. And, yeah, as long as we have a lot of security and we're both sleeping with an eye open."

"Check and check." We were in an elevator. I didn't feel amorous; I just wanted Martini to hold me. He shifted me so I could wrap my arms and legs around him. "Just hold on, baby," he said softly. "We'll be in bed soon."

"Mmm hmmm." His arms were around me, one supporting my bottom, the other my neck and upper back. It reminded me of when I was little and my father would carry me to bed. "You're going to be such a good daddy."

"I hope so. And soon." He hugged me. "As soon as you're ready."

"Not tonight."

He laughed. "No. I don't even think we're practicing tonight."

I thought about that. "Maybe later." I yawned against his neck. "Sleepy."

"I know, baby."

We were in the bedroom, or at least I assumed we were, because Martini laid me down on a bed. He didn't undress either me or himself, just lay down and pulled me next to him. I draped over his body, held onto his shoulder, and went back to sleep.

I woke up, all senses alert. I could feel Martini was awake, too. He slid his hand over my mouth, and I nodded. It was dark in the room, just a tiny nightlight glow, meaning we were in the middle of the night.

I listened hard. I could hear Martini's breathing, shallow, to stay quiet. I was doing the same. But it was there, at the edge of my hearing—breathing that wasn't ours. I had no clear idea where my purse was, so no way to get to a weapon.

Martini still had his arm around me, and he tightened his hold. I relaxed as much as possible—it was easier for him to move me that way.

The advantage we'd have, the only one, was that we lived here and our intruder didn't. I wasn't confident this would be enough.

Something was different—the breathing was closer. Martini rolled me over him and us both off the bed, and he hit the intercom button while he shoved me behind him. This took less time than I needed to blink.

"Yes, Commander?" Gladys' voice came through the com.

We looked around the room. We were alone in it as far as we could see. "Intruder, somewhere on level fifteen," Martini said.

"Are you endangered, Commander?"

"Potentially." The lights came on like it was midday.

"Security on the way."

I looked around during this exchange. Where would some-one be able to go in such a short time? I didn't doubt some-one was in here with us—I might be wrong, Martini might be wrong, but we were rarely wrong at the same time. Plus, there were too many intruder possibilities for me to assume we were just jumpy.

The closet could work, but the door was open, it wasn't all that big, and we were on the same side of the bed as it was, so we should have felt the intruder go by. I looked back at the bed. It seemed so obvious . . . but we weren't looking there, were we?

I nudged Martini and pointed to the bed. He gave me a look that said I was crazy. I shrugged—probably, but it was worth a shot.

He didn't want me near the bed, and he didn't want to let go of me. I could tell by the way he was moving, or not moving. Oh, well, impetuous was apparently my middle name. I pulled out of Martini's hand, jumped on the bed, and started bounc-ing. Impetuous, yes. Stupid? Not so much.

It didn't take long, I heard someone make an "oomphing" sound. "Come out, come out, wherever you are."

Martini rolled his eyes. "Only my girl." He grabbed a pair of my stilettos from the closet and sent them under the bed, hard and fast.

"OUCH! Stop!"

"Crawl out and maybe we won't kill you," Martini growled. I didn't stop bouncing. It was kind of fun.

"Make her stop."

"Not just no, but hell no. You're the one who's in here try-ing to kill us," Martini added. "Why should we make it easy for you?"

"I'm not here to kill you, Your Majesty."

I didn't stop bouncing, but Martini and I exchange the clas-sic WTF look. "His majesty would like to have that proven," I shared between bounces. "We start, on this world, by showing our faces. Actually, we start by knocking and being admitted, not doing some alien form of B and E, but you know, whatever works."

Someone crawled out from under the bed, opposite from

the side Martini was on. I leaped onto his back, wrapped my arms around his neck, and, as he started to flip, my legs around his waist. Tucked my head and held on.

I'd held Martini like this, many times, when his reaction to the adrenaline harpoon was too violent and he was a danger to himself and me. Whoever I had in a full body lock tried to get me off, but he wasn't as strong as Martini by a long shot. I tightened my hold, particularly the hold on the neck, and started to choke off his air.

Martini was right there. "You okay, baby?"

"Yes. Get a gun and shoot him. Or her. Whatever it is I'm holding."

Whatever it was flipped so it was on hands and knees and I was in the air, so to speak.

"Male, unless it's a shapeshifter."

"Stop . . . her . . . emissary . . . friend . . ."

"Our friends knock, you creep. Our enemies, on the other hand, love to pull this kind of crap. Jeff, a little help?"

"You're doing so well. And you look great doing it, too. Love that outfit. If it gets wrecked, I'm buying you another one."

My opponent stopped struggling. "Not an enemy. An emissary." He sounded pained, as though I'd insulted him.

"Heard you the first time, dude. Didn't care then, don't care now. You snuck in. That makes you an enemy, means someone out to harm us. We have a lot of them."

"I'm not one."

"Right. Jeff, really, I have to kill him, or you have to help."

"Oh, kill him."

"Your Majesty, that would not be wise."

"You keep on calling me that. Wouldn't know why."

"Your name is Jeffrey Stuart Martini . . . on this world. However, you have a name on another world, and you are the next ruler there."

Martini sighed. "Thanks for stopping by. Give my loathing and complete lack of interest to the folks back home. We'd love to invite you to our wedding, but, gosh, we've already booked the room, and we're full up. Now, I'm going to knock you out, so I don't have to worry about you hurting someone I care about. No hard feelings."

"No, wait!" Too late. Martini clobbered him, and we went down onto the floor.

"Um, Jeff? Dead weight on my arms and legs."

He lifted us both up, I detached, and he dumped the body on the floor. Security chose this moment to arrive. "Commanders, are you all right?"

"Yeah, thanks for the speedy arrival." Martini had the sarcasm knob up to eleven.

"Sorry, sir. We had some other issues."

"What?" We asked in unison.

"Variety of small issues."

"Describe them. In detail." Martini shifted me to his hip and I wrapped my legs around his waist.

Gladys came on the intercom. "We have a variety of unknown A-C personnel in custody, Commander Martini. All claiming to be emissaries from the home world."

"How many?"

"With the one in your room, Commander Katt, an even dozen."

"How did they land without our noticing?"

"Cloaking, I assume, Commander Martini. We have confirmed NASA picked up nothing, but we have done some molecular scans. We have three cloaked ships perched on the tops of Animas, Hatchet, and Chiricahua Peaks."

"Fabulous," Martini snarled. "Take him to a holding cell. We'll be up in a minute." Security did as requested. "Gladys, please make sure they're all together—I don't want to have to wander around too much."

"Yes, Commander. I've alerted the Pontifex and Commander White as well."

"Thanks." The com went dead, and Martini sank onto the bed. "Great, they're here. Perfect timing, too."

"And, boy, do they want you."

He shifted me so that I was in his lap with my legs around his back. "I don't want them. Only want you."

I leaned up and kissed him. "You have me, Jeff. I promise."

He held me tightly. "I won't let them take you away from me."

I hugged him back. "I won't let them take you, either. We'll be fine. I'll bring along my hairspray and some Everclear."

Martini managed to laugh. "I do love how you think."

CHAPTER 26

MARTINI SIGHED. **"GUESS WE'D** better get moving."

"I want to change."

"Why? You look beyond hot."

"I look naked with some fabric hanging off my shoulders."

He gave me a wide grin. "Yeah. Like I said . . ."

"Jeff, they're going to test me. I know I'm going to fail, but I should at least try to represent."

He shook his head. "Good luck, but okay. However, I want you to wear that again. A lot."

"You didn't mind everyone staring at me?"

"Nah. As long as you're coming home with me."

I felt his forehead. "You okay?"

Martini kissed me, long, deep, and hard. Couldn't help it—I started grinding against him. He pulled me closer in to him. "Yeah," he said as he ended the kiss, slowly. "I just felt everything you went through when you thought we'd lost James. Life's too short and uncertain. I'm trying to give up the jealousy. It's hard, but I'd rather put the effort into making you feel safe and happy."

"I don't mind that you're jealous. All that much. I just don't want you to think I want anyone more than you. Because I don't." And after my talk with Reader in the clothing store, I could say that confidently again. I felt the worry about making the wrong lifetime decision slip away. I ignored all the other wedding-related worries—we had bigger problems right now.

He kissed me again. "Mmmm, I'd love to tell you to prove

that, but duty calls." He said the last two words like we were going to clean out a pigsty. Of course, I shared his opinion.

He lifted me off his lap and put me on the ground. "Armani fatigues or my own clothes?"

"Do we care what they think?"

"No, I was asking what you wanted."

Martini grinned at me. "Have I mentioned how much I love you recently?"

"Yeah, but it never gets old." I took my clothes off in the closet. Hoped the A-C Elves would get this outfit cleaned fast.

"Oh, go for the fatigues. You look so hot in them."

"And they're not sheer. Tito might not recognize me." Martini laughed. "Jeff, do you think these dozen are going to be it?"

"No, and you don't either." He had that right. "I think, no matter what, we have a world of hurt coming toward us."

"Yeah. At least the emissary wasn't Moira's mate. I want to be heavily armed when we cross paths with that chick."

"Me too. Speaking of which, your purse is in the living area." I came out of the closet as he got up and went to get it. Martini put it down on the bed. "I want to make sure it's okay. It was out of your control for a while there."

"I need my heels. You dump, I'm going to scoot under the bed."

He did as requested while I dropped to the floor. "Wow. I can't believe what you manage to stuff in here." He sounded awed.

"I told you. It's big and made of cheap leather, so it's strong and sturdy. I can fit anything in there."

"Hmmm . . . including something alien."

I almost bumped my head on the bed frame. "What?" I reached for my shoes and stopped. "Jeff?"

"Yeah."

"I'm not alone down here."

The bed disappeared. Martini lifted it, and, I was sure, in deference to all my stuff on it, put it aside as opposed to throwing it across the room. Now that I could see clearly, I for sure wasn't alone. There was a small thing in front of me. Quivering.

"What is this?" It wasn't something from Earth. I hoped it wasn't an interstellar snake. Or bomb. Or worse.

"What the hell?" Martini bent down and put his hand out.

The quivering thing sniffed, then crawled into his palm. He pulled me to my feet with his other hand.

"What is it?"

"I think . . ." He dug his phone out. "Christopher, sorry, where are you? Oh, good. Look, do you remember that pet thing your mom used to tell us about? Yeah, that. What did it look like, and how big? Amazing. Yeah, I think I'm holding one. Get down here, will you?"

"So that's a Tribble?"

"Huh?"

Oh, right. They weren't into science fiction, humorous or otherwise. Guess all the shows and movies were too much like documentaries. I decided not to try to explain. "It's not dangerous?" It didn't look dangerous, but I'd seen enough movies. The probability it could go killer or instantly reproduce into the thousands seemed high.

Of course, it looked a lot like a tiny kitten with really, really fluffy fur, only no ears and the eyes looked more like black buttons than cat's eyes. And it had no tail. But otherwise, just like a fluffy kitten. Or a fluffy ball with tiny legs and paws. If it were a plush toy, it would be the hottest thing for Christmas with little girls. I wondered if Martini would get upset if I suggested we talk to Chuckie about starting a plush line and decided he would.

"No, not dangerous that we were told." Unlike Security, Christopher had used the real hyperspeed to get to us. "Wow, Kitty, you're dressed. I was getting used to the negligee look."

"It's an outfit. For wearing out to clubs."

"You're okay with her wandering around naked?" he asked Martini.

Martini shrugged. "I look at it as her using all the weapons at her disposal."

"One flash and he's a changed man." Christopher laughed. "Fine, no argument from me. So, how'd we get the pet?"

"What's it called?" I wanted an answer, since Tribble seemed out.

"My mother called it a Poof."

I looked at them. "You're kidding."

"No." Christopher had the grace to look embarrassed. "It's a stupid name, at least by Earth standards, I know."

Martini put the Poof into my hand. "Must be a girl's pet." He looked like someone had just tried to put hair bows and a tutu on him.

"I tackled a guy, remember?"

"What?" Christopher yelled. The Poof trembled.

"Uh, I think you're scaring it."

"Oh, great. Let's get this thing back to its owner, shall we?" Martini turned to go, and the Poof leaped out of my hand.

"Jeff!"

The Poof landed on Martini's shoulder as he was spinning back toward me. It looked happy there.

"Why is this thing on me? Is it attacking and I just can't tell?"

"Um . . . no." I got a funny feeling. "Wow. Your mom had one, Christopher?"

"When she was little, yeah. I think it died or something. She didn't bring it here."

The Poof looked at me and closed its eyes. I listened. Yep. "It's purring."

"What?" Martini tried to look at the Poof by twisting his head, but it was so small, he really couldn't see it. "Why is it purring?"

"Um . . . I think it thinks it's yours."

Christopher started to laugh.

"Christopher? Just guessing, but I'll wager there's one of these waiting for you, too. Paul and Michael and their sisters might have one, too. One each."

Christopher stopped laughing. "What are you talking about?"

"Corgis."

"What?" They both shouted. The Poof whimpered and tried to crawl under Martini's collar.

"Get this thing off me!" He was doing the there's-something-crawling-on-me dance. I tried not to laugh. Failed.

"Jeff, stop. It's scared. Calm down, and it'll calm down." He did as requested and the Poof stopped trying to hide.

"What did you mean by corgis?" Christopher asked.

"The Queen of England has her corgis. I'm betting the A-C royal family has their Poofs." Reader and I were going to have a field day with this when he was back up and running. "You know, the Royal Pet."

"Oh, my God. Kill me now, right now." Martini sounded like he meant it.

"Let's get upstairs and see if I'm right." I tried to sound soothing. The snickers probably didn't help.

"I'm remembering this for later," Martini said darkly as I put the stuff back into my purse.

"Jeff . . . wait. You said there was something alien in my purse."

"Oh, hell, right. This thing distracted me." He grabbed my hand before I could touch the alien thing. "I think it's a tracking device, but it's not anything familiar to me." He pulled out Chuckie's alien-detector—the piece turned red.

It resembled a small feather or leaf, only it was thicker and seemed made out of a mass of fibers. They glowed, just a bit.

Realization dawned. "That's why she kissed me."

"Come again?"

"She kissed me to distract me and slip this into my purse. She said I wasn't the target. But they knew they would find the target through me. That means Moira's mate knows exactly where I am. Which also means she's somewhere around here."

Martini pulled out his phone and made some calls, with the Poof happily settled back on his shoulder. Christopher shook his head. "I can't believe this. Any of this. Jeff can't wander around with that thing on him—he looks like an idiot. I'm not wearing one, either. We're the damned heads of Field and Imageering."

"Not the Lords of the Dance? Are you sure?"

"I love you, but I may kill you." Martini hung up, grabbed a washcloth, put it around Moira's tracker, and put it in his pocket. "Let's get upstairs and start the next round of torture."

CHAPTER 27

WE DID A FAST CHECK BEFORE we left the level. Moira was still sleeping the sleep of the very drugged, and we still had a lot of A-Cs on Security duty around her cell and the drainage pipe entrance. I made Martini and Christopher test the guards for being real A-Cs. None of them asked Martini about the Poof but I could tell they all wanted to. So could he.

"I hate my life, have I mentioned that?" he asked as the three of us went up in the elevator. He kept his arm around my shoulders, which I didn't mind at all, though it did make me wonder if his no-more-jealousy resolve was going to disappear fast.

"Could be worse. You could be the one whose brains were bashed in." I was relieved I could say this calmly and without wanting to cry. Knowing Reader was going to be okay was a huge relief. I tried to remember the thing I knew I'd forgotten about all that. Couldn't. Decided we had more pressing matters. "Maybe we can get a straight answer out of the emissaries as to what's going on with Moira and the rest of the Free."

"Can't wait," Martini muttered.

We arrived at one of the science floors. The holding cell was easy to find: It was surrounded by A-Cs, all of them talking quietly to each other, so the hum was pretty loud. One of the older Dazzlers saw us coming, and her mouth dropped open. "Jeff, how did you get that?"

"Unwillingly."

Her eyes were wide. "Do you know what it is?"

He didn't answer, so I did. "We think it's a Poof."

She nodded. "Yes. Only the royal family and their closest retainers are allowed to have them. They're very rare."

Martini winced. "Oh. Good. You know we live in America. No royalty here." She nodded, but she didn't seem convinced. We kept on moving.

Reached the holding cell to see a dozen people in it. The cell was really one of their big fishbowl conference rooms, adapted for security issues. The main difference was it had an individual intercom system attached to it.

The prisoners were dressed in what I called Renaissance Faire Spiffy. They looked like something out of that time period but not quite accurate. Seeing the men in hose and long, loose-fitting fancy shirts was interesting. I didn't think I'd ever want to see Martini in the garb, but he would fill the hose out a lot better than the examples before me. The women were going for a similar look, only with a little Grecian Formula thrown in. It was as if they'd taken a look at our historical dress and tried to imitate it, with limited success.

All of the prisoners were decent-looking. Interestingly enough to me most were not as good looking as our Earth A-Cs. "So, the looks, for the most part, resided with your race?"

"I suppose. Maybe you're just jaded." Christopher sounded amused.

Martini laughed. "She's used to looking at me. All others fade away."

"True." I squeezed his waist. "However, I've seen a lot of A-Cs, male and female, and while these are all attractive, they are not drop-dead gorgeous. Your father is, but these, not so much."

"I hate it when you mention that you think my dad's hot," Martini muttered.

"Jeff, you look exactly like him. If I think you're hot, it stands to reason I think he's hot. I am not lusting after your father. I'm just happy to know how hot you're going to look as you get older."

He hugged me. "That's okay, then."

White joined us. "Interesting. I see you've dressed, Miss Katt."

"Yes, I decided to keep the outfit for when I have to convince you of something."

"Good, anticipation is the key to any good relationship."

"Mister White? Why are most of them not as hot looking as your people?"

"Bluntness is your specialty. No idea. They look normal to me."

"They don't look unnormal to me. But they don't look like all of you, either."

"Granddad wasn't all that great, if you recall. Maybe we just have a concentration of hotness. Does it matter?" Martini was looking at the Poof again.

"Hopefully not."

He hit the intercom button. "Hi, there. Who the hell are you and why are you here? And how soon are you leaving?"

The guy I recognized as having been in our room stepped forward. He was nursing a lovely black eye. "Your Majesty, we are here to begin the rites of passage for your intended."

"Nice. I don't plan to have her do them. Don't plan on any of you sticking around. Don't plan on going back to the world that exiled us. Rot in hell. Have a nice day."

"Harlie has accepted you."

"Harlie?"

I looked up at Martini's shoulder. "Here, Harlie." I put my hand up, the Poof purred and jumped into my palm. "Good little Poofy thing. Meet your new pet, Jeff."

"You will refer to His Majesty as My Royal Lord at all times!" A woman's voice rang out from the back of the holding cell. She stalked up to the window, and it didn't take an empath to tell she was furious. "How *dare* you speak to him casually?"

"Oh, you have *got* to be kidding me!" I was ready to lunge through the window. Test one—failed. Test one—pissing me off. Could not wait for test two.

White stepped up to the intercom. "Excuse me. Who are you, and why do you believe you have the right to give anyone on Earth orders?"

"We are the emissaries from the royal court. You, as an exile, have no right to speak to us." She actually turned her back on White and walked to another part of the window.

"Five minutes, that's all I ask. Me and my Glock. Trust me, Mom's been teaching me how to shoot really, really fast."

"Tempting as that is," Martini said through clenched teeth, "I'll be the one kicking their asses."

"You're the king, My Royal Lord."

"Do not start." He let go of me and went closer to the intercom. "You, come back here."

She turned around and stalked over. "Yes, Your Majesty?"

"First off, I'm fascinated that you exiled my entire race here, you're insulting my religious leader who also happens to be my uncle, and yet you're somehow thinking I'm your king. Secondly, if you ever speak to anyone on Earth, particularly the Sovereign Pontifex, that way again, I'll kill you with my bare hands. Oh, and I know how, believe me. Finally, I don't know who you people think you are, but unless you start giving us some explanations, and quickly, I'm going to order you all put to death. Got it?"

She gave him a small, very self-satisfied smile. "You are so like your grandfather, Your Majesty."

Martini lunged at the window. I thought he was going to break through. Christopher and I both grabbed him. "Jeff! Jeff! She means the other one! Not ours. Well, ours, but the other ours! The one who stayed on the home world!" Christopher was shouting, which he had to, because Martini's growl was already at "enraged bear" and about to go to "lion takes over the veldt."

"She means your father's father, Jeff!" I was shouting too. We weren't calming him. At all. Of course, in his mind, Bitch Leader had just compared Martini to Ronald Yates, aka Mephistopheles, aka the Supreme Fugly. The rage was understandable.

"Jeffrey, let it go." White spoke softly.

Martini stopped, took a deep breath, and let me and Christopher pull him back. "Sorry." He was shaking.

The emissaries looked shocked, other than the one I was calling Bitch Leader. She looked amused. "Your Majesty has a temper, I see."

"Really. I mean it, Jeff. Let me in there. I'll do Crane Opens a Can of Whupass, they'll never know what hit them."

"They can kill you." Martini's voice was low. He was staring at the emissaries, and I'd never seen so much anger in his expression before.

"Maybe. I want in."

"I don't want you hurt, so no."

"Easy way or hard way, Jeff."

"I don't want you to shoot them. We don't know what else they're bringing."

"You mean besides stress and high blood pressure problems?"

"Yeah."

"I won't shoot them. They won't kill me. Let me in. Please."

"Why?"

White nodded to one of the security guys, and the door opened. "Miss Katt."

I detached from Martini and went in. Harlie went with me. "Dudes, nice to see you." The door shut behind me. "Now, let's cut the crap. You have no intention of approving me. I have no intention of passing your tests. So what is it you expect to get out of this whole ridiculous endeavor?"

Bitch Leader came over to me. She was a lot bigger. "You insignificant peasant! How dare you—"

"Blah, blah, blah. Heard it all before. I'm an American, you moron. We wrote the book on insignificant peasants making good. I'm also not an idiot. And I'm also not buying it."

I walked through them. There were exactly two who fit the mold. The one with the shiner and another guy. I pointed to them. "You two are the only actual A-Cs here. So, what, are the rest of you shapeshifters from Planet of the Really Pissed Off Amazons, also known as The Free, or are you some other delegation combo? 'Cause you're not all from the same place my aliens call home."

They all looked at me in shock, Bitch Leader included. She recovered fastest. "How . . . how dare you insinuate—"

"Stow it. I'm a human. Want to know the biggest way our A-Cs differ from humans? They are drop-freaking-dead gorgeous. My little friend over there with the black eye, and this other guy here, they're pretty hot. The rest of you? Um, well, you're not barking, but you're not going to win any prizes against Jeff, Christopher, or the rest of the A-C gang."

"There is more to our culture than looks," the guy with the black eye said.

"Oh, right." I slammed my open palm onto Bitch Leader's chest. "One heart." I walked around the room and did the same thing. None of them tried to stop me. "Okay, we have eight with two hearts, two with one, and icky, two with three hearts. I don't even want to know. However, that means you're not all from A-C."

I looked at the two with three hearts. They were both wearing really ugly matching necklaces. I pulled them off their necks and was faced with what looked like giant iguanas. Iguanas wearing stretchy body suits and standing on their hind legs, but still, iguanas. Giant iguanas that looked pissed off in the way only an iguana can.

"Jeff?"

"Yeah, baby."

"I'm not screaming because they're sentient. But I'd really love it if you would, you know, set phasers on full or something."

"We do not kill except in battle," Iguana Number One said to me.

"Right. Talking is good. Our iguanas don't talk. As a rule."

"We are not iguanas," Iguana Number One said huffily. Iguana Number Two just glared at me.

"Right. Komodo dragons?"

"How dare you—" Bitch Leader was giving it a go again.

"SHUT UP!" I couldn't do the Martini bellow, but I was pretty good. They all cowered. "Aww, it's okay, Harlie." The poor little Poof was cowering, too. "I'm not mad at you. Unless you're going to turn into something horrible. Then we might have to agree that I cook you." I patted it gently. Harlie purred and rubbed against my hand.

Bitch Leader lost it and lunged at me. As I jumped out of the way, Harlie leaped off my hand, gave a growl worthy of Martini, and turned into a much, much bigger Poof. A Poof with lots and lots of teeth. It had Bitch Leader in its jaws within moments. Then it turned to me and cocked its head. Its head was about double the size of its body. It looked like a fluffier bigheaded kitten with no ears or tail, only a kitten that could chomp a normal person in two with ease.

"Ummm . . . first off, is Harlie a boy or a girl?"

"They don't have sex, per se," the guy with the black eye said. "It's going to kill her."

"I know. I wanted to be able to say good boy or girl as soon as Harlie's done."

"We don't want her dead."

"I do." I looked at him. "So, let's get this clear. You all come clean, right now, or I have Harlie the Attack Poof eat you. I'll bet Harlie's hungry, aren't you, Harlie?" I cooed this last line. The Poof purred at me. It was a really loud purr now that it was Martini-sized.

I felt something nudge my ankle and looked down. Sure

enough, there were a few more Poofs down there. "Do they replicate in water or if they eat too much or something?"

"Uh, no," Black Eye said. "They're androgynous and can mate with any other Poof. They only mate when a royal marriage is imminent, however."

"Sort of normal." For a freak world, but that's what I was living in, so, normal. I bent down and the other Poofs climbed into my hand and crawled up on my shoulders. "I count six more here. I guess that's one for Christopher, one for Paul, one for Michael, one each for the Gower girls . . . and that leaves a spare. Who is the spare for?"

No one answered. "Okay, let me ask that another way. Someone tells me who the spare is for or I tell Harlie to enjoy its big, nasty snackage."

Bitch Leader decided not to play chicken with me. "It's for you."

CHAPTER 28

"**H**MMM . . . INTERESTING. SO, let's see if I can guess what's going on, shall we? Oh, but before I do, Christopher, I really need Chuckie. In here, with me."

"On it."

"Why?" Martini asked.

"I like the help with the conspiracy theories."

"And," Chuckie said, "there are none better than me with that. What, Martini? I was in the back of the room."

"Oh. Fine." He didn't seem all that fine with it. So much for that no more jealousy promise. "Not jealous, just worried," he snapped.

"Right." Chuckie came in. "Okay, Kitty, what have we here? I mean, other than giant iguanas?"

"We are not iguanas!"

"I think they're Komodo dragons."

"We are neither!"

"They're giant lizards, Chuckie. We'll leave it at that."

The giant lizards both looked really angry. I picked up one of the spare Poofs and looked at the guy with the black eye. "What's this one's name?" The giant lizards calmed down instantly.

"So," Chuckie said. "Back to the theories?"

"Sure. We have a delegation of twelve here. Two are clearly from Jeff's home world. Two are obviously from the Giant Lizard world. I'm betting the other eight are from other planets in the A-C system."

Chuckie wandered the group as I had. "Interesting rings,"

he said to three of them. "Take them off and give them to me. Or we'll insist on learning the rest of the Poofs' names."

They did, and the moment they were in his hand, they turned into what looked like walking jackals who were really into the Ancient Egyptian look. "Chuckie, meet the emissaries from the Dog Planet."

One of them bared its teeth at me. One of the Poofs jumped off my shoulder and turned huge. It stayed in front of me, but the point was clear. The jackal stopped its growling.

"Jeff, I *love* these Poofs. They are like the greatest things ever!" All the Poofs started to purr, including the big ones.

"They seem to love you, too, baby. Hope that lasts."

Chuckie gave everyone a very evil smile. "Okay, let's make it easy. The rest of you, take off your image shifters, will you? We don't have all night."

No one budged. "Poofikins? Will you help Chuckie for me?" The Poof in front of me trotted next to Chuckie and bared its many teeth at the others in the room. A couple of bracelets came right off, and, voila, the Cat People were represented. They were wearing leather cat suits. I wondered if they were being ironic or really went with this look on a daily basis. "Wow, it's a regular menagerie in here. Someone get Paul, please. And triple the guard on James."

"Here, Kitty," Gower's voice came from the com. "Jeff already called for me."

"Good. So, I see four of your planets represented. Who's missing? Or, rather, who's from what world? You're from Alpha Four, right? And Moira and her whacked out girlfriend are from Beta Twelve?"

"Right on both. The Giant Lizards are from Beta Thirteen. We'd call them Reptilians here."

"Wow, sounds like Giant Lizard to me."

"Yeah, well, it's a more polite word. To them."

"If I decide we like them, I'll worry about being polite." The Giant Lizards still looked pissed. One of the other Poofs hopped down, turned big, and sat in front of me. "I love the Poofs. I want that on record. Poofs are the greatest things to hit the solar system. After the A-Cs, I mean." Poof purring continued unabated. The two nearest my neck rubbed against me. It tickled, thankfully, not in an erotic way.

"Thanks, I'm touched." Martini sighed. "So, back to why everyone's here?"

"Not quite. Paul, the jackals from the Dog Planet and the walking felines? They are?"

"From Beta Fourteen and Fifteen, respectively, Canus Majorians and Feliniads."

"Major Doggies and Cat People. Got it."

Gower sighed. "The others are, I'd guess, from Alphas Five and Six."

"Do the Alpha Fives and Sixes have one heart or two?"

"One."

"Then one of our party of humanoids isn't being honest. Poofies? I think we have a mean lady I will not like even more than I do not like Bitch Leader in Harlie's mouth." All the Poofs jumped down and turned big. "What do my Poofies like to eat best?" I asked Black Eye.

"Um . . . uh . . . meat." He sounded worried. Good.

"Wow, how convenient!"

Chuckie laughed and patted the Poof near him. It purred at him. "These are great, I have to admit it."

"Wonderful." Martini was muttering, but not that quietly.

"Jeff, hush."

"Fine, fine. They like Reynolds because you like him, right?"

"I hope so. Because I don't like anyone in this room at the moment, other than Chuckie." The Poofs, to a fluffy thing, started to growl, very softly. The one by Chuckie moved in front of him. "See? Poofs are wonderful."

Black Eye swallowed. "Uh, please don't let them eat us."

"Give me a reason not to. Start with having the shapeshifting Amazonian bitch unmask."

Shocked looks all around. Other than from one person, one of the humanoid women. She stood up straight, shimmered, and a taller, older version of Moira was standing there, complete with the spiky blonde hair and the Xena/Wonder Woman body suit and boots look. "I am not your enemy," she said quietly.

"Right. Chuckie, get behind me. I'm serious, by the way."

He did as requested. "This is an emasculating feeling."

"She'll emasculate you more than I ever would."

"No," the shapeshifter said, "I will not."

"Met your sister, or mate, or whatever she is. Don't believe you."

She shook her head. "They are not here on my order."

My order. "What's your name?"

"It cannot be pronounced—"

"Oh, give it a rest! We know! We know! We've had A-Cs on Earth for decades. All humans working with them are really clear that we are just too damned slow to catch your fabulous languages. Let me mention that what humans are really good at is turning inferiority complexes into mass crusades of destruction. Now, before I tell my adorable Poofies to have a delish breakfast, stop, all of you, with the 'we talk too fast for your pitiful ears' crap and give me names that I can understand that you will also actually answer to. Or die. And I mean that literally."

Poof growling went up a notch or two. I wondered if they required grooming or had nonmatting fur, and if they would be happy sleeping on their own pillows or in a nice big pet bed together.

"Baby? I don't want them in our room, okay?"

"I do."

"Think about it, for a minute, while the prisoners stop wetting themselves."

I did. "Okay, when we're sleeping, how about that?"

"Maybe. Folks, she's not joking. She's protective, tired, and upset. One of her best friends almost died today because of a shapeshifting lunatic, and I'm not in there to restrain her. She doesn't follow orders. So do what she says. 'Cause I don't care what happens to any of you."

The shapeshifter nodded. "I apologize for my subject's actions. I am Queen Renata of the Free Women. And we are here as emissaries for the Planetary Council, not as emissaries of Alpha Four."

CHAPTER 29

CHUCKIE LEANED DOWN AND WHISPERED in my ear. "We have an elaborate ruse. But you knew that. Find out who has the most to gain."

"Interesting. Paul?"

"Yes, Kitty."

"I'd love to chat with ACE, please."

Gower sighed. "Fine." There was a pause. "Yes, Kitty, ACE is here."

"ACE, are these the evil beings you said were heading for us?"

"No, Kitty."

"Are they evil? As in, get them off our planet before they try to kill us all evil?"

"No, Kitty. They are very afraid."

"Would they stop being afraid if Chuckie, the Poofies, and I left the room?"

"No, Kitty. They are afraid of what has happened and what might happen."

I thought about it. "ACE, this is one of those you want to tell me but can't times, isn't it?"

"Yes. Kitty will figure it out without ACE's help." ACE sounded really confident.

"Um, okay, great. As always, thanks very much, you're the best, no more questions and so forth."

"Moira is waking up. Please have someone make Moira sleep again." ACE sounded freaked out.

I heard Martini bark some orders. "ACE . . . where is Moira's mate?"

"ACE is not sure, Kitty."

"Is she in any of our strongholds or around our people in Sin City?"

"No. ACE is not sure where Moira's mate is." ACE still sounded frightened.

Chuckie whispered again. "Or figure out who has the most to lose. This is a power play, but it doesn't make any sense yet."

I gave this more thought and took a look at Queen Renata. "ACE . . . they're off their planet because their net went haywire, didn't it? Because the leader of the Free Women figured out how to play nicely with others. And some of the Free Women don't want to play nicely with others, especially with male others. And the PPB net agreed with them. Is that about right?"

"Yes, Kitty." ACE sounded relieved. "ACE knew Kitty would discover the truth. Kitty thinks right."

"Yes," Chuckie said out loud. "She does." I heard Martini muttering under his breath.

"Yes, good. Okay, please have Paul correct me when I'm wrong on this, but otherwise, go back and relax. Or whatever it is you do in there."

"Yes, Kitty." There was another pause. "Well," Gower said in his own voice, "that was fun."

"So, Queen Renata, how long ago did your protective net start talking to people?"

"Several years ago." She closed her eyes, and when she opened them there were tears there. "For so long we struggled, unable to understand why we were held away from the stars. We knew we could reach them and that we had in the past. We blamed our males, for their aggression."

"But without them, you turned just as aggressive, didn't you?"

"Yes. But we believed ourselves right." She heaved a sigh. "As my mother gained the throne, she saw us for what we were: brutal people, bound only for vengeance. She knew this was not the right way. Through her leadership, we began to hate less and try to forgive more."

"She sounds very wise. And strong."

"She was." Queen Renata looked around. "She sent a message to the other planets, asking them to help us, to forgive us, to teach us how to be less warlike and more peaceful. They sent us help, support. But they would not remove the net. My mother understood—centuries of danger are not removed in a few years."

"What were the reactions?"

"Our people were divided. Over time, however, as the other planets sent gifts—helpful things that made our lives better—most came to my mother's way of thinking."

"But some didn't."

"It was the net." Black Eye was speaking.

"Dude, you have a name?"

"Yes. Gregory." He sounded peeved. "Can I go on?"

"Sure, just figured your parents named you something other than Black Eye or Wimpy."

Chuckie laughed. So did Martini and Gower. Gregory didn't look like he enjoyed the joke. "If I may?"

"Go for it, Greg."

"Gregory." Said through clenched teeth. Nice to have the proof—planetary thing, not just my A-Cs' hang-up.

"Whatever."

"The PPB net is sentient. It . . . became self-aware and started speaking to some of the planet's inhabitants. I'm sure you can't understand, but—"

"Um, Greg? I'm going to speak very slowly, and we'll see if *you* understand. You know the net you folks on Alpha Four put around Earth?" He nodded, a shocked look on his face. "Well, I was just chatting with it. It's in one of our people, while still being around our world, and it likes us. A lot. We like it, too. It's not keeping us in any more. It's doing it's best to keep people like you out. If it let you through, consider yourselves lucky. We're a team, our sentient superconsciousness and us. All alone out here together. We are all very tired of being treated like dirt and only paid attention to when you want something from us. Keep that in mind before you speak again."

"In simpler terms," Martini snarled, "if you talk down to any of us again, her in particular, you're Poof Chow. Got it?" I was so proud—he'd come up with Poof Chow all on his own.

"Uh, yes. Apologies, Your Majesty."

"And stop calling me that!"

"He really isn't into the whole forced royalty thing, Greg. Maybe you should, you know, get on with your condescending explanation."

"The net went nuts and thinks it's God," Bitch Leader snapped. "Can you have this thing let go of me?"

"Name, rank, planetary number?"

"Uma, head delegate from Alpha Six."

"Okay. Harlie? Be a good Poofie and put icky Uma down, okay? No snack right now." Harlie spat Uma onto the floor then trotted over. Clearly for pets and lovies. Which I gave it. In abundance. The purrs were loud. From all of the Poofs. "So, Uma, you were saying?"

"The net went crazy, started talking to the more militant on the planet. Considers itself God, tells them so." She stood up and brushed herself off.

"Tells them to go kill all the men, right?"

"Yes."

"So, you're all here, why?"

"To crown the new king of Alpha Four." She said it like it was obvious.

"But you're not *from* Alpha Four."

"We represent them," Gregory said. I looked at him, and the rest of them. Yep, eyes were not looking at me, faces were turned away, the usual. On the humanoids, anyway. The Giant Lizards were pretty stone-faced, the Major Doggies looked smiley or snarley, depending, and the Cat People looked smug. I didn't know yet if this was just how they looked naturally or how they happened to feel right now.

"So, for some reason, Alpha Four needs a king so badly that they're willing to go across the galaxy to pull up the last person in a line—who happens to be from the religious sect they cold-bloodedly exiled with extreme prejudice—and in addition, they asked the entire solar system's diplomatic corps to help out?"

"Yes." Gregory was looking at me, but his eyes were shifting all over the place. Chuckie was laughing softly.

"And, somehow, the rulership of Alpha Four doesn't care about the fact that if Jeff goes back, all the exiles go back, too?" They wouldn't, but then, Martini wasn't going in the first place. But it was a good question.

"Uh, yes. That's fine. All is forgiven. Their work here is done." I saw the Cat People's expressions—they were as unimpressed with Gregory's lying as I was.

"So, are the parasites still hitting the ozone shield?"

Gregory nodded. "Slowing down, but yes." He seemed relieved. He shouldn't have been—I could tell he was finally telling the truth.

"So Chuckie remains the Conspiracy King, not that I ever had a doubt, and all this is an elaborate ruse. You don't represent the Alpha Four government at all. There is no way they want all our Λ-Cs back. As long as there are parasites, they want our A-Cs right where they stuck them, on Earth, with all of us dealing with the superbeing problem. In fact, I'm betting they, either don't know you're here or, worse, they're coming after you with intent to blow us all up. Which is it?"

I stared at Gregory. He tried to stare back. I was much better at it. "We're . . . not sure . . . entirely." He stared at the ground.

I turned to the only one I figured was going to tell me an approximation of the truth. "Queen Renata? What's your guess?"

She nodded. "Prepare for interplanetary war."

CHAPTER 30

THE OTHERS IN THE ROOM SEEMED UPSET when Queen Renata shared reality with us. I heard silence behind me—our Earth A-Cs were thinking, and so was Chuckie.

Left me to handle the human side again. Always the way. "So, wonderful beings who have arrived in three cloaked spaceships that were somehow landed on the top of the same three peaks my team and I just visited a day or so ago, I have one question."

They all looked at me. The Poofs were, to a fluffy thing, growling quietly.

"What is it you hope to gain from Earth by showing up and pretending to be the actual royal shipload from Alpha Four?"

No one replied. Shocker. I looked over to where Martini was. "You know, we're back to three freaking plans."

"Yeah, baby, I picked that up."

"The one in front of us, whatever the royal family is really doing, and Moira's, right?" Chuckie confirmed.

"Yep."

He wandered the room again. One of the Poofs trotted along with him. I was almost willing to forgive the Emissaries from Hell for coming—I'd wanted a pet of my own. Now I had seven. Well-trained ones. I hoped they were housebroken.

Chuckie got to the back of the room and turned so he was facing me. "Move them into planetary position, would you? In relation to their suns and each other."

Like I was going to be able to do that? "You heard the man,

move it." Poof growls emanated, beings moved their butts. "Paul, make sure they're right, okay?"

"Sure, Kitty."

While they were moving about, a question nagged. "Greg, why did you bring the Poofs along?"

He sighed. "Because they're customary."

"Do they really only mate when a royal wedding's on the horizon."

"Yes."

"Mister White?"

"Yes, Miss Katt, from what I recall, that's the case."

"And they're really rare?"

"Yes," Greg and White said in unison.

"Interesting. So, you brought a rare, royal-family-only animal—seven of them, really. Enough for all the potential royals on Earth and Jeff's intended."

"Yes. Protocol. Maybe you've heard of it." Gregory was almost as snarky as Christopher.

"What position in the royal court do you hold?"

Gregory was silent and wouldn't look at me.

I noticed the other A-C wasn't looking at me, either. He was looking at his feet. "You, what's your name?"

He looked up. "Alexander."

"What positions do you and Greg here actually hold, Alex?"

He winced at the nickname. "Alexander."

"Best of luck with that. Welcome to Earth, Alex. What positions do you and Greg hold within the Alpha Four royal court?"

He didn't answer. I got up closer to him and took a good, long look. Same with Gregory. They were both about my age, so younger than Martini and Christopher. Physically they fell between those two as well, but were about Christopher's height and leaned more toward the wiry side as well. Hair like Christopher's. Facial structure like Christopher's. And at least one of them snarked like Christopher.

"So, Alex, who's older, you or Greg? I mean, he is your brother, right?"

Alexander swallowed hard. "Yes. My older brother." He wasn't lying.

I got closer to him. Eyes were green, but you could see the blue flecks in them this close. Christopher's eyes, nose, and mouth were his father's, but not his eye color. Went to Gregory. One eye was pretty well shut, but the other was the same, green flecked with blue. He glared at me. Christopher's Glare #2, as a matter-of-fact.

I did one last comparison. I thought about my mother, since she, and I, looked like Christopher's late mother, and I tried to see if they could look a bit like her. Or me. I got a reasonable yes. Not a lot, but enough.

"Jeff, are you seeing what I'm seeing?"

"Not so much, baby. What are you seeing?"

I turned around and started to laugh. Christopher was glaring. Glare #2.

"Look at Greg here . . . then look at Christopher."

He did. "Oh, are you kidding me?" Martini sounded beyond annoyed.

"What?" Christopher was still glaring, but it had shifted to #5.

Martini rubbed his forehead. "Why are they *here*?"

"I don't know." I turned back. "Greg, Alex? This just seems like an incredibly complex plot merely to get to vacation with the distant relatives."

They both looked hugely guilty. Chuckie came over and took a look. "Amazing. Genetics are really something."

"Yeah."

"What?" Christopher snapped. "I'm not clear on what you're driving at, Kitty."

"Greg and Alex here are your cousins, Christopher. Possibly as close to you as Jeff is. On your mother's side, of course."

"Are you kidding me? What are they doing here?" Christopher sounded exactly like Martini, only a bit less bellowy.

"Well, boys? Both Jeff and Christopher have asked you the same question. Why the hell are you here?"

They didn't answer. Chuckie did. "Let's list our options. There's been a coup of some kind on Alpha Four. The royal family has been overthrown or is fighting to retain power. The ruling monarch is dead or dying. The people are not accepting whoever is supposed to take over. They're going outside the norm to bring in Martini so that he can act as a messiah. Or, more likely, they've come here to drag Martini back so he can be their martyr. You take your pick from those options."

The two A-Cs were quiet, but they also weren't looking at us. The other delegates were quiet, and all looked nervous. I could tell that Chuckie had hit the real reason in his list of options, but I couldn't tell which one had been our winner.

Chuckie's voice was low and very menacing. "But know this—Martini, White, all the others? They report to me now. And I don't let terrorists steal my people. You try to take anyone by force or coercion? We'll show you that there is no planet more frightening to deal with when angry than Earth."

"They're all in position, Reynolds," Gower said.

Chuckie nodded and walked through them. "Where are the suns, exactly?"

"Greg, put three of the Poofies into sun positions."

He glared at me. "Why?"

"Because if you don't, I'll break your neck." Chuckie was right behind him. "And I can. I may be human, but I'm trained to take out aliens."

Gregory started to try something, but Chuckie had known it was coming, apparently. Gregory was on the floor in a heap.

"What did you do to him?" Alexander shouted.

"What I'll do to you, all of you, if we don't get some immediate cooperation." Chuckie turned as he was talking so he could make eye contact with them all in turn. "Understand— until proven otherwise, you are all considered enemies of Earth in general and the United States in particular. I have orders to exterminate with extreme prejudice any alien threats I feel pose a short- or long-term problem. You pose both. Cooperate or I kill you. It's that simple."

Alexander looked over to Martini and Christopher. "How can you let him threaten us this way?"

Martini let a slow smile creep across his face. "I don't have a choice. He's the boss. I report to him." I saw the realization that Martini wasn't lying cross all the delegates' faces. It was kind of nice to see that Chuckie had been right. Again. "Now, show three of the Poofs where to stand to be suns."

One of the Major Doggies nodded and went to three points in the room. A Poof went to each location. Harlie stayed by me, and the one I'd called Poofikins stayed near Chuckie.

Chuckie came back beside me and took a long look. "Gower, the other planets, how many of them are inhabited?"

"Alphas Seven and Eight, Beta Sixteen. Ten inhabited planets in total."

"Why aren't the others represented?" Chuckie's eyes were narrowed.

Alexander answered. "They are not advanced enough. Beta Sixteen and Alpha Seven seem to have grasped that there is life on other planets in the system, but we won't interact with them until they have made some realistic attempts to contact us. Alpha Eight is at Earth Bronze Age level."

Something Gower had told me months ago waved to me. "Who are the ones with long-range space flight? Besides Alpha Four, I mean."

Animal types all nodded their heads, and Giant Lizard Number One spoke. "We and the Feliniads have had such abilities for decades. The Canus Majorians have joined us in that skill in the past decade."

The Major Doggie who'd positioned the suns spoke up. "We originally had no desire to explore past our own solar system. Events have shown it to be necessary."

Uma chimed in. "Alpha Six still has no interest in traveling beyond our system."

"We have no desire to leave our planet," the last woman, who hadn't identified herself, offered.

"What's your name?"

"Lenore. But," she added, "some of us from Alpha Five do understand that we must, from time to time."

"And Beta Twelve is hot and heavy to get back out there, right?" Queen Renata nodded to me. "So, what will your people do to the three planets that aren't as advanced as the rest of you?"

Queen Renata shook her head. "My loyal subjects? They will not harm them. The dissidents? They will slaughter if they can."

"So why are you all here, not there?"

Silence and a lot of shifty looks.

Chuckie sighed. "They like drawing it out, don't they?"

"Yeah. I'm sure it relates to the real plan, and you know how much they don't want to tell us that."

Gregory was coming to. Alexander helped him up. He looked a lot worse for wear. "Why are you fighting us?" he asked blearily.

"Because we don't trust you. At all."

He managed to shoot a glare at me. "We've come in peace."

"Right. And I'm actually Angelina Jolie, I'm just playing this role shorter, fairer, and with a lot less sex appeal."

"Oh, don't sell yourself short," Martini said. "I think you're a lot sexier than she is. You have better curves."

"Yes, she does," Chuckie and Christopher added in unison. Martini muttered a bit, but at least he wasn't growling.

"Thanks, I'm feeling all tingly. So, Greg or Alex, since you represent the reigning superpower in your solar system, lay it on us. We're big kids, we can take it. And, if not, we'll just kill you. So, you know, we win either way."

CHAPTER 31

THEY DIDN'T ANSWER. But I was thinking. I'd had to do a lot of thinking like this over the past year, and it was starting to come naturally to me. Being human and not an A-C, I liked to do my thinking aloud and share the fun and deepness that was me with everyone within earshot.

"Since we have two males somewhere in the royal line standing in front of us, it can't be that they've run out of potential king options. We also have what I assume are hot Poofs, because if they're that rare, then they're valuable, and we have seven of them."

"Works for me," Chuckie said. He was still examining the living solar system in front of us.

"What do you mean about the Poofs being hot?" Alexander asked.

"Hot, stolen, removed from their owner's possession without said owner's consent, lifted, shifted, grabbed and bagged."

"Oh. We didn't steal them." He was telling the truth, from what I could tell. "They were given to us. But . . ."

"But?"

"Amazing." Chuckie looked over at Martini. "I heard about the first one. It bonded to you, didn't it?"

Martini shrugged. "I guess."

"No, Harlie did, Jeff. Harlie likes Jeff, right?" The Poof started to purr up a storm. All of them joined in.

Alexander nodded. "They didn't bond to me or Gregory. That's why we knew—" He stopped himself.

The light dawned. "That's why you knew you had to come

and find someone they would bond with? Because they're a part of the succession process?"

"Yeah." Alexander looked down.

"Shut up," Gregory hissed.

"Oh, Greg, stop it." I went back near them. "There's a reason Moira and her mate are here, isn't there? A reason you know about. All of you." He wouldn't look at me. I dropped my voice. "If anything happens to Jeff or Christopher, I'll hurt you in ways you've never imagined. I'll make it last for what will seem like forever. I'm a human, you know I can do it."

He looked right at me. "I know you won't. He might," he nodded toward Chuckie. "But not you." He swallowed. "We've been watching you, all of you."

I kept my eyes on Gregory's face. "Queen Renata, Moira and her mate, and however many of your other dissidents, you arrested them, didn't you?"

"Yes."

"Because they were planning to kill the king of Alpha Four, correct?" Gregory drew in his breath.

"Yes."

"But the sentient net let them out, didn't it?"

"Yes."

"Is the king dead?"

"He lives, but just barely."

"And Moira and her mate escaped, with the help of the sentient net, and made it here. I'll bet they used the gate that sent my A-Cs here all those years ago. It's locked to us, but not to the home planet."

"Yes," Renata confirmed. "As far as we can determine."

"Greg? Why is the Queen of the Amazonian Nutcases the only one willing to tell me the truth?" He swallowed but didn't reply. "No worries. I know why. Because, unlike you, she's not a gutless coward."

I spun around and walked over to the door. "Let's get out of this room, Chuckie and Poofs." It was that or I was going to try to kill them. The door was opened, and we all exited. The delegates stood there, still in solar system formation. "Take a look, folks. You're never going to see a better collection of cowardice and guilt anywhere." I was so angry I was shaking.

Martini came over and pulled my back against his chest. "Okay, I can already tell I'm going to hate it. What's going on?" The Poofs went back to tiny. They all crawled up and onto my shoulders, though Harlie went onto Martini's.

"Want me to do it?" Chuckie asked softly.

"Yeah." I had to keep my teeth clenched. Martini gently moved some Poofs and started rubbing my neck.

"We're looking at a bid for power gone wrong." Chuckie leaned against the glass. Like Martini, he made this look comfortable. "White's cousins presumably expected to advance to the throne. Martini, however, has a more direct claim to it. He also chose a bride."

"Setting off the Alpha Four Alert System," I added.

"Right. Meaning that the most direct male descendant was going to get married and presumably start having some babies. Which would strengthen that line even more."

"I don't want to go back there, so why does it matter?" Martini asked.

"Old men get funny notions." I looked up at him. "Maybe he feels sorry, or wishes he'd seen his son's family, or seen you grow up. You're the son of the son, the direct line." I looked into the holding cell. "And unlike the options on the home world, you're not gutless. You're brave and strong . . . and a leader. So's Christopher. Either one of you would be a better choice for ruler than the two in the room in front of us. But you, especially. You've been leading the A-Cs here for over ten years."

"And they've watched you the entire time," Chuckie added. "Which is why the king, when he was attacked, decided it was time to revive the long-distance relationship. And why your cousins in there decided it was a great idea to hire some assassins to kill you."

"Jeff? That tracking thing's in your pocket. Can you take it out?" He did. "Queen Renata, is this from your world?"

She came to the glass, and Martini opened the washcloth and showed the feather-leaf thing to her. She nodded. "It is. How did you come by it?"

"Moira stuck it in my purse after she'd almost killed one of our operatives, that best friend of mine we mentioned earlier. By the way, what's her mate's name?"

"Kyrellis. She is extremely deadly."

"We guessed. So, when did the rest of you come on board? Before Moira and Kyrellis killed your leaders or after?" Okay, so I couldn't shut up and let Chuckie do all the talking.

"After they killed the head of Alpha Five," Uma, of all people, answered. "We realized we'd created a monster we couldn't stop."

"Yeah, I figured Greg wasn't doing this on his own. So you're all pretty much traitors to your home worlds, is that right? Other than Renata, who is somehow along for the ride."

"I am along because the assassins are my responsibility. They killed my mother, first, before they went to Alpha Four. I had to become queen far earlier than I had ever planned . . . or desired." Queen Renata looked very old and tired for a moment, but then she recovered herself. "These did what they felt was best," she indicated the others in the room. "Alpha Four is old and powerful. They control the rest of us. Many chafe under their hand."

"We can relate."

"This council was formed to expand the other planets' self-determination."

I looked back up at Martini. "You come from the bossy stock, I see."

He snorted. "You should talk."

"So, Alpha Four's got a battle cruiser after you guys, with good reason. And, of course, they don't know if we're with you or against you."

"Against," Martini said dryly. "But, you know, they never listen to what we say."

"Figure Alpha Four assumes we started it," Chuckie added. "Only those of us who know Martini would believe he wasn't interested in a kingship."

"Too freaking true. Meanwhile, Greg there gave Moira and Kyrellis the heads-up that the most potent males in the line were here on Earth. They're gunning for Jeff, Christopher, Paul, and Michael, for sure. They'll probably try to wipe out more of the family, just in case."

"I doubt Greg talked to them directly," Chuckie corrected me. "I'd guess Uma had a hand in it. She seems Moira's type."

Uma gave him a dirty look. "Alpha Six has a female-led government, yes."

"Which probably saw the benefits of aligning with the fanatics. You know, I'm all for following the *Feminist Manifesto*, but nowhere in there was the suggestion made that we kill all the men and make do without them."

Uma shrugged. "Your world, your rules."

"Right. And our rules say you're a bunch of traitors, to two solar systems."

"Your Majesty, we beg for clemency." Gregory bent onto one knee. Alexander followed him, somewhat unwillingly.

"I'm not the king. I'm not going to a world that only wants me when it's convenient. And you can rot in hell for all I care. You're endangering the world I care about and the people I love on it. You're lucky I don't just kill you right now and offer your dead bodies to whoever else shows up." Martini was furious, but he was calmer than me, which was sort of surprising.

"Please forgive us," Alexander said quietly.

"How much did you have to do with this plan?" I saw his expression and got a funny feeling.

Alexander shook his head. "I support my brother."

"Does your brother know you're the one who triggered the Royal Proposal light show back on the home world and here on Earth?"

Alexander's eyes went wide. "I . . . don't know what you mean."

"Open the door!" Chuckie and Martini shouted in unison. There was a lot of that going on. Too many alpha males in one small space.

Security flung it open, and the Poofs pretty much flew into the room, turning bigger as they did so. One tackled Uma before she was able to get Alexander with the knife she was holding, another knocked Gregory aside, and the others surrounded Alexander, with much growling and the showing of sharp teeth.

"Good Poofies. Anyone else want to try to kill someone? No? Smartest move I've seen you people do yet. Poofies? Bring Alexander out, please. Oh, and take that nasty weapon away from the mean lady." The Poof on top of Uma growled in her face. She dropped the knife; the Poof picked it up in its jaws and trotted out of the room behind the rest of them, looking very pleased with itself.

I gave lots of Poof lovies, then turned to Alexander. "Sucks to be you, dude, but you could have given us the heads-up a lot sooner, you know."

He shook his head. "He's my brother. He wanted the kingship so much . . . I didn't realize he was out of control until it was too late. I did what I could." He looked at Martini. "I'm sorry. For all of it."

"So, who can we trust besides you?"

Alexander shrugged. "I'm not even sure you can trust me. So much has gone wrong . . . but Queen Renata is trying to fix things."

"So are we," one of the Major Doggies said. "I am Willem. We have the support of our leader."

"Support to try to kill the Alpha Four royal family?" Chuckie asked pleasantly.

"No," Willem said. "Support to fix the damage we have caused."

One of the Cat People spoke up. "I am Felicia. We as well are along to help."

I looked at the Giant Lizards. "You speaking up there, Iguanodon?"

"My name is Neeraj. This is Jareen. We do not appreciate your way of speaking to us, human."

"We don't appreciate Giant Lizards coming by trying to screw our world over. So we're even." I thought about it. "How do they spell their names?"

Alexander sighed. "Yes, each name is the other name spelled backward. It's a mating thing on their world."

"So, they're married? Which one's the girl?"

"Jareen is my female," Neeraj said, clearly pissed off. "She is the most beautiful Reptilian on our world."

"Yeah, well, Jeff thinks I'm hot, too, but he didn't rename me Ffej."

Martini laughed. "Oh, but it's so cute, so you."

"We are not amused," Neeraj said.

"We don't care," Martini said pleasantly. "We don't like you."

"You know, they're all going to say they're here to help." Chuckie looked back at Alexander. "Who, besides Queen Renata, do you recommend we trust?"

Alexander sighed. "They all need to help you, because they can't go home unless this situation resolves in a positive way."

"Interstellar war bad for the image?"

"Yes. But, I wouldn't let anyone but Renata out of the room right now, if that's what you're asking."

"Alexander, how can you do this to us?" Uma shouted.

He closed his eyes, but didn't turn around. "I still have a shred of honor left, and I want to hold onto it."

"You are not my brother any longer," Gregory said. He sounded hurt and furious.

"I know." Alexander looked like he was trying not to break down.

"Jeff, what do you think?"

Martini sighed. "Let Renata out. Alexander's telling the truth, and she's not our enemy. Leave the rest of them in there." He pulled me back, out of the clutch of people, bent down and whispered in my ear. "I can't tell on the lizards, dogs, or cats. I need to be around them more to see if I'm filtering their emotions correctly. There's more going on than Gregory's told Alexander; I can feel him hiding something. Lenore is basically clueless, and Uma's a raving bitch, but you already knew that."

"Umm hmmm." Him nuzzling my ear was really turning me on, scary interstellar plots or no.

He laughed softly. "I love how, no matter what, you can always focus on the priorities."

"I want to go to Vegas." And spend time in the huge suite. Spend time making like bunnies in every portion of the huge suite. It felt like ages since Martini had made me scream and beg for more.

He kissed my ear. "Put on that outfit and tell me that."

I turned around. "You'll be mine to do with as I please?"

Martini grinned. "Probably." He looked at my shoulders. "Okay, they're cute, they're cuddly, and they're great at protection, so, as long as we don't discover they turn on their masters for some weird reason, you can keep them."

"Oh, thanks! By the way, Poof Chow? Jeff, that was awesome."

"You're rubbing off on me. I like it, don't worry."

"I'd rather rub on you."

"I *love* how you think."

CHAPTER 32

"I DEMAND DIPLOMATIC IMMUNITY and to speak with your Diplomatic Corps!" Gregory shouted, giving imperious a good run.

I snorted, but Martini looked uncomfortable. "Is this going to be a time when we're again glad that Chuckie's in charge?" I asked him quietly.

"Yeah." Martini jerked his head at Chuckie, who came over to us. "This could be a problem."

Chuckie shook his head. "Not for me. They're suspected terrorists, not sanctioned diplomats. So, no chats with your Diplomatic Corps allowed."

White joined us. "If, however, Gregory is truly a member of the royal family, and I have no doubt that he is, his request is one we must agree to."

"Why?" I asked as Gower, Christopher, Alexander, and Queen Renata came over to us as well. "Chuckie just said he's identified as a terrorist, and we all know the Alpha Four head honcho or honcha isn't going to confirm anyone along as having true diplomatic immunity. And even if they do, why should we care? And even if we were nice and let Greg chat it up with the A-C diplomats, so what?"

Everyone stared at me, Chuckie included. I got the impression this was something that I was supposed to know, meaning it was in one of those huge sets of briefing materials I'd been ignoring for a good year now. Hey, I really hadn't noticed any lack in my ability to get the job done. However, I saw no reason to either share that I still hadn't read said information or not to get an answer. I stared right back.

White heaved a sigh. "Our Diplomatic Corps has great power within our society. Not only do they provide much needed protection and interference for us with the various world governments, but they hold sway with our people. While the Office of the Pontifex can and does make decisions, as do the Heads of Field and Imageering, if the Diplomatic Corps isn't in agreement with those decisions, then the rest of our people will not be in agreement."

Chuckie was nodding, so he clearly knew about this. "So they're more like Congress?" I asked him.

"Close. More like the British Parliament. The Diplomatic Corps is in place to provide a check and balance against the Alpha Centaurion monarchy."

"So, they're a full-on A-C thing, not just an Earth A-C thing?"

"Correct," White said. "And since Gregory and Alexander are both confirmed to be citizens of Alpha Centauri, they fall under those laws, which means that if they wish to speak to our Diplomatic Corps, then they may do so."

"Even if they're traitors to two solar systems?" International politics was bad enough. Interstellar politics was starting to give me a headache.

"I'm with Kitty," Chuckie agreed. "I have more than enough precedents to not only deny them access to anyone but to ship them off never to be seen or heard from again."

White looked pained. "I'm sure you do, but . . ."

Martini sighed. "But it could cause us more problems than letting him speak with the Diplomatic Corps." He pointedly looked around. There were still a lot of random A-Cs here, watching the show with rapt interest. "Because our people here know, someone who's anti the Pontifex or doesn't like something Christopher or I do is going to find out, and then we have internal issues I'd like to avoid." He shook his head. "Under the circumstances, just one should be sufficient, wouldn't you think?"

Alexander nodded slowly. "The Head Diplomat would be my suggestion."

"Isn't that Robert Coleman?" I wasn't a fan of the Colemans, other than Doreen, who wasn't speaking to her parents and was also hugely happy about it. "Who's married to that bi—"

"Yes!" Christopher interrupted quickly. "The ones who tried to force Jeff to marry their daughter. Them."

"Dude, I've already failed all the protocol tests."

"Why make it worse?" he muttered.

Alexander managed a weak grin. "The Diplomatic Corps are used to getting their way. They can be . . . quite forceful."

"So, they don't use diplomacy so much as strong-arm techniques?"

I got a lot of blank looks. Chuckie just laughed. "In that sense. Diplomats have jobs that entail more than just shaking hands and smoothing over problems. Besides, the power they're used to is within their own A-C community. In Washington and elsewhere they do function as a protective layer."

"So, they're the bulky, ugly sweater your mom makes you wear when it's really cold out, even though you'd rather not?"

Queen Renata smiled. "A very apt description."

"I like her." I looked back at Chuckie. "Does that mean we have to bring in Mister Coleman?"

"I don't particularly want to. I'd like to know the ramifications with Alpha Four if we do or don't acquiesce."

"My great-uncle is not in condition to deal with this, due to the attack on his life. My mother and the Chief Councillor are. And since Gregory is my mother's eldest son . . ."

Chuckie heaved a sigh. "Got it. Alpha Four's already angry enough. Why make it worse?"

"Who's the Chief Councillor and what's his job description?" I didn't get a lot of glares or exasperated looks, so I figured this wasn't in the briefing papers, or if it was, it wasn't given a lot of space on the pages.

"When we were on the home world, the Chief Councillor functioned as the liaison between the monarchy, the Diplomatic Corps, and the other sovereign planets," White said. "While the goal is to have someone in that position long-term, it tends to be a short-term post."

"Why? Death or desertion?" Retirement seemed out.

"Usually resignation." White shrugged. "It's a difficult position without a great deal of popular public support."

"It's still that way," Alexander agreed. "Our current Chief Councillor has been in place for the past decade, however."

I considered this. "Why? What's going on that's made whoever's in that post seem either like the greatest option around or so necessary that things'll go to pieces if he takes off?"

Alexander looked uncomfortable. "Nothing out of the ordinary." This was mumbled. I wondered how they managed to lie to each other and why they were even trying to lie to us when it never worked.

Chuckie smiled at me. "I'm so proud." He looked at Alexander. "I want the answer, too. Now."

Alexander nodded. "My great-uncle has . . . certain views. Many feel those views are outdated."

"We are all tired of living under the yoke and control of Alpha Four," Neeraj said from the holding cell.

"No one turned the intercom off?" Chuckie sounded exasperated.

"It would not matter," Willem said. "We can hear you through the glass."

"We're a good twenty-five feet away," I pointed out.

Willem shrugged. "We can still hear you. Clearly."

"All of you, or just the Major Doggies?" We all got closer to the holding cell. Clearly, stepping away hadn't made a difference.

Willem looked like he really wanted to snarl at me, but he glanced at the Poofs on my shoulders and controlled it. "We Canus Majorians have the best hearing, but the Feliniads and the Reptilians also have hearing above that of any others in our solar system."

Felicia nodded. "Those from Betas Five and Six are much closer to Earth people in terms of abilities."

I wondered if this meant they were closer to us in terms of ability to be treacherous, but I didn't voice it. "They have one heart, so that makes some sort of sense. How's your sense of smell?"

Willem grinned. "We all know what you had for your last several meals."

Felicia sniffed. "Not that we can create enthusiasm for your choices."

"Sorry, we'll round up some interstellar rats for you. Oh! Quick thought! They're probably in the room with you right now."

Chuckie and Martini both chuckled while Felicia's eyes narrowed, and she flexed her claws. I got the impression she was willing to see if she could take the Poofs, which was, all things considered, sort of impressive.

White cleared his throat. "However, the issue at hand is the current political situation. Feel free to share that with us. For example, there was no Planetary Council before we left, but I have no idea what may have changed since then."

"I'd bet not much." Chuckie looked at Queen Renata. "Because I don't buy that the Alpha Four government has ever okayed a Planetary Council."

She nodded. "They have not. We are all considered dissidents, in that sense, not just my planet."

"Well, not completely," Alexander corrected. "The Reptilians and Feliniads are considered allies, particularly when it comes to dealing with the other planets."

Chuckie looked over at the prisoners. "Do you agree with that assessment?"

Neeraj, Felicia, and Willem came to the window. The others started to move, I looked at a Poof on my shoulder, and they stayed put. "We would, to a degree," Neeraj said. "We and the Feliniads have been sentient and space-traveling almost as long as those from Alpha Four. However, because they successfully reached space and the other planets in our system first, they insist they are the leaders. In all things."

"Some of their laws we don't mind," Felicia said. "Most we do."

"None are allowed to travel the solar system without Alpha Four's permission," Willem added. "Let alone go beyond."

"How did you all get here, then? How did you have interstellar ships at hand? Or did you jack some Alpha Four ships along with the Poofs?"

Neeraj glared at me. "Our ships are our own. We all are capable of interstellar flight on our own, and Alpha Four allows us to build our own vessels."

"Because they might need us," Felicia added.

"Do the parasites show up on your worlds?" Martini asked.

Neeraj shook his head. "We all have ozone shields protecting us. One of the gifts from Alpha Four."

"And something they could remove if they chose to," Willem added.

"Wow, bossy *and* nasty. What a fun combo. But, no one's answered my question about the Chief Councillor."

"His name is Leyton Leonidas," Alexander said.

"Say that five times fast."

"I'm sorry? I don't understand you," he said politely.

"Few ever do. So, what's Leonidas done to stay in the job so long?"

"He has walked a careful line between support of the monarchy and support of planet's rights," Queen Renata answered. "He is truly a great man."

Coming from the Queen of the Amazons, I had to figure this meant Leonidas was beyond impressive, at least in terms of his political skills.

"Queen Renata is correct," Neeraj agreed. "His skills have kept all the planets in check since well before the attack on Alpha Four's monarch."

"He also suggested the idea of the Planetary Council," Felicia added. "Though that's not widely known among the people. Any of the people."

"You're all high up in your world governments?"

They nodded. "None of us are the leaders," Willem said. "We are more like him." He pointed to Gower.

"The high-level, in-the-know advisers?" That's what Gower was for the Pontifex, in one sense. More nods. "So, not really diplomats like you told us when you got here." Though, of course, Gower was probably the head diplomat on Alpha Team.

"We are here on a diplomatic mission, in that sense," Queen Renata said. "We desperately need Earth's help."

"To do what?" Martini asked. "Because if it's to bring back a new king of Alpha Four, you're out of luck."

"No," Felicia said. "What we truly need is protection and emancipation from Alpha Four's control."

"But I'm not sure you've earned that," Chuckie said. "You've come in disguise, undercover, and have lied about your intentions. We don't tend to support governments that do that."

Felicia snorted. "Oh, really? Let us give you a term I know your country is familiar with. We are freedom fighters, requesting assistance to remove ourselves from the yoke of tyranny."

"Wow, you're good." Hey, I was impressed.

Felicia looked extremely smug. "Radio waves travel."

"So we've heard. And that reminds me, we still have to figure out what Kyrellis is doing."

"I would like to question Moira," Queen Renata said. "Perhaps I can get some information from her you could not."

Chuckie shrugged. "Fine with me." He smiled the evil smile I was fairly sure my mother must have taught him. "I'd like to question the 'freedom fighters.' Without a lot of witnesses. And before we have anyone from the Diplomatic Corps in attendance."

The emissaries looked a little worried, especially when Martini smiled. Apparently my mother had taught him the scary smile, too. "You're the boss."

CHAPTER 33

ALL NONESSENTIAL PERSONNEL WERE SENT back to their jobs, guards were doubled around the holding cell and given orders to do whatever Chuckie said, and we took Queen Renata down to visit Moira. Wasn't my preferred plan, but it had to be tried.

"I don't think Moira's going to see the light."

"I'm sure she will not," Queen Renata sighed. "However, I must try."

"Think Reynolds will get more out of the rest of them?" Martini asked me quietly as we headed down in the elevator.

"Yes, and even if he doesn't, I know he's still studying the A-C system, so he'll get something from that."

"Getting it memorized?"

"He already has it memorized. He's doing analysis now, I assume. While doing the interrogations."

"You think he walks on water, don't you?"

"Wow, that sounds so jealous. I'm going to pretend it wasn't said with so much sarcasm. And, no. I know how smart he is. Jeff, he's in an incredibly powerful position, very young. He's not there because he has connections—my mother didn't know aliens existed before I met you, remember?"

"Yeah." He sighed as we got out of the elevator and headed for Moira's cell. "And, as much as I hate to admit it, I know he's brilliant. He's also a pain in the ass. But, and I really hate admitting this, he was right about being in charge. It's been helpful."

"It'll probably be more so. But that means he's got a big

target on him now, too." The worry crashed over me like a
tsunami.

"Nice to know you care."

I stopped walking. The others continued on. "That wasn't
funny."

Martini sighed. "I know. And I know you're worried about
all of us, not just him. I'm trying with the jealousy, okay? It's
just . . . they all want you." He looked lost and lonely.

"Jeff, what's wrong?"

He pulled me into his arms. "I think we're missing something, and it's going to cost us. Like we missed what was going
on and James almost died."

My brain kicked, hard. "Oh, my God. That's it!"

"What? What's it?"

I pulled out of his arms and ran to catch up to the rest of
our crew. "Alexander, Renata, were any of you in Las Vegas,
New York, or Los Angeles in the last day or so?"

They looked at me as if I were insane. I was so used to that
look by now that it didn't even faze me. "No," Alexander said
slowly. "We only arrived a short while before you captured
us." Queen Renata nodded.

"Renata, would you say Kyrellis has more restraint than
Moira?"

She gave a bitter chuckle. "Hardly. Kyrellis is the leader of
the dissidents. She has no restraint whatsoever."

"So it would be hard for her to enter a room full of men,
while pretending to be a man, and not hurt them?"

"It would be impossible for her to be around a man and not
kill him," Queen Renata said dryly. "I wish it were otherwise.
But she was the head of our armed forces before she believed
God was guiding her."

"Alex, you set off the light show on your home world,
right?"

"Yes."

"Did you do the one here?"

"No." He sounded confused. "I assumed one of His Majesty's retainers had done so."

"Jeff. My name is Jeff. You can call me Mister Martini, Martini, or Jeff. Even Jeffrey. If you call me or refer to me as Majesty, Highness, or Your Royal anything, I will kill you with my
bare hands."

"I told you, he's really not into the royalty thing. Okay,

so no one from our Interstellar Dirty Dozen set off the light shows over the past year or impersonated Christopher. Kyrellis and Moira wouldn't have been able to enter any A-C facility without going all *Kill Bill,* and I don't credit either one of them with the stealth involved to impersonate the Catering department so they could drop off the bugged pineapple."

"Kyrellis is more . . . straightforward, yes," Queen Renata confirmed.

"So, who pretended to be me, then?" Christopher asked. "We can't identify anyone out of our own people."

I thought back. "They've been here a year. A year of working as spies. And what do spies do in a foreign country?" I didn't need Chuckie here to answer that question. "They do their best to blend in. They don't wear the Armani Fatigues. They don't act like A-Cs. They look and act like any other hot guy." I felt stupid and somewhat offended.

"Who are you talking about?" Martini asked.

"Remember those two good-looking guys at THEhotel who were smiling at me? One held the door for us, probably because he'd just gotten back from New York via his personal floater gate. The other was coming from the elevators, probably after having delivered the food and interstellar pineapple to Chuckie's room."

Martini closed his eyes. "I can't really remember much about them. I was trying to ignore them." He shook his head. "I didn't notice their heartbeats, one way or the other."

"I saw them again at a craps table when James and I were heading out to go shopping. And one of them *knew* I was there, even though his back was to me." I wondered if he was an imageer-empath combo, or if they'd just been keeping a watchful eye out. Figured we'd probably end up finding out, one way or the other.

"Could just be coincidence," Martini said doubtfully.

Chuckie didn't believe in coincidence and neither did I. "Trust me, they're the actual spies for the Alpha Four royal family. And they've been here at least a year, maybe longer."

"If so, I don't know about them," Alexander said. He wasn't lying. But he did look worried. "I don't know if Gregory is aware of them or not."

"I'm actually betting not. Because he's been stupid, and I doubt he wants the king or the Chief Councilor to know." And I was betting at least one of them, if not both, knew. Another thought occurred. "Alex, why did you land your ships where you did?"

"We assumed we were supposed to—traditionally, the light display indicates where visiting dignitaries will sit to observe the royal nuptials. The one peak was quite difficult."

"Hatchet, yeah, it would be." So, someone had suspected a coup of some kind was coming at least a year ago—or had been planning one. Interesting. I looked in Moira's cell. She seemed awake but fuzzy. "I need to get in there again."

"Are you sure?" Queen Renata asked. She sounded worried.

"She's strapped down and I'm not without the skills."

"She's strapped down and if she wasn't, she'd break Kitty's neck, but, yeah, let her in. Baby, please remember that you are not up to taking her, okay?"

"Fine, fine. Need in, now." Security opened the door, and I trotted inside. The door was shut before I realized six of the Poofs were inside with me. I realized it because they all started growling, softly, but with great menace. "Yeah, I don't like her either, Poofies."

Moira stirred. "You. Has my mate destroyed yours yet?"

"No. We're giving her time. How long did you watch us before you tried to kill my friend, the one you thought was my lover?"

She looked at my shoulders. "What are those?"

"No idea what you're talking about. How long did you watch us?"

"They are staring at me. Growling."

"No idea what you mean. How long did you watch us?"

"I watched you all arrive. Why are they on your shoulders?"

"Nothing on my shoulders. How many of us arrived?"

"Your lover and his other lover and another man," she spat the words. "Then two beautiful women with six beasts. Then you and him," she looked at Martini. "We will kill him, all of them." The Poof growling increased. "Why don't they like me?"

"What are you talking about? So, what did you do, after we all arrived?"

"I waited. My mate knows how to destroy a more numerous enemy."

"I'll bet she does. So, you waited and then what?"

She gave a drugged giggle. "Then you and your lover came

out. It was so clear he was the one you loved the most, and he loved you most, too." She looked right at me and smiled. "It was so easy to follow you. But to watch him paw you and see you enjoy it, to see you dress you like you were his whore, to see you fawn over him—that was not easy. I enjoyed hurting him. I made him think I was his other lover. I attacked him in that hideous form. He thought his other love was jealous and was the one who killed him." She smiled beatifically.

I'd heard people say that something made them so mad that they saw red, but I'd always thought it was just a saying. It wasn't. Moira's joy in letting Reader think it was Gower who'd tried to kill him made me feel as if my head were going to explode from rage. The room looked red, and all I could see was her throat and how easy it would be to rip it out.

The Poofs jumped off my shoulders and turned large and in charge. To a one they were growling and had all their teeth bared. Moira looked at them and started to scream in terror. "They want to devour me!"

"They do, don't they?" I forced myself to calm down, at least somewhat. "Where was your mate while you were watching us? Tell me, and I won't let them eat you."

She shook her head. The Poofs moved closer and she sobbed. "Please, no. Take the monsters away. My God, my God, help me!"

I waited. Nothing. "Your God's not here yet, Moira. I think it's coming, and when it does, there will be some hell to pay. I'm going to make sure you pay it. Now, answer me—where was Kyrellis when you were following us?"

Her whole body jerked. "How . . . how do you know her name?"

"We have her. And we'll kill her unless you tell me where she was. She won't tell, but I'll do all the things I told you and more if you don't. I'll let them eat her, slowly, in front of you. From the feet up." I had a feeling the Poofs would do it, too, if I wanted them to. I hoped we'd stop Kyrellis before I wanted to.

Moira sobbed. "Don't hurt her!"

"You didn't care about James. You wanted to hurt him. You were happy to hurt him, happy that it was breaking my heart. Why should I care about your feelings?" She didn't have an answer, and I hadn't expected one. "Now, tell me—where was Kyrellis while you were following us?"

"If I tell you, will you promise not to hurt her?" Moira was begging.

"Yes."

She nodded. "She was setting the bombs." Oh, good, we were officially at DEFCON Worse. I almost felt kindly toward the spies—they'd only planted bugs.

"What bombs and where?"

"Bombs to destroy you all." She said it calmly.

"WHERE?" The Poofs all snarled.

Moira looked at me as if it were obvious. "At the palace."

"Palace? What palace?"

"Where you all live."

We lived here and Caliente Base. No one would call either a palace. A horrible feeling came over me. "You think where we were when you attacked James is the palace, don't you?"

"Of course." She smiled. "Even if you have Kyrellis, the bombs will go off soon."

"How soon?"

"When your sun is high. Fitting time to see a kingdom die." She looked happy again.

I couldn't help it. I leaned close to her and spoke softly. "Moira?" She nodded. "You know how I said I wouldn't hurt Kyrellis?"

"Yes." She sounded uncertain. Maybe she was looking at my expression.

"I lied."

CHAPTER 34

I **RAN OUT OF THE ROOM,** Poofs behind me. "Drug that crazy bitch. Renata, forget it, we have bigger issues!"

"What the hell is going on?" Martini asked. "Your stress levels are off the charts."

My phone rang before I could reply. Why now? I dug through and answered it, while I ran for the elevator, the others behind me. "Hello?"

"Kitten? Where are you?"

"Dad? Now's a terrible time. I'm at the Science Center."

"Why aren't you in Vegas?"

We were in and I hit the button for the launch area. "Heading back there at warp speed, Dad." I thought about it. "Why?"

He sighed. "Your mother's waiting for you, and from what I can tell, things are a little tense with Jeff's mother."

I went cold. "What do you mean, Mom's in Vegas?"

"Well, Kevin told her about how some of Jeff's people were going to be there, and we figured it might be a good way to get to know them. She's not alone. Your Aunt Karen and Aunt Ruth are with her, and Nana Sadie and Nona Maria are there, too."

"Daddy?" I never called him Daddy any more unless I was freaked beyond belief.

He knew that, and I heard his voice shift. "What, Kitty? What's wrong?"

"Call Mom. Get them out. All of them, out. Evacuate the entire complex. Tell her to do it fast." I looked around wildly. "What time is it?"

"About eleven in the morning, why?" Christopher was giving me the look that said I was scary and strange.

"Dad, get them OUT! Do not go there yourself, you understand me? You stay away from Vegas and get them out of there!"

"Okay, I'll call you back." He hung up, and I hit the stop elevator button, then hit the one for the holding area.

"How bad is it?" Martini asked me quietly. "Your terror is so high I can't read you correctly."

"Worse than you can imagine." The doors opened and I bolted out. "Chuckie!"

He ran to us. "What's wrong?"

"We have spies," Christopher offered. He didn't sound like he thought this was worth panicking about.

"We have a lot worse than that." I reached Chuckie and grabbed his arm as my phone rang again. "Dad, did you reach them?"

"No. Your mother didn't answer. I tried several times. Either she left her phone in the room or they're in the casino and can't hear it. Should I call the hotel management?"

"No. I'll take care of it. Keep calling, keep me posted." I dumped my phone into my purse. "Everyone's there. Jeff's parent's, Paul's, Michael, my mother, my female relatives, the rest of Airborne. The Amazons weren't the ones bugging your room. They were the ones setting bombs up to go off in the palace at the height of the sun." I was shaking and shaking Chuckie. It didn't seem to help.

"What palace?" Chuckie asked me, looking as confused as everyone else.

Martini grabbed my hand. "GLADYS!" The man was the king of bellowing

I heard the com activate. "Yes, Commander."

"I want this live to all A-C personnel, all A-C bases worldwide, *now*!"

"Live, Commander, go ahead."

"This is Commander Martini. All active Field and Imageering agents to Las Vegas immediately, unless dealing with a superbeing. If so, kill it, leave it, and get to Vegas. Bombs spread throughout, at least, the Mandalay Bay complex. We have no more than an hour to save tens of thousands, including our own people. Anyone who doesn't pull weight answers to me when it's over. Bombs are alien in nature, likely to look like something imitating nature. Move out, NOW."

Gower and Tito appeared. "Ready," Gower said.

Christopher grabbed Chuckie, and we all took off at hyperspeed for the launch area. Ran the stairs instead of the elevator—it was faster. Realized I should have mentioned it on the 15th floor. Decided to worry about the bigger issues.

"The entire city of Las Vegas imitates something," Christopher said as we waited for an open gate and the humans all dealt with the aftereffects of the hyperspeed. Apparently all the gates had been calibrated for Vegas by the time we got up here, but there was a huge stream of A-Cs pouring through them, and we were at the back of the line. "The bombs are going to be impossible to find."

"I can help," Queen Renata said. "I will know them."

"We need more than one person."

"Chuckie, how many of those alien-detector things do you have?"

"On me? One. At my office in Headquarters? Plenty."

"On it," Christopher said. He grabbed Chuckie, and they disappeared.

"Where're they going?"

"Operations," Martini answered. Meaning where the Head of Security hung out. Meaning, I assumed, Gladys had a personal gate. Martini didn't seem concerned, so I decided to focus on the bigger problem.

"What if the alien-detector things don't work on the bombs? If only Renata can recognize them, we're in trouble."

"The others could assist as well," Queen Renata said.

Alexander shook his head. "Not Lenore or Uma. Lenore has no idea, and Uma's more on the side of Kyrellis than us."

"What about the lizards, dogs, and cats?"

"They could, yes." He looked uncertain. "Gregory could, too. We've seen the bombs."

Martini grabbed two random A-Cs. "Get the prisoners in the holding cell. Everyone but the two women who look humanoid. The rest I want here before I go through. That's fifteen seconds, tops." They disappeared. "Describe the bombs."

"They can look like more than one thing," Queen Renata said. "But they will normally resemble a large, spiky fruit. I believe you call them pineapples here, or at least, your world's equivalent."

Martini and I looked at each other. "What, are pineapples the universal fruit of badness or something? I think they're tasty."

He shrugged. "Easier to find."

"Not at the Mandalay Bay."

"Good point."

The A-C agents were back with the rest of Animal Planet. "Long story short—Kyrellis is about to blow up what she thinks is Jeff's palace. It's not, but we have a lot of innocent people in it as well as people we care about personally. Alex and Renata seem to think we can trust you, even Gregory, to help us find and defuse the bombs."

Willem nodded. "How many?"

"No freaking idea. Figure a ton."

He looked to his Major Doggie companions. They nodded. "Wahoa, Wrolph, and I will help. We should be able to hear and smell them."

"Loud and smelly in a casino, guys."

"I am a girl," Wahoa said.

"Sorry, didn't count the teats, okay?"

She looked at Queen Renata. "This is the ruling class of this planet?"

Martini and I exchanged another look. "Not so much, no."

Neeraj spoke. "They are the protectors, not the rulers. It is why he," he indicated Martini, "is so upset by the insinuations he is king." He looked at me. "The Iguanodons will assist."

"You have a sense of humor in there after all?"

"The one you call Chuckie explained yours to me. Where is he?"

"Bringing stuff to help out," Christopher said. He and Chuckie were dragging bags of devices.

"Good choice on the Reptilians, Canus Majorians, and Feliniads," Chuckie said quietly to Martini. He pointedly looked at Gregory.

"I have the science team making more," Christopher told Martini before he could respond to Chuckie. "We'll have enough for every agent within fifteen minutes."

Felicia came closer to me. She walked just the way I expected a cat on its hind legs to walk, only a little smoother. "Arup and I will help. We understand how the assassin thinks."

"Because you think like her?"

She gave me a fangy smile. "Because we have dissidents

on our world, too. Arup and I are the Chief Inquisitors. And I chose that word purposely."

"Nice. So, you and Torquemada going to hurt my people along the way?"

"Not if we can help it."

We were at the gates. I grabbed Gregory. "What's your plan?" Chuckie dropped his bag and started to walk rapidly toward us.

Gregory didn't answer. Alexander spoke. "Their families are in what the assassin thinks is a palace. You've been given a chance to regain some honor, Brother. Answer the question. What do you plan?"

Gregory pulled away from me as Martini shouted, "Stop him!"

Chuckie lunged, but it was too late. Gregory was through the gate.

CHAPTER 35

MARTINI CURSED. "YOU SAID to bring him along why?" he snarled at Alexander.

"I tried to warn you," Chuckie said.

"Nice if you'd been clearer about it," Martini snapped. "Or faster."

"No time for the alpha male fight right now, guys, please. We need to focus." I grabbed Martini's hand and pulled him through the gate. It sucked, but I was too frightened to care. We landed in a bathroom, but not at McCarran. I could tell—it was too nice. The hell with subterfuge. I walked out behind the rest of the A-Cs.

Of course, women and men coming out of a bathroom might not cause a lot of stir, but walking dogs, cats, and lizards would. Martini had the same thought as me. "How can they help us if they get arrested for being aliens?" he asked as Willem exited the stall.

"On it, Martini," Chuckie said, as he came out. He tossed Willem a ring; Willem put it on, suddenly looked human.

He nodded to us. "I will contact you if I find any I cannot defuse."

"How?"

He grinned like a wolf. "We have ways." Then he disappeared.

Chuckie handed the rings to the other two Major Doggies, the bracelets to the Cat People, and the necklaces to the Giant Lizards. They all said they'd contact us and all disappeared. The Giant Lizards stayed together, the Cats and Dogs did

not. Queen Renata shapeshifted and raced off as well, several
A-Cs with her.

"Okay," Martini said. "I want everyone fanned out. We
need to find the bombs, but we also need to evacuate in case
we can't. Reynolds, you need to get to the head of the place
and tell them to get the people out."

"Jeff, this is Vegas—they won't believe him until it's too
late. Besides, I have an easier way. Fire alarms."

"What?"

Chuckie nodded. "She's right. It won't clear out everyone,
but it'll clear out a lot of them."

"Fine." Martini grabbed the next several A-Cs who were
coming through and told them to find every fire alarm and
make it go off. The sounds started immediately.

"We need to go through the hotel, especially THEhotel,
where we're all staying. It's a good bet some of our team are
still up there, and they might not leave."

"Who?" Christopher asked Martini.

I wanted to say me, but I was the one who'd talked to
Moira. "Alexander, can you take Chuckie and do that?"

"Yes."

Chuckie nodded. "That's fine. Has to be me, Martini, or
White, or they won't listen anyway." He gave me a long look.
"Hope they're listening to me now, by the way."

"They will. Chuckie . . . my mom's here, and both my grandmothers, and . . ." I couldn't talk.

He took my hand. "And Martini's parents, and Gower's. I
know. We'll get them out, Kitty. I promise." He nodded to Alexander, let go of my hand, and they disappeared.

"Tito, take Paul to the mall. Check it, all of it, but especially around the store I was in, the one where the alarms were
going off. They'll have put at least one bomb there."

"Yeah. I have some ideas where they might have stashed
others, too," Tito said.

"How so?"

"There was this guy . . . he was odd and nasty. Sort of threat-
ened me when I got near him, then said I wasn't important
enough to worry about. I'm thinking it might have been the
other shapeshifter. And I know where he, or she, went, 'cause
I watched."

Gower managed a chuckle. "Kitty, good job on the hiring."
He grabbed Tito and they were gone.

"What are we doing?" Christopher asked.

"We're looking for Kyrellis and Gregory."

"What?" Martini and Christopher were in unison again.

"We have at least a thousand agents here, plus Chuckie and Tito, plus all our new Animal Planet friends. Kyrellis is a lunatic of the highest order, but I promise you this—she wants to watch this place go up in smoke, see all the people die, feel the pride in a job well done."

"What about Gregory?" Christopher asked.

"He's either running away or trying to find her." Something rubbed against my neck. "Oh, are my Poofies okay?"

"Is now really the time?" Martini asked through clenched teeth.

"Yes. Poofies, you have to be very careful. Harlie? Do you remember the man who gave you to Jeff?" Harlie mewled at me. I took it for a yes. "Good Poof! I want you and the other Poofies to find him, find Gregory. If he's being bad, you stop him. If he's being good, some of you watch him and some find me or Jeff or Christopher. Okay?"

Much Poof purring came back at me. Then they were gone, just like everyone else.

"They have hyperspeed?" Martini asked as we started out of the bathroom finally.

"No idea. Maybe they turn invisible. Don't care. They're smart, and I think they'll find him."

"Why'd you give him the benefit of the doubt?" Christopher asked as I scanned the casino. No sign of anyone I knew, no sign of an Amazonian assassin.

"Because Jeff said he was hiding something. Could be bad, possible that it's good."

"What are the odds?" Christopher asked dryly.

"Don't know. I just know he's your blood, so I'm hoping there's more of you in him than not." I closed my eyes. "Have to think. If I were a psycho Amazonian assassin, where would I go to watch the show?"

"We could search everywhere in the time this is taking," Martini said urgently.

"Jeff, stop. Psychos and megalomaniacs are my forté, remember? They all wanna hang with me." It would have to be close. She wouldn't want to miss the show. "Make sure they search the entire complex—Mandalay Bay, Luxor, and Excalibur."

Martini and Christopher were on their phones, barking orders.

The Excalibur, New York New York, MGM Grand, and Tropicana were the four casinos on this corner. But they'd all be too close, especially if she'd set up the entire Mandalay complex to go. "Have them check all the casinos on the corners, too." Martini and Christopher barked more orders.

Where would she go to watch? Where in this town would someone like Kyrellis feel comfortable? Or at least feel she could control herself from killing all the men in order to watch her fireworks display? I had to think. Figuring out what the psychos did for kicks was my job, really.

Too stressed. Think about what I did know. Moira and Kyrellis were insane. Fanatics. Amazonian lesbians who really loathed men deep in the bone. Military trained. Why had Moira hurt Reader? Because he was, according to her, pawing me. But she'd pawed me and hadn't seemed to think that was an issue.

I was trying too hard. I had plenty of lesbian girlfriends. Like most of my friends, I wasn't in constant contact, but I certainly could remember what they'd talked about. They talked a lot like my guy friends talked, liked many of the same things. Of course, none of my gay girlfriends were loathing man-haters; they just preferred boobs and such. Oh. DUH. I opened my eyes.

"Boys? You like chicken wings?"

CHAPTER 36

"NOT REALLY," MARTINI SAID. "Also, think we should, you know, save the innocents and all before we stop to have a snack."

"And that's why I'm the one the psychos all wanna hang with. Can I lead if we're running at hyperspeed?"

"Sure."

I grabbed his hand and we took off. Too revved up to get sick from the hyperspeed, so that was a bonus. Raced out and down the Strip, made a right on Tropicana and raced to the goal—Mecca for most straight guys and lesbians—the Hooters Hotel and Casino.

"Are you kidding me?" Christopher shouted. "Why are we here?"

"Because Kyrellis is here. Waiting and watching and enjoying the view before she really enjoys the view."

"What are we looking for?" Martini asked. "She's a shapeshifter. She could look like anyone."

I thought about it as we raced through the casino. "She'll look like herself, as much as possible. She thinks she's in the clear, and she's had hours here to assure herself of that."

"She knows we have Moira," Christopher said.

"No, I don't think she does. I think she thinks Moira has me. Jeff, you still holding that tracking device?"

He cursed. "Yes. I forgot I had it."

"That's great. Put it into my purse."

"Hell, no!"

"Put it in my damn purse, Jeff! And look for a strong, big

woman with spiky blonde hair. Figure she'll look like she's in the WNBA." He muttered but dropped the tracker in as requested.

We looked around. Nothing that seemed to fit. "It's close to noon," Christopher said urgently.

My brain waved at me. "The roof. She'll be on the roof. This is a small place, she has to get up high to see things go down."

We raced for the stairs. The door to the roof was locked. Martini wrenched it open and we went through, back outside under the close-to-noonday sun. We came around to face the Mandalay Bay, and there she was. Her back was to us, but from what I could tell, she was built like Martini and about the same size. Only, she was a bit larger, and potentially more muscular. I got a bad feeling in the pit of my stomach.

"Kyrellis."

She turned around. "I know you." Spiky blonde hair, violet eyes. I got the impression the Free Women had made do without their men via a cloning process. She smiled, and it was a very evil smile. "You brought them to me. What a good little girl you are. Maybe I will not kill you. Maybe I will let you stay with me and my mate."

Oh, right. She was an assassin. And she wanted to kill Martini and Christopher. "Guys? Please get out of here."

"No." In unison again. Not too loud, but with a lot of meaning from both of them.

"I can't see her do to you what Moira did to James."

"She won't," Martini said. "We aren't being lured and fooled."

"She will." Gregory's voice came from behind us. I looked over my shoulder. He was behind us. The Poofs were with him, but they weren't big or growling. They were trembling.

"So, you have them attached to you after all, Greg?"

"No. I just know how to control them." He had Harlie in his hand, fingers held in an unnatural position. I assumed this meant he was doing something to prevent Harlie's ability to go large or toothy. He was squeezing it tightly and it was clear he could squeeze tighter. "Threaten the leader, the followers do your bidding."

"Yeah, that's the bad guy plan in a nutshell."

Gregory shrugged. "Just because none of you can see the advantages to ruling the strongest planet in two solar systems doesn't mean I can't."

"Kyrellis, why are you working with a man?"

She shrugged. "He has . . . helped us. My God feels he is worthy in Her sight. Not to touch us, but he will be an ally we need."

"Boy, are you gullible."

She smiled her evil smile. "No. I am powerful. As you will soon see."

She shimmered, and there was another Martini standing there.

"Oh, great," he muttered. "Don't use the Glock."

"I'm sure that's her plan. Jeff, please, get out of here."

"I love you. Please remember that." He ran toward her and the two of them started fighting, all out, with clear intent to kill—but at human speeds. Gregory's attention was on the fight, and Christopher took advantage of his distraction by body-slamming him. Unfortunately, A-Cs were strong, and they were fighting at hyperspeed instantly.

I realized I'd never seen Martini fight, other than the one time he and Christopher had gone at it, and that had looked a lot more like the fight Christopher and Gregory were currently having—blurry guys rolling around on the ground. I had no idea who was the real Martini—they were both good fighters, scary good.

Body slams, double punches, kicks, lunges—they could have gone into the light heavyweight class in the UFC and taken the division easily. Tito was in the featherweight class, I was pretty sure, but he wasn't here to pass along any clues as to who to put my money on.

I gathered the frightened Poofs and put them into my purse. "It's okay, Poofies," I lied. I pulled the Glock out, just in case.

I saw something small fly through the air. It was Harlie, and it was heading for the edge of the roof. I dropped the Glock and my purse, kicked off my shoes, and ran. I'd been a sprinter, and I was still great over the short distances. Caught the Poof in the air, had to come to a screeching halt. Didn't achieve it and went over the edge.

Lucked into something to grab onto. One-handed. Small ledge, too far from the roof to get back up there. Far too far away from the ground to want to let go. "Harlie, be a good Poof and get on my shoulder." Harlie scrambled up as requested, and I managed to get both hands on the edge, just in time. Got toes on not much. Felt like glass.

Okay, this wasn't good. Tried to use my toes to support, didn't work. At all. The edge wasn't all that secure, and I was in trouble. I couldn't call to Martini or Christopher—not only were they dealing with murderous opponents, but my screaming could cause them to be fatally distracted.

Of course, my plummeting to my death wasn't going to sit well with them, either. Right before I started to scream, whatever I was leaning my toes against disappeared, and I felt hands on my feet.

"It's a chick," a male voice called. "Gimme a hand."

"Help!"

"Hang on, sweet cheeks, we got you." I felt someone near me and risked a look. A big guy wearing a USC Trojans T-shirt was inching along the ledge next to me. He put his arm around my waist. "Got her, guys. Let go, babe."

I did and grabbed him. Built like Martini. Thank God. Several pairs of hands pulled us inside. Inside what turned out to be a big suite. "Wow, thanks. I can't tell you how great your timing was."

The guy who'd saved me grinned. "Trojan football at your service, hon. I'm Len."

Lots of big guys, all athletes. Fairly drunk, but I wasn't going to complain. "I'm Kitty, and I need your help. I mean, again."

"You a dealer here?" another one asked me.

"No, why would you think that?"

"Some of the Hooters girls don't wear the shorts and stuff," he answered with a grin. "And you have the job requirements filled."

"Filled well!" another voice called. There were affirmations around the room that my rack was all right by Trojan football.

"Dudes, seriously. I'm a Federal agent and we have a terrorism situation going on." I looked around and saw the room clock. 11:50 a.m. "We have ten minutes to save thousands of people. Can you please help me?"

Len gave me an up and down. "Federal agent?"

"Undercover. My badge is on the roof. Along with my partners. Who are potentially losing fights to the terrorists. Look, thanks for the save, I have to go."

"Oh, come on." One of the others said, getting in front of me. "Why go now?" He was one of the drunker guys. He was also a linebacker if I was any judge.

I picked up the threat. I didn't have time for it. "Let me go or come with me. The only options."

"C'mon, Kyle, get out of her way," Len said.

"You're only the QB when we're on the field, Len." Kyle looked as though he was used to being a problem.

"I don't have time for the gang rape plan, okay? I'm not kidding, thousands are going to die."

"Sounds great." Kyle had a few guys backing him.

Len came up behind me, took my hand, and pulled me away. "Mine, then. Okay? Now, get out of the way."

"We're a team. We share." Kyle finished his beer, tossed the can, and put out his hand. One of his buddies slapped another into his huge ham-hand. He popped it and started drinking again.

"I have to get out of here. There's no time."

Len tried to move me out of the room, but the line stopped him. "Who's gonna know?" Kyle asked.

"I will," Len said. I looked behind us. Len had some backers. They weren't as big as Kyle's backers, and Kyle's were all clearly more wasted.

Time to improvise and hope Gregory hadn't caused too much damage. "Harlie? Be a good Poof and help me get back to Jeff."

The Poof jumped off my shoulder and turned Martini-sized. It didn't growl, though. It roared.

"Holy shit!" Kyle and his guys fell back. I took the opportunity to run for the door.

Len came with me. "What the hell is that thing?"

"Experimental protection weapon. Top secret. Come if you're helping, otherwise, thanks again for the save." I bolted for the stairs.

There were pounding feet behind me. Len and his crew were following me. I could hear the line screaming. Good.

Ran up the stairs, saw the door Martini'd ripped off its hinges. Good, right spot. Reached the roof to see the fighting still going on. Grabbed my Glock and tried to figure out who to shoot.

There were two Martinis fighting. Both were hurt, one more than the other. But I couldn't guess who would have done more damage between the real Martini and Kyrellis. Christopher and Gregory were rolling on the ground, blurry but there. So they were tiring. I pointed to them. "Guys, get them separated. One's a bad guy, one's another Federal agent. The Fed's in a black Armani suit."

The football players ran over and surrounded Christopher. I stopped looking. Hopefully that would turn out okay.

"Kyrellis!" They both looked at me. Damn, that didn't work. "We've found all the bombs." Lie, but maybe it would cause a reaction.

Did. They both went back to hitting each other. Hard. One landed a great uppercut and the other staggered back, toward the edge. I wanted to run and grab him, but what if it wasn't "my" Martini?

"Hey, Kitty!" I turned at the sound of Len's voice. They had Christopher and Gregory separated. "Who's who?"

I ran over, and pulled Christopher out. "He's the Fed. Keep this other guy under control. Hurt him if you need to." I looked at Christopher. "You look awful."

He shrugged. "It'll pass. How's Jeff?"

"Um . . . no idea." We stepped a little closer. "Have you seen him fight like this? Can you tell who's who?"

Christopher studied them. "She's imitating his fighting style. No way to tell." He sounded as worried as I felt.

"Great. Find out if we're going to have an explosion."

He pulled out his phone and I inched closer to the fight. The Martini who was more hurt got knocked to his knees. The other one slammed his fist into the side of his head. He went down.

"Jeff?"

The one standing looked at me and nodded. The one on the ground groaned. I went to him and pointed the Glock at the one standing. "Say something." The Martini standing rolled his eyes. But he didn't speak. And I didn't hesitate.

CHAPTER 37

KYRELLIS TRIED TO RUN, but I hadn't been joking—my mother had been working with me on rapid firing techniques. I hit her torso and kept firing. By the third bullet, she shimmered and turned back into herself. By the eighth bullet I gave up on the torso and hit a knee. She went down.

"Christopher, need you and the guys, and my purse!"

Christopher pulled some of the football players off Gregory, and they covered Kyrellis. Len ran my purse to me. "That was weird and amazing."

"Thanks. Need your help." I dug through for the case where I kept Martini's adrenaline. Got it out, filled the huge needle. Ripped his shirt open. "He's going to start thrashing, and he's really strong. You need to help me hold him."

"Okay. Will you tell me what's going on later?"

"Possibly."

Martini's eyes fluttered open. "Baby? Were you sure that wasn't me?"

"Hush, Jeff. Of course I was sure. Why do you think I waited until you were on the ground?"

"Gee, thanks."

"I meant I had to wait to see if the Martini standing was going to speak to me or not. I didn't want to distract the real you."

"I feel like crap." He was gasping. I knew this scenario well.

"It's okay. It'll be okay." I, as always, hoped. I bent down and did my ritual. Kissed his forehead and said, "I love you,

Jeff," against his skin. Then I reared back and slammed the needle right into his hearts.

He bellowed and started thrashing. "Shit!" Len flung himself onto Martini's body. "You weren't kidding!"

I heard the sound of running feet and felt the roof shake. Looked over to see the linebackers coming our way. "Oh, great." I was trying to hold Martini's upper body and get the harpoon put away without getting hurt or killed.

Kyle's eyes were wide and he looked as though he'd been scared sober. "I think that thing wants us to help you." His voice was squeaky. I looked around him and saw Harlie, still huge and mad, herding the rest of the team to us.

"Help hold him, but don't hurt him."

Kyle and a couple others dropped and held. I got the harpoon put away, then put Martini's head onto my thighs. "It's okay, Jeff. Come on back, baby." I stroked his head and tried not to worry about how badly Kyrellis might have hurt him.

It took a few minutes, but his thrashing slowed, then stopped. "Get these guys off of me," he growled.

I nodded. "Thanks, guys." They stood up. "Jeff, how badly are you hurt?"

"Oh, a couple of broken ribs, my head's killing me, I think my shoulder's dislocated. You missed a lot of brutality. She only imitated my fighting style when you were around to see it and be confused."

"Wish you'd said something. I could have shot her."

"Love you, know you're becoming as good a shot as your mother. Didn't want to get shot by you, and, shockingly, didn't want you saving me. It's bad enough that the Amazon beat the crap out of me." He closed his eyes. "You know, I'm officially tired of having to be rescued."

I kissed his forehead. "Retire, and then I won't have to."

He managed a laugh. "Right." He opened his eyes. "Any of you jocks know how to put a shoulder back in?"

Len and Kyle both nodded. "Really?" I found that hard to believe.

Kyle shrugged. "I'm premed."

"Oh, come on."

"I am. And, I'm sorry I was a jerk." He mumbled that one.

"What did he try?" Martini was growling.

"I almost fell off the building. Len and the rest of his team saved me." I figured it wasn't worth getting upset over. There were so many other issues at hand.

Len and Kyle sat Martini up, then Kyle did some push and shove move with Martini's arm and Martini bellowed again. I winced. "Thanks," he said through gritted teeth. They helped him up, then Len helped me up. Martini's eyes narrowed. Oh, good, back to jealousy. Oh, well, at least he was alive and reasonably unscathed.

I heard a shriek from Kyrellis. "What have you done?"

I looked around. Nothing was crumbling; nothing was going up in smoke. "Christopher?"

"They're pretty sure they found all the bombs. An unreal amount—she had to have been planting them for twenty-four hours straight." Christopher's voice was clipped; he was in full Commander Mode. "Tito's hunch was right—she'd rigged the mall. The rest of your hunches were right, too. She hadn't rigged the other casinos outside of the Mandalay complex, but she'd set the bridges to blow, I guess under the impression it would cut the 'palace' off."

"You are one whacked-out chick."

"You will pay for this," she snarled.

"No. I think you and Moira will. We've had her in custody for quite a while. You know, while you were hanging out, eating chicken wings and ogling the Hooters girls? I've been mentally torturing her. It was great."

Kyrellis lunged at me, but the football players held her in check. "Get these beasts off me!"

"Nah. I'm almost tempted to let them have fun with you. But that would be wrong, and the men I work with would be appalled, so I won't."

"She in the WNBA?" Len asked me.

"No. She's an Amazonian superbitch from another solar system." Why lie? I was pretty sure Martini was going to have to give the team a different memory.

"You're kidding, like Wonder Woman?" This from Kyle.

I took a look at his expression. Wow, you never knew when or where a kindred spirit would appear. "Yeah, only Wonder Woman wanted to protect the Earth, and she wants to destroy it."

"That thing from her planet?" he asked, as he pointed to Harlie, excitement radiating from every pore.

"Nope, from theirs," I pointed to Martini and Christopher,

both of whom were giving me the looks that said I had a big mouth and was insane.

"Babe, really, I was drunk off my ass. Total apologies, okay? In fact, someone should probably kick my ass." Kyle was sincere. It was touching in a weird way.

"I'll be glad to," Len said. He had a sarcasm knob just like Martini, and it was on, as near as I could tell, full.

"Do I want to know?" Martini snarled.

"No. Guys, really, we need to get our alien lesbian psycho and the wimp traitor over to the proper authorities."

"Need their help with it," Christopher snapped. "They're both too strong for us alone."

"You got it." Len barked some orders, Kyle did the same. The line took Kyrellis; Len's boys took Gregory. Len and Kyle both helped Martini. I took Christopher, who wasn't as steady as he was trying to pretend he was.

Got my purse and shoes, checked on the Poofs. They were all asleep, cuddled around Harlie, who was back to small. "Why didn't you have the Poofs attack?" Christopher asked me.

"Uh . . ." Damn. Hadn't occurred to me. For all I knew, I might not have had to catch Harlie, either. Possibly the Poofs could fly along with all their other skills.

Martini laughed. "Ow, that hurts. It's okay, baby. You found a football team. I'm sure they were as helpful. Slower, but still, helpful."

"Trojan football always here to help," Kyle said. "So, what planet are you guys from?"

"Far, far away." Martini sighed. "Later, okay? I hurt." He glared at me. "Stop enjoying helping Christopher."

"Jeff, for God's sake."

I had Christopher's arm around my shoulders. He hugged me. "Jeff, the jealousy promise. What was it again?"

"He had that chat with you, too?"

"Yeah. He fails all the time, but he's trying." Christopher grinned. "I think it's flattering. He actually seems to think you're biding your time before you dump him for me." He looked over his shoulder. "I think I'll land her tonight, Jeff."

"Hilarious. Have I mentioned my head hurts?"

"Oh, Jeff, stop." My phone rang, and I dug it out, moving Poofs as gently as I could. "Dad?"

"Kitty, I reached your mother. They're out, over at the MGM Grand. What's the status?"

"Pretty sure we found all the bombs, have the bad guys of the moment in our custody, I'm okay, Jeff's hurt but not badly, as least so he says, Christopher's about the same."

"How are James and Paul?"

"Paul I don't know, but I think he's okay. James . . . James is going to be okay." I filled my dad in on what had happened as we inched down the stairs to the elevators.

My father's voice was shaking. "I'm heading to the Science Center. You all have too much going on. I'll stay with him."

"Oh, Dad, thank you so much." My dad was the best, truly.

"It's no problem, kitten. I know how much James means to you. Should I call his parents?"

"No. They . . . don't understand, or know what he does. It would be harder for him if they were there."

"Got it. I'll be with him. I'll bring the pets, that way I don't have to wait for someone to come take care of them."

"Okay, Dad. Richard's either there or at Home Base. Call him and he'll get a room for you. All the active agents are here, so you'll be on your own."

"Not a problem. Call me when you can."

We hung up, and the elevators arrived. I got a funny feeling. "Jeff, are you okay with the stairs?"

"Why?"

I looked at Kyrellis. "She's shot, but she's still got fight in her. Gregory's a sneaky little bastard. The team's willing but untrained, and we can't all fit in the elevators together."

Kyrellis gave me a look that said I was her newest target. "No prison will hold me. My God will free me, as She did before. Then I will destroy these while you watch. And then destroy you."

"Blah, blah, blah. Heard the same crap from Moira. She's in our custody and gave away your plot. I'm still debating whether or not to just have the Poofs eat you both, so shut the hell up. Jeff, the stairs?"

"Yeah, I'm with you. And I can do it."

"No one does it better than you." I refrained from adding in more about our sex life, at least out loud. I wondered how long it was going to be before he felt up to anything and hoped it wasn't going to be too long.

"Glad you still think so. And, trust me, soon." He grinned at me. "Love your laser focus on the priorities."

I shrugged. "It's a gift."

CHAPTER 38

IT TOOK A LONG TIME TO GET DOWNSTAIRS. Hooters wasn't the tallest hotel in town, but we had a lot of people to get from here to there, two of them were trying to escape, and four of them were hurt.

Kyrellis had eight bullets in her, but she wasn't bleeding to death. We hadn't done anything for her, so apparently the Amazons were faster healers than the A-Cs. By the time we were down, Christopher and Gregory both were looking better. Martini, not so much. I tried not to worry and failed utterly.

We decided to wait there and went into the Hooters restaurant. I enjoyed my feelings of inadequacy while waiting for the still-mobile rest of Alpha Team to arrive. We got a lot of looks from the patrons, but the Hooters girls were, to a one, hotter than any Vegas showgirl, and they were plentiful. The customers gave us the initial glance, then went back to the view they'd come to see. I had to remind the football players to keep an eye on the prisoners.

Martini and Christopher, however, weren't looking at the Hooters girls. They were talking on their phones, barking orders, keeping things moving. I wasn't talking, I was thinking. I was getting tired of thinking, but someone had to do it, and we still had alien plans active.

Chuckie and Alexander arrived first. Chuckie took one look and shook his head. "How did you get an entire football team helping you?"

"Talent. We need real security on Kyrellis. She's got eight bullets in her, and you'd never know it."

"We'll take care of it. Your families are all fine. Once I found your mother, things moved faster, of course."

"Thank you." I wanted to just curl up in Martini's lap and pretend this had been a TV show. No such luck, of course.

"Don't mention it. Glad to ensure this wasn't a tragedy."

"How did the hotel management deal with all this?"

Chuckie shrugged. "As your mother knows, flashing the big Federal agent badge solves a lot of issues. For some reason, when people see Central Intelligence Agency, they get amazingly cooperative. They were relieved the terrorists weren't able to destroy their properties and agreed to use an electrical fire in the basement as the excuse. Most of the guests have been comped a free meal for their inconvenience, and everyone's heading back to their gambling."

"Good, so business as usual."

"Pretty much." He looked around again. "How's Martini? He looks like he had the crap beaten out of him."

"He sort of did. He and Kyrellis got into it. But he'll be fine." I really hoped.

Alexander looked at his brother, who was glowering. "He did not try to help?"

"No, he was all over Kyrellis killing Jeff and Christopher. He and Christopher got into it, but they were more evenly matched."

"This is all my fault. I should have told someone, anyone. And sooner than this."

I studied his face. "How old are you?"

"Twenty-two."

"Wow, I thought you were older."

He shrugged. "No. Gregory is thirty."

"And thought he was younger."

"Sorry." Alexander rubbed his forehead. "What can I do to help?"

"Get the rest of the emissaries rounded up. I want to be sure they're helping."

Chuckie snorted. "They helped, believe me."

Before he could expand on this, Gower, Tito, Tim, Lorraine, and Claudia came in. Lorraine took one look at Martini and cursed. Impressively. She'd been spending a lot of time with the pilots.

She started doing some medical things to Martini while Claudia checked out Christopher. Gower gave me the run-down. "Found all the bombs, at least, if any are missing, they didn't go off."

"Kyrellis was expecting an explosion when we figured, so I think we're good."

"Hope so, but the Canus Majorians and Feliniads are still searching, just in case. They each have two field teams with them, so they should be good."

"How'd you get rid of the bombs?"

"Spatiotemporal warp."

"Come again?"

Gower grinned. "The Reptilians have the ability to create spatiotemporal warps between mated pairs. Once we started finding the bombs pretty much everywhere, they fired it up, and we tossed the bombs through."

"Going where?"

"I asked, don't worry," Chuckie said. "It's a complex scientific answer. You want it, or you want to trust me on it?"

"I want to trust you on it."

"So I figured."

"Where's Queen Renata?" Chuckie and Gower both started to cough. "Um, guys? Where is Renata? It's a clear question."

Tito shrugged. "Don't know why they're acting like that. She's with your mother and all the other women. Total girl bonding."

"Oh. Goody."

"At least," Tito added, "I think it's your mother. The woman who's clearly in charge anywhere she goes and also looks like you? The one who could probably kick everyone's ass, including the Amazons'?"

"Yeah, that's my mom. She's not that horrid."

He grinned. "Wasn't an insult. I think she's awesome."

"Me too."

"Oh, there were some men with them, too. It's pretty much turned into a party. Your mother wanted your father to come out, but he told her about James. I think the plan is your father will come to Vegas with James when he's up to traveling." Tito smiled at the look on my face. "Sooner than you think. Might be sooner than a week. The medical stuff the A-Cs have is incredible. And James is healthy, strong, and wants to get well. Said something about having to take care of his girlfriend's wedding."

I managed a laugh. "Good to hear." I looked around. "What are we going to do with the psycho Amazons?"

"Queen Renata is all for killing them." Gower sounded serious. I looked at his expression. He was serious.

"Um, Paul? I think that might pose issues, don't you?"

"Yes. However, they *are* her subjects."

"And they're on *our* world. So, no. Not yet, anyway." Chuckie's voice was pleasant and casual, but I picked up the knife and it was clear.

Gower did, too. He shrugged. "Fine with me. But we have other problems as well."

"True," Chuckie said with a sigh. "We have no idea when the Alpha Four team will be arriving, but I think it'll be soon."

I shook my head. "I think they're already here. At least some of them, anyway."

"What do you mean?" Chuckie sounded tired and a little annoyed. I remembered that he hadn't been with us when I'd figured out who the spies were.

Martini and Christopher both heard me. "I'm still not sure I buy who you think the spies are," Martini said. "Are we done yet? Ouch!" This was directed to Lorraine.

"Me either," Christopher agreed.

"Spies?" Chuckie asked.

"We'd be done if you stopped jerking away." Lorraine had Martini's shirt off and was doing something to his rib area. He looked bruised all over. I started to worry about certain important body parts. Parts I knew Kyrellis would have taken particular aim for.

Martini flashed a grin. "I protected those. Trust me."

"Okay." I figured I'd test later. And give them tender loving care should he be in pain. I stared at his chest, and it did to me what it always did—I wanted my mouth all over it. "Can we go back to the hotel any time soon?"

"Almost done," Lorraine snapped. "Not my fault you all get banged up so much."

"Spies?" Chuckie asked again. "I'm still waiting to hear what you're going for, Kitty. Besides Martini, I mean."

Martini waved. "Eyes up here." I looked up, and his grin went wider. "Not that I mind, but you were going to share your latest theory with Reynolds."

"Huh? Oh, right." I took a deep breath and was rewarded by seeing Martini's eyes shift downward. "Up here."

"Yeah, yeah." His eyes weren't moving up, but I didn't care. There were a lot of impressively filled out tank tops in this place, and he was only looking at me. I was great with where his eyes were.

"Do you two ever stop?" Christopher asked.

"Not really."

"I'm really losing patience," Chuckie said. "Mind actually telling me what you're talking about?"

I filled him in on my theory about the two hunks who'd been flirting with me, including the fact that these two had probably been on Earth long enough to have learned how to blend in.

Chuckie nodded slowly when I finished. "It makes sense, and it ties up several loose threads. Or will if we can find them. Could you pick them out of a lineup?"

"Possibly, but since they can put images over themselves, we're probably not going to get the opportunity until they're ready to let us know they're around."

"Why were they so obvious?" Christopher asked. "I mean, you and Jeff were both aware of them."

"Overconfidence," Chuckie answered. "For all we know, they've been around all of you far more often than you realize."

"Fabulous," Martini muttered.

"It's the only theory that fits so far," I pointed out.

"True." Chuckie sighed. "Oh, we found out what that dish was."

"The Gruel of Grossness?"

Chuckie laughed. "Yes, that one."

"It's from Alpha Four," Alexander confirmed. "It's considered quite a delicacy. Boiled tapeworms."

Everyone within earshot, human and A-C alike, gagged. "You have tapeworms that big?" I had to stare at Martini's chest again to get my stomach under control. Worked like a charm. Lord, the man had incredible pecs and awesome abs.

"They're nothing like the ones here on Earth. But, yes. However, once the property was cleared, Charles and I went back and checked. The dish was drugged. It's being analyzed now for what it was drugged with."

"How could you tell?"

Alexander shrugged. "It smelled wrong."

I didn't want to know. "Okay, we already had a good idea

they weren't our friends. Why did you two go back?" I wasn't wild about the fact that Chuckie had risked himself for a non-lifesaving reason, and I realized it showed in my voice, at least if Martini growling was any indication.

Chuckie smiled. "Nice to know you worry. It wasn't a risk, Kitty. We had time—the fire alarms had sent most of the hotels' occupants out. I didn't want to lose the evidence."

"Evidence like that isn't worth you dying for. This was a huge, scary situation, and you can act as nonchalant as you want, but the danger was real and so was the risk."

Chuckie shrugged. "As emergencies go, this one, and I'm sure Martini and White will agree with me, while challenging, wasn't the worst we've ever seen."

"What a comfort."

Gower laughed. "You know, Kitty. Routine."

CHAPTER 39

A PHALANX OF A-CS CAME TO TAKE KYRELLIS into custody and back to the Science Center. I wasn't wild about her being there with both my dad and Reader in the same facility, but no one wanted to risk her getting loose at Area 51. She was drugged up before they left Hooters. She required double the drugs that Moira had, according to Martini and Chuckie, which didn't make me feel any better.

Gregory was also escorted back to Dulce under heavy guard. He, Uma, and Lenore were to be put into separate cells, all on the 15th floor, like Kyrellis and Moira. I felt less happy about this, but, again, there was no place else secure enough.

Surprisingly, neither Chuckie nor Martini felt the need to do anything to the football players from a memory standpoint. They got the "thanks of a grateful nation" speech from Chuckie, a "thanks for taking care of my girl, and if I find out you did anything I wouldn't like I'll come and hurt you for it" speech from Martini, and the "we strongly recommend you forget about this" chat from Christopher.

Len and Kyle grabbed me before they went back up to their suite. "Kitty, what are the career opportunities with your organizations?" Len asked.

"Why? You're both in an excellent school and are likely to go pro. I mean, SC has a great football program."

"Sure, but it's not the same as what you guys just did." Len shrugged. "Saving the world, doing it undercover, aliens, action—it sounds great."

"What's your major?"

"Engineering."

"Really? You smart or just pay someone to take your tests?"

"I'm at SC on a scholarship. I started out with a merit scholarship, since I'm a walk-on. So, yeah, I'm smart."

Kyle nodded. "He's a brain. I'm not as smart, but I make up for it by studying."

"You study?"

"In between beers, yeah." He looked worried. "You know, really, I don't try to attack girls all the time. Ever. It just seemed so . . . weird."

"And you were drunk off your ass."

"That too."

"My guys can't drink. It'll kill them. We're not big on the alcohol or drugs, smoking, or steroids. Pretty organic and natural."

Kyle nodded. "I can do that."

"You're premed, though."

"Yeah, and that alien chick took a ton of bullets and is still standing. Your guys were banged up, and now all but your boyfriend are looking fine, and he looks a hell of a lot better than he should. And your doctors are smokin' hot."

Couldn't argue with him. In the match-up between Dazzlers and any other women, Hooters girls included, the Dazzlers were always going to win. I called Chuckie over. "Give them your card, will you?"

"Why?"

"They would love to be recruited out of school. They may not work with us, but I'm sure they could fit into your side of the house."

Chuckie gave them both a long look. "You, fine," he said to Len. His eyes narrowed as he looked at Kyle. "You . . . straighten up. You ever threaten a female again, not only will I not recruit you, I'll send someone around to take you out."

Kyle nodded. "You got it. If I stay clean, what are my chances?"

Chuckie sighed. "Pretty good. Big, smart, eager, and willing is a rarity." He gave them both his business card. Len hugged me, and Kyle shook my hand, then they trotted off. "You sure you're not bucking for Gower's job?"

"Nah. Just a lot of talent in Sin City right now."

"Yeah. Martini didn't go to human schools, so he's mostly

buying that those football players were gentlemen." Chuckie looked right at me. "I'm not. How close were you to being in real trouble?"

"Well, Harlie was with me, so not as much as I could have been. Len was protecting me, and he had some backup."

"Right. And the line were the problem, led by Kyle?"

"Yeah. Look at it as proof of his leadership. I don't know if he was just blustering or would have gone through with it. But he didn't, and he came to help. Oh, and he's a total comics geek."

"So that's where you two bonded. Okay, I'll consider them. Believe me, though, I'll be watching him."

Chuckie seemed really upset. I put my hand on his arm. "Are you okay?"

He sighed. "Not really." He looked down. "I know Martini thinks I like being here with you." He looked back up at me. "But I don't. Because I'm not with you. He is."

"Why did you choose this location, then?"

He grinned. "Because it bugs the hell out of Martini. And I enjoy doing that."

I rolled my eyes. "I'm not going to even try to follow the logic."

"Fine with me. So, how many A-Cs do you think we have here? I mean that we don't want or know about?"

"No clue. At least those two, maybe more. They must have used the same gate the Amazons did."

"I've added some C.I.A. personnel into the Science Center."

"Oh, Chuckie, come on."

"Not to take over." He sounded exasperated. "Try thinking like you, or me, not Martini, for just a minute, okay? We have three to five interstellar criminals in the lowest level of that place. A level with external access, as you, White, and your fly-boys have all confirmed. I want some humans there I can trust to kill without hesitation."

"You think they'll get out?" My stomach clenched.

"I think they're going to try. I also have C.I.A. around your father and Reader. And the Pontifex. Again, to protect them. I know the A-Cs have been vulnerable before, but nowhere near as much as right now."

I tried to think the way I knew he did. "You worried this was all an elaborate ruse to get them inside the Science Center?"

"I think it's possible. There are too many variables, but

there's more going on, you know it, I know it. We had to pull every active agent out of the field and put them here. I don't even want to consider how much could have been affected by that. However, it's my job to figure that out. So you'll have to accept that I'm going to put humans I can trust into these alien strongholds, to ensure they remain strong."

"Not your enemy. Not saying you're wrong. Chuckie, you're really . . . tense."

"Yeah." He looked at Martini then back to me. "Can't imagine why."

I forced myself to look past jealousy and try to figure out what he was worried about in regard to Martini. "You think Kyrellis was taking it easy on Jeff, don't you?"

"Yeah, I do. Not that I want him dead, but he's doing pretty well. Better than Reader."

"James was fooled."

"Yeah, but not as much as you may think. I've had a chat with him. He was lured out by Moira pretending to be Gower, but the moment Gower didn't talk to him, Reader was on guard. He thought he was fighting an A-C imageer, not an Amazon, but he knew he was fighting someone. She was just more than he could take."

"He's human. Jeff's an A-C. They're a lot stronger, and they heal amazingly fast."

"I know." Chuckie sounded exasperated again. "But Moira almost killed Reader with one blow. One. There was only one hit on him—she smashed his head into a wall, and it almost killed him. Kyrellis is bigger, stronger, and older, meaning she's far better trained. She's bigger than Martini, stronger than him, and wants to kill him for a variety of reasons. But he walked out of that fight pretty much under his own steam. It doesn't add up."

"I'll spend a lot of time worrying about it."

"I'm not trying to make you worry needlessly."

"No, I think you're probably right. So it's not needless."

"I want guards in your room."

"Not just no," Martini said, coming up to us. "But hell no."

"You explain it to him." Chuckie sounded ready to actually lose his cool.

"No need. I heard most of what you said, and I'm touched." Martini's sarcasm knob was set to high again. "But I think I can handle anything they want to throw at us."

"Can Kitty? Because, let's be honest here, she's what I care about, and you know it. She lucked out with Moira in that dressing room because they wanted her alive. Figure they don't any more. She's got no hyperspeed, no extra strength, no double hearts, no fast healing. We're lucky as hell we aren't attending Reader's funeral. Luck, like lightning, rarely strikes the same place twice."

"You saying I can't protect her?" Martini was starting to growl.

Chuckie got right up in his face. "I'm saying that six months ago, it was luck that you got to her in time. Yeah, you beat the rest of us. But if you'd been a split second later, she'd be dead. I'm saying that we may be in Vegas, but I'm not willing for you to ever gamble Kitty's safety on your damned ego again. Kyrellis let you off easy. There's a reason, and I'm sure when we find out what it is, it won't be good for any of us. You're a pawn in some interstellar chess game, and we don't know if we've stopped it or just opened up our king to be taken."

They looked ready to go at each other. But something Chuckie had said struck me oddly. "Chuckie? Why do you think Jeff's a pawn?"

"Because he's not the king, and we all know it."

"You're right, he's a knight. So's Christopher."

"And you're the queen."

"What are you?"

"Bishop." Chuckie turned away from Martini. "What are you getting at?"

"Put the players on the board. White moves first, so we're black."

"Gower's our other bishop. Reader was a rook."

"Richard is our king."

"What are you two going on about?" Martini sounded confused and annoyed.

"Chess. Jeff, you know how to play it. Help us. Who's our other rook?"

"We replaced Reader with Tito. Call him the rook." Chuckie started talking faster. "Tim, the flyboys, your girls, they're the pawns."

"They're more powerful than that," Martini protested.

"A pawn can take the king," Chuckie snapped. "I'm talking about power on the board. Tito's new, and he already has more influence than the pawns do."

"I can get our side, Chuckie. But until we know who the opposition's king really is, we don't know who the power players really are."

"Who has the most to gain?" Chuckie shook his head. "It's always who has the most to gain—or lose. Find them, you find the key to everything else. And we need to find them fast, because my gut tells me we're running out of time."

CHAPTER 40

WE WANTED TO TAKE A LIMO BACK TO THE hotel because Chuckie and Martini both wanted to powwow, and we didn't feel confident about avoiding spies, bugs, or interstellar terrorists any more. Getting one was the issue.

"We've got no available agents," Tim told Martini. "Everyone's still doing clean-up and prisoner transfer, or fixing what they were in the middle of when we had to call them here."

Martini looked at Chuckie. "Think you can put a limo on the expense account?"

Chuckie shook his head. "I don't think we want to do that." He wasn't looking at Martini. The rest of us turned to see what, or rather, who Chuckie was looking at. Our personal paparazzo was barreling toward us, crocodile grin on full.

"I thought we got rid of Mister Joel Oliver," I shared. "James had Security take him away."

He snapped a picture before any of us could move. "What did I miss?" he asked, as if he were part of the team.

"What did *we* miss? How is it you're not in jail or something?"

Oliver chuckled. "Really, so naïve. That's cute. Babe, if a bribe doesn't work, then my newspaper simply makes a few calls and I'm out."

"Blackmail pictures?" Chuckie asked.

"Oh, and more." Oliver beamed. "So, what's the real story about what happened here?"

"Weather balloon," Chuckie said.

Oliver snorted. "Of course. That's the C.I.A.'s official statement?"

Chuckie's eyes narrowed. "We aren't giving you an official statement about anything or for any agency."

"Why are you insinuating anyone here is with the C.I.A.?" Martini asked.

"Same reason I'm 'insinuating' half of you are aliens. Because I know."

I wished Reader were here. He'd handled Oliver a lot better than we were. What had he done? We'd smiled, posed, and called Security. Well, it was worth a shot.

I put my arms around Martini's and Chuckie's waists. "Smiles, everyone, smiles!"

"What's with the Mister Rourke voice?" Chuckie asked.

"Not exactly *Fantasy Island here*," Martini added.

Oliver laughed. "Mister Reader is much more comfortable in front of a camera." His smile disappeared as he took another shot of all of us. "Much more comfortable than you are, Mister Reynolds. I can hardly find any photos of you at all." He winked at me. "But you're in every one of the few there are."

Martini started the low growl that usually led to a much louder roar. This wasn't going as I'd hoped.

There was a loud whistle, and we all looked. Tim had gone to the valet area and procured a limo. At least one of us was thinking. "Let's go," he called.

Oliver was still blocking our way, and Christopher knocked into him. "Get moving or get run over," he snarled.

Oliver backed away. "Care to make any comment for why there were thousands of aliens in Las Vegas this morning?"

"Movie stunt," I called over my shoulder. "Casting call for the next *Ocean's Eleven* sequel." We piled in while Oliver took more snaps as we drove off, Tim giving the driver directions to head downtown. "How do we stop him from printing our pictures? I mean, I doubt the government wants proof of things like Chuckie being with all of us on the front page."

"You have no faith, do you?" Christopher said. He sounded smug.

Chuckie laughed. "You could alter the film just by touching the camera?"

Christopher shrugged. "No." He grinned. "I could, however, cause all the film to become exposed. He's got nothing now. I exposed the roll in the camera and all the film on him."

"How?" Everyone other than our driver looked at me. Everyone had the "duh" look going. I thought about it. "Oh. Hyperspeed."

Chuckie shook his head. "I worry about you sometimes." He looked at Martini. "I don't think we want our driver sharing."

Martini nodded. "I don't want us sharing until we know this vehicle's safe. Tim, have our driver pull over."

The driver pulled off onto a side street. We piled out. While Chuckie and Christopher searched the limo for a variety of nasty things, Martini gave the driver a lot of money and a strong suggestion to walk to THEhotel and wait for us and his limo to return. The driver wandered off, the limo was declared safe and clean of bugs, Tim took the wheel, Christopher took shotgun, and the rest of us settled in.

Even with those two in the front seat now, what with me, Martini, Chuckie, Gower, Lorraine, Claudia, Alexander, and Tito in the back, it was cozy. I was between Martini and Chuckie, which I knew Martini wasn't happy about. But there was too much going on to worry about seating arrangements. We could worry about those for our wedding once we had the latest alien invasion schemes thwarted.

"Reynolds, where do you want me heading?" Tim asked.

"Where you were heading us already. Downtown. I'd tell you to leave the Strip, but I think we'd be too conspicuous on the regular city streets."

We turned back onto the Strip. "Got it, casual wandering on the way." Tim sounded as though this was a normal order. I wasn't used to us just meandering anywhere, however.

"Why?"

"Because we need time to regroup." Chuckie sounded tense, which was a rarity. "Since tragedy's been averted and White's taken care of the annoyance, let's get back to the real issues still at hand. What's the likelihood that Gregory can demand to see your Diplomatic Corps now that he's clearly a traitor to both Earth and Alpha Four?"

"I'm honestly not sure," Martini answered. "We haven't dealt with anything like this during my tenure as Head of Field."

"I believe I could convince my mother that Gregory was

acting dishonorably," Alexander said. "And Councillor Leonidas would undoubtedly see things from your perspective."

"I got more about him out of the emissaries," Chuckie said. "He's playing a dangerous game, but it appears to be for the overall good of the Alpha Centauri system, not just Alpha Four."

"Why would he do that?" I asked. "Wouldn't that make him a traitor to the Alpha Four monarchy?"

"No," Alexander said. "My great-uncle is perceived by some to be . . . unstable."

"Is he?" Gower asked.

"No," Chuckie answered. "From what I got from the Reptilians, Canus Majorians, and Feliniads, the king of Alpha Four is shrewd. He's been in power for a long time. The Free Women's attack was something no one seemed to have seen coming."

"Councillor Leonidas warned about it for years," Alexander said. "He has never felt the PPB nets should be around any planet, Earth included."

"So, is he pro-Earth?" It would make him the only being in the A-C solar system who was, apparently, but it was worth a shot to ask.

"I would call him more pro-planetary freedom. While he, like the rest of us, does not want the might of the Free Women brought down upon us, he has counseled for years that holding people prisoners in the way we have is not conducive to their becoming peaceful members of a greater solar and galactic community."

"Think Winston Churchill," Chuckie said to me. "Only the A-C version."

"So Leonidas is a better ruler than the king, isn't he?"

Alexander looked uncomfortable. "Those kinds of questions are not voiced on Alpha Four."

"Because dissidents are eliminated with extreme prejudice," Chuckie added. "They were actually being benign to our Earth A-Cs by sending them all here."

"I hate my family," Martini grumbled. Alexander looked stricken. "Not the family here," Martini added quickly. Alexander didn't cheer up. "Oh, and not you. Probably not your mother, either, unless she's just like your brother or great-uncle."

Alexander shook his head. "She's more like me. My mother has been very . . . alone since our father died." His eyes clouded. "I believe our great-uncle may have had a hand in his death, but I was only a child when it happened, and I could be mistaken."

"Assume you're not," Chuckie said briskly.

Gower nodded. "Even without confirmation from Richard or our parents, I know the royal family was very ... stringent ... in how they dealt with what they considered insubordination."

"Wow, what a great bunch of folks they are. Let's not plan to visit."

"Most of our people are like yours," Alexander said. "They want to live their lives in peace and enjoy their loved ones and the fruits of their labor." He sighed. "Councillor Leonidas has protected our people from my great-uncle's whims, as much as he could, at any rate. He protects my mother, too."

"Leonidas actually runs the day-to-day," Chuckie added. "Which is why he's been able to influence the formation of a Planetary Council."

"You sure he's a good guy?"

Alexander nodded. "I believe if you knew him, you would feel he was trustworthy."

"So far," Chuckie said, "Leonidas seems like the only thing that's prevented Alpha Four from doing even more damage than they've already managed." Tim was winding us through the streets of downtown Vegas, and Chuckie sighed. "We're no closer to knowing what's coming, let alone how to defend against it. Leonidas can be the biggest booster of Earth and planets' rights around, but the king's word is the law."

"Maybe Jeff needs to accept the kingship," Lorraine said quietly. "That would stop all the badness, wouldn't it?"

"I'm not going there," Martini growled. "I'm not going there alone, or taking everyone back with me. Alpha Four isn't our home, Earth is."

"There is no one else," Alexander said. He sounded desperate. "If not you, or one of the others here who are in the bloodline, then we lose the monarchy."

"Sounds like a good thing to lose. Give the idea of democracy a try."

"No, it won't work that way," Chuckie said quietly.

Gower nodded. "The other planets may not like the control Alpha Four has, but without it, they'd all fight like ..."

"Like cats and dogs and dragons?"

"Exactly." Gower shook his head. "Alpha Four remains in

power because, in reality, the other planets want them to be in control."

"They'd like more say in their self-determination, but I agree," Chuckie said. "From what I got from them, what they object to is the current king's tightening of the screws, as opposed to Alpha Four's leadership. They'd all welcome Leonidas as leader."

"Which is impossible, as he is not in the bloodline," Alexander said.

"Could he marry in? I mean, if he's protecting your mom already, why not?"

Alexander looked as though he'd never considered the idea, and now that he had, he wasn't a fan. "Ah, I have no idea."

"He'd lose his position," Gower said. "The Chief Councillor can't be a member of the royal family. He wouldn't really be considered royal, though any children would be."

"If they had any," Tito said. "I'm not sure how long an A-C woman can continue to bear children, but if it's Alexander's mother we're talking about, the chances would be slim if she was an Earth woman."

Alexander still looked like this was a discussion he'd never imagined having and never wanted to have again. "I'm sure my mother isn't interested in the Councillor. He's old enough to be her father." He sounded just this side of horrified.

"You'd be surprised at the age gaps some happy couples have." Alexander's look of horror increased. I considered sharing that his parents had done the deed in order to have him and Gregory, too, but decided to take pity. "But if you haven't seen any romantic sparks, let's assume there aren't any."

We were heading back up the Strip. "Not that anyone asks the driver's opinion," Tim said, sarcasm knob up to full, "but I think the fact that we have A-C spies around who can tell the incoming A-C space cruiser filled with A-C warriors exactly where to attack is a bigger deal than playing the royal dating game."

Alexander looked uncomfortable. "I doubt it will be filled with Alpha Centaurion warriors."

The way he said it made all of us look at him, including Christopher, who turned around in the front seat. "Just who would it be filled with, then?" he asked Alexander, Glare #1 in full force.

Alexander gulped. "The best warriors in the system. The Free Women."

Before anyone could freak out, Gower's phone rang. We all let Alexander's pronouncement sit on the air while Gower gave some one-word replies and did a lot of grunting and Tim drove us back to the Mandalay complex.

Gower hung up. "That was Richard. The Diplomatic Corps is on site in full force. Only Robert has been allowed to talk to Gregory."

"Thank God for small favors," Martini said. "I'm calling them the least of our worries right now, though. Let's deal with the question of what to do when the Free Women army arrives."

There was a lot of silence. "Renata could call them off," Chuckie said finally.

"Not if they believe her to be a traitor." Alexander looked miserable. "I know Councillor Leonidas wouldn't send a battle cruiser after us. I doubt he'd send any ship. He knew we were coming to Earth to ask for your help, under the guise of the Wedding Protocols."

"Queen Renata thought there was a ship after you, though."

"There was." Alexander gulped again. "I believe my great-uncle sent it, though. And if I'm correct, then he would have told the Free Women that their queen was a traitor . . ."

"And that would mean they'd consider themselves, what, honor-bound to kill her and anyone she was with?" I knew I'd guessed right by the look on Alexander's face. "Oh, goody. How far behind you were they?"

"Far." Alexander perked up. "We received a transmission when we left our solar space, advising us that a ship was being sent to follow."

"Leonidas giving you fair warning?"

"I believe so, yes."

"One ship to handle three?"

Martini snorted. "If Kyrellis was any example, Renata could take every one of the rest of the Planetary Council and all of us besides all on her own. God help us if we actually have a regiment of Amazon warriors coming here."

I looked at Gower. "Well, we'll fall off that particular bridge when we're pushed."

He nodded, and I had a feeling he knew what I was thinking. "Exactly. Or as we like to call it, routine."

CHAPTER 41

MARTINI AND I WERE BACK IN OUR HUGE SUITE in the hotel. C.I.A., A-Cs, Chuckie, and Martini had all gone over it—it and all the rest of the two floors our personnel were on—and came up with nothing.

Tito was installed in a room for his own protection. He'd gone home to get some things under heavy guard. We didn't want to lose another power piece.

Per Chuckie, my mother was briefed, had discussed the situation with Queen Renata, had the P.T.C.U. on high alert, and was doing all sorts of other high-level, need-to-know stuff Chuckie and Mom both felt I didn't need to know.

The rest of my family, having heard thirdhand that I was all right, were all back inside the casino. I felt the love. Then again, I figured my mother had a good idea of what state my hair and clothes were in and had decided discretion to be the better part of scaring the crap out of my grandmothers.

I settled the Poofs on one of the couches with instructions they were to be good and get some rest. Many purrs and mewls earned them some lovies, then they went to sleep. They snored, but it was low and cute. Everything about them was cute. Hey, I was all over cute with huge teeth when it was protecting me.

The bathroom had a gigantic tub. It said it was big enough for two, but it looked big enough for ten. It was set up for soaking, too—not only were there inclines to lean against, but also inflated pillows strewn about. "When was the last time we showered?"

"No idea, baby. The hours are all running together."

"I don't want to find out how bad I smell. You still sore?"

"Yeah. And you smell like roses, as always."

"That bad, huh? Let's take a bath, okay?"

He grinned at me. "I think I can manage to enjoy that. Just have to make a phone call. Be right back; get the water running."

"Make sure the line's secured and all." I was getting paranoid.

"C.I.A. took care of that. I figure Reynolds will hear my conversation, but no one else will." He left the bathroom, and I started to fill the tub. They had some great stuff in the bathrooms here, and I dumped all the expensive bath salts in. They foamed, scented, *and* relaxed, per their packaging. I'd worked as a marketing manager before I'd joined Centaurion Division, so I didn't expect much from the hype. But there were instant bubbles, and the scent was nice. I was hoping Martini would help with the relaxation part, so I didn't care as much about that being accurate.

I got out of my clothes. They were filthy and ripped—thankfully I'd been in the Armani fatigues and not my Aerosmith shirt. I was amazed I hadn't been arrested as a vagrant. But it made it easier to see why Chuckie hadn't trusted the football players. I risked a look in the mirror, was glad I hadn't looked earlier, and thanked God the family was distracted by the lure of the slot machines. Considered that I looked damned good for falling off the top of the Hooters' tower and decided to take that as a win.

Martini was still on the phone—I could hear him talking but not what he was saying. I decided I didn't want to wait any longer. I stepped into the tub and settled under the water and the bubbles. It felt great. Leaned my head back against a pillow and closed my eyes. Felt even better.

The water turned off and my eyes opened. Martini was standing over me. His upper body looked completely healed, no bruising remained, which was a relief. "Sorry to wake you." His voice was a purr.

"Was I asleep?" He was still in his pants, which I found disappointing.

"Yeah. The tub's so huge it didn't overflow."

"Water's nice. You coming in?"

He gave me a slow, sensuous smile. "I plan on it." My

breathing got heavy. He undid his pants slowly. By the time they were unzipped, I was starting to writhe in the water. By the time they were off, I was panting for him, and I could easily confirm that all his equipment looked better than fine and completely operational.

He sat at the edge of the tub. "You need anything? Before I come in?" His voice was low and silky.

"Oh . . . Jeff . . . please . . ." He was good. I was ready to go over the edge and he hadn't even touched me yet.

Martini put one hand on either side of the tub by my head and shoulders. "Please what, baby?" His face was near, his eyes locked with mine, his mouth close, but not touching me.

I licked my lips. "I need you." I gasped this out.

The predatory smile that made me weak was on his face now. "You sure?" He moved his mouth slowly around me, almost kissing me but not quite. My mouth followed his, trying to get his lips to touch mine.

"Jeff, please . . . don't . . ."

"Don't what?" he said near my ear, his breath hot against me.

"Don't . . . don't . . . I can't . . ."

"Can't what?" he purred. I felt his breath on my neck.

"I can't wait any longer." It came out like a wail.

Martini put his face in front of mine again. His eyes were smoldering. "Never let it be said that I made you wait for anything." He put his mouth onto mine so quickly I jerked back unintentionally. But his hand was there and caught my head as his lips covered mine and his tongue slammed into my mouth.

He'd had me on the edge, and this was all it took. I screamed my climax into his kiss, while my whole body shook. I barely registered as he came into the tub with me and put his knees on either side of my hips. My arms went around him automatically and my hands clutched at his back, and still our kiss went on.

Martini kissed me until my body's spasms subsided. Then he slowly pulled away. "Water's nice." He sat back and settled in. He never took his eyes off mine, and his expression was still predatory. He put his hand toward me. "C'mere, baby."

I took his hand, and he pulled me to him. I slid on the porcelain, and he flipped my legs over his thighs, wrapped his other hand around my waist and pulled me up onto his lap. I slid my lower legs back so I was straddling him now. He had both hands on my waist. I grabbed his shoulders, back to panting for him. His smile was the sexy half-snarl he got where he reminded me of a jungle cat ready to eat me. I moaned. I wanted him to take me in any way he wanted, as long as he was inside me.

He knew, of course. Either I was already gone enough to satisfy him or he was being kind to me, because he didn't make me suffer any longer. He pulled my hips down and slid himself inside me.

My head fell back and my back arched. My wailing started immediately. Martini kept his hands on my waist and moved me up and down. He shifted a bit, and his mouth was on my breasts, one then the other. He licked, sucked, nipped, and easily caused another orgasm to crash over me.

I managed to straighten up. He leaned away from my breasts and gave me another half-smile. I grabbed his face in my hands and kissed him, hard and frantically. His hands slid off my waist and up my back while I thrust on him wildly. He growled and pressed my body down in time with my wild rhythm. It didn't take long before another orgasm slammed through me.

Martini slid his hands up, over my breasts and neck to my face. He gently pulled my mouth away from his. "Turn around." He lifted me, spun me, and put me on my knees in front of him. I grabbed the side of the tub, and he slid back inside me while I moaned his name. His hands roamed my back then slid around my body, to stroke my breasts and stomach. He pulled me up slowly, so that my back was against his chest. I reached up and grabbed his shoulders.

One hand still toyed with my breasts, but the other trailed down my stomach, as his fingers traced circles on my skin. They slid over me, in time with his thrusts. My head went back against him, and my breath came in gasps, interspersed with short, sharp cries of pleasure. I couldn't tell how long he kept me like this—the feelings were too intense for me to be able to focus on anything except how he felt on and inside me.

He changed his rhythm a bit and rocked me inside and out—I started to wail in earnest. "That's right, baby," he growled softly. "You know what I want." His thrusts and strokes became harder and faster. I screamed his name as he roared and erupted inside of me, triggering an orgasm so intense I thought I would go insane from pleasure.

Our bodies shook together, each throb from him causing shock waves to course through me. We were locked together in this erotic frenzy for what seemed like hours. Finally, though, our bodies slowed and the feelings subsided and, with them, my ability to stay upright.

I started to slide down into the water, but he was ready for it, and his arms cradled me. Martini turned me back around and held me against him. I nuzzled the hair on his chest as he slid us back under the water. He slid me between his legs, and I wrapped one arm around his waist while the other held his shoulder. He stroked my hair and kissed my forehead.

The water was cool, and I felt him shift and fill the tub up again. The warmth of the water and his body, the sound and feel of his heartbeats, and complete erotic exhaustion made my eyelids heavy. I wasn't asleep, but I was so relaxed I could have been.

Martini's hands slid over my skin as he stroked and massaged me. He shifted me again, so my back was against his chest, my head against his shoulder. I was sitting on his lap with my legs between his. He kissed the side of my head while his hands continued to perform a sensual massage.

"I should be doing this to you," I murmured.

"Later." His voice was low and silky again. "I feel fine, and right now, I want to feel every part of you."

"Okay, whatever you say." I reached up one arm so I could run my fingers through his hair and stroke his face. He kissed my hand as it went by, then went back to nuzzling the side of my head.

"I say you're mine to take care of. In all ways."

"Yes, Jeff. Only yours. Only and always yours."

"Good answer." I could feel him smile against my skin. "I think I might like baths as much as showers."

"Mmmm, me too."

One hand slid between my legs, and he started to massage there, while his other hand rubbed and teased my breasts as his tongue traced my neck. My moans started and didn't stop until I again sounded like a cat in heat. He didn't stop until my climax subsided and I was limp against him.

We considered washing off, but the shower for twelve was right there and we didn't want to make it feel slighted. In deference to the fact he'd only made me orgasm about six times in the tub, Martini ensured that I still loved a shower and a variety of screaming orgasms were had by all.

A human man would have been close to dead after this kind of performance, but Martini was just getting started. His theme seemed to be to see how long he could keep me screaming and docile at the same time. We dried off, if I counted his tongue running all over my skin as drying. By the time he was carrying me out of the bathroom I was helpless to do anything other than mewl or whimper and let him do whatever he wanted with me. What he wanted was to make love on the humongous bed. I found the strength to go on and have a few more mind-blowing orgasms, just to show I was a team player.

We were collapsed around each other when there was a knock at the door. I groaned. "Can I wake the Poofs and just have them eat whoever's there?"

"Nope." Martini kissed me deeply and got up. This room had everything, including nicer bathrobes than I'd ever seen in my life. He put one on and headed to the door.

"Jeff, you want to take a gun or something?"

"Nope." He sounded amused.

Men. I heard him open the door and talk to someone. There were so many people trying to hurt us, I got worried. What if it was a shapeshifter? A rogue imageer? Some lunatic with a loaded pineapple? I dragged myself out of the bed and put on the other robe. It felt like velour or silk or silk velour. It was huge on me, but I decided not to care. It was comfy as all get-out.

Martini was still talking to whoever it was, and I figured I'd better see if I needed to bring him some pants or a Glock or something. Gave my hair a fast brush—didn't want to give the visitor heart failure by looking at me.

Martini's voice was friendly and cheerful, and, as I walked out, the thought that maybe this was someone he knew, like, God forbid, his mother or father, waved weakly to me from the fuzziness that was my overclimaxed mind.

I got to the living area and, sure enough, it *was* his father.

CHAPTER 42

"**H**I, KITTY," ALFRED SAID with a wide smile. "Nice to see you."

I had nowhere to run, so went for casual. "Hi, Alfred. How goes the gambling?"

"Not as well as things up here," he said with a wicked grin. The exact same wicked grin his son had. Martini was a little taller than his father, but otherwise, he was an exact replica, including personality.

"Dad, stop drooling at my fiancée." Martini shook his head. "Does Mom know you lust after my girl?"

Alfred rolled his eyes. "Always with you it's the jealousy. I don't lust after Kitty, Son. I'm just pleased you're marrying so well." He winked at me. "Don't tell him about our trip to Aruba, okay?"

I couldn't help it, I laughed. "Secret's safe with me." I noticed Alfred had a large clothing bag with hangers in it. "Doing some shopping for Lucinda?" It was from the same store where I'd sort of bought my naked-in-fabric outfit.

Alfred grinned and handed the bag to me. "No. Picked up some things for you."

"For me?" I took the bag and looked at both of them. "Um, why?"

Martini shrugged. "Why not?"

They both had the exact same expression on their faces: they were pleased with themselves but a little worried about my reaction. I thought about mentioning how exorbitant the prices at this store were, but it dawned on me that if Martini cared about it, he wouldn't have had his father pick up whatever it was he'd picked up.

"Okay. Um, I'll just go into the bedroom and take a look."

I sort of backed away, resisting the urge to look in the bag. Truth be told, there hadn't been anything in that store that wasn't sexy and appealing. As I walked past the sofa, there was a mewling and the Poofs put their heads up. They saw me and started purring. I picked Harlie up and petted it. As I did so, it spotted Alfred.

Confirmed the Poofs had hyperspeed, because Harlie gave a huge mewl of what sounded like joy to me, then all the Poofs were all over Alfred, purring and rubbing on him.

"Where did you get these?" he asked me.

"Long story. Jeff, you want to cover it or want me to?"

"Check out the bag. I'll bring my dad up to speed." I could tell he was getting worried that I wasn't going to like whatever was in the bag, so I nodded and trotted into the bedroom.

I resolved to love whatever it was, because even if it was somehow hideous, Martini had clearly gone to some effort, and so had his father. I poured the bag's contents onto the bed and started to laugh.

Okay, he'd loved the outfit Reader had picked out for me, because there was another one in here. There were also bags from other shops. Alfred had been spending the time since Martini's phone call cruising the mall.

Lingerie, shoes, a couple more incredibly sheer and sexy outfits, it was all here. The shoes fit and were comfortable, which amazed and relieved me. The lingerie were all my size, fit well, and looked great on me. It also matched the outfits.

In addition to the sheer and shiny short-skirted outfit I now owned two of, I was in possession of a glittery little black dress and some of the sexiest black pumps ever, as well as silver sandals with a lower heel that went with a white Grecian type long dress with a silver belt set right under my breasts. It was extremely complimentary to my rack—I could wear this and fit in at Hooters without a problem. I could wear all of it and fit in just fine in any spot in Vegas. I couldn't wear any of this at home, but then again, maybe I'd put them on and let Martini rip them off the moment after. They were that sexy.

I was unsure if I was supposed to model each outfit or not. I had no issue modeling them for Martini, but with Alfred in the room it seemed kind of awkward.

"Wear the black one," Martini called to me.

"Erm, Jeff? How—"

"Empath. Try to keep up."

"But that was a *thought*."

He laughed. "You were confused. Baby, you broadcast your emotions."

Okay, right, Mister Superempath. I considered suggesting that maybe too much sexual fulfillment made me slow but decided to keep that one to myself. I also considered mentioning that I wasn't sure I believed him, but I really decided to hold that one for later.

I put the black outfit on, hung the others up in the still ginormous but less empty closet and went out front.

Martini's expression was worth every penny he'd spent. His eyelids dropped and his mouth curled into the jungle cat snarl. I didn't have to look down to know my nipples had gone hard, just looking at him looking at me. I decided to love this outfit.

Alfred coughed. "I'll just leave you two now. You look wonderful, Kitty. Jeffrey, remember, you're meeting all of us in an hour at that Russian restaurant."

"Right." Martini looked like he hadn't heard a word his father had said.

Alfred grinned. "And then you're going to pass Kitty around to every man there."

"Right." Martini was *not* paying attention. I tried to remind myself that this outfit was a weapon to be used for good. I'd have been cracking up, but I was too busy trying not to orgasm from Martini's expression alone.

"And then Mister Reynolds is going to take her to Australia."

"Right."

"Kitty, you okay with that plan?" Alfred was trying not to laugh.

"Yep. We'll see you in an hour at Red Square. I have no idea why you want to go there, it's a vodka bar."

"The human side of the family would like to imbibe a bit, and we're capable of being around alcohol and not drinking it. Your Nana Sadie is looking forward to going there." I heard the "father chide" in his tone.

"No argument, they have great food."

Martini hadn't stopped looking at me. I got the impression he was seeing my mouth move and hearing noises from me

and his father, but his brain wasn't engaged at all. I shifted a
little and watched his eyes follow me. It was official; this was
an outfit for the ages.

"Yes, so Mister Reynolds said. We have the entire restaurant booked. So, we'll order what for you?"

Alfred was a great father. I wondered if Martini had managed to realize that yet. "We'll both start with borscht. Tell
Nana Sadie it's not as good as hers but it's close. We'll both
take iced tea."

"Jeffrey, you like borscht?"

"Right."

Alfred was laughing silently. "Wonderful. Well, see you two
in an hour. Or so." Alfred went to the door. "Son? Jeffrey? I'll
just let myself out."

"Right."

Alfred was chuckling as he left. The door shut, and Martini
was out of the robe and on me. There were advantages to hyperspeed. We didn't get to the bed or even leave the room. He
had me up against the wall with my legs wrapped around his
waist in moments. The lingerie was all easy access and he had
it opened and was inside me within another moment.

He was out of control, but it was flattering—and arousing.
His thrusts were hard, fast, and frantic, as if he couldn't get
enough of me quickly enough. His mouth ravaged my neck,
specifically the spots that made me howl.

His body was moving so fast inside me that my orgasm felt
like it came out of nowhere—one moment being pounded by
a sex god, the next screaming from sexual fulfillment of the
highest order.

I triggered him and he bit my neck, which spiked my orgasm higher. Any time this happened I felt like I would faint,
and this time was no exception. The room spun, and I held
onto him as our bodies' spasms continued unabated.

Finally things slowed back to normal, and Martini let me
slide down his body and back to the floor. I nuzzled his chest.
"So, I should return this?"

He laughed and slung me gently over his shoulder. "Sure."
He nipped my behind, and I giggled as he carried me into the
bedroom. "As soon as I've made love to you in it for another
year, year and a half, why not?"

"I love how you think."

CHAPTER 43

IN AN HOUR, GIVE OR TAKE, I brushed my hair and marveled at how this dress hid wrinkles. I'd already felt the money spent was more than worth it, but it was nice not to have to change into something else.

Martini had his standard suit on, but because I'd begged, he was just carrying the jacket, and he had the shirt unbuttoned to the middle of his chest and the sleeves rolled up to about midforearm. Wasn't my fault that this was the second time he'd had to dress. He looked too good to pass up the first time. Only the clock prevented me from insisting he looked too good the second time, too.

I took another look in the mirror. "Are you sure it's okay for me to go have dinner with your parents dressed like this?"

"Sure, why not?"

"It's kind of . . ."

"Totally sexy?" Martini was grinning.

"Um, yeah. I mean, it's a little much for dinner with the folks, isn't it?"

"My dad picked everything up for me, and he saw you in it before. He didn't seem to mind, and I can promise you he wasn't upset, I'd have noticed."

I doubted that, based on Martini's reactions when he'd first seen me in it, but I kept this to myself. "Maybe we should stop and find some kind of wrap or something."

"Nah." Martini draped his jacket around me. "How's that?"

It seemed workable; it was black, the dress was black, why

not? I really put the jacket on and rolled up the sleeves. "I'm bringing the eighties back, I think. All I need is a fedora."

"Mmmm, let's be sure to pick that up sometime soon."

It didn't really say, "completing the ensemble," but under the circumstances, I took my purse along. The hell with a handbag—the last time I'd tried that I'd been chased through the Arizona desert by sociopaths. I took the Poofs along as well. I didn't know what else to do with them, and I figured they needed to eat.

I was heading for the door when Martini grabbed my arm. "Baby, wait a minute."

I turned around. He had a funny look on his face. "Jeff, are you okay?"

"Yeah." He drew me over to the couch and sat us down. I took my purse off and put it on the table—it didn't seem that this was going to be quick. "I just wanted to . . . ask you something." He looked nervous and worried, so, despite my best efforts, I got nervous and worried.

"Okay. What's wrong?" My throat felt tight. Had I done something?

He stroked my face. "No, baby, you haven't done anything wrong." He closed his eyes. "You'd think it would be easier this time around."

"What? What would be easier?" I tried not to panic and failed utterly. It was stupid and silly, and I could remember that whenever the logical side of my mind had a say in the matter—but the oldest fear I had about my relationship with Martini was that he really didn't want to be with me for me but wanted me only because I was a human and so exotic and forbidden. This worry skipped and laughed out of my deeper consciousness where I'd shoved it away for the past six months and danced through my mind. It shared that Martini was breaking up with me, again, and that this time, he meant it.

"Oh, Kitty . . . no, baby, no." He pulled me into his arms. "Baby, how can you think that? Especially after all this time?"

"What's wrong? What do you need to tell me? Are you mad at me?" My voice was heading to the dog-only register.

Martini pulled me into his lap and held me tightly. "Shhh, baby. No, nothing's wrong. I didn't mean to scare you. Kitty, I love you so much . . . for you, not because you're a human. Because you're everything I ever dreamed of and never thought

I'd find. I never believed you'd love me or choose me over everyone else."

I wrapped my arms around him. "Then what do you need to tell me?" I was shaking, and the logical part of my mind mentioned we hadn't gotten nearly enough sleep in the past many hours and maybe I needed some.

"Ask you." He reached into his pants pocket. "I need to ask you something." He rocked me. "Baby, please, relax. It's not bad. At least, I don't think you'll think it's bad." I heard uncertainty in his voice, faint, but there.

I nodded and sat up in his lap. Be a big girl, calm down and deal. Okay, I could handle that. Hopefully.

Martini stroked my face, then slid his hand to rub the back of my neck. He got a funny smile on his face. "You know what the most flattering thing in the world is? To me, anyway?" I shook my head. "That you're somehow afraid I'm going to decide some other woman's better for me than you. I've been in love with you since I met you. Baby, we mate for *life*. We make the commitment, and it stays there. It doesn't go away."

"But I can't wear the necklace anymore because someone hates me." I started to cry and felt like a moron.

"I know, baby. And it bothers me, but you didn't take it off because you wanted to. You took it off because you had to." He kissed my tears away. "Kitty, oh, baby, stop. You're too tired. I should have let you sleep."

"I didn't want to sleep, I wanted to make love to you."

He laughed softly. "And you wonder why I think you're the most perfect woman in the universe?" He took my hand and put something into it, something small. "I wanted to do this more romantically, but I think, under the circumstances, let me just say I hope you like it, and if you don't, the store is open twenty-four/seven and said we could exchange it any time."

I looked down to see a ring. A diamond ring. Stone not too big, marquis cut, excellent quality from what I could guess, gold setting with an intricate design that enhanced the stone's beauty.

"I know you like the traditional cut better," Martini said softly. "But since that's what Reynolds had for you, can you manage to forgive me for not wanting to give you something exactly like it?"

I couldn't talk. It was beautiful, and I felt both beyond happy and fairly stupid at the same time. He took the ring out

of my palm and slid it onto the ring finger of my left hand. It
fit perfectly and looked real, not like paste, which was why I
hated large stones.

Brain finally kicked in, and I flung my arms around his neck
and kissed him wildly. He wrapped his arms around me. "Can
I take that as a yes?" he asked when we finally pulled apart.

"Yes. Jeff, I love it. But why, and why now? You didn't have
to buy this for me."

"Yes, I did." He leaned my head against his shoulder. "Your
family doesn't understand our customs, and I know they think
you've been deluding yourself. No ring means no commitment
to humans. I verified that with James, by the way, and Michael.
They're all here, but the moment I realized you couldn't wear
the necklace again, I knew I had to give you something—for
your peace of mind, mine, and your family's."

"When did you have time to shop for this?"

"I went down to the mall about fifteen minutes after you
and James. I figured it was the best time. I'd picked it out when
I felt your terror with Moira, told them to hold it, and ran for
you. I had my father make sure it was held, and he picked it
up when he got the clothes for you. I picked the clothes out
while waiting for backup with Moira. Had to do something to
fill the time."

"No complaints. You know, your dad loves you so much,
Jeff."

"Yeah, I've picked that up. Finally."

"Are your blocks down?" I tried not to sound worried.
Failed.

"No, they're all up and functioning. You've just helped
me . . . filter a little better when it comes to my parents, that's
all."

I felt pleased for a moment, then I had a horrible thought,
and my stomach clenched. "If you'd gone down first, or with
me . . . Moira would have gotten *you*."

Martini held me tighter. "No more what ifs. At all. It's bad
enough we almost lost James, but I don't want you living with
that kind of worry, especially since it's based on nothing. 'What
if' doesn't help anything, and it changes less."

"Okay, I'll do my best. Jeff?"

"Yeah?"

"How are you reading my mind all the time?"

He sighed. "I'm not. I just pay attention to you—because

I love you. And, like I said, you broadcast your emotions." I could hear evasion in his voice.

"And?" He didn't say anything. "Jeff, I know there's got to be an 'and' in there."

"Okay, fine. I just didn't want you to worry."

"About what?"

He took a deep breath. "The drugs the Club Fifty-One people gave me?"

"Yes? The ones that could have killed you and pretty much drove you crazy? Hard to forget those drugs." I tried not to let the dread take over. Failed.

He hugged me more tightly. "They're out of my system, but . . . they affected me."

"How?"

"Remember how I told you they enhanced my powers to where I could feel every emotion you had and almost see you?" I nodded. "Well, I still can, but with even more . . . depth. I can't read your mind, exactly, but pretty close. Only you, though. With everyone else it's the same as in the past, maybe a little more enhanced than before. So," he added dryly, "I knew what the football players were up to. I just decided to trust you on it."

"I call that personal growth."

"You okay with it?"

I thought about it. "Yeah, I am. I kind of like it, in a weird way."

"Sums up our entire relationship."

"Pretty much. What about your healing?" He'd been amazingly active awfully soon after his beat down from Kyrellis.

Martini grinned. "That's another positive—my regeneration has sped up. I'm stronger, too, and a little bit faster than I used to be." His expression changed to quietly upset. "I'd say it was all worth it if I hadn't come so close to losing you forever."

I hugged him. "It's in the past. Everyone's here and fine, and that's what matters. And as long as the only aftereffects make you more awesome, I'm good with it." I looked at the clock. "We'd better get going. We're late."

"Dad knew we'd be late."

"I didn't think you heard anything he said."

"He knew I was giving you this tonight." He leaned back. "What do you mean, what he said?"

"You agreed that I was going to be passed around to every man at the restaurant and then go to Australia with Chuckie."

"I did not!"

"You did. Your dad will confirm it." I laughed at his expression. "But, under the circumstances, since you really are planning to marry me, I think I'll save myself for our wedding night and stay here with you."

"Thank God you like the ring."

CHAPTER 44

WE WERE ONLY ABOUT THIRTY MINUTES LATE to the restaurant, which I thought was doing pretty darned well for us.

Our party did have the entire place, but it was small, and there were a lot more of us than I was prepared for, so it was packed. I looked around. "Oh, my God, Jeff. My entire family is here."

"I don't see your dad."

"Everyone else. And I do mean everyone. Oh, my God . . . Uncle Mort's here. And so is Richard! What is going on?"

Christopher spotted us and shoved through the crowd. "Took you long enough. My dad was getting worried about you." He gave Martini a meaningful look.

"Yeah, sorry." Martini put my hand out toward Christopher. He grinned. "Told you she'd like it."

Martini shrugged. "Nice to be sure."

Christopher hugged me. "Congratulations again."

"Thanks. Why is the world here?"

"Well, on our side, nobody blew up, and we occasionally like to celebrate that kind of success. On your side, they like our side, and the vodka martinis are reputed to be great." Christopher grinned at my expression. "Seriously. Your mother's still having a little trouble with Aunt Lucinda, but your grandmothers are getting along with her like they've known each other all their lives." He looked to Martini. "Your sisters and their husbands are here. The kids aren't."

Martini sighed. "Pity. I'd like to see *them*."

"Yeah, me too. Reynolds is dealing with the guys, though. Amazingly enough, they don't seem to bother him."

"He spent junior high and high school being attacked by big jocks. He knows what makes them tick. And how to deflect them."

"Yes, Reynolds walks on water. Got it. Let's get in and be seen before we get bawled out for being late." Martini took my hand and led me through to the back. This didn't go quickly. Every relative of mine we passed had to have an introduction.

My mother's sister, Karen, spotted us, and the ring, when we were about halfway in. I loved her, but she had a big voice and used it to share with all that Martini was indeed going to make an honest woman out of me.

We were mobbed. Fortunately, my entire family was aware that I liked smaller stones, but even so, I heard some comments about the size of the diamond. "Big stones look fake on my hands." I repeated that at least a dozen times before I got a glimpse of my mother.

She was way in the back with a woman I took to be Queen Renata, Martini's parents, and both sets of my grandparents. Mom looked happy, but I knew her, and she was faking it. I pulled Martini's head down. "Something's up with Mom. We need to get over there."

"I could throw you, but otherwise, I think it's going to take some time. Yes, sorry, we've been engaged for almost six months already." This to my Aunt Ruth, who was reading Martini the riot act for us sending out wedding invitations before I had a ring. "Look, she's wearing a ring." He shoved my hand in Aunt Ruth's face.

"And not much else. Katherine Sarah Katt, what are you doing wearing next to nothing to your engagement party?" So much for Martini's jacket providing adequate coverage. Oh, well, it'd been worth a shot.

I opened my mouth to give some sort of reply, but Aunt Ruth barreled right on. "Not that I can tell it's an engagement party . . . no decorations, no gifts, no engagement cake." She shook her head. "I've never been to an engagement party without a lovely cake."

"Engagement party?" Christopher was on my other side, and he kicked my foot. "Ow!" Aunt Ruth's eyebrow lifted, and I scrambled to recover. "Um, sorry about the cake, Aunt

Ruth." I'd never known she was an engagement cake aficionado, but the learning never seemed to stop for me.

She rolled her eyes. "Charles explained it was impromptu, and the chef and staff didn't have time for something proper. Honestly, I'm more upset by your attire or the lack thereof."

"Jeff bought this outfit for me."

She sniffed. "I'll bet."

"It's really expensive."

Aunt Ruth rolled her eyes. "Charles has money, too." Oh, hell, there it was, out in the open. "Charles wouldn't have waited six months to give you a ring. And he wouldn't have dressed you like this."

"Wow, gotta get to Mom. Love you, Aunt Ruth, thanks for the stress." I dragged Martini through the crowd.

"What's with 'Charles has money, too'? I thought you said you two never dated!"

"One fling for one week, Jeff, okay? But he's been my friend since we were thirteen."

"I've been friends with a lot of women no one suggests I would be better off marrying."

"Aunt Ruth has views."

"What views are those?"

"Chuckie would convert to Judaism if I asked him to." Great, religion out in the open, too.

"So? You don't even go to temple!"

"I don't go to mass, either. Get ready, here comes Aunt Carla."

My mother's other sister descended on us. I didn't like her as well as Aunt Karen. "What's this I hear about you two finally getting engaged?" She hugged me and gave Martini an obvious up and down. Then she looked at Christopher, who was still covering our backs. "That one, not this one?" And this was why.

"Aunt Carla, meet Jeff. The man I'm marrying. This is his cousin, Christopher. A man with many excellent qualities whom, however, I am not marrying."

"Christopher's more your type. So is Charles."

Martini started growling, and Christopher winced. "Aunt Carla, Chuckie and I are still good friends. Okay?"

"Your mother told me he proposed and you turned him down. I can't believe you were willing to throw away years of friendship with a brilliant, successful man who worships you for some good-looking stud." Aunt Carla made Aunt Ruth seem demure.

"He's a great-looking stud, Aunt Carla." I hid behind Martini, dug through my purse, and pulled out my cell. "Daddy?"

"What's wrong, kitten? Are you all in danger again?" It was so loud in the restaurant I could barely hear him, but he sounded freaked. Of course, I'd called him Daddy, because I was freaked.

"Daddy, we're at our engagement party I didn't know we were having, and you're not here, and James isn't here, and . . ."

"And you've run into your Aunt Ruth?"

"And Aunt Carla."

My father almost never cursed, but when he did, it was impressive. "I knew it was a mistake to tell them anything. Your mother and I were trying to explain how you'd met Jeff and how he proposed, and of course Charles was involved and . . ." He sighed. "James wants to talk to you."

"Girlfriend, what's going on?"

"I'm at our engagement party, and you and my dad aren't here, and it's horrible." I didn't care if Aunt Carla heard that. She was busy telling Martini and Christopher how great Chuckie was, and how he'd convert to Catholicism if I wanted him to. "My aunts are telling Jeff I should be marrying Chuckie, or Christopher, or anyone else. I love my ring, and people are asking why the stone is so small, and I can't get to my mother."

He laughed. "Families are hell. Don't worry, it'll be okay."

"How so?"

"Your dad and I will be there shortly."

"James, you can't leave the hospital!" I shouted that out, and both Martini and Christopher spun toward me.

"I'm fine. Clean bill of health."

"That's impossible." There was something in the back of my mind that said it wasn't impossible, but I couldn't remember what it would be.

"Yeah, I know. Your dad got here and we've been playing cards the whole time. In between worrying about all of you."

"James, how the hell can you be sitting up?"

"Don't know. Don't care." He was quiet for a moment. "I think I should know, but . . . well, doesn't matter. The doctors are a little freaked out, but there's nothing wrong with me at all any more. Other," he added, sounding seriously pissed, "than the fact that I'm bald."

I managed a giggle. "Yeah, Paul said you'd be upset."

"Can't wait to hear the comments. Anyway, Kevin stopped by to check on me. He'll be coming with us." There was something in his voice.

"James, what aren't you telling me?"

"You'll find out when we get there. Don't tell Paul, unless your shouting alerted him already. I'd like to surprise him."

"Trust me, it's packed in here and unbelievably loud. Paul might not even know I'm here, and he sure hasn't heard any of our conversation. Your surprise is safe."

"Love you, babe. See you soon, and then your dad and I will fix everything."

I hung up, dropped my phone back into my purse, patted the Poofs, grabbed Martini and Christopher, and plowed on toward my mother, leaving Aunt Carla in mid-insult.

"This is really fun," Martini said. "I can't wait to hear what your grandparents have to say to me."

"I'm not enjoying being bachelor number three," Christopher added. "You didn't tell us your family worshiped Reynolds."

"I didn't know." I thought about it, though. I'd always bragged about him, because I was so proud of him. They all knew him, and while I was apparently the densest girl on the planet sometimes, perhaps they'd realized he was in love with me a lot sooner than I had. Wouldn't have been hard, since I hadn't realized it until he'd asked me to marry him. The second time. Guilt and its BFF Stress waved to me. They were loving this party. Me, not as much.

We reached my mother's table. "Hi, Mom, am I high or is our entire freaking family here?"

"Other than your father, yes, pretty much." Mom took a deep breath. "Kitty, could you, perhaps, introduce Jeff and Christopher to your grandparents?"

I was still holding both their hands, and as so many people, Chuckie included, had pointed out, Christopher had been more my type when I was in school. My Nona Maria beamed at him. "You must be the lucky boy who's marrying our Katherine. I told you he'd be decent, Dominic." This to my Nono Dom, sitting next to her.

Nana Sadie nodded enthusiastically. "Yes, we've heard so

much about you. See, Abraham? He's a nice-looking boy." My Papa Abe nodded with a bit less enthusiasm.

I saw Mom put her face in her hands. Alfred was wincing. Even Queen Renata looked shocked and uncomfortable. Christopher and Martini both were stunned into silence. Me, I wanted to die. This was worse than anything I'd ever imagined. I knew it would be bad, but this . . . I was one more word away from bursting into tears and running screaming into the street—and Reader wasn't here yet to stop me.

For whatever reason—fate, karma, ironic justice—I made eye contact with Lucinda. I didn't know what to expect to see in her expression—triumph, maybe hatred, disdain, victory. She smiled at me, but it wasn't a vicious smile at all. It was warm and understanding. Then she winked at me and turned to my grandparents.

"Your Kitty is such a lovely girl, and she had so many suitors, I'll admit we were wondering if our nephew would win her. That's our Christopher on Kitty's right. But our Jeffrey seems to have managed to catch and keep her eye. That's him on her left. I know he's a little bulkier than you all seem to think Kitty's attracted to, but you know, a woman's tastes change as she gets out of school."

I could see my mother out of the corner of my eye. She sat back up and looked both shocked and relieved. Renata let out the breath she'd clearly been holding. Alfred looked as though he was finishing a prayer of thanks. I was still afraid to look at Martini.

"Oh!" my grandmothers chorused. They both looked to my left and obviously checked Martini out.

"Handsome boy," Nana Sadie said.

"Very. Tall, too. Big and strong." Nona Maria beamed. "Should give our Katherine healthy babies."

"How many little ones are you planning?" Papa Abe asked. "And can you afford them? A man needs to support his wife and children."

Nono Dom nodded. "Our little kitten needs a big tomcat to take care of her and keep her under control." He was serious, and I tried not to die of embarrassment. "You up to that?"

I heard the best sound in the world right about now— Martini laughed. "Yeah, I think so. As for kids, I want a lot, but we figure we'll take one at a time and see how it goes."

"How soon for the babies?" Nona Maria asked. Eagerly.

"Um . . ."

"Oh, soon. But, you know, not too soon." Martini sounded completely at ease. I was still considering the benefits of spontaneous combustion.

"We're not getting any younger," Nana Sadie said, rather sternly. "I want to see my great-grandchild before I die."

"Nana, you've been saying that for years. You have tons of great-grandchildren."

"Not from you. You're my Solomon's only child. I want to see your babies before God takes me home."

Nona Maria nodded her total agreement. "We'd hoped Angela would have given you some brothers and sisters. You need to have more than one baby, and soon."

"I liked being an only child."

"Children need siblings." This from Papa Abe, who had strong views on this.

Christopher cleared his throat. "Ah, I'm an only child, too."

"But you had Jeffrey," Lucinda said with a small smile. "Christopher's like our other son. We were so lucky the boys are the same age and always were each other's closest friend."

"Cats need kittens to make a home." Nono Dom had been making cat jokes since my mother had introduced her parents to my father. Right up until this evening I'd loved them. Now I was considering the benefits of calling myself Kathy.

Martini leaned next to me. "Stop worrying. I like being your tomcat."

This was a relief, but it was clear my grandparents were willing to ask us about our reproductive choices for the foreseeable future. However, before they could continue, we were all interrupted by a shout from Lorraine. "James, what the *hell* are you doing out of your hospital bed?"

I breathed a sigh of relief. "Thank God, the cavalry's here."

CHAPTER 45

MOST OF MY SIDE HAD NO IDEA who Reader was. Everyone else, of course, hadn't expected to see him moving, let alone walking, talking, and joking, for days. There was pandemonium.

Gower got to him first, partially because I thought that was right and partially because short of Martini tossing me, I had too many people to shove through to have a hope of getting to him sooner than next week.

It was good that my dad and Kevin had Reader flanked, because he was being swarmed. I felt someone's arm go around my waist and lift me off the floor. "Coming through," Martini said, then just shoved people out of our way.

"I think you'll be impressing my Nono Dom with this tomcat move." Martini flipped me onto his hip and I wrapped my legs around his waist. There, back to our normal position for a chaotic situation. He bent his other shoulder a bit and plowed on through. "You could have played football with moves like this."

"Would that have meant I got you earlier in life?"

"Nah, I didn't date football players." Much.

"I can tell when you're lying."

He got us within range of Reader. It was a shock to see him without hair, but I'd been right—it would take total disfigurement to make Reader anything less than a twenty on a scale of one to ten.

Reader spotted us and flashed his best cover-boy grin. "Jeff, what're you doing with my girl?"

Martini flipped me down in front of him. "Marrying her, unless you turned straight in the hospital."

Reader pulled me into his arms and held me tightly. "No, but you're still my girl," he whispered to me. "Love the outfit. Jeff must have gone shopping."

I hugged him back and leaned my head on his shoulder. "Oh, James, I'm so glad you're here."

He rocked me and kissed the side of my head. "I know."

"Who is this, and why is he pawing Katherine?" Aunt Carla was on the scene.

"He's one of her best friends," Martini answered calmly. "The one who *doesn't* want to marry her. Hey, look. There's Brian, her old boyfriend from high school. He's an astronaut now. He's with his new girl, but, you know, maybe you could go and see if he still wants to marry Kitty, too. I understand he's a good Catholic boy, so right up your alley."

I didn't let go of Reader, but I cringed. Before I could come up with anything to say or do, someone else handled the situation.

"Carla, what a pleasure. Have Angela and I mentioned how much we love Jeff and how happy we are that he and Kitty are getting married?" Dad sounded amused and somewhat disdainful, but not angry.

"Somewhat." Aunt Carla sounded as if it didn't matter.

"Good. I think we also mentioned her very close friend, James Reader? The former international male model?"

"Oh. Him." Aunt Carla heaved a martyred sigh. "I still don't understand why she didn't choose Charles. Wealthy, brilliant, successful."

"I think it's because she's in love with Martini," Chuckie said from somewhere around us. I chose to keep on cringing into Reader's shoulder. It was comfortable, and I could pretend I wasn't here.

"Charles, maybe you can talk some sense into her, then." Boy, Aunt Carla was really on a tear. I had no idea why.

Reader did. "You're aware that the Martini family's loaded, aren't you? As in, Martini and Rossi? Old Italian money. And a lot of it."

"OH?" Aunt Carla's entire tone changed. "Really? Well, why didn't you say Katherine was marrying well, Sol?"

"We did. We said she was marrying a good man who loved

her and would cherish and protect her. As far as Angela and I are concerned, that's what matters."

"Right. I keep forgetting your humanitarian views. Well, carry on, though, if I were you, young man, I'd keep an eye on those two." I assumed she was saying this to Martini about me and Reader, but I chose to keep my cringe on full.

Silence for a few seconds. "You can come out now, Kitty." This from Kevin.

"I like it here, think I'll stay."

"More than a little jealous over here."

Reader laughed. "She's just making me feel better about being bald, Jeff."

"James, I hadn't even noticed."

"You lie like a wet rug, girlfriend."

"Really, the jealousy? It's on full."

"Give him a break, Kitty." This from Christopher, who must have joined the party while I had my eyes closed. "You know he had the jealousy talk with James, too. And Kevin. And Paul."

I was still holding on to Reader, but I opened my eyes and looked over my shoulder. "James and Kevin I sort of get. But *Paul*?"

Martini shrugged and didn't look all that embarrassed.

"I think I should be offended, somehow," Gower said with a laugh. "You thought I was hot when we first met."

"Paul, I still think you're hot. I am never joking when I say that if you and James want to go bi and expand the marriage to include me, I'm in. Barring that, however, Jeff sort of has the edge."

"Which everyone other than some of your family seems to understand," Chuckie said. "Martini, two things. One, you owe me for spending the last two hours with your brothers-in-law. Two, God, man, you have my sympathies. I've never met men more jealous of someone else's success in my life, and that's saying a lot."

"Thanks, and consider us somewhat even. I just got to hear about how great you are from just about every one of Kitty's relatives. They think you walk on water even more than she does."

"Jamie? Kitty? Can you two stop making everyone, including me and Jeff, think you're coming out about your illicit affair and sort of separate?" Gower sounded like he was only kind of kidding.

"She's hiding." Reader laughed. "Babe, there are no relatives around other than your father. I think the coast is clear."

"Okay, hope you're not wrong." He let me out of his arms. "Thanks for defusing Aunt Carla."

He grinned as Martini pulled me next to him. "Spent enough time around people like her, it was easy to spot. If they lead with the money, that's what they care about." He rubbed his hand over his head. "I need a freaking hat."

"You carry bald off well."

"It's gay."

"You *are* gay. And so's Paul. And he's bald, and he looks hot, and you've never minded bald on him." I knew why he didn't like it, of course, but I wanted to hear him say it.

"Two baldies is totally gay, okay?" Reader looked disgusted, and more so when we all started laughing. "You mentioned this to them?" he asked Gower.

"Maybe once." Gower put his arm around Reader's shoulders and pulled him close. "Bald over dead? Bald is great, Jamie."

"Yeah. So, how's the party been?" Reader was looking around, and I noted his eyes were lighting on everyone from Alpha and Airborne. I shot a glance at Kevin. Same thing. Well, he was our other rook, after all.

Looked to Chuckie. "You want to tell us what's going on, now that all our side of the board is here?"

He smiled at me. "No. We have time. Let's eat. We'll need the fuel."

"You know, mystery statements like that make it hard for me to get excited about food."

Martini stroked the back of my neck. "You sure we have the time?"

"Yes," Kevin said. "Though none of our team should be drinking. I've already passed the word to the humans on Alpha and Airborne. Oh, and Serene's briefed, too."

"Serene's coming along on whatever we're doing that none of you will tell me about?"

"Yeah. And Tito. Geez, I'm down and you replace me with the maintenance guy? I'm touched." Reader grinned at me. "He's great, Kitty. Good choice."

Dad sighed. "Kitten, really, enjoy this party. As much as you can."

"The doom and innuendos are really causing the word 'enjoy' to leave my vocabulary."

Kevin sighed. "Look, Reynolds, just tell her. She'll handle the news just fine, and maybe be able to relax."

"Go ahead," Chuckie said. Ah, this was a protocol issue, and Kevin was still reporting in to Chuckie like the rest of us.

Kevin looked at me. "Our NASA team picked up radio transmissions. We've translated them, accurately, and confirmed against molecular disturbance. We expect a spaceship of significant size to arrive from the Alpha Centauri system within the next twenty-four to forty-eight hours."

CHAPTER 46

"**O**KAY, YEAH, LET'S EAT."

It was worth it to see every one of their jaws drop.

"Uh, great." Chuckie looked sort of dazed.

"Wow, dudes, you crack me up. First you're all *Mission: Impossible* and then you're shocked when I take the news the way you said I'd take the news."

"We don't believe you," Reader said.

"Well, I could start screaming, but I don't think it'd do us any good. Besides, I think better on a full stomach."

"Think?" Kevin asked.

"The plots. Geez, guys, keep up. The mystery imageer spies who are bugging us and giving orders pretending to be Christopher, the laser light show, the so-called emissaries, our whacked-out Amazonian assassins, political intrigue in the A-C system—there's clearly something bigger going on. We have less than twenty-four hours to figure out what. And, as I said, I think better on a full stomach."

I heard a sleepy mewling coming from my purse. "Oh, right. Can someone find out what the Poofs like to eat? I'm sure they're starved."

Christopher called Alexander over, and my Poof concerns were explained. "Any meat should be fine."

"Alex, they're from your world. What, I'm supposed to toss them a steak?"

He shrugged. "Sure. Or some chicken. If it was once a living beast, they'll eat it. They're carnivorous."

"Okay. So, food for me and a dead cow for my Poofies. Should make the waiter's night."

Chuckie shrugged. "The moment I realized this had turned into a party of epic proportions, I got the buffet going. Help yourselves."

"Chuckie, did you pay for this?" I didn't want him to, and I knew without asking Martini wanted that even less than I did.

Chuckie grinned. "Yes. Compliments of the C.I.A. You're all operatives, and this is part of our cover."

"I like how he thinks," Reader said with a laugh. "Come on, let's get some food and try to help Kitty think right."

It was there, on the tip of my mind. "James," I said as we shoved our way to the buffet, "what do you think's going on?"

"No idea." He took a plate and passed another one to me. "God, I'm starving."

"Me too." We worked our way through the buffet options. "What commonality is there in everything that's going on?"

"Girlfriend, you're the brains of the operation, remember?"

"No, you are too, and you know it. Does your head still hurt?"

"Honestly? No. I feel great. I don't even have a scar; your dad pointed that out."

I looked his head over. How could he not have a scar? His head had been bashed in. But he was right–he looked just fine. I wanted to worry about it, but there were bigger issues. "Chuckie says we have to find who has the most to gain or the most to lose."

"Earth has the most to lose." Reader said this calmly, as he snagged some Chicken Kiev.

"Why so?"

"It's our planet that's being invaded. We don't have long-range spaceflight that can guarantee us safe passage to another planet. The gate's locked on the A-C side of the galaxy, so no way to get through there. Whatever's happening, it's happening here, and that sucks for us."

And there it was. Pretty much perfect clarity. "I know what's going on."

"Uh-huh. Do you think that stuff's safe to eat?"

"Yes, it's goulash. James, did you hear me?"

"Yes, you know what's going on. Fill the plate, sit down, eat what's on the plate. Starving here, and I want to have the food, in you and in me and the others before you explain what's really going on, because experience tells me the minute you *do* explain it, food and rest are a thing of the past."

"Fine." Couldn't argue, it was true.

We finished loading the plates and squeezed in at a table. Happily, we could set our plates down. I put one of the three Chicken Kiev pieces I'd taken on the ground and put the Poofs down there to eat. From the purring, I assumed they liked it. By craning my neck I could see my mother's table. Dad was there now, and Mom looked a lot better. I got a warm feeling inside—A-Cs weren't the only ones who mated for life.

Martini, Christopher, and Gower managed to shove in with us. I had to sit on Martini's lap, but I didn't mind. Everyone had brought extra for the Poofs, which was good because they were eating up a storm. Chuckie came by with a plate of raw chicken that also went under the table. He stood and ate.

"I know what's going on," I told him as I stuffed in some cabbage rolls. Red Square had what I'd call "regular nice food," too, but they could pull out the Russian and related specialties when they wanted to, and this meal was excellent proof.

"Good." Chuckie took my empty plate, wandered off, and came back with it filled up. With everything I liked. Martini muttered only a little bit.

"No one seems to care that I know what's going on."

"Baby, we're all starving, and we know we have time. You gonna finish that Kiev?"

"Yes, but have it anyway." He speared it quickly, and it disappeared from his plate almost as fast. Martini rarely used hyperspeed to eat; all the A-Cs were trained to do "human" things slowly from birth, so I knew he was starving. Well, we had been amazingly active for hours on end. I put my last cabbage roll onto his plate.

Chuckie grinned, wandered off, came back with another loaded plate. He put it down in the middle of the table. "Group feeding trough." This food disappeared quickly, and Chuckie waved someone down. A waiter managed to get near us. "Can I get more of the main dishes over here?"

"Yes, sir." The waiter hustled off.

"Nice to have them at your beck and call," Reader said in between mouthfuls.

"Pay to have a place closed for your own private party, tell the chef to pull out all the stops, the only goal being all the good food and drink that the guests can eat be available and coming nonstop, and add that money is no object—you get treated right." Chuckie beat me to the last cabbage roll on the group plate. "More's coming, and I'm bigger than you," he said with a laugh.

"Where's Kevin? Bet he'd like to know what I think's coming."

"He's with your parents," Chuckie told me. "And we're all fascinated. I'm wondering how you're missing the part where we're surrounded by your relatives and at your engagement party, though."

"My surprise engagement party."

He grinned. "Pontifex White, Mister Martini, Senior, and I thought it was appropriate. And, again, it's a great cover. Your mother felt it would make her job easier, too, so we're approved up to the Presidential level."

I would have been impressed by our importance, but the waiter arrived with four laden plates and I was too busy trying to get food to care about it. The men cleared them to their own plates before he could set them down. I managed to snag a couple of cabbage rolls before they were all gone but got stuck with a lot of potatoes and goulash.

I looked at Martini. "Did you know about this?"

"No. You eating that goulash?"

"Go for it." I wolfed down my cabbage rolls and eyed the ice bar with a touch of nostalgia. It was exactly that, a bar made out of ice, to keep your vodka martinis nice and frosty. Chuckie and I had come here every day when we were in Vegas.

"Hate your line of thought," Martini muttered as he snagged some potatoes off my plate.

"Just occasionally miss having a drink."

"So have one."

"Right. Like I want to risk killing you? Or, worse, not being able to kiss you?"

He grinned. "Okay, love this line of thought." He kissed me, then finished the rest of my potatoes.

I looked around some more. "Chuckie, how did my entire family get out here? I mean, my cousins are all here, not just my aunts and uncles and grandparents. The only ones missing are the kids under eighteen, 'cause I see the older ones. At the bar. Drinking." Lucky things. I wanted to give the ones under twenty-one a severe talking-to, but they'd know it was because I wasn't having a drink myself, so I let it pass.

He shrugged. "I think your grandparents called them. Apparently it wasn't sitting well with anyone that they hadn't met any of Martini's family. Once they did and could confirm that Alfred and Lucinda seemed to believe you two were really getting married, it snowballed. The more of your side that came out, the more of Martini's side Lucinda called in, basically."

"Huh." Most of my family lived in the West, so it wasn't a long flight or even drive to get here for most of them. But some of them had come from farther away. "What day is it?"

"Thursday." Chuckie gave me a long look. "You slept last, when?"

"No idea." My brain was whirring. "I think I know the rest of the plot."

"Great. Is there anything for dessert?" Martini had finished everything on my plate and his.

"Yeah." Chuckie made some signals and two waiters appeared, laden with dessert plates, teacakes, and some other things. I couldn't identify the other things because the men devoured them before I got a good glimpse. Fine. I liked teacakes. I took a few and clutched my dessert plate to my bosom.

"No one cares what I think," I muttered to my teacake.

"We care. You gonna eat that other one?"

"No, Jeff, I took it for you." He ignored my sarcasm and snagged it.

"Thanks, Reynolds, call those waiters back, will you?"

"Geez, I've never seen you guys eat like this."

"Kitty, we haven't eaten in at least twenty-four hours," Gower said patiently, as he grabbed some dessert off the new platters the waiters brought by. "By the way, ACE says he's fascinated by what you think and is waiting patiently for us to finish so you can share it with us."

"At least someone cares."

"He says we have the time to eat," Gower added, as he started in on what looked like German chocolate cake. I had no idea—the platters were never getting close to me.

Finally the men seemed somewhat satiated, and by that I mean I could see some of the food on the platters before it disappeared. Then I heard a sound I didn't like.

"Everyone!" Nono Dom shouted. "We need to have a toast!"

"Oh, no. Please not this." The Poofs were done eating and I put them back into my purse so I could run as soon as I needed to.

"Oh, relax," Martini said as he finished the last teacake on the table and leaned back. He pulled me closer to him. "This is the fun part."

"Is it?" I knew what my family's toasts were like. Long. Detailed. Embarrassing.

I was saved from finding out how bad it could have been because an A-C who looked fairly familiar came up to us. I was pretty sure he hadn't been at the party all this time.

"Commander Martini?" He seemed stressed, and I felt all of us shift from relaxed to alert.

"Yes, what's up?" Martini had his Commander voice on.

The A-C took a deep breath. "The prisoners held in Dulce. They're gone, sir."

CHAPTER 47

WE ALL STOOD UP. "ARE THEY in the complex?" Martini asked, while Chuckie went off to pull our teams out.

"No, sir. We've already checked. They're gone completely."

"Did anyone get hurt?"

"No, ma'am, Commander Katt. Not even Security."

"Then how did they get out?"

He shook his head. "We don't know. Security wasn't alerted. Including the agents on the floor with the prisoners."

"Where are the dogs, cats, and lizards?" I asked Gower.

"Here." He pointed out some people I realized were the aliens, all of whom were moving through the restaurant to the exit.

"Well, that's convenient. I have to go say good-bye to my parents and grandparents."

"I'll come with you. Christopher, contact Gladys, I want her info. Tell Commander White the rest," Martini snapped at the A-C. He took my hand, and we started to the back.

My family could tell something was going on. "What, they don't like toasts?" Nono Dom asked as we got closer.

"No, Nono, that's not it. We have an . . . emergency." This was going to suck. Because I hadn't told Martini just what it was I'd been telling my family I did for work now.

"What kind of an emergency that calls you away from your engagement party?" Papa Abe asked, in the tone of voice that said it couldn't possibly be important enough for me to get a free pass to leave.

I took a deep breath.

"Our main client just rejected the full ad campaign and is threatening to go to a larger agency," Reader said calmly from behind me. "Business-ending kind of stuff, unless we get right on it." He shrugged and gave them the cover-boy smile. "You know how it goes when you own your own company. There's always something threatening to end your world and put you right out of business. They won't settle for less than me and Kitty, and since half of our creative team is here, we're going to have to go into full-on 'save the world' mode."

"What James said." I didn't look at Martini. "So we have to go. Hopefully we'll be back tomorrow. Everyone's staying at least the weekend . . . right, Mom?" I looked straight at her. "Since that's the idea, isn't it?" I looked at Lucinda, too. They both looked hugely guilty.

"What's going on?" Martini asked me quietly.

"Ask your dad—he's in on it, too."

"In on what?" Martini sounded confused and suspicious.

"Tell him about it on the way," Reader said with a lot of authority. "We don't get moving, we're out of business. Permanently."

"Right. Mom, can I steal Renata and Kevin, please? The only thing the client liked about the campaign was the two of them. They're into the unprofessional model/real person look."

"Sure, Kitty." Mom gave me a long-suffering look as I glared at her. "It wasn't my idea, okay? But it's not out of the question, either. You haven't put any deposits down anywhere yet."

"Invitations are out." Renata and Kevin were saying quiet good-byes to my grandparents. "And we sort of have a deposit out."

"We aren't charging you to come to our home," Lucinda said dryly. Yeah, okay, I'd given up, and we'd asked Martini's parents if we could get married at their estate. It would suck for my family, but we hadn't found any place else we actually both liked. Reader, in particular, felt us getting married in Florida was insane.

"It's been taking you two forever to make any kind of decision," Mom added in an exasperated tone.

"And pretty much everyone invited is here, yes, got it. Wow, the timing is just so impeccable and all. I'll ponder why you all thought now was such a great time to spring this on us while I go try to save the . . . business. Back in a while." I hoped.

My dad shook his head. "I was with James."

"You helped."

He smiled. "I did. Take care of things, call us if you need us—we'll have our cell phones on us at all times."

"Thanks." I hugged my family good-bye, asked my mother to make some phone calls for me, Martini and Reader hugged my parents and Martini's and shook hands with my grandparents, and then we left.

Chuckie was at the door, ushering our teams out. He looked at me. "I didn't have anything to do with it."

"But you knew it was going to happen."

"Only tonight when I realized they were all here."

"Okay, we're out. What the hell is going on?" Martini was growling. "Not the invasion, what you were talking to our parents about. And what the hell have you told them you've been doing?"

Reader laughed. "She told them she and I started our own marketing agency. Small but with a high-paying customer base. Easier explanation than what we really do. And as for what's going on, jeez, Jeff, think about it."

Chuckie was counting noses. "We have everyone. Brian, you sure you're coming along?"

"Yeah. Hey, Kitty, Jeff."

"Bri, nice to see you. Michael riding herd on you?"

"Like always," Michael Gower said. "You know, you dragged my parents out here and you still haven't talked to them."

He was right. And I needed to. "Back in a flash. Michael, can you introduce me?"

"Sure." We trotted off. I heard Reader and Chuckie explaining the obvious to Martini. He was starting to bellow as we got back inside the restaurant. "He's a little slow sometimes," Michael said with a laugh.

"Caught us both by surprise. I'm just clearer on how my family works."

"You okay with it?" He took my elbow and led me toward an interracial couple about my parents' age. The man was typical A-C handsome, and I could see a resemblance to Alfred. The woman was stunning in her own right—skin the same color as her sons', beautiful features. They were with two younger Dazzlers, same skin tone as their mother and the boys.

"Yeah, I think so. Not sure about Jeff. Paul wasn't kidding—human external genetics rule, don't they?"

"Yes," Mrs. Gower said with a knowing smile. "They do." She stood up, as did the rest of the family. "Paul and James have told us so much about you. I'm Ericka, this is my husband, Stanley, and our girls, Abigail and Naomi."

Shook paws all around, then everyone except Ericka sat back down. "Sorry to be rude, but we're at the usual end-of-the-world-as-we-know-it time, and I need to ask you two things."

"Go ahead," she said with another knowing smile. "I can guess both."

"Oh, yeah?"

She nodded. "Yes, it's worth it. Yes, it can be absolute hell, and the extended, nosy, always-there family can be torturous. But once you're in, you're in, and they'll love you like the rest of the clan and die for you if they have to. Paul was a lot of work, but, honestly, Michael was more. He got more of the human side in his personality," she added with a laugh. Wow, she was good or I was obvious.

Michael shrugged. "Playing the field's allowed."

"Not like you play it," Naomi said with a snort.

"So," Ericka added, "while you're likely to get powerful children, I don't agree with Lucinda's concerns. I've heard enough about you to feel confident you can handle it. And your parents are clearly capable of helping."

"Not to mention Jeff."

"Yes. Now, your other question? No, this never happened when Stanley and I got married. Nothing like it."

"Anyone expect something to happen?"

Stanley shrugged. "Somewhat, but we'd been exiled. Once Ericka and I got married and nothing triggered, we assumed the cut was complete."

"Why did you? Get exiled, I mean, you personally? You're from the royal family side of the house. I wouldn't have thought you'd have been asked to leave."

He gave me a small smile. "I agreed with Richard, about religion, about how people should live. The rest of those on our home world may want to act civilized now, but our history was brutal, and some of that was still retained. The way we demanded that the other civilizations in our solar system toe the line we'd drawn or be controlled by us, things like that."

Alexander had said as much when we were in the limo. I thought about ACE and the other PPB net, how they'd been created, what they'd been sent to do. "Yeah. I can see the brutality's still there."

Stanley shrugged. "Richard's not a brutal man. Yates wasn't either, until he lost two wives."

"Two?"

"Yes. And while there's no proof, most of us believe they were both murdered."

"Why kill his wives?"

"Yates was probably the target, both times." Stanley sighed. "I know you're in the middle of another crisis. All I can say is, it's probably not due to your engagement . . ." His voice trailed off, and he got a funny look on his face. "Oh . . . no . . . it can't be." Stanley stood up. "Alfred!"

Alfred came over; Richard White did as well. "Thought you'd left, Kitty," Alfred said with a worried smile.

"Did, came back, getting info."

Stanley grabbed Alfred's arm. "Think back, way back. What were the rituals for marriage? Not in our grandparents' day, but early on."

"They were brutal," White said quietly. "They were a reason our ancestors broke away from the world religion and world leaders."

Stanley looked pale. "Alfred, think about it. You, more than the rest of us, would have learned this."

Alfred's expression was both confused and horrified. "What you're talking about was done thousands of years ago. Why in the world would they pull them up now? And for my son and his intended?"

This didn't sound good. "Um, should I just guess, or are you going to share?"

White closed his eyes. "Everything that's happened has been a test."

"Come again?"

He opened his eyes and I saw rage and fear in them. "Tests. All of them. Tests of you, of your ability to lead." His voice was clipped. Stanley and Alfred were nodding. They looked ill.

I decided arguing was stupid. "Why would they test the incoming spouse?"

"To be sure said spouse would be strong enough to help rule, to provide strong children, that sort of thing." Stanley sounded sick. "But they were so long ago . . . I'm sorry, we should have realized anyway."

"No. None of this is the fault of anyone here."

"The modern tests were more like you all were expecting—protocol and deportment." Stanley's voice was shaking.

"You know," Michael said. "All the things you were going to flunk."

"Too damn true. But this is less about Jeff's wedding than about succession, right? I mean why they're pulling up the old stuff."

"No idea," Stanley said.

Ericka was on her phone. "Yes. Get all the children, theirs and ours. Yes." She looked at Alfred. "I'm moving them to your home, is that okay with you?"

"Yes, please," Alfred said briskly.

Ericka went back to her call. "Yes, go to Alfred's. Highest threat levels. Yes. Thanks, Gladys." She hung up. "Okay, all the children, yours and ours, are sequestered or getting there. Gladys will be with them."

"Gladys isn't at the Science Center?"

"No. She was called to NASA Base earlier tonight," White replied. "She can still monitor it, however."

I looked at Michael. "I wonder if that's how the prisoners got out?"

He shook his head. "No idea." He pulled out his phone and made a call.

White spoke again. "Miss Katt, I do believe this is about succession. I spent some time with Alexander. His brother clearly wants the throne. The ruling king doesn't agree. Alexander does not want the throne and has already refused it. Therefore, succession must be fought for. They could stall it off before, but now . . ."

"Now the Free Women went nuts and started a galactic war, so things need to be speeded up. Because rulers are dead or dying, and someone strong has to take control."

"Yes." White shook his head. "I don't know why they won't leave us alone."

"Because they don't consider us their equals. We're their garbage dump. Gregory started them off, somehow. I know it." Though I had a strong feeling he'd had help, even if Gregory himself didn't know it.

"I'm sure he did. Alexander feels very responsible."

"Jeff said he was clean. So to speak." Another though occurred. "Can I get your cells programmed in?" I had a feeling I'd want to talk to Ericka or Stanley soon.

Ericka put out her hand, and I gave her my phone. "I'm programming in all our numbers, including Abigail's and Naomi's. And we'll make sure every A-C here stays near a human counterpart." I took my phone back and dropped it in my purse. Thank God for cell phones. Our whole operation would go down without the phone system.

I got a funny feeling in my stomach. "Mom!"

She came over. "I thought you left."

"Trying to. I need the P.T.C.U. to monitor all the telecommunications industry. I'm betting it's going to go down, and soon. I have no idea if we can keep it up or not, but whatever system the A-Cs are on has priority. Oh, and keep Richard with you and Dad, please. They're after him, of course."

Mom nodded, but Stanley seemed confused. "Why do you think they're after Richard and not Jeff?"

"Well, they're after all of us, but Richard's the king, and they can only win if they take the king. Gotta dash, great meeting you all, hope I see you again and we're all still alive. If we lose telecommunications, make sure you get the families out of here. The fight will head here, if they can do it, because they know you're all here."

Mom looked at me. "This went from bad to worse, didn't it?"

"Mom, we've been at DEFCON Worse for hours. Ericka, Stanley, this is my mother, Angela, just in case you haven't met. Mom, listen to them and get caught up; they sort of know what's going on."

I grabbed Michael, and we ran for the door.

"I've talked to Gladys," Michael told me as we worked our way out of the restaurant. "She cleared all nonagent personnel out of Dulce when she went to Florida. All the human children in your family are there now, including the ones who were here in Vegas with their parents. All other American personnel are spread out at Caliente, East, NASA, or Home Bases; she's left the other worldwide bases as is, but they're all on alert. Security seems okay, but they have no idea of how the prisoners escaped, and Gladys feels Security wasn't infiltrated."

"What's her power?"

"Jeff hasn't told you?"

"If I knew, why would I ask?"

"She's a combo, dream-reader and empath. And she's trustworthy."

"She's Lucinda and Richard's sister, isn't she?"

He laughed. "Yeah. But from his second wife."

"Can we trust her?"

"Yes, believe me. And the children couldn't be safer—God help anyone who tries to hurt someone Gladys has under top priority protection."

"NASA Base is where? The Martini compound?"

"I thought you only asked if you didn't know."

"Whatever."

Michael grinned. "Well, it's actually connected to the Martini estate, but they can and do function separately."

"One day, I'll get this all straight." Maybe. We reached the others. "Okay, we're officially at DEFCON Oh My God. Ancient history for any A-C history buffs in attendance. Chuckie, we need to get to the area in New Mexico and Arizona between the peaks. That's where they'll be landing."

He nodded. "Figured. On it. Martini has a floater gate coming; we were just waiting for you."

"Weapons of all kinds coming in from Home Base," Martini added. "Issue with jets, though. Need to send the flyboys to Home Base if we want jets."

I shook my head. "No, they'll just shoot them out of the air. I think we want to keep our opponents on the ground." I looked at the other emissaries still with us. "We need to know, right now, if you're with us or against us."

"With you." Queen Renata sounded confused.

I checked out the other's expressions. "Jeff, what are they feeling?"

"Confusion, baby, just like the rest of us. Alexander, too."

"Okay . . . Gregory indeed had more going on. He's started an ancient Alpha Four succession ritual to claim the throne. The Planetary Council are pawns in that, and so are the Amazonian assassins. Problem is, they're all out, and their reinforcements are coming."

"Great." Chuckie sounded as though he was getting a migraine.

"But it should be official Free Women warriors," Alexander said. "Not any who side with the dissidents."

"I promise you, we've got the crazy ones coming."

"How do you figure?" Martini asked.

"Because I think this has been planned for a long time, much longer than anyone from the Planetary Council here realizes."

"Great." Chuckie sounded as if the migraine was getting worse.

"It'll get better. Assume they'll knock out telecommunications first. We're extremely reliant on it, and Gregory knows that now. Everything going on so far has been a part of the succession test, triggered because we're getting married."

"Great." Martini was joining Chuckie in Migraine Land.

"They'll want to take out Richard. He's here, and my parents and others will be staying with him."

"Why my father?" Christopher sounded angry and afraid. I could relate.

"Because he's the head of your religion. If Jeff wins, they will want to force him to go back to Alpha Four. Richard, as the religious leader, would be able to support Jeff staying here. Without him, your entire race crumbles. At least in their minds."

I looked to Gower. "Paul, I need to talk to ACE." It was time to confirm what I was pretty sure Gower and I both already knew.

He nodded and twitched. "Yes, Kitty, ACE is here."

"The sentient net from the Free Women planet is on its way, isn't it? That's who you meant when you said 'she' was evil. Not Moira or even Kyrellis, but your godlike counterpart, who considers itself female."

"Yes, Kitty." ACE sounded both relieved and scared. "ACE wanted Moira to stay unaware so Moira could not bring Moira's God to us any faster."

"It's not a god, ACE, any more than you are."

"She is freer than ACE. And more ruthless."

"We'll handle it, ACE."

"ACE will help. ACE will have to." I heard the fear.

"You'll handle it, too. We won't let them destroy you, either, ACE. I told you that—I won't desert you, ever."

Alexander cleared his throat. "I know the succession ritual you're speaking of. But we haven't practiced that for centuries, millennia, even."

"But they're still available for use. And your king is hurt and dying. And you refused the crown, and he knows Gregory is unfit. So . . . he said yes, in the hope that we'd handle his problems for him. Just like always."

"Gate's here, baby. Using a big one, so we can all pretty much go through together."

"Okay, Chuckie and Christopher first, you and me last. Everyone else, remember that the humans must have an A-C near them or there's a good chance they'll be dead fast. Tito, Planetary Council members, Alexander—welcome to what it's like with us. Now's the time to back out and stay with our families. We won't hate you, as long as you help protect the people we love. Everyone else, you've all been here before— let's remember that this is *our* world, not theirs."

Everyone nodded. "Don't dawdle," Christopher said to Martini and me. It was almost a ritual now, and I managed to laugh.

Chuckie and Christopher went through, then the rest of our fighting force, including Tito and the others. No one hesitated. No one but me.

Martini pulled me into his arms. "You okay with getting married this weekend?"

"It'll give me something to live for."

"Yeah." He held me tightly. "You're the human I'm staying near, you know."

I shook my head. "The power pieces don't get that luxury, Jeff. We're lucky we have a lot of extra pawns. But they're gunning for the power pieces."

"Maybe so. But a knight's job is to protect his queen." Martini bent and kissed me. It was slow, deep, and sensuous and I never wanted it to end. But it did. Everything ended, after all.

Martini stroked my face. Then he lifted me up into his arms, I buried my face in his neck, and we walked through the gate and toward the things trying to kill us.

CHAPTER 48

WE EXITED THE GATE IN THE MIDDLE of the desert. It was the end of April, but it was still cold at night, and I was glad I had Martini's jacket on. He put me down, and the idea of changing out of four-inch heels seemed like a smart one—too bad it hadn't occurred to me before we'd gotten here.

We were lucky—the moon was full. We had a plethora of weapons with us, but I didn't think they were going to matter, or help.

"Okay, we're here. Early, hopefully. So, what's going on?" Chuckie was looking around while my flyboys handed out weapons to everyone. "You know, we're out in the middle of nowhere in the middle of the night with an invisible gate for an exit. Was this wise?"

"No. But they're going to be here shortly."

"We still have hours," Kevin protested.

"No. We are supposed to think we still have hours. They knew we'd intercept the communication. They'll be here soon. What time did the light show start up?"

"Midnight. On the dot." Chuckie sighed. "Okay, so that's when they'll show again, right?"

"Right. I need our Animal Planet helpers."

"You are lucky Charles explained your sense of humor," Willem said, as he and the others came closer to me. "We could call you naked apes, you know." All of them were back to their normal, unaltered forms.

"Go for it. Like I'd care? We need you guys to move your

ships. They're gonna get smooshed if you don't, and we have to have an escape plan."

Willem barked an order. Literally, he barked. Wahoa barked back, then she and Wrolph took off toward Chiricahua. It was miles and miles away, but I got the impression they'd be back soon.

Felicia and Arup nodded. "We will be back as well." They ran off, but toward Animas.

"So, Iguanodon? What's the status for your ship?"

Neeraj smiled. I was impressed. It was both scary and nice at the same time. I wasn't sure I ever wanted to see it again. "We do not need to be in our ship to fly it." He and Jareen did something funky between them, and I felt a very large thing fly over us. "Our ship is near. Would you like it uncloaked?"

"Can the Alpha Four folks see it through the cloak?"

"Yes."

"Then uncloak away."

They did. It looked a little like a lizard with wings. "Wow, did the folks who created *Star Trek* hang with you guys?"

"I'm sorry," Neeraj said. "I don't know what you mean."

"No worries. Few ever do."

"Would you like the lights on?"

"Sure, as long as we can turn them off right away if we have to." Neeraj nodded, and we were bathed in light. Something resembling a cat's paw and a dog's head landed on either side of the Flying Lizard. They put on their brights, too. "You know, why is it humans make rockets that look like bullets, but all of you imitated yourselves?"

"No idea," Neeraj said. "You think strangely."

"Yeah. I think right, too." I thought about this. "I think I know what ACE's counterpart is going to be doing."

"Can't wait to find out," Martini said. "You going to share anything or just keep the rest of us in suspense until we die?"

"Boy, are you testy tonight. Feeding you was the wrong idea, I guess."

He shook his head. "I was happier with the toasts coming than this, I can say that."

"Me too. Okay, fine, let's break it down." I took a deep breath. "This is all a chess game. Accept that, and it becomes easier to understand. We're playing chess for the same reasons that someone would challenge Death to a match—it's the only shot we have."

"Kitty, that was amazingly unclear, even for you." Tim was next to Reader. "You need some tunes or something?"

"Yes, but not just now. Look, chess, everyone know the game I'm talking about?" Most of the heads nodded. Chuckie spoke quickly and quietly to the heads that didn't nod, and I continued. "Okay, it's a game of strategy, of intellect. And in order to win, you have to be cagey. It's rare to win a chess game by just barreling toward the other side's king. You have to create action on all parts of the board, so your opponent is distracted from your true main gambit."

"Is the main objective finding a new king for Alpha Four?" Chuckie asked me.

"No. Though even Gregory thinks it is. But he's not actually the one moving the pieces on his side of the board."

"Who is?" Martini asked me quietly.

"The person with the most to gain *and* lose." I looked at Alexander. "How long ago was the king of Alpha Four hurt?"

"Months," Alexander said promptly.

"And he's Jeff's grandfather, so he's older than Alfred, so he's in, what, his seventies or eighties?"

"Older," Alexander admitted.

"Wow. An old man in his nineties is attacked by the Amazonian Assassin Squad, and he's still managing to hang on to life. Amazing will."

Martini cursed. "You are kidding me!"

"I wish, Jeff. Just think what you'd all be like if you were still on the home world."

"We'd suck." Christopher's voice was shaking with rage. "That's why he wants my father dead."

"Yes, because the one person who could actually come back with the authority to lead thousands isn't really Jeff or you . . . it's the religious leader who's been doing it in exile for decades. Richard is the one who leads the hearts and minds of the entire A-C population, including the hearts and minds of the people in charge of all operations."

"So the king isn't hurt all that badly?" Kevin sounded suspicious.

"No, and it's obvious now." Chuckie's tone was one I was very familiar with. He was in full-on Conspiracy Mode. "But, the question is, who does the king want as a successor?"

"No one."

Everyone looked at me. The spaceship floodlights made it really clear that everyone, even Chuckie, thought I was nuts.

I sighed. "Guys, I'd like everyone to meet Paul Gower. Paul, come next to me, please." He did, while giving me the crazy girl look. "Folks, what's the most unusual thing about Paul?"

"Oh, God, tell me you're wrong." Reader looked freaked. Finally, someone else got it.

"I'm not wrong."

"Kitty, James. Answers, now." Martini was growling and in full Commander Mode.

"Jeff, I birthed ACE into Paul six months ago. Paul's suffered no ill effects. Neither has ACE. But I'll bet that if we bothered to check, Paul's longevity has been increased. Also, ACE is part of our world and so thinks more like we do. More to the point, he's joined with a group who are, truthfully, pacifistic at their core. But the other PPB net was around the most warlike, angry world out there. We assumed it became sentient and aware and took on the anger of the world it surrounded."

"But it didn't, did it?" Reader asked. "Because the plan is to get rid of all the potential heirs to the throne here and now."

"Well, the net *is* angry, but it's more than that. I'm fairly sure it's being controlled, not doing the controlling, at least, not all of it."

"Who could control the net?" Alexander asked. "They're created to stand alone and do what they're programmed to do."

"But they're sentient, and a sentient being can always change its mind. Plus, the person who created the net could always find a way to control it, or create a fail-safe. Or merely program the net to obey at the right time." Paul and I could control ACE, to a degree, anyway, but I didn't share that out loud.

Instead I looked around at all the emissaries. "The plan is to get rid of all the other planetary leaders. And to do that, there needed to be an assassination squad. There were plenty of the best warriors around, in captivity on Beta Twelve. That's why I know it's the rest of Kyrellis' crew who're coming on that ship—it's what they were created for, why their net talked to them specifically and told them what to do and who to listen to. The king of Alpha Four will join with the PPB consciousness from Queen Renata's world and rule everyone, in both the A-C and Earth solar systems . . . potentially forever."

Everyone looked horrified and a little ill. No one from the A-C solar system, however, looked all that surprised. From all we'd heard, this was business as usual for Alpha Four.

I looked at Chuckie. "So Earth has the most to lose, and the king of Alpha Four has the most to gain. Everything else, as always, was an elaborate ruse to keep us distracted from the real goal and what's really coming."

"I'm so proud," Chuckie said with a small smile. "All those years, you really were paying attention."

"To everything you ever said, yeah." I looked back to Alexander. "I forgot to ask and you've never said—what's Jeff's good ol' granddad's name?"

"In your language, my great-uncle's name would translate to Adolphus."

I was quiet for a moment. "Wow. That's so fitting it's scary."

"So, why was Reynolds' room bugged?" Christopher asked me.

"Hitler's royal A-C counterpart and the PPB net haven't joined yet. I think Kitler wants to be sure he's got a great story for the rest of the solar system's inhabitants. You know, something like 'Earth killed all your leaders and diplomats and all the heirs to my throne, so for the good of us all, I'm going to get some superpowers and fix everything.' So, I assume he wanted to know if we'd figured it out or not as well as keep tabs on us."

"Kitler?" Neeraj asked. "Who is that?"

"Adolphus . . . Hitler . . . King Hitler . . . put them together, it's Kitler, also known as our Supreme Bad Guy?"

"Oh. This is more of your humor." Neeraj didn't seem amused.

"So to speak," Chuckie added.

"So the Planetary Council is also a target?" Queen Renata asked, possibly to change the subject.

"You are, Renata. The rest of the gang are all identified as being close to their world leaders, so assume every member of the Planetary Council with us is in danger. Kitler's agents here on Earth set off the laser light show not to announce a royal wedding but to set Gregory off and into motion. Alexander doing the Royal Messenger thing on the home world helped them, which is why Alexander is still alive. Oh, I'd guess Uma's in with the Reigning Megalomaniac. The PPB has to filter through a woman to go wherever it's going to end up, plus someone has to be feeding Gregory ideas. She was too good about focusing all of us on the protocols issue—you will refer to him as My Royal Lord my ass, sort of thing."

"Uma is the sister of Alpha Six's ruler." Queen Renata sounded ill, and angry. "They murdered my mother for this insanity."

"Babe, they're just upset they didn't murder you, too. Your dissidents do think they're talking to God, though. I've seen the fanaticism up close and personal, and it's real. I've also talked to ACE in my head, and if I didn't know what ACE was, I wouldn't have a hard time believing I was talking to God."

"Especially if ACE said he was God," Gower added dryly.

"So this has been planned for a year?" Alexander asked. "Because the first announcement lights went off a year ago."

"Alex, you don't plan to take over all the sentient inhabitants of two solar systems on a whim. This is a complex plan. His Royal Megalomaniacness has been planning it for years, maybe before you were born. I mean, why don't you want to rule?"

He shrugged. "My great-uncle spent much time telling me how onerous it was, how thankless." I saw the light dawn. "He talked me out of it, didn't he?"

"Yes. Welcome to the team, big guy. We'll do the blood oath and pinkie swear rituals later, but trust me when I say you come from really nasty stock. They must hate you—you're a lot more like Jeff and Christopher than your own brother."

He nodded. "I've heard that I wasn't like the rest of the family most of my life."

"You know, we need to protect Alexander, Martini, White, and Gower, but Reader is still going to be target number one," Chuckie said calmly.

"Why?" Reader asked, but so did a lot of the others. It was like we had our own echo even though we weren't in a canyon.

"Because Paul and Kitty both love you, and ACE is in Paul and worships Kitty." Martini's voice was clipped. "And anyone spying on us would know that. That's why you were the target in the first place, James. To cause emotional trauma, to remove the person they both rely on. To ensure that ACE had to deal with that kind of loss and horror alone—because the two people who could best talk ACE through it would be out of their minds with grief." He looked at me. "I hate my family."

"Not the family here, Jeff."

"True."

"Sins of the father," Brian said softly.

"Will be delivered like unto the fourth generation." I didn't go to temple much or mass ever, but I knew the Bible. "Yeah. Jeff and Christopher are the fourth. It ends here. Tonight. One way or the other."

CHAPTER 49

"I HAVE ONE QUESTION." Christopher sounded thoughtful.

"Shoot."

"What is the point of the Poofs?"

"Good question. No idea. Alexander?"

He looked embarrassed. "They wanted to come."

"Beg pardon?"

Alexander sighed. "Harlie has been around for a long time, before Gregory was born, maybe longer. It was always listless. I assumed it was because it was so old. When the announcement light triggered, it was the first time in my life I saw Harlie excited. There was one other Poof alive, and it was excited, too. When I realized it was up to me to make sure the people knew we had another royal elsewhere who might be able to take the crown, the Poofs mated. That's how we got the other six."

"How did you get them out of the palace, let alone here with you?"

He shrugged. "I told you, they wanted to come. Only the person they're attached to can control them, so if they want to go somewhere, they go. The other Poof, Tenley, stayed at home."

"Protecting your great-uncle?"

"No, my mother. They seem more attached to females than males. Tenley has been my mother's since her marriage was announced."

"Can we trust them?" Chuckie asked.

"Been helping us so far. But, to be sure, who did Harlie belong to?"

Alexander shrugged and shook his head.

Martini coughed. "My father." He sounded embarrassed.

"I'd call that a big yes, then." I pulled the Poofs out. They looked at me and purred. Then, one by one, they jumped. Harlie went to Martini, and the one I'd called Poofikins stayed with me. The others went to Christopher, Gower, Reader, Alexander, and Chuckie.

"Why is one with Reynolds and not, say, me?" Michael asked. He didn't sound upset or jealous, just curious, which I considered massive personal growth.

"Because they're going to be gunning for the seven of us. Not that they will ignore the rest of you, but they want to take the seven of us out."

"Why?" Tim asked.

"Because we're the power pieces on the chessboard." I figured Alexander had replaced Kevin because he was a legitimate threat to King Adolphus' plan. With Reader back in action, we had two spare rooks. I hoped I wasn't going to have to pull Tito or Kevin in, though.

"I hate being a pawn," Tim grumbled. "Pawns get sacrificed."

"Not my pawns." Martini looked at the Poof. "Do me a favor and hide in my pocket." Harlie purred at him and hid as requested. The other Poofs did the same, going into the men's pockets. Poofikins hopped into my purse.

"Break down their side of the board," Chuckie said to me.

"Knights are Kyrellis and Moira. Bishops are Gregory and Lenore. I know everyone thought she was clueless, but I'm betting she had some emotional overlay on her to block Jeff. After all, she said she was related to the now-deceased ruler of Alpha Five, so figure she's in on it, too. Plus, Alexander didn't trust her, so when in doubt, go with your gut. Their rooks will be the two imageers who infiltrated us, the guys I spotted in Vegas. I'm betting only two, by the way."

"Why?" Christopher asked.

"There's not enough distraction and destabilization of our side for too many more to be likely," Chuckie answered. "It's possible there are more of them, but I'm with Kitty, probably safe to assume just the two."

"I practiced with Christopher and Queen Renata," Serene

said. "I can tell who's who if I've ever seen them before, even if they're shapeshifted or have an image overlaid."

"Great work, Serene! You're going to have a tough job, though, no matter what. I want Tim, Tito, Kevin, and Brian protecting Serene, by the way. The moment they realize she can figure out who's who, she'll be target number one."

"Who's their queen?" Chuckie asked.

"Uma."

"You're kidding." Martini snorted.

"Bitch Leader is the queen. Trust me."

Queen Renata nodded slowly. "Yes. If I understand your meaning. She was influencing Gregory. It was subtle, but now that I can see the whole web, it was she who drove more decisions, though Gregory would tell you it was him."

Willem and Felicia nodded as well. "Renata is correct," Felicia said. "But we are more than pawns."

"Not in this game. Your death or survival is meaningless to Kitler. In that sense, it's meaningless to us. The difference is, we know you, have fought with you, and so are attached to you. He knows this about us—they've been watching, after all. But if you look at it from the point of a game of strategy, unless you can affect the outcome of this battle, you are not involved."

"We are good fighters," Willem said. "Why would you think we would not be able to assist, even turn the tide?"

"Because," Martini snapped, "I want you guarding the queen."

"Jeff, I'm going to have to fight."

"Not if I can help it." He looked at all of Animal Planet. "Seriously. You want to help? Keep her safe, and keep her out of it."

"I agree," Chuckie said. I glared at him. "What? You think any of us want you actually fighting these people?"

"I'm not without the skills."

"You are in comparison to what we're up against," Christopher snapped.

Willem and Queen Renata exchanged glances. "We will protect as you request," Willem said. I was surrounded in moments.

"Great. Nothing's here yet. I think I can get out of the group huddle." They backed off but stayed nearby.

Jerry brought over some extra clips for my Glock. "Just in case," he said with a grin.

"You guys all weaponed up?"

"Yep. The pawns have all agreed—we don't plan on dying."

"That's the mind-set I want." I was with Martini—I didn't want to lose anyone from our side.

Chuckie and Martini were discussing strategy, and the conversation was getting animated. I went to them, Animal Planet trailing me.

"We need to stop them here," Martini said.

"No argument. I'd like an idea of how." Chuckie looked around. "Do we need to call in more agents, yours or mine?"

"No." They both looked at me. "Look, they're the white side, okay? Accept it. We have no freaking idea of what they're going to throw at us, just that it's going to probably hurt. So our initial strategy has to be a reactive one. I don't like it any more than you guys do, but that's the reality. If we need more backup, we'll call for it."

"If they don't knock out telecommunications," Chuckie said.

"Too late," Kevin was holding his phone. "Just tried to call for backup. No signal, no connection, nothing."

"They're almost here, then." I grabbed Martini's hand and pulled him out of the group. Animal Planet followed. "Um, guys? Appreciate your slavish devotion to your assigned positions, but a little privacy?"

"Oh," Willem said, sounding embarrassed. "Apologies." They backed off.

I looked around. We weren't the only couple having that "this may be good-bye" chat. Animal Planet seemed to catch on, too, and apparently only Wrolph was mateless on this journey. "I hate these people."

"Me too, baby." Martini wrapped his arms around me. "Promise me you'll stay out of it."

"Jeff, I can't promise that, and you know it. They're gunning for me, under the laws of this ritual. I know I'll be getting involved."

"You'll have to get through your honor guard first, and they seem dedicated, thankfully."

I leaned my head against his chest. "They'll be gunning for you, too, you know."

"I know. I'm used to it."

"You know, in all the movies and TV shows, the happy couple always loses a member either right before or right after they get married." I hated where my mind went during times of trouble.

Martini picked me up, and I wrapped myself around him. "It'll be fine, baby. I promise. They've thrown worse at us, and we've been fine."

I knew this was a blatant lie and that Martini knew it was a lie as well. I chose not to mention it. We held each other tightly for far too short a time. Then he kissed me deeply. Like every kiss of his, it was fabulous and arousing, and I didn't want to stop. The fear that it could be the last kiss of his I'd ever have didn't make it better, though—it made it bittersweet.

We probably wouldn't have stopped, but suddenly there was wind and a roaring. We broke apart a bit and looked in the sky. A ship worthy of an Imperial Battle Cruiser from *Star Wars* appeared out of nowhere, hovering over us. Three shuttles disengaged from it, circled us, then flew off. I could tell they'd gone to land on the three peaks chosen for their little game of Interplanetary Risk. The battle cruiser rose up, disappearing as it did so. I assumed it was still there, merely cloaked again.

Martini set me down. "Be good, be careful, and stay in the back. Run if you have to. Get through the gate if you can. And remember that, no matter what happens, I love you, and I always will."

He ran away from me at hyperspeed before I could say anything. But it didn't matter—my superempath knew how much I loved him.

A whole lot of people appeared in front of us. More than we had. I spotted the power players—in the back, like a lot of ours were.

Gregory's voice rang out. "Let the Ritual of Worth begin!"

CHAPTER 50

MOIRA JUMPED OUT IN FRONT and started for us. To my horror, and Martini and Chuckie's obvious shock, Christopher did the same. They headed straight for each other.

A variety of people from the other side charged out as well. "They're all Amazons," Serene called. "They look like humans, but they're not."

Animal Planet surrounded me, but I had a good view of what was going on anyway.

Our side was using a lot of guns, mostly semiautomatics. The problem was, the Amazons could take a lot of punishment. "How many bullets will it take to down one of your people?" I asked Queen Renata.

"Many. We are . . . enhanced."

"No kidding." Martini was barking orders, and our team was fanning out. Kyrellis leaped over a clutch of others and headed straight for him, but he wasn't looking in her direction. "Jeff, look out!"

He turned just in time, and they were at it. This time I could tell she wasn't holding back. He wasn't, either, and he'd picked up a lot from their last fight, because he was dodging her strikes better.

"We need to help them."

"We need to stay back," Felicia said. "As your mate requested."

I looked at the last place I'd seen Christopher. Now there were three of him, all fighting with Moira, but I had a feel-

ing they were all hitting the real one. "Serene, who's the real
Christopher?"

"The one on the left!" Reader and Tim heard her, and they
both ran toward this clutch of bodies. "Now on the right! No,
don't, that's him!" Serene lost it and ran at hyperspeed. She hit
into Christopher and tackled him.

Reader and Tim hit the fake Christophers, hard, and they
shifted to look like what I'd expected them to be—the two
guys from THEhotel. Nice to be right, hoped Tim and Reader
would really hurt them. Human versus A-C was an uneven
fight, but my guys had been working with A-Cs for a long time
and were doing pretty well.

The rest of the guys who were supposed to be guarding
Serene were over there now, and that brawl became hard to
follow.

Not a lot of gunshots any more, not just from this group
but all of our side seemed to have stopped shooting. It made
sense—everyone was too jumbled up to shoot without a
real risk of hitting our own side. The fight was now the old-
fashioned kind—hand-to-hand, edged weapons, blunt instru-
ments, completely brutal.

Gower ran to me and shoved in. "Kitty, take my hand!" I
did and felt a power flow I'd experienced once before. I felt
someone hold me up, saw Queen Renata grab Gower and
hold him upright, then it stopped.

"Paul, are you okay?"

"Yes," he said slowly. "It can't last, but it's necessary. ACE
knows what Jeff doesn't."

I nodded. "It's all about being strong enough to marry in,
right?"

"Pretty much." He squeezed my hand. "You'll do fine. I
have to go help Jeff." Then he disappeared. I saw him slam
into Kyrellis just before she could stab a long, glowing stick
into Martini.

"What the hell is she using?"

Martini rolled away just in time. Since I was wearing his
jacket, I could see him clearly because of his shirt. This meant,
of course, that others could see him clearly, too.

"A battle staff," Queen Renata answered.

Martini was on his feet; he and Gower were trying to
get around the staff, but Kyrellis was good with it, and they
weren't having a lot of luck.

"Why do the ends glow?"

"They are supercharged and cause more damage."

An end hit Gower, and I heard him shout. He wasn't down or out, but I knew he was hurt.

"Wow, did George Lucas spend time with you guys?"

"I don't follow you."

"Few ever do, Renata. Got any more of those puppies lying about?"

"Yes, I brought some with me, in case we faced resistance."

"Where they at?"

"In Neeraj's ship."

"Iguanodon, can you get stuff out of your ship without leaving the field of battle here?"

"Yes, but why? Our instructions are to stay back and guard you."

"And the eight of you, all primed for serious butt-kicking, you're alright with that? You're good to, you know, fly across space to come here and hang in the back and watch the battle but have nothing to do with the outcome?"

There was a lot of shifting of paws and swishing of tails.

"I have four dogs and three cats, and while they don't walk upright or talk or anything, they'd all be in it if they were here. And did I mention that iguanas and Komodo dragons can be really nasty?"

More paw shifting and tail swishing, with a little muttering added in.

Chuckie and Alexander were engaged with Lenore and Gregory. It was sort of even, or would have been if there hadn't been three extra Amazons helping the other side. Only Moira and Kyrellis had the staffs.

"Why don't the grunts have the battle staff?"

"It has to be earned."

"I'm a brown belt in kung fu. And I've been staff trained." Okay, sort of a lie. Not on the staff trained, on the belt level. I hadn't tested for brown yet. Because I kept missing the test for end-of-the-world crap. But I was ready, my sifu said so. Well, he'd said I was ready to learn if I was really up to brown standards, but I took that to mean I was ready for black and just needed to hurry it up.

"I don't know—" Queen Renata was interrupted by a bunch of battle staffs dropping to the ground in front of us.

"I'm with the Naked Ape," Jareen said. "Let's get in there

and kick some evil overlord butt." I realized it was the first time I'd heard her talk.

I grabbed a battle staff, and so did she. "Jareen, I think this is the beginning of a beautiful friendship."

She gave me the Iguanodon smile. "Neeraj never wants to let me do anything, either. Because I always end up saving him."

"Ain't it the truth, soul sister? But you have to love them anyway. Especially when they're totally hot."

"You can tell Neeraj is hot?" she asked, sounding surprised.

I shrugged. "He said you were the queen of hotness on your planet. Didn't figure he was barking, therefore, by your standards."

Queen Renata showed me how to activate the battle staff. It was easy. It felt like any other staff, but seemed weighted like a javelin. No worries, my sadistic track coaches had wanted everyone to know how to do every single track and field event, so in case someone was sick, one of the rest of us could cover. The less said about my pole-vaulting the better, but I hadn't been awful at javelin.

Our side was getting pummeled. I saw two of my flyboys down, Joe and Walker. I also saw Lorraine kicking butt while protecting them. "Can one of you hyperspeed a battle staff to the three A-C girls on our side?" I felt someone go past me and looked around. Wrolph and three battle staffs were missing. Lorraine started spinning something. Claudia next, then Serene.

Wrolph was back. "The second female needs help." He meant Claudia, I assumed, because she was surrounded. Wrolph didn't wait for anyone to comment, he disappeared again, and reappeared next to her.

"So, guys? You gonna let Wrolph have all the fun and the glory?"

"Our side is not doing well," Willem admitted as more Amazons appeared.

"Our side's about to lose. This is where, in chess, the queen comes in."

"The queen also comes in when you're about to win." Felicia pointed. Uma was there with the new contingent of warrior women, and she was swinging something that looked remarkably like a battle ax. She was also glowing.

"Three guesses where the Free Women's PPB net is currently being housed, and the first two don't count."

The others around me all nodded. "It's time to fight," Queen Renata said. "To avenge the ills done to our people and to save the lives of our new friends."

They took off, with a lot of snarling, hissing, yowling, and banshee screaming. Only Jareen and I were still standing there.

"I'll stick with you," she said. "At least for a while."

"Works for me, girlfriend." I pulled my iPod out of my purse while I took my shoes off. "Not being rude, just need some tunes." I took Poofikins out and put it into the pocket of Martini's jacket. Reality told me my purse had to stay here and hold down the fort by itself.

"I understand. Same here. Our players are a little different, but the effect is the same." She fiddled with something, and I heard faint, odd sounds.

I tuned my iPod to my new Fight Songs mix. Ironically enough, 'We Want the Airwaves' by the Ramones was song number one. "All ready?"

"Yes."

"Then, Jareen? Let's go show these interstellar assholes how Naked Apes and Iguanodons do things out here in the wild, wild West."

CHAPTER 51

WE TOOK OFF. I was a hurdler with a perfect four-step and she was a Giant Lizard, but we were in complete sync with each other.

We hit the people around Chuckie and Alexander first. I should have had more trouble with the staff than I was. This dawned on me when I sliced off an Amazon's head right before she could break Chuckie's back.

"Thanks," he gasped. "What the hell are you doing?"

"Kicking butt and taking names. You know, routine." I slammed the staff into another Amazon's stomach. It went through her. Jareen lopped her head off and finished off the third Amazon. I had to figure ACE was helping me, and I decided if there was ever a time to let the superconsciousness give you a major assist, it was now.

Lenore and Gregory took off, running toward Uma. Alexander looked awful. "Chuckie, you have to get him out of the battle, and you have to stay with him and protect him."

"What?"

I grabbed his lapel. "Think! No ruler on Alpha Four means complete destabilization of that solar system. Guess what planet will lose?"

"Ours, got it." He grabbed me and held me. "Be careful."

"I will. Get to some sort of defensible point. I'm sure we're going to have more wounded. I'll send them to you. Protect them—and yourself," I felt compelled to add. I was noting a little too much willingness to take the bullets from Chuckie, and I liked that attitude from him only slightly more than I liked it from Martini.

He nodded, grabbed Alexander, and went back to where I'd been with the Animal Planet folks. I had a bishop and a rook out, and from what I could tell, half of my pawns.

"We need to clear out the extra pawns," Jareen said.

I had to agree. There were a lot of them. "I'm open to ideas."

She cocked her head at me. "Even if they're crazy?"

"I'm the queen of the crazy ideas, babe."

"Good. Stand back and be ready." She stepped away from me then started twirling her battle staff over her head. "Do what I'm doing!"

I did. It was like a funky baton. It was also speeding up. A lot. We spun for what seemed like forever but reality said was only about thirty seconds. I noted that the extra Amazons were bearing down on us. All of them.

"Throw it toward them . . . now!" Jareen shouted.

We both did. It was really impressive. The staffs spun like dervishes but with a clear intent to maim if not kill. At least, Jareen's was. Mine was sort of flying straight but without a clear goal.

"Aim it!" Jareen snapped. I looked over; she was moving her hands around as if she were doing some funky fake kung fu move. I did the same, and suddenly my staff was also actually doing its job.

"Do I want to know how this is working?"

"Tell you when we have the time. I can't keep this up forever."

I had to figure that beings that could create spatiotemporal warps and move big ships on their own could also affect a couple of space-aged javelins. The battle staffs were slicing through Amazonian necks as if they were made of butter and the staffs were hot knives. I'd have been grossed out if I hadn't known exactly what said Amazons were going to do to my people if we didn't decapitate them.

The staffs flew back to us; we spun them again, and did the whole weird thing again. And again. The Amazons tried to shift their locations, but the staffs went where we wanted them to. They were close to impossible to avoid in this manner, for which I was thankful—I didn't credit myself with enough skill to thrust and parry effectively from a distance. I just kept on doing whatever Jareen was doing until we'd lowered the number of extra Amazons down to very, very few.

Those few broke off and headed for other melees while our staffs sailed back to us again, nice as you please. "These are wicked cool boomerangs."

"Yes, but they only work like that for crowd control. We have to use them like true battle staffs now, we'll be in too close."

Jareen and I headed for the dog pile that had Reader and Christopher in it. It was the next closest, and the rest of the Animal Planet folks had gone to support Lorraine and Claudia, except Neeraj, who was with Martini and Gower. The three of them weren't making a dent in Kyrellis.

Sadly, the group we went to wasn't doing much better against Moira and her assistants. "Yo, freak chick! Why don't you fight someone your own sex?"

She spun toward me and smiled widely. "My mate says we should keep you."

"Good luck with that." I ran toward her, flipped in mid-air and landed with my feet on her chest. She fell back, and I somersaulted over her to land on my feet. Yeah, ACE was definitely spotting me.

This didn't slow Moira down much, but it got her away from everyone else. I saw Jareen start kicking random Amazonian butt and the others manage to regroup. Tim was hurt, and so was Christopher. "James, get them out of here! Go to Chuckie."

Serene was still up and fighting. Maybe the battle staffs responded well to women, not just Jareen and the Amazons, because she was a lot better with it than I'd have expected. Reader and Kevin started to get the others moving. Brian was down, and Serene was standing over him, keeping an Amazonian pawn and the two image-changing A-Cs at bay.

Moira charged me. I planted the staff and used it to let me slam both feet into her stomach. She flew back, still away from the others, which was what I wanted.

Jareen finished off the spares, then leaped over to Serene. She sliced the Amazon down the middle, then she and Serene each took one of the A-Cs. They shifted to look like me. Serene gave a snort of disgust and stabbed hers through the heart. Jareen grabbed the one she was fighting by the head and gave it a vicious twist. The A-C went down. I was glad he didn't look like me any more, since he was lying on his front but his face was staring at me. For certain it was the guy who'd held the door for me at THEhotel. The one Serene had killed was indeed the other one. Good. Flirting was not an issue. Fake flirting really pissed me off.

Serene and Jareen each grabbed an arm and dragged Brian back. I had no idea where Tito was.

Moira was on me again, and now it was just the two of us. There was a variety of staff-to-staff slamming that didn't do much other than make my arms feel like they were jolting out of their sockets. The staff spinning had been a lot more fun and much easier on the limbs.

"You will enjoy being with me and my mate." She spun and tried to kick my legs out.

I jumped and landed safely. "I doubt it. I like men. Big, strong, manly men. In fact, I like their hands all over me. And their other parts inside me."

She was young and easy to bait. "You disgust me!" She charged, I sidestepped and hit her in the stomach with the side of the staff. Knocked the wind out of her, but she grabbed my staff and wrenched it out of my hands, which knocked me back and down. Now she had two, and she was good with them. Moira grinned. "Get ready to die."

I was in the same crouch I'd spent years in—my feet and hands were set just the way they were in the sprinter's blocks before the gun went off. I let her get a little closer, then pushed off with all my strength.

I hit her stomach and took her down. Grabbed the pressure points on her arms and squeezed for all I was worth. Lucked out that they were in roughly the same place on her as on a human. Her hands released the staffs.

Moira flipped us, so she was on top of me. She felt as heavy as Martini and she was definitely as strong. But I had to wrestle him all the time after I harpooned him. I wrapped my arms and legs around her and held on.

"Mmmm, I like this," she said against my neck. I was sort of surprised—in my experience, anyone being this close to my neck would cause me to start to lose control. Apparently not when I was fighting for my life. I was thankful for small favors and worked to get out of the under position.

I heard someone shouting instructions. To me, I realized. "Move, move, move! Don't let her hit your head, block with your arms!" It was Tito, and I did what he said—just in time. Moira rained some blows down, but they hit my forearms. She reared back, and I slammed the heel of my hand into her nose. It knocked her back.

"Release your legs!" I did as Tito said, pulled my knees to my chest, and slammed my feet into her sternum. She went onto her back and off of me. I scrambled to my feet and grabbed a staff as I did so.

"Tito, you okay?" I couldn't see him. Anywhere. I looked around to see someone rolling on the ground with Gregory.

Moira tried to get up; I kicked her in the head and sent her flying back. Tito was on top of Gregory, pounding him. Moira flipped onto her feet, I slammed my staff into her side, and she went down again. Tito was still pounding Gregory—A-C or no A-C, Gregory wasn't looking like he had much, if any, fight left.

Moira crawled to her hands and knees and went for her staff, but I kicked it away. "You won't fight me equally?" she asked. Tito was off Gregory now, and Gregory wasn't moving at all.

I thought about it, spun the staff, and rammed it right into her head. "No. Oh, and, by the way?" I pulled the staff out. There was a huge hole in her head, and I felt confident she was dead. "When I punched you, that was really for me. This was for James."

CHAPTER 52

TITO AND I LOOKED AT EACH OTHER. "Grab a staff, not that you seem to need one."

"Never hurts." He picked up Moira's.

"Is Gregory alive?"

"No." He shrugged. "I'm used to someone tapping out or a ref telling me to stop. Got carried away." He didn't sound upset about it.

"Restraint is not exactly my watchword, either." I took a good look around. Claudia and the Major Doggies had cleared out their portion. I could see bodies down, but they didn't look like ours. Glanced toward where I'd sent Chuckie. We had a lot of people over there, and most of them looked like crap.

Jareen ran over to me. "We have just two battles still going on." She pointed. One was Martini and Neeraj against Kyrellis. And the other was Lenore and Uma against the Cat People and Queen Renata.

Kyrellis did a leaping splits kick and hit Martini and Neeraj in their guts. They both went down. She swung her staff up, over Martini. He wasn't moving.

"KYRELLIS!" I bellowed as loudly as I could. She stopped and turned. I bent down and yanked Moira's head up by her hair. "Guess what?"

She arched back and screamed. It sounded how I figured a thousand banshees in an echo chamber would. And while she was occupied, I decided to see if the rusty javelin skills were up to the task. Did the little run, aimed, and threw. Kyrellis wasn't looking at me or at the staff heading toward her.

Jareen and I ran forward. I didn't have to ask her plan. Get our guys, get them out of the way of danger. My impromptu javelin hit just as Kyrellis straightened up. Unfortunately, it speared through her hip, meaning she wasn't dead.

She bared her teeth at me. "I will kill him in the worst way possible." She spun her staff and aimed it right at Martini's groin.

Jareen's staff hit Kyrellis' and knocked it out of her hand. It fell, missed Martini by a hair, and rolled away. Kyrellis snarled and pulled my staff out of her body. Now she aimed it at Neeraj. I decided it was my turn to represent again and went for the long jump.

Hit Kyrellis in her chest. Due to her injury, it knocked her down. Due to her being the Amazonian Super Bitch, she held onto the staff. I tried to scramble away, but she got me, dragged me back, and slammed me up against her, my back to her chest. She also wrapped her other arm around me and started to squeeze. My arms were free, but the best I could do was lock my hands against her chin to keep her from head-butting me.

I had perfect clarity. I could see Tito drag Martini away and Jareen do the same with Neeraj. Others ran up to help them. I saw Claudia slam adrenaline into Martini's chest, heard him bellow, saw Claudia and Tito throw themselves on him, saw Jareen do something to Neeraj to bring him back to consciousness. I had the clarity because Kyrellis was squeezing the life out of me, and I got the feeling I was getting to see everyone before she crushed me to death.

"I will make you pay," she whispered. "My God will take you to the depths of hell."

"There a lot of men in your hell?" I gasped out.

"Yes. They will have their way with you constantly."

"Sounds like heaven to me." Maybe I'd luck out and when Martini died, he'd end up there. I could spend eternity with him ravaging me.

She snarled at me. "I am not confused by you. You are a warrior. You don't belong to any man." She spat the word. "You belong with us, with the Free Women."

"I like Renata. I could hang with her. You, not so much."

"Renata is weak."

"She's your queen." I was starting to black out.

"I serve my God."

"Your 'god' is taking orders from a man."

"You know nothing about my God."

"I know everything about your god."

"I will not kill you," Kyrellis whispered to me. "I will save you and show you the true way."

I found myself wondering what ACE was doing, since I wasn't feeling like I was going to survive this encounter. Then again, death might be better than what I guessed Kyrellis had in store for me if she let me live. My arms were weakening, and my vision was at pinpoint. I wasn't out, but I was close. I wondered when I'd feel my ribs crack.

I heard a crack, and Kyrellis let go a bit. I took a breath— the crack hadn't been my ribs. My vision came back a little. Someone was on his knees next to us, hitting Kyrellis in the head. With his bare fists. He was doing damage . . . and he was growling.

She released me and shoved me away, presumably to focus on the stronger threat. Martini was high on adrenaline, and he was at "lion takes over the veldt" with his roar. His hands were moving so fast I couldn't see them anymore. Kyrellis was still in it, and she managed to grab him around his waist and use that to turn herself and get onto her knees.

Before she could capitalize on this, Martini made a double fist and slammed his hands down on the back of her head. He did this until she stopped moving—then he did it some more.

I could breathe, and nothing seemed broken. My feet hurt, but I'd run around barefoot in the desert before; I could ignore it. Good. I got to my hands and knees. "Jeff." He didn't stop. "Jeff, baby . . . stop. I think she's dead."

He looked at me and his eyes were wild. "I know what she wanted to do to you."

"It doesn't matter now." My body was shaking. "Jeff, it's not over."

Martini took Kyrellis' head and twisted. If she hadn't been dead before, she was now. He threw her body away and grabbed me. His hearts were pounding, and he was shaking. I held him and let him rock me for a few moments.

A scream rang out. We both turned toward the sound. Tito had, as near as I could tell, just broken Lenore's neck. Claudia had Wrolph's arm around her shoulders and was trying to get him back to the others. Queen Renata, Felicia, and Arup were nearby. But the scream was from Uma. She was swinging her ax in a circle, and as Claudia and Wrolph got closer, I could see he'd been slashed.

"Tito, down!" I shouted as loudly as I could, and he ducked. Uma's ax whizzed over his head. He rolled away, but she was after him. Queen Renata planted her staff and used it to steady herself as she swung her body toward Uma. She connected with Uma's side and staggered her enough that the next swing of the ax also missed Tito.

"GET OUT!" Martini bellowed.

Tito didn't argue, he ran. But the other three didn't. Uma turned and started bearing down on them again. She looked uninjured, and she was still glowing.

Uma hit Felicia. Felicia screamed, a cat's shriek of pain. Arup managed to grab her. He lifted her into his arms and ran back to the others. Uma's ax just missed him.

"Jeff, we have to get Renata away from her."

"On it." Martini ran at hyperspeed. I couldn't see him, but I saw Queen Renata go flying just before Uma's ax cleaved her in two.

I stood up. "Bitch Leader!"

Uma looked at me. "You. How dare you still stand!"

"It's a human thing. We Americans pride ourselves on it." I picked up a staff. "We're all over the scrappy attitudes. The get-knocked-down-and-get-back-up mind-set."

She smiled. "You will not get up again."

I shrugged and used it as an opportunity to relax my back and shoulders a bit. "Your side's down. Just the White Queen to protect her king. I still have active pieces on the board."

"They can't help you."

We were close to each other. Not close enough for the weapons to hit, but close enough that we didn't have to scream.

"They aren't supposed to help me, are they? Not now."

"No. You will face me as your final test."

"Babe, you know, you can stop with the My Royal Lord crap, I know the plan. I know what's inside you and what King Creepola has planned. I also know that you're going to be very expendable once you send your god-in-the-machine inside him."

She laughed. "But that presumes I will let him have this power. We have discussed it—the power is better in a woman. Stronger, more ruthless."

"The power doesn't have to work like that. It can protect and serve and love."

"Your planet is weaker than mine, your power is weaker than mine, and you are weaker than me. I will enjoy killing you."

"Uma? Got one thing to say to you." I shifted into a fighting stance. "Bring it."

CHAPTER 53

AS I WAITED FOR UMA TO MAKE A MOVE, ACE spoke in my head. Kitty, ACE wants Kitty to know that Kitty and ACE will be fighting together now. Kitty will see things as ACE can see them, do things as ACE can do them.

Come again? ACE? Haven't you been helping me all this fight?

No, Kitty. ACE did not need to.

Wow. I really was black-belt material.

ACE spoke again, and he sounded embarrassed. Kitty is very . . . lucky. That is good.

Maybe I'd wait to go for the brown-belt test.

ACE thinks that might be wise.

Geez . . . I didn't even have to actively think the thought with ACE inside. I wondered if Martini could read me like this now.

Not quite. Jeff is very upset. All the others are very upset. Why?

The other consciousness and ACE have blocked everyone out. Kitty and Uma will fight alone now. No one can help Kitty.

Other than you.

Yes.

That's all I'll need, ACE.

ACE subsided, but I could feel him there. It was as though my whole mind expanded to see every living thing in the world and beyond. It was startling and amazing and a little frightening. Distracting, in a way, but a scary Valkyrie with a loaded ax can really pull you back into the moment.

Uma ran toward me, and I knew we were moving fast, but it seemed slow at the same time. I looked into her eyes, and I could see the other consciousness there. It was filled with hatred and anger, and it despised me, despised us, despised ACE most of all. By taking a name ACE had become more human, and so the other one loathed ACE.

Uma's ax swung, I dodged, and it whizzed by me. I flipped the staff toward her stomach. She twirled, and the staff missed. She kept spinning, the ax swung toward my head. I ducked and spun the staff toward her legs. Uma jumped and landed farther away.

This went on for what seemed like moments and hours at the same time. I was tired, but stopping wasn't an option.

The song in my ears changed, and I realized I still had my iPod on. I'd been so involved with staying alive that I hadn't noticed. Aerosmith's "Nine Lives" came yowling on. I started to laugh.

"What is funny?" Uma hadn't hit me yet, but I hadn't hit her, either.

"God likes me."

"Your God does not exist. Only power exists."

"You know, every time I fight some fugly monster or crazy bitch like yourself, Uma, someone tells me there is no God. But I know they're wrong."

Uma lunged at me, but I managed to jump out of the way. As I did, I realized we weren't on the ground any more. We were floating in the air.

Looking around at the view was stupid. Uma slammed into me, with her body, not her ax. I was lucky that way. Not so lucky that I didn't lose hold of my staff. It fell, and apparently it didn't get to float if I wasn't holding it. I saw it hit the ground and stick in the sand.

I rolled and kept rolling, Uma's ax just missing where I had been a moment before. I started to feel like a hamster in a ball.

AC/DC's "Back in Black" came on. Fitting—I was the Black Queen, after all. I managed to roll and shove away against nothing to get far enough way from Uma to get to my feet. I started running.

I was a sprinter, and I was staying in front of her. But the superconsciousnesses had created some sort of weird bubble around us. Which meant I was running in circles, but circles in any direction, including the impossible ones. Laws of gravity seemed suspended, but the ax was still missing me, so I was good with it.

ACE, any shot of us doing something more proactive? Just asking.

If ACE does, she will attack the others.

An odd thought occurred. ACE . . . name her. Name the other consciousness.

ACE cannot do that, Kitty! ACE does not have the right.

Why not? I name stuff all the time.

Uma was almost on me. Decided to see just how out of whack with the laws of physics we were. Instead of running, I jumped. I was standing upside down on the air, so the ground looked like the sky to me. I jumped for the ground.

It worked. I was across our Super Hamster Ball, and I hadn't gone splat.

Decided all the talking in my mind was getting old. "ACE, name her!"

"Who are you talking to?" Uma shouted at me while she barreled toward me.

I jumped again, in a different direction. "I'm talking to ACE. He's in me. Like Lilith Fair is in you."

"That is not her name!"

"Well, she didn't pick one, neither did you. ACE and I like Lilith. Sort of fitting."

"Stop using that name!"

Wow, this really bugged them. Good. "Lilith and Uma, sittin' in a tree, trying to kill poor little Kit-ty." Hey, wasn't the greatest rhyme, but I was trying to stay alive here.

This continued for a bit, me taunting, them trying to kill me. I didn't have a weapon other than my speed and my mouth, both of which were running down. The ball of nothing we were in shifted—I got the impression Lilith had won some fight she and ACE were having at the same time, a fight I couldn't comprehend but could just feel in the background—and I went flying.

Landed flat on my back. Facing the ground. The trippiness was what I expected hard drugs to do to a person. Found myself glad I'd never indulged and swore to never start. My stomach didn't enjoy the view.

The wind was knocked out of me, so I got to see how upset and frightened everyone on the ground looked. Chuckie, Tito, Reader, and Michael were restraining Martini. All the other males from Earth were down, though they appeared to be alive. Animal Planet was fifty-fifty on the sexes. Bottom line— our side was battered.

Uma thundered toward me, ax up. She swung, I dodged. Swing, dodge, swing. I was still on my back, and her legs were straddling me. I wasn't going to luck out much longer.

I saw someone extract from our group—Jareen was running, toward our bubble if I was any judge. There was something on her shoulder, and I realized it was a Poof. I wondered if Poofikins was alive or squished in my jacket pocket, but I was too busy dodging to say anything.

Jareen grabbed my staff out of the ground. "Kitty!" She threw it, with a lot better aim than I had. It pierced the bubble we were in and sailed right for me. I grabbed Uma's leg and used it to help slide myself under her. Rolled, jumped up, and grabbed the staff as if I'd done this move a thousand times before.

Chose not to marvel. Spun and stabbed, just as Uma was spinning, ax over her head, and coming for me.

The staff went through her stomach. All the way through to the middle and stuck there. I leaped back as she stared at me. "I . . . cannot die."

"Wanna bet?"

The ax fell out of her hands and tumbled to the ground. She grabbed the staff with both hands and tried to pull it out of herself. The bubble we were in started shaking.

Uma looked at me again. "I . . . cannot die. She . . . promised."

"She lied." I watched the light go out of Uma's eyes. "Sayonara, Bitch Leader." I looked around. "ACE, we going down?"

Yes, Kitty. Lilith is still fighting to survive.

I thought about what I knew from when we'd first found ACE. "Take us down, to Jareen." The bubble started to lower. "Soul sister! Need your help, if you're up for it."

Jareen nodded, but Lilith still had some power, because our bubble shifted, far away from Jareen and the others. It was shaking, and I saw Uma's body tumble out and hit the ground, staff still inside her. I knew she was dead.

I also knew when the bubble was gone because I started to tumble as if gravity was back and seriously pissed that I'd ignored it for so long. I closed my eyes and winced. This was going to hurt. A lot.

But it didn't hurt all that much. Because instead of hitting the ground, I fell where I'd been falling for the past year—into Martini's arms.

"Ooof!" Okay, it wasn't the most smooth or romantic thing he could have said, but I was okay with it.

"I'm not that heavy!"

"Baby, you're not heavy at all. You just fell a long way." He was shaking. "I hate it when you do that, you know." I shifted and wrapped my legs around his waist. He grinned. "But I so love it when you do that."

I kissed him, hard. But not too long. "Jeff, you have to get me back to Jareen."

"I'm right here." So she was. Forgot, all these folks had the superspeed. "Naked Apes are really into public displays of affection. It's nauseating back there, and here, and you've rubbed off on the Cat People and Major Doggies, too."

"Jeff, meet Jareen, my new best friend forever. Jareen, we need to channel Lilith the Bitch Goddess through you. Jeff, need to get down." Martini released me unwillingly.

"Er . . . while that sounds great, I think I'll choose not becoming like Uma."

Kitty, we must do it now. ACE cannot contain Lilith any longer.

"Has to be now. Jareen, it goes through you, and you birth it. Somehow. Otherwise, Lilith will be around and able to join with someone like Uma, or someone worse."

Jareen looked apprehensive, at least as much as a Giant Lizard could. "Why me?"

"Because you're just like Kitty," Martini said. "Only green and with a tail. But personality and brainwise? You're her twin."

Kitty!

"ACE is freaking, Jareen. Please." I took her hand.

She nodded. "Okay. Tell Neeraj—"

We didn't get to find out what she wanted us to tell him, though I could guess, because her head went back sharply. Martini caught her before she went down. She was rigid, but because ACE was inside me, I could see a glowing substance funneling into her. It went in golden, but it came out all the colors of the Pantone Matching System color book.

I watched the color motes fly through the air. They swirled around everyone with us, then everyone on the planet, then the planet itself. I watched via ACE, so I saw the colored pieces of Lilith's consciousness swirl through our solar system then move off, toward Alpha Centauri.

It is done. Lilith is scattered. ACE sounded sad.

Are we safe from her?

Yes. Lilith is one with the cosmos now and can join God.

Interesting. Even the superconsciousnesses got to go to Heaven apparently. Even the ones who'd tried to take over the universe.

God forgives.

Oh, right. ACE heard more than top-layer, focused thoughts. How could God forgive her?

Once Lilith was . . . birthed . . . Lilith saw all and so could understand Lilith's wrongdoing. And repent. ACE sounded a little unsure on this point, and I decided we could table the rest of our intergalactic comparative religion course for another time. However, ACE still sounded sad.

Do you envy her?

In a way. But ACE pities Lilith more. ACE has what Lilith did not.

Love.

Yes. Because of Kitty.

No. Because of ACE. You loved Earth before you met me, ACE. You cared and protected and mourned its inhabitants as your own. *You* did that, not me, not Paul. You could have told us you were God and we would have believed you. But you didn't, because you also have humility. If you want to leave us, I'll birth you. But if you want to stay, we would be happier.

ACE wants to stay. ACE has a home here, and a purpose.

Jareen groaned and came back. "That sucked. Did it work?"

"Yes, good job. You birthed a demigoddess and saved the universe."

She grinned at me. "So, from what I gather for you guys, routine."

CHAPTER 54

"LET'S GO HOME," Martini said.

"It's not over, Jeff."

"Looks over to me."

"Where's the battle cruiser?"

"Good point." Martini looked up. "I don't see it, but that might not mean anything."

Kitty, the ship has taken its shuttles and is heading back to Alpha Centauri.

Why?

The rules must be followed.

They have rules and follow them?

Yes. Does Kitty wish a listing of the rules?

No, ACE. I'll take your word for it. Of course, our game has rules, too. I told Martini that the ship was gone.

"Good, so we're done."

"No. We have to take the king."

He groaned. "How? He's on Alpha Four."

ACE?

Yes, Kitty. Who should come?

All, if they can stand the trip.

Many are hurt, but all can survive it.

And come back?

If they choose to. There was evasion in ACE's tone.

I know what's coming. And what I have to risk.

Very well.

Billy Idol's 'Cradle of Love' started in my ears as I felt ACE gather us all up, dead bodies included.

"Fitting song." Martini put his arm around me.

"You can hear it?" I wondered if my iPod was too loud.

"I think we can all hear it. ACE must like your musical taste. Someone should."

We time warped. That's the only way to describe it, though we didn't have to dance or anything. But once we were all in ACE's bubble, so to speak, we shifted. I could see the planets, stars, and empty space whiz by us, but I got the impression I was the only one who could.

We landed at a plaza in front of a place that made Martini Manor look like welfare housing. Frankly, it made the Taj Mahal look skimpy. Huge, white, built on the side of a hill— the architects had wanted to make darned sure that when you stood at the bottom of the many steps leading up you knew you were an insignificant peasant.

"Guess this is your family estate."

"Yeah." Martini sounded awed. I did my best not to feel anything about that.

A crowd appeared around us. It parted a bit as a group of people came down the stairs. One was old and leaning on a cane. I didn't buy that he needed it and figured this was King Adolphus.

I looked around. Our group was all on its feet. Sure, some of our group were being held up on their feet, but we were still standing. On cue, Elton John's "I'm Still Standing" came on.

"Barely," Tim called out. The others chuckled. Nice to know ACE wanted to share my tunes with everyone. I wasn't sure they worked for the others like they did for me, but I didn't have any time to worry about it because King Creepola was in front of us.

The king stopped at a stair landing about fifty steps above us and looked around. "The Rituals are completed!" His voice boomed. He wasn't bellowing like Martini—it was more like he was speaking through a super-duper sound system.

"How's he doing that?"

"Troubadour." Martini sounded as unimpressed with that skill as Christopher had when he'd told me about it. "Vocal projection is one of the traits."

"Well, that explains a lot." Most actors don't want to give up the gig of a lifetime, after all. I detached from Martini. "Wait here, Jeff."

I took off my headphones, put my iPod into a jacket pocket,

and started up the stairs at a trot. The king was glaring at me.
I didn't care. He wasn't getting to win with no pieces left on
the board. I did have a question, though. ACE, how is it I can
understand him and see him move at human speeds?

ACE is providing translations for sight and sound. All will
understand and see each other.

You rock. I looked up. Sadly, I was still a lot of steps away
from the king.

"You are found not worthy," he said to me, voice still
booming out.

I shrugged and kept on going. No one tried to stop me.
Reached his level without panting. My track coaches had
lived by the train and pain method. Fifty stairs was nothing,
I'd learned to do two hundred at a go.

"You are not worthy in my sight," he said. Close up he was
kind of icky. If I stripped away decades, he might have once
looked good. Now, he looked old and shriveled. He didn't have
old person smell, which confirmed to me he wasn't nearly as
decrepit as he was acting. Happily, I didn't see Alfred in him
anywhere, so I could comfort myself that, should I ever get
married to him, Martini wouldn't age like this.

"Yeah, and you're really gross, but, hey, we can't have everything." My voice was booming, too. "Wow, you a walking
microphone or something?"

"Hardly," he snarled.

ACE is projecting Kitty's voice.

Thanks, big guy. I looked around. "Nice view. Bet it's better from way up top there. So, just to bring the populace up
to speed with the *Reader's Digest* version of current events,
you've been plotting to overthrow the entire solar system's
planetary leaders, toss a godlike superconsciousness inside
yourself, then rule everyone forever from on high. Did I miss
anything?"

"How dare you?" He was bellowing, but still, Martini did
it better.

"Oh, blah, blah, blah. ACE? Any way you can save us all a
lot of time and needless blathering and just show the folks at
home what's been going on across the railroad tracks?"

I felt something radiate out of me. There were gasps and a
lot of muttering. I felt it circle this world and send itself out to
the other worlds in the solar system. Thanks. Hope it wasn't
overkill.

They deserved to know.

King Adolphus glared at me. Not up to Martini's standards, let alone Christopher's. "You are still found unworthy."

"Whatever, Kitler. It's time to pick the successor."

"I am not dead." He snarled at me. "But you soon will be." He raised his cane up over his head.

I heard a growl. First one, then several. Poofikins burst out of my pocket, landed in front of me, and went Martini-sized. The other Poofs all joined it, bodies and teeth set to full. I had a Poof blockade between me and the king. All growling.

Adolphus started to back up, but a new growl announced another Poof. I assumed it was Tenley since it showed up behind the king. "I think the Poofs have a different view, Dolph-man."

"I am the ruler here!" he thundered.

Poof growling increased. "Doesn't seem like they care. Or agree. Could be that they know there are several options down below us, all better fit to lead and rule than you ever were, as near as I can tell."

I didn't want Martini picking up anything from me right now. ACE, can you make sure Jeff can't feel what I'm feeling?

ACE has already, Kitty, since Kitty chose to come here. ACE understands.

Thanks.

Adolphus was back with the thundering. "Citizens, you must destroy these invaders and traitors!" I checked—nobody moved.

"I don't think they like you much any more, Kitler."

"I am the sanctified ruler!"

"Sanctified? Dude, did you miss it? Your Amazonian Assassin Squad's been destroyed, literally, so you have no fighting force to support you. Your battle cruiser's on the way home, pretty much devoid of personnel. Your demigoddess is declawed and defanged. You aren't going to get to join up and live forever, sorry not so much."

"You are a failure as a future queen," he snarled at me. "Even if he stays, you will not stay with him."

"I know." I did. My throat was tight and I wanted to cry about it, but I'd realized where we were heading as soon as I saw the outline of the real plan.

Adolphus looked at me. His expression was familiar; I'd seen it a lot for the last year or so—enraged insanity focused solely on me. I was the girl all the psychos and megalomaniacs wanted to hang with, after all.

"You. This is all your fault."

"Pretty much, yeah. That's how I roll, Trouble Chick to the Rescue, sort of thing. Destroy the decades' worth of planning in a couple of days. Yep, sounds familiar."

"I will destroy you."

"Already tried. Already failed. You saying you're ready to go head-to-head with me now?"

His answer was to lunge for me. I didn't have to answer back. The Poofs did it for me.

Adolphus was devoured. There weren't even any bones left. The Poofs finished up, burped discreetly, then went back to small. They trotted over to me and purred.

I had no choice.

CHAPTER 55

I **BENT DOWN AND GAVE THE POOFS** lots of pets and lovies. "Good Poofies!" I mean, I wasn't going to argue with the save. And they were so proud of themselves. The purring was almost deafening.

I stood up to see a man and woman near me. Tenley mewled and jumped onto the woman's shoulder. She was about Alfred's age, maybe a bit younger. I didn't have to ask if she was Alexander's mother. He looked just like her.

The man was older than she was, but not as old as Alexander had insinuated. That this was Leonidas wasn't a question in my mind—he wasn't a big man, but he radiated intelligence, authority, and confidence. He looked around and raised his arms. "The Poofs have spoken!" His voice carried just like Adolphus' had. I assumed that the troubadour talent went naturally with a political bent.

"Excuse me? The Poofs chowed down, but they didn't speak."

He nodded solemnly. "When a ruler is deemed unfit by the Poofs, it's proof that a new ruler must be found."

I processed this. "You mean the Poofs' role in the succession process is more than just making more Poofs?"

"Yes."

"What about the king's Poof?"

"Sadly, Heinrich passed on to its greater reward many decades ago."

I let the myriad comments I could have made slide. Give

me credit for the diplomatic effort. "So you're okay that they turned Adolphus into Poof Chow?"

He cleared his throat. "I would phrase it more that we are aware of the vital role the royal Poofs play in the control and progression of the monarchy, and while we are saddened that our last king has met his end, we rejoice that we will shortly crown a new king."

"Wow, you're really good with the doublespeak."

I got a nod that was more like a bow. "You flatter me. I am Chief Councillor Leonidas."

"I guessed."

Leonidas' lips quirked, but he kept the solemn going. "May I present Princess Victoria?"

She did the little head bow. "And you are?"

"I'm Kitty. Sorry about Gregory." Sort of not really, but it's what you're supposed to say to someone when you've killed her son. "Not so sorry about King Megalomaniac, though, I have to admit."

"He should have known better." I assumed she meant the king. "Who killed Gregory?"

Tito was next to me, Gregory's body in his arms. "I did." He laid the body down and stepped back. "And I'd do it again. He was trying to destroy our world and your world, too." ACE was projecting everyone's voices, as near as I could tell.

Victoria nodded solemnly to Tito. "Your guard is forgiven."

"My guard?"

"She means me," Tito said. "Thank you, Your Highness." It dawned on me that Tito was staying up here in case someone else tried anything. Gower was right, I did hire well.

"Love the Poofs, I must say."

"They are very loyal." Victoria closed her eyes. "Alexander?"

"I'm here, Mother," he called to her. He was still in the Plaza, and Chuckie was holding him up. "I fought against Gregory, against our king. And I have aligned with these people now. And for what they stand for and believe in."

Victoria looked straight at me. "I saw what you showed us. We do have laws," she said quietly. "My uncle was a traitor and the reason my eldest son is dead. He did nothing when my grandfather forced my sister and cousins, forced his own son, to leave our world. If Alfred were here, this would not have happened."

"True. But he's not."

"His son is." Leonidas pointed to Martini. "Have you come back, to rule us as we should be ruled? To protect this world and solar system and all who dwell in it?"

I turned around and wiped my face of all expression, at least I hoped I did. This was why I'd wanted ACE to block my emotions from Martini, after all—I didn't have any place in the decision he had to make.

Martini looked around. There was a lot of whispering and pointing. Kitty, they will accept Jeff, if Jeff declares.

I know.

"You want me to declare as king of this world?" Martini shouted. ACE projected his voice, too. There was a lot of murmuring, and I heard some agreement.

"Yes," Victoria said. "We need a strong king to lead us."

"Really?" Martini looked around again. "You kicked my family off this world and exiled us to Earth. You set that planet up, set us up. And now that Granddad's proved to be exactly what you deserved, you want a change in the leadership?"

"Yes," Leonidas said. "Not only Alpha Four, but the entire solar system requires strong, compassionate leadership. You are clearly a leader, and a good one. We need you. You are one of us as you can never be one with Earth. We ask you to take your rightful place here, where you have always belonged."

"Gee, tempting offer. Of course, let me guess—I can't bring my family back here, can I?"

"You would be the king," Victoria said. "You could do as you wished. Let me show you what you would rule." She waved her hands, and it was as though a big screen opened up above us and we were watching IMAX. The Doobie Brother's "'Takin' It to the Streets" came on. Clearly ACE enjoyed having a soundtrack.

Alpha Four was pretty amazing—deserts, yes, but they were beautiful, more than Earth's. The seas were blue, and the industry was mature and functioning. Every part of the world was rich in something, and it seemed prosperous.

The images on Victoria's super-IMAX changed, and we saw the solar system. I'd seen it before, six months ago when ACE had moved through me to join Gower. It was an intricate and intriguing place, each planet moving in a strange dance with the others. Victoria showed us glimpses of the other worlds as well, each different from Earth, each one fascinating in its own right.

She returned us to the palace and what I assumed was the royal city where the king would live. It was beautiful, impressive, lush. Nothing like a room in the Dulce Science Center or Caliente Base. A very little bit like what Martini Manor was like, but on a grander, better scale.

Now we saw the people, and it was odd to see so many of them. They all looked pretty great to human eyes, though I could tell some were happier than others. In fact, it was clear that not all the people were happy.

Victoria closed her hands and the images disappeared. "See what you would rule over? Alpha Four leads the other planets. You would be the most powerful man in this galaxy. You could do whatever you wished, bring your family here, do more than that."

"Like what?" Martini asked. "You showed me a lot of nice things. I saw the people making them happen. It's not all perfect here."

Leonidas shrugged. "Then come rule us and make changes. The king's word is law—you could enact any reforms you felt were needed." I didn't doubt that Leonidas had an entire list of suggested reforms on hand. If he was truly as Alexander had described, I figured Leonidas was praying Martini would say yes, because he'd finally get as king the kind of leader he was himself—the good kind.

I tried not to think about what Martini was going to choose. He was a protector, had been all his life, and now an entire solar system needed him. A solar system I couldn't stay in. The one thing I knew Adolphus had said that was true was that I'd failed the tests for marriage. Martini couldn't be king here and marry me. But then, he was the person who'd really taught me that the good of the many comes before the good of the few.

Queen Renata was next to Martini, and she whispered something in his ear. He nodded, and she whispered some more. He nodded again, then Queen Renata went and spoke to Christopher, Gower, and Michael.

Martini looked around. Christopher, Gower, and Michael were next to him. "I'd like to see what the others in the bloodline have to say about this."

Christopher nodded and stepped forward with Michael's help. "I respectfully decline the kingship of Alpha Four, for me and the descendants of my line. I will serve Alpha Four if my acknowledged leader serves or requests it, and I will not if he does not." He put his hand on Martini's shoulder.

Michael helped his brother get to Martini's other side. "I speak for my brother and myself," Gower said. "We respectfully decline the kingship of Alpha Four, for us and all the descendants in our lines. We will serve Alpha Four if our acknowledged leader serves or requests it, and we will not if he does not." Like Christopher, he put his hand on Martini's other shoulder.

Victoria and Leonidas looked back at Martini. "The others have declined," he said. "You are the only hope our world, our system has. What is your decision?"

Martini didn't look at them when he answered. He looked straight at me. "I respectfully decline the kingship of Alpha Four, for me and all descendants in my line. I have another life, and it doesn't belong here, so neither do I."

CHAPTER 56

I MANAGED NOT TO BURST INTO TEARS. ACE is allowing Jeff access to Kitty's feelings again.

Thanks, big guy.

Victoria was standing there in shock. Leonidas didn't look shocked—he looked worried, and a little hopeful, at least when he glanced at Alexander.

I took a deep breath, let it out, and felt in control enough to talk. "Think that covers the Earth blood. Alex, what's your plan?"

"I respectfully dec—"

"Dude! Not a good plan!"

He looked at me in confusion. "But . . . I don't want it." I saw Leonidas out of the corner of my eye—he was tensed and focused. I could practically feel him trying to influence Alexander's decision. But no worries, that's what I was there for, and unlike the Chief Councillor, there weren't any repercussions they could use against me.

"Alex, want has nothing to do with responsibility. You know why Jeff and the others declined? Because this world is no longer their responsibility—Earth is. But this is your world, and these are your people. Leadership isn't about wanting—that's what screwed up your great-uncle. Jeff and Christopher don't want to have to run everything—they do it because they're the best at what they do, and our world needs them."

"I don't want to rule the way my great-uncle did," Alexander said.

"That's a great start. But there's only one way to achieve that."

He gave me a long look. "I thought I could stay with all of you."

I shrugged. "Unlock the freaking gate. I'm sure we'd be open to the occasional visit back and forth. Provided both sides called first and made sure their respective houses were cleaned and tidied."

"Alexander has already refused the crown," Victoria said quietly.

"So what? Unless this world's ready to hail Queen Victoria, then they'd better hail King Alexander pronto. Or else I have a queen standing right down there who could probably rule this planet as well as her own." Queen Renata grinned at me.

"There is precedent," Leonidas said. "From centuries ago. But since Alexander has refused the crown already, the people must agree." He sounded worried.

"Not the Poofs?"

Leonidas pointed to one of the Poofs. "This one has accepted Alexander." How he knew I had no idea, but I assumed they had their ways. The Poof so identified purred, loudly, which seemed to make both Leonidas and Victoria happy. This was really a freak world. "Therefore, the only remaining protocol would be approval by the majority."

The chanting started softly. It was started by our guys—Tim and Reader specifically—but no one seemed to notice. I didn't mind. By the time it grew loud, everyone was chanting it. "King Alexander!"

"Does that work?" I asked Leonidas.

He nodded and smiled. "Yes. I believe we can safely say the majority of the population have approved the new king."

"Democracy along with the monarchy. Nice."

"It works for us . . . when the right monarchs are in place." I noted Leonidas hadn't projected that for the crowd. "Thank you."

I didn't reply because Chuckie had helped Alexander get up the stairs to join us. "Nice display of calm." ACE didn't broadcast this. Thank God. "Am I a bad man to admit I was hoping Martini would accept the crown?"

"No, I'd have been sort of hurt otherwise."

Chuckie grinned at me, then turned to Victoria. "Your

Highness, here's your son. Alexander, nice meeting you. Remember that the C.I.A. is now watching you."

Victoria hugged Alexander and started crying. I looked at Chuckie and raised my eyebrow. He gave me a very nice smile and an almost imperceptible nod. I was impressed and hoped the bugs worked long range. It was Chuckie, of course, so the likelihood was high that they would.

Alexander laughed. "What can I do to thank you?"

"Well, start with no longer making us the dumping ground for all your freaking problems." I thought of something. "ACE, remove the Alpha Four Ozone Shield. Leave the ones up on the other worlds, though." My voice was projecting again. I looked up and saw a shimmering high up in the sky that broke apart and disappeared.

There were gasps of horror from the crowd. "Oh, you don't like that? Well, here's what Earth doesn't like. We're really freaking tired of being the Alpha Four trash bin. That's over now. Deal with your own parasitic superbeings. We'll tell you how, if you want to send an emissary, Alex. One that we approve and who doesn't come disguised and to do damage to us."

Chuckie nodded. "Earth has more weapons than perhaps you're aware of. Don't put up another PPB net around us; don't interfere with us any more. We like the A-Cs we have, and if you asked nicely about immigration, we might consider letting you come on over. But we will exterminate with extreme prejudice anyone coming to make us your battlefield ever again." He was talking to Alexander but looking at Leonidas. I got the impression they were communicating on the super-smart-guy channel in some way.

Alexander nodded. "Your requests are fair, even the removal of the Ozone Shield. Once we know the parasitic threat has truly stopped, we can put it up again. And, perhaps, share it with you as well."

"That we would appreciate." I looked around. "Time for us to go."

"Already?" Victoria sounded shocked. "But you just arrived. None of you from Earth have been here before. You are that uninterested in other worlds?"

"Hardly. We're hot and heavy for the new world experience. We're also battered and banged up, and some of us have things to do and all. We know the way here now, if you catch my drift."

"I will open the gate to you," Alexander said. "You will be able to come when you choose or have need." He looked a little lost. Victoria still looked shocked. Leonidas looked as though he was fine with our taking off.

I spit in my hand and held it out to Alexander. "Spit." He looked at me like I was crazy. So did Victoria and Leonidas. Chuckie started to laugh. "Dude, spit. It's gross enough." He spit, gingerly, in my hand. I grabbed his hand and shook, did the whole gangsta thing. It was really impressive in a totally icky way. Alexander tried not to gag. "It was spit or blood. You're bleeding but I'm not, so . . ." He nodded. I figured he was afraid he'd barf if he talked. "Pinky up."

"What?" he asked weakly.

I raised mine. "Pinky. Up. How hard are these instructions?" He did as I said. I wrapped our pinkies. "Earth and Alpha Four—we have each other's backs from now on. Agree?"

Alexander looked at Chuckie. Who grinned. "Agree and say the same thing."

Alexander nodded. "Yes. Earth and Alpha Four, we have each other's backs from now on. Agree?"

"Yes." I shook our pinkies. Alexander still looked confused. Victoria looked more shocked. Leonidas looked as though he was trying not to laugh. I looked at Chuckie. "Aliens are weird." I let go of Alexander's hand. He wiped his on his shirt. I wiped mine on his shirt, too.

"What was that about?" he asked me.

I shrugged. "We could do the whole long diplomatic crap and argue over pieces of paper for decades, but it all comes down to the spit shake or the blood oath and the pinky swear. They're as binding as any piece of paper and, honestly, probably work better."

"We are allies now?" Alexander seemed very confused. Leonidas, however, looked quietly pleased.

"Yeah! See? The first thing you did as the new king was create an alliance with Earth. Dude, you rock!"

Chuckie coughed. "I'll send you a note about the ramifications, Your Majesty."

"Thanks, Charles. I think I'll need it."

"I believe I'd like a copy as well," Leonidas said.

"Absolutely." Chuckie and Leonidas were smiling pleasantly at each other. I got the distinct impression they were weighing and examining each other in a lot of ways I was missing. "Are you staying on as King Alexander's Chief Councillor?" Chuckie asked finally. He didn't sound as though he was going to disapprove if Leonidas said yes, but I also wasn't sure if he'd disapprove if Leonidas said no.

Leonidas shrugged. "That's up to His Majesty."

"And the people," Alexander added.

Either ACE had projected this or Victoria or Leonidas had, because I heard murmuring from the crowd. They seemed pleased.

"Oh, I'm sure the people will be very happy with Chief Councillor Leonidas staying on," Chuckie said. "From what you've said, he has the people's well-being foremost in his mind."

Leonidas gave Chuckie one of their formal little head bows. "From what we've seen, Mister Reynolds, you function in a similar capacity." Even knowing they'd been spying on us for a long time, it was still a shock to hear him use Chuckie's name as if they'd been introduced.

I tried to figure out how what someone in the C.I.A., even Chuckie, did could be compared to what Leonidas did, but before I could, Alexander's face lit up. "Maybe you could stay here and become my adviser?"

Chuckie looked interested. I could guess that some others with us were, too. And, surprisingly, Leonidas didn't seem against the idea. "That could prove helpful. I'm sure we could learn a great deal from each other."

Chuckie opened his mouth. I beat him to the reply. "No."

"No?" Chuckie and Alexander chorused. The unison thing was getting to me. Too many alpha males in small spaces equaled bad for Kitty's sense of propriety.

"No. Because you have to learn to do it on your own. Could Chuckie stay and help you guys out? Sure, he'd be awesome. Some of the others would, as well. But you need to rebuild Alpha Four, not rebuild it into Earth: The Alpha Four Experience. Maybe once you're stabilized. Let's see how you do on your own before we send one of the guys we need to you, okay?"

Alexander nodded. "That makes sense."

"It does?" Chuckie asked.

"Yes. Besides, I think Alexander has a Chief Councillor here already who knows what's going on in this solar system a lot better than any of us, even you, would." Leonidas gave me a pleasant smile. "And I don't want said Chief Councillor learning even more about us than he already knows."

His eyes narrowed, though his expression remained pleasant. "I don't follow you."

I snorted. "You'd learn as much from Chuckie as he'd learn from you. That's great, but now's not the time. You all need to prove that we can trust you before you get to pick this particular brilliant brain."

Leonidas gave me a long look. "Understood." He cleared his throat, straightened up, and bowed to Alexander. "Your Majesty, if you are willing, I would be happy to stay on as Chief Councillor." It was clear from what he did and how he said it that this was an official moment of protocol, and that the response wasn't in question.

Alexander gave the little head bow. "It would be an honor for us if you would remain in this position of responsibility, respect, and confidence."

I could feel the crowd around us relax. "You sure this is the right way?" Chuckie asked me quietly."

"Yes. You can spend your summer vacation here another time. Now shut up, and let's go home."

Is Kitty ready? ACE asked politely.

I looked around. Almost. "Victoria, what happens with the Poofs?"

There was much Poof mewling and whining at this question. One of the Poofs, the one Leonidas has identified as Alexander's, jumped onto his shoulder. The others scattered—back to Martini, Christopher, Reader, and Michael. Poofikins stayed with me. The last one whined and jumped onto Chuckie's shoulder.

Victoria chuckled. "They are attached."

"I'm not from Alpha Four, and I'm also not marrying in," Chuckie said.

She shrugged. "Attached Poofs pine without the one they are attached to with them. Harlie was listless for close to fifty years. If it is attached to you, it's yours. Take it as our gift of thanks."

"Thanks, I think." Chuckie seemed confused.

"You named it, didn't you?"

He shrugged. "Calling it 'it' or 'you' seemed stupid."

"What's its name?"

He coughed and mumbled something.

"What? Missed that."

He glared at me. I stared him down. "Fluffy."

I ran through all the things I could say. "Fitting."

"Yeah." Fluffy purred at Chuckie. "Fine, yeah, back in the pocket." Fluffy disappeared.

Victoria smiled. "They attach to the one who names them."

I hadn't considered Poofikins a name, but, apparently, it was. Worked for me. "You sure you can spare them, though? Tenley's been around a while, right?"

"Yes, but they can live for hundreds of years." I heard Martini groan. "We will be fine with the two we have. And, if not, we can always ask one of you to visit."

"Wow, Poof breeding. A new career option. Has to be better than this saving the world stuff."

"Is there money in it?" Chuckie asked.

"Doubtful, but who knows?" Victoria laughed. "You think strangely."

"Welcome to hanging with humans."

Tito bowed to everyone. I hugged Alexander and Victoria and shook hands with Leonidas. Chuckie tried to shake hands with Victoria and Alexander, but they both hugged him. I thought about it. "I'm sure everyone else would like to say good-bye. Would you mind walking down to them? Under the circumstances, I mean."

"Of course." Alexander headed down with Tito's help, Victoria went after him. Leonidas, on the other hand, stayed put.

"Mister Reynolds, before you go . . ." Leonidas gave Chuckie a hug, in a manly way, but it lasted a lot longer than normal. I was positive he was whispering something in Chuckie's ear. Of course, the fact that Chuckie nodded when they were done, then winked at me, was a clue, too.

"Do I want to know?"

"Tell you later, boss girl."

"Yes, you will." We went down to the others. Leonidas still stayed put. As we walked, he started talking. Sounded like the typical "bad things have happened but we've overcome, and we have a great new king and he rocks" speech. There were no hints that Alpha Four might want to retaliate or argue about our taking down their ozone shield. I hoped that would remain the case, but I wasn't prepared to place a bet on it.

Michael was done with his part in the farewell hugging, and his Poof was sitting on his shoulder. I thought about it.

"So Paul didn't name the Poof who was with him during the fighting?"

Michael looked embarrassed. "I named it for him."

"Can't wait. Spill it."

"Fuzzball."

"Again, fits." I figured I'd ask Christopher and Reader what names they'd given theirs later. Reader was too far away, and Christopher was in the midst of getting the "you look just like your mother except" song all relatives seem to love doing. Victoria seemed to think he wasn't getting enough to eat, which, considering we normally ate at the Dulce Commissary of a Million and One Food Options was sort of funny. Christopher didn't seem uncomfortable with the attention, of course.

Martini got a different kind of farewell, from both Victoria and Alexander. Fond, but very formal. Even their hugs were more formal than for anyone else. I decided to worry about this later.

Though Martini, of course, caught the worry. At least if his wink at me was any indication. He nodded, and I knew what that meant.

"Victoria, Alex, Leonidas, it's been real. We need to roll, however."

Kitty is ready now? ACE asked.

Yep. Let's rock and roll, big guy. I looked around at my team. We all looked as though we needed a really long vacation. "Guys, let's get our bedraggled flock out of Dodge."

I felt ACE gather us up where we were standing. He tossed me, though, straight at Martini. Who caught me easily, flipped my legs around his waist, and kissed me. We did a reverse time warp, I guess. I wasn't paying attention to anything other than Martini's kiss. And this time, since it wasn't going to be the last kiss of his I'd ever have, it wasn't bittersweet—it was the best ever.

CHAPTER 57

I **FELT A GENTLE JOLT.** Martini ended our kiss. "You actually thought I'd choose them over you?"

"You're a protector. Good of the many and all that."

"Not over you. Never again—no one and nothing else over you—you understand?"

I nodded and again managed not to cry. Martini shifted me to his hip, and we took a look around. ACE landed us back pretty much where we'd been. All of Animal Planet was still with us, which made sense since their ships were here.

Kitty, ACE must go back to Paul. If ACE stays any longer with Kitty, ACE will destabilize.

I understand. ACE? Thank you again. For everything.

Our world to protect and love.

Yes. I looked up at Martini. "Jeff, we need to get to Paul."

Gower wasn't that far away from us. He looked crappy. Reader helped him over. "Hope he can handle the transfer back."

"I can," Gower said. He put out his hand and I took it. The heavy-duty electric charge went through me and finally stopped. I leaned my head against Martini's shoulder until the dizziness and nausea passed.

Gower straightened up. I saw his body repair itself even faster than A-C normal. "ACE doesn't like you hurt?"

"Nope. Thankfully." Gower looked around. "We need to get everybody healed."

"Let's see if telecommunications is back or if we still have reason to curse Bitch Leader and her gang." My purse was nearby, but Martini pulled his phone out so I didn't have to get out of his arms. I was more than okay with this.

"I have a dial tone." Martini looked around. "We need to verify that all bases are still secured." He was back to full Commander Mode. Other phones came out, and it was business as usual.

Martini dialed. "Dad? Yes, we're all still alive. Yes, all the nice people from the A-C solar system, too. Yes, they're dead. Your father, too," he added quietly. "Huh? Yeah, the Poofs, ah, ate him." Martini's eyebrow rose. "Okay, yeah, we all agreed with their choice. Yeah, no loss at all, believe me. Kitty installed Alexander as the new king. Yes, we were on the home world. No, we didn't want to stay. Long story."

He sighed. "Yes, I brought it back with me," he muttered. "I'll give it to you when we see you. What? What do you mean it's mine now? I don't want it!" Martini was quiet, but the look on his face said he was losing whatever argument he was having with Alfred.

"Yes, of course I'll take care of it," he said finally, in a tone of total resignation. "Kitty has one, too. So do some of the others. Look, can we talk about this later? What do you mean it's important? I think the safety of our people and our bases is more important. Fine, fine, look, really, is everyone in Vegas okay? Uncle Richard? Kitty's family? Good. How about the kids? Good. Okay, we'll clean up here, be back there sometime in the next few hours. What do you mean you'll all be up? It's the middle of the night! In fact, it's heading toward dawn. What? Are you kidding me? Okay, fine, fine. Go back to the craps table, so sorry to bother you with all that end of the world stuff. Yes, love you, too."

He closed his phone. "Well, that was . . . odd."

"Is your dad okay that his father got . . . eaten?"

"Yep." Martini shook his head. "Apparently Leonidas wasn't making nice and covering up in regard to the Poofs. If the Poofs eat anyone in the royal family, it's because they've made a determination a better ruler's at hand, just like he said. So, if you're eaten, you deserved it."

"Wow. That's a lot of power given to fluffy bundles of fur."

"Tell me about it." Martini eyed Poofikins, who'd crawled up onto my shoulder. "You sure you want to keep them?"

"The Poofs rock. They ate Adolphus, not you, me, Alexander, or Renata."

"Good point."

"How's everyone else?"

"Oh, just *fine*. They're all at the craps tables. Apparently your Nana Sadie is a craps queen and has been showing off her technique. The few who aren't playing craps are either at the blackjack tables or, God help us, in the baccarat room."

"Who's in the baccarat room?" Kevin and Chuckie both started to snort laughter. "Oh, no. You're kidding me. My mom's playing baccarat?"

"Gotta figure," Kevin said with a grin. "We call her Jane Bond at the office." I learned new things about my mother every day. "By the way, Jeff, thanks again."

"For what?" Martini asked.

"For getting my wife and kids stashed with the others in Florida. I just talked to her—the kids are all having a blast, but she was glad to be there to give Gladys a hand."

"You're part of the team, you get the same security," Martini said with a shrug.

"Never stop appreciating it."

I could see the Animal Planet folks were getting ready to leave. "Jeff, need down for a minute." He released me slowly. I found my shoes and grabbed my purse. There, properly dressed again.

Felicia was hurt, but she was going to be okay. Willem and Wrolph were both injured as well but also seemed likely to recover. Wrolph was being tended to by Claudia again, and I got the distinct impression he had a crush on her, if his tail wagging when she looked at him was indicative.

Neeraj was looking beaten up, but not too terrible. The rest of the Animal Planet folks were similar.

"You all leaving now?" I tried not to sound disappointed and failed.

Queen Renata nodded. "We have done what we came to do, in that sense. You have many things to get back to."

"Yeah, uh, that's sort of why . . . hang on a second." I stepped off a bit and dug out my cell phone. "Mom? How's the baccarat room?"

"Fine. I'm winning. This is a bad time."

"I'm alive. We saved the world."

"Good. Need to concentrate." Nice to see where her priorities truly were.

"Mom, did you ever get a hold of Amy, Sheila, and Caroline for me?"

She heaved a sigh. "Yes. Sheila was flattered that you wanted her to be in your wedding, but what with the delay in your making any kind of decision, she's had time to find out she's expecting number four and would rather die than try to shove into a bridesmaid dress, even though she's probably only barely showing. They can't come, either, expenses. And her husband would be insulted if we offered to pay."

"Okay." I couldn't be hurt—reality was what it was. "How about Amy?"

"Can't come now, can't come in six weeks. Talked to her right before telecommunications went down worldwide. She was assigned a huge case because, let me mention, she wasn't able to say when exactly she needed to come to the States until it was too late. She can't leave for the next few months. Career-making kind of thing." Amy was a corporate lawyer working in Paris for one of the huge conglomerates. The only stuff she did was career-making, so again, not a surprise. "She's sending you an overwhelmingly too generous gift to make up for it."

"Okay. That'll be nice. Caroline?" I held out no expectations.

"Caroline could have come in six weeks because she apparently knows you well enough to have arranged for a week off any time one to four months from now."

"Wow." Cool. I had three bridesmaids. "That's a perk."

"Well, the senator loves her. I wouldn't expect anyone else to get that kind of consideration. *However*, at this moment she's in Paraguay with a full senatorial team on a fact-finding mission, and even if they'd let her leave, by the time she could get here, it would all be over."

"Ah." Okay. Back to two bridesmaids. "Such is life. What facts are they finding?"

"It's need to know, and you definitely don't." Mom's tone shifted. "Kitten, are you really okay?"

"I think so. I'll know in a few minutes. Go back to the baccarat, Missus Bond."

"Hilarious. Love you. See you soon, I hope."

"Yeah. Love you, too." As I hung up, Reader ran over to me.

"Girlfriend, Jeff's asked Kevin to be in the wedding party,

too. I tried to shut him up, but he was clueless. I'm amazed he hasn't asked Reynolds at the rate he's going. You want me to get him to retract?"

"Hopefully not." I went back to the Animal Planet girls. Reader came with me. I grabbed Jareen. "This request is going to make me sound like the most friendless soul in two solar systems. I have a lot of friends. Most of them don't know what I do or who I hang with. My two best girlfriends from high school and my best girlfriend from college can't come to my wedding for a variety of human real-life issues. My other two best girlfriends are already in my wedding," I pointed to Lorraine and Claudia.

"But Jeff's got, at last count, six guys standing up with him. I'll understand if you don't want to, or if you want to just get home and out of our boondocks part of the universe, but . . . I'd really like it if you'd be my maid or matron of honor. Maid is if you're single, matron is if you're married."

Jareen cocked her head. "But he's your best friend." She pointed to Reader.

"Yeah, he is. But on Earth, he's a guy so he stands on the guy side. He'll be up there, but with the other men. Same with Chuckie. Can't ask him since he's a guy."

"The person of honor?"

I shrugged. "Soul sisters are hard to come by."

She grinned. "I would love to. Neeraj would be better off if we didn't travel for a few days anyway."

I hugged her. "Thanks. No one I'd rather have up there with me than a Giant Lizard."

"I look forward to seeing how the Naked Apes join together. I am a matron. Neeraj and I have been mated for a hundred years."

"Wow, really? You look like, twenty-five. In lizard years, I mean."

She grinned again. "We live a long time. In lifespan comparison, I am about your age."

"Works for me." I moved off to Queen Renata, Felicia, and Wahoa. "This will sound like—"

Wahoa put her paw up. "We Major Doggies have really good hearing, Friendless Naked Ape. Remember?" She grinned as only a dog could. "Dogs are supposedly man's best friend on this planet, but I only get to be a bridesmaid?"

I laughed. "Had to go with the soul sister."

Claudia snorted. "We've known her longer, and we're only at bridesmaid rank." She grinned at me. "We know it's because you couldn't figure out which one of us to ask without hurting the other's feelings."

"How did you know that?" Reader coughed. "Oh." Duh. Reader was pretty much taking care of everything. A suspicion tickled, but I let it pass for now. "Felicia, will you be up to it?"

She nodded. "Your doctors are very good." Lorraine had been working on her. "I would be honored. All Naked Apes need a good Cat Person around."

"Renata?"

She smiled at me. "I am honored to be a part of this. Besides, I'm on the Giant Lizard vessel."

"What do we wear?" Felicia asked.

"Ummm . . . no idea whatsoever."

Reader coughed. "Handled. Trust me. Or will be."

"You're just Mister Helpy Helper, aren't you, James?"

He flashed the cover-boy grin. I noted it worked on all the females, even Queen Renata. Figured he knew that and used the power for good. "Babe, let's just say that someone has to take care of things and leave it at that."

Martini came over. "We have medical teams on the way, should be here momentarily. We've gone too long without full medical on some of the injured."

"Are we losing someone?" My stomach clenched.

"Me, to pain, agony, and boredom," Tim called out.

"Me, too," Jerry said. "The rest of the guys are complaining that they're not in the wedding party, Jeff."

Martini opened his mouth.

"NO!" Wow, Reader and I were now doing the unison thing.

Martini snapped his mouth shut.

"Sorry, guys. The only way that would work is for you to draw lots for which two of you were putting on a bridesmaid's dress. I'm out of females I want up there with me." I thought about it. "Well, I could add on one more."

"Great!" Martini said.

"One, Jeff. Only one."

"Great!" He looked really guilty.

"Jeff . . . who did you already ask?"

He mumbled something.

"Come again, can't hear you."

"Alexander."

I let that one sit on the air. "Um . . . *how*?"

Martini looked hugely guilty again. I tapped my foot. He heaved a sigh. "I asked ACE to ask him. He said yes. He's really excited about it." He looked guilty and embarrassed. "I just want it to be . . . special."

"And huge. Fine." I thought about it. "He just became king because his great-uncle was Poof Chow. The solar system's in disarray. We're getting married really soon. How the hell can he come?"

Martini shrugged. "No idea, but he said he could."

Chuckie joined us. "It'll be fine. From what Leonidas told me, he's been waiting for this day."

"You two weren't chatting all that long."

"He implanted the information."

"What?"

"It's something many of us are able to do," Martini said quietly. I'd known Terry had put an implant into Martini, of course. To find me, as it had turned out. And I'd also known he'd passed that implant along to me. It just hadn't occurred to me that other A-Cs could do it as well.

"Oh. They don't hurt," I added, because Martini was looking the way he always did whenever the implant subject came up, which was guilty and ashamed. "And they're useful."

"Yes, they are," Chuckie agreed.

"You didn't pass out." I had, when Martini had put Terri's implant into me.

Chuckie shrugged. "I think it's different when you're forewarned. I felt a little woozy, but it wasn't an issue. And, I have a clear understanding of the political situation in the entire Alpha Centauri solar system. Or," he added with a grin, "I have the view Leonidas wants me to have."

"He *is* a politician," Martini said. "You sure you can trust anything he told you?"

"Most of it correlates to what we've been told already. I'll confirm the rest with the Planetary Council. I assume they're staying for the wedding?"

"Yeah, because—"

"You're out of bridesmaid options, and they all know what's going on," Chuckie finished for me.

"Right as always!" I'd said that too cheerfully, if Martini's low growl was any indication. "But I need one more," I added quickly, before the growling got louder. "Be right back. Behave," I added to Martini as I raced off. Hey, I'd had enough fighting for one night.

I looked around, found her, and trotted over. "Serene, you willing to be one of my bridesmaids?"

She looked shocked out of her mind and pleased beyond belief. "Really? You really want me? After all the . . . stuff . . . from six months ago?"

"You were drugged. Jeff was too, and I still want him. So, yeah. I didn't ask before because I had no idea Jeff was going insane with the groomsmen numbers." I looked at Brian, whose head was in her lap. He was still hurt, but he looked as though he might pull through. "Bri, I don't care if Jeff begs you. Unless James or I say yes, you are to say no if he asks you to be a groomsman. Oh, and stop playing dead."

"Got it." He grinned. "I just like how Serene takes care of me."

She giggled. "I like it. And, yes, Kitty, thank you so much for asking me!"

"Thank you so much for saying yes. Oh, and, I'd like you to join Airborne, while I'm thinking about it."

"Why? I'm a scientist."

"You're an explosives expert and the only A-C capable of seeing through both shapeshifters and imageers with an overlay on. I call those vitally strategic skills we need at the highest levels. You can fool around in the lab on the off days."

"You ever stop with the hiring?" Reader asked.

"You find the talent, you grab the talent before the competition does."

"Right. Reminds me, we need a good story for your family."

"Ugh. Let's get everyone healed up or at least headed that way first." An impressive number of Dazzlers were appearing out of nowhere. They fanned out and started doing very fast things. Gurneys appeared. All my pilots were loaded onto them, with much whining and complaining. Tim and Christopher were also gurneyed up with a lot more whining and complaining.

Tito was in great shape and having a field day. He'd already been taking care of the flyboys and was trotting around explaining injuries and symptoms.

Animal Planet got gurneys, too. "What are we going to do about the ships?"

Chuckie sauntered over. "Already handled. If you folks would be so good as to cloak them again, the C.I.A. will ensure no one comes by to disturb them."

"Just to put tracking devices on them?" Neeraj asked.

Chuckie smiled. "Of course not."

Jareen nodded "Because they're already on."

Chuckie shrugged. "It's a living."

I heard some bellowing. Martini was being forced onto a gurney. "Excuse me." I trotted over. "Jeff, stop it."

"There's nothing wrong with me!"

"Claudia had to harpoon you. I'm sure Kyrellis at least cracked some of your ribs. If what we're expecting is coming, wouldn't it be nice to go into isolation now, so that, you know, you're awake, alive, and functioning?"

"But I don't want to leave you alone."

"I'll keep James with me, okay? Or the girls. I have to find a dress. Trust me, I'll be busy." The panic about the dress hit again.

He caught it, of course. Strangely enough, it calmed him down. "Okay. You'll be okay?"

"Yes. Does Harlie go into the isolation tank with you?"

"No. Out of the pocket, take care of Kitty."

Harlie crawled out, rubbed up against Martini's neck and chin, purring like mad, then jumped to me and hopped into my purse.

Martini pulled me to him and kissed me. "You be good."

"I'll do my best, Jeff."

He stroked my face. "I wanted to go back and take a bath."

I laughed. "If we're really getting married in about a day and a half, then you'll have to wait anyway."

He kissed me again. I was ready to let him take me here in front of everyone. Truly, the man was the god of kissing.

Martini pulled away slowly and looked quite pleased with himself. "I always want to make you feel like that."

"I'll make sure it's in the wedding vows."

CHAPTER 58

THE ALIEN SPACESHIPS WERE CLOAKED and being guarded by a lot of buff guys in dark camouflage fatigues. The rest of our equipment was back in Area 51, and the injured were at the Science Center, whose personnel had returned from wherever they'd gone for lockdown. Martini was in isolation with Security around him, just in case.

I wasn't with him for a variety of reasons. Isolation meant isolated, of course, and I needed to rest and regroup and all that good stuff, too. But the real reason was that the isolation chambers creeped me out beyond belief. I'd rather fight Bitch Leader again than have to watch them put Martini into the scientific cross between Frankenstein's lab and *The Mummy's Tomb*, complete with extra special effects including tubes and wires running into his body and head. Supposedly this was harder to observe than experience, and I had no desire to put it to the test.

Kevin, Chuckie, and Gower assigned teams to search the Science Center from top to bottom, including the old water pipe. No bombs, bugs, or anything else strange were found.

"Still want to know how the prisoners got away," Chuckie fretted.

I thought about it. "Oh, duh. Paul, ask ACE if Lilith did it."

Gower twitched a bit. "Yes, ACE is pretty sure the other superconsciousness removed the prisoners. He apologized for not mentioning it before. Even a superconsciousness can get distracted, apparently."

"No worries. Solves that problem." I had a much bigger one. "I need to go shopping."

"Kitty, when did you sleep last?" Chuckie looked concerned.

"I don't remember."

Reader put his arm around my shoulders. "I'll take care of it."

"But James—"

"I'm fine. I had a lot of rest. You get some sleep. Then we can take care of everything else. I'll line up the dress options while you and your many bridesmaids take a breather, okay?"

"You conspired with the families to get us married this weekend."

The cover-boy grin was in full force. "Of course. You two were heading for a disaster. Eloping to Vegas is a great plan."

"Eloping with our entire families and almost all our friends?" A thought occurred. "What about my friends most of you don't know about?" It was one thing not to ask my other sorority sisters to be bridesmaids. It was another to move my wedding up by six weeks and not share that news until after the fact.

Chuckie shrugged. "I know all your friends from college. Already did the list comparison with your mother. Those who received invitations in the mail were advised that things had been moved up. Most of them will make it."

"How?" I looked at Chuckie and Reader suspiciously. They both contrived to look innocent. "Who's paying to get them out here?"

Chuckie grinned. "It's amazing how we need a really good cover story for what's gone on here, something to distract attention away from interplanetary and terrorist issues. A huge wedding is just the thing."

"How did the C.I.A. get involved in my wedding day?"

Reader grinned. "You invited Reynolds and your mother."

"Good point. I'm almost afraid to ask what else is coming."

Reader shrugged. "It did spiral a bit out of what I'd originally planned, yeah."

"I don't want to know, do I?"

Reader kissed my forehead. "Probably not. Let's get you into bed." He nodded to Chuckie and took me to the elevators.

"I thought Jeff was going to stay on Alpha Four."

"I don't know why." We got into the elevator. "Man lives for you."

"He'd make a good king."

"Probably. Doesn't matter. He declined."

"Because of me."

Reader hugged me. "Yeah. He made the first selfish choice I've ever seen. About time, too."

"But he's the leader."

"Even leaders deserve to be with the person they love." We got out on the 15th floor and went to the Lair. "You think you'll be okay down here?"

"Well, you could stay with me, but I think that would cause Jeff and Paul some major issues."

He laughed. "Yeah."

I remembered something I'd wanted to ask. "What did you name your Poof?"

He looked embarrassed. "Doesn't matter."

"Oh, come on. I'll find out Christopher's, too, you know."

"I'm sure. Gatita."

I thought about it and did a translation. "That means Kitty in Spanish."

"Yeah, it does." He kissed my forehead. "Go to sleep now. I'll come and get you by midafternoon. If you wake up sooner, just call me."

"Okay."

Reader grinned. "Trust me. I'll have everything taken care of, and anything you don't like we'll be able to change. Okay?"

"I'll trust you."

He grinned again, kissed my cheek, then left, closing the door quietly, but firmly, behind him. I took a deep breath, let it out slowly, and the exhaustion hit. Staggered to the bedroom, stepped out of my shoes, lay down, purse, jacket, dress and all still on, and went to sleep.

I woke up and could tell I wasn't alone. It was light in the room, but I had no idea what time of day it was. Tried to figure out if I was in trouble and where the other entity was. There was pressure on my chest. I managed to move my head a bit and look down. To see Harlie and Poofikins asleep between my breasts, curled around each other. Harlie looked at me, purred, curled back up, and went back to sleep. I decided to follow suit.

Woke up again and knew I wasn't alone, and this time I knew it was someone other than the Poofs. I opened my eyes and looked around. No one I could see. Sat up, got to hear much Poof grumbling as they tumbled from my chest to my lap. Still no one in the room. But the bedroom door was closed, and I'd left it open.

I moved the Poofs back into the jacket pocket that didn't have my iPod in it, got my Glock out of my purse, and got out of bed as quietly as I could. Checked the closet and under the bed—nothing. Crept to the door. Opened it like I'd seen Chuckie do, from the side so the wall would block me, pointed the Glock out.

"Whoa there, Superagent Girl. Gun down. It's a big crime to shoot your superior."

I pulled the gun back. "Chuckie, what are you doing here?" I dumped the Glock back in my purse and walked out to the living area.

He was sitting on the couch, arms stretched out on the back, watching TV with the sound very low. "Got some sleep, then woke up and couldn't get back to sleep. Reader brought me down here with, of course, the message that if I put moves on you, he and many others would conveniently forget I was their superior and rip me a new one, literally, and so on."

"Why are you watching TV?" I yawned and went to the fridge. "Coke or Cherry Coke? Or whatever?"

"Coke. And I'm watching it to relax and maybe fall back asleep. Duh."

I opened the fridge and grabbed a Coke for him and a Cherry Coke for me. Took the straw that was in the door for me, didn't bother for him. Tossed him his can.

"Hey, Dudette, you have to stop doing that. I hate it when it sprays."

I snorted. "Payback's a bitch, and so am I." I plopped down on the couch next to him. "So, what're we watching?"

"Reruns. *Lifestyles of the Rich and Famous* right now."

"What, are you and Jeff on some scary wavelength? I thought he was only separated at birth from Jerry."

He shrugged. "I like it. I've been to a lot of the places they show. It's interesting to me to see what they were like a few years ago."

"Yeah, you are the one with the big money."

"So's Martini. You'd better get used to it."

"He lives a lot more simply than his parents do." I thought about it. "Like you."

"Do you want to?"

I thought about this. I knew Chuckie well enough to know this wasn't casual talk. "I don't know. Comfy middle class has always been fine. I like the Lair. I like Dulce and Caliente

Bases. Of course, I really like the maid service, but it's fine here. Like the dorms, only for grownups."

"I miss the coed floor sometimes."

"I miss having you right there sometimes. But, why are you asking about living arrangements?"

He sighed. "Martini is going to want to give you the best of everything, shower you with gifts, buy you an expensive house, the works. And I know you. That will sound great to you for a little while. Then your father's training will kick in, and you'll realize you don't need ten thousand square feet even if you have a bunch of kids. You'll feel guilty for wearing designer clothes when other people can barely afford shoes. And he won't understand, because you liked it before."

"What makes you so sure of all this?"

"I know him. Not like you do, but as a professional, a peer, if you will. I've seen how he is with you—which is nothing like he is with anyone else. He's been to C.I.A. headquarters a lot. Every time, he's charming to the women, nice to the men who aren't his peers, and pissed off with me and anyone who technically has a higher rank than he does."

"So?"

"So, he could have landed any woman there. He's got a lot more charm than me, and every woman I work with and around thinks he's great-looking and would give their right arm for a shot at going out with him."

"Are you telling me I should be worried?"

He laughed. "Not about his eye wandering, no. He really is a very focused individual. I've seen his 'everything's great, no worries' act. It's just that, an act. But because he's focused and you're the one he's focused on, he's going to be putting that energy into making you happy."

"Is that bad?" I was wondering where Chuckie was going with this.

"No." He sounded exasperated. "But he's only known you a year. I have half our lives' experience. I can say without a doubt that it would take you quite a while to adjust to my lifestyle. Could you? Sure, because I know the things to do to make you feel right about it—we come from very similar backgrounds—and I'm fairly unostentatious. Martini is too. However, he grew up with a father who showered his wife with everything and lived on a huge estate. He comes from royalty, for God's sake, and even though he didn't know it, clearly Alfred's imitated that lifestyle as much as he could within Earth-American standards."

"I guess."

Chuckie made another sound of exasperation. "The clothes you've been in, as an example—how comfortable are you in them?"

I thought about it. "Well, I like that Jeff thinks they're really sexy."

"And I saw your expression when you looked at the price tags. You were ready to cut a vein open. You look sexy in a concert T-shirt, Kitty. You just woke up and were sleeping in your dress and a man's jacket, you have total bed hair, and you're still sexy."

"Gee, um, thanks." I started to get up to brush my hair, but he pulled me back down.

"I've seen it. For years. We lived next door in the dorms, remember? Hell, even when you joined the sorority and moved in there, you looked like this half the time when I came by."

"Yeah, I always liked to look my best. Fine, point made. And, yeah, I love these clothes, but I wouldn't want an entire wardrobe of them."

"Right. You love them because they're a special indulgence. He may be an empath, but unless you set the stage right away for how you want to live, long-term, he's going to err on the side of extravagance, and that's going to cause major marital issues for the two of you down the road."

"Why are you telling me this?"

He shook his head. "Because I love you, idiot. You chose him over me, fine, I'm a big boy, have to learn to deal, but, hey, I'm still around should he screw up. Of course, he chose you over ruling an entire solar system. Let's be real—first the guy saves you at the last moment from a raving sociopath by running over a hundred miles and turning himself into the Hulk, and next he passes up total galaxy domination for you. There is no way I can ever up his ante, and he's not even doing it in competition with me—he's doing it because he loves you so much."

"Sometimes I think he thinks he's competing with you."

"He's jealous as hell, yeah. Can't blame him, really. Even the gay guys drool over you."

"James doesn't drool."

"Right. Put it this way: I can understand why Martini and Gower wonder about the two of you."

"Humph."

"Play coy; it's cute, and doesn't fool me." He hugged me. "I love you, okay? Yeah, romantically, but also as a friend. And that's all I'm getting, the friend part. So, as your friend, instead of letting you make a mistake that could cause that 'mating for life' idea to seem passé, I'm giving you the talk your parents can't, because they have no experience like this, and the one your other friends won't because they aren't aware it's an issue."

I hugged him back. "Okay, fine. And thanks. I'll make sure to get the ground rules on extravagance set early, okay?"

Chuckie kissed my forehead. "Good." He let me go. "Now go get changed, and please, God, brush your hair. I promised Reader I'd get you over to him once you were up and functioning."

"I thought you said I looked sexy like this."

"Only if we're going to fall into bed together and you're going to realize you don't love Martini and run away to Australia with me."

"Love you, but no."

"That's what I figured. So, go make yourself presentable even to those who don't want to jump your bones."

"You are *so* smooth." I got up to go into the bedroom.

"That's why I'm one of Australia's most eligible bachelors."

"Really?" This was news.

He shrugged. "Yeah. Just means all the bimbos and gold diggers come calling."

"We'll find you a nice girl."

"No. I found a nice girl. She just chose a nice alien instead." I opened my mouth, but he put his hand up. "You don't apologize for falling in love with a good man who'll take care of you and die for you if he has to, Kitty. Real men know how to take it."

I leaned down and hugged him tightly. He held me, but not too long. I straightened up and went to the bedroom. "You are a real man, Chuckie. You always have been, since we were thirteen years old."

CHAPTER 59

I GOT INTO THE BEDROOM and was rather proud of myself for not feeling overwhelmingly weepy. I was glad I'd had this talk with Reader already, because there was a part of me still afraid of getting married. I wasn't afraid to marry Chuckie—the comfort level was so high with him that it wouldn't seem awkward.

On the other hand, the uncertainty and potential risks that would come with Martini were both appealing and a little scary. On the other hand, the sex more than made up for a little apprehension.

I went to the closet. The sexy outfit I now owned two of was there and clean, and there were shoes to match. The A-C Elves really were top-notch. Decided to go for it and hoped Martini would get out of isolation soon and be happy about my outfit choice.

"Chuckie, do I have time to take a shower?"

"Yes, please," he called. "The others might lie to you, but, trust me, you need one, unless your new fragrance is Eau de Rank."

"Thanks ever, Mister Smooth Operator."

"If I were smooth, I'd have told you I'd shower with you. Close the door—I'm human, and there's only so much temptation I can take."

I shut the bedroom door and the bathroom door. Took one of the faster showers of recent times. Of course, the rare showers without Martini were, by their very nature, faster than what I'd become accustomed to. Dried off, combed the hair into a severe ponytail, found lingerie in the drawers that matched the naked with fabric outfit. It made me look only slightly less naked, but I decided to call it a win. Shoes fit, all was well. Poofs and iPod transferred from Martini's bedraggled jacket to my purse, ready for action.

"Good lord, do you hate me or something?" Chuckie asked the moment I was out of the bedroom.

"What? What's wrong with how I look?"

"Not one damn thing. God, you like to torture a man, don't you?"

I rolled my eyes. "Oh, cut it out."

Chuckie sighed and stood up. "You need some sort of covering if you're going to wear that."

"We're going to Vegas, right? I'll fit in there."

He took my shoulders and turned me around. "God, it's as bad from the back. Really, go put on some clothes."

"I don't have a wrap, okay?"

"Find one. Before I rape you." He gave me a gentle push toward the bedroom.

"Fine, fine." Went back to the closet. The Elves had been by. There was a light jacket that could work with the outfit, at least as a cover-up. I put it on. "Thanks, uh, whoever you are."

Went back out. "Better," Chuckie said. He shook his head. "And you wonder why Martini's the most jealous man on the planet? Good lord." He took my elbow and led me out of the room.

We got in the elevator, and I was happy to realize I just wanted Martini out of isolation and in here with me. "We are going to Vegas, right?"

"Yes. All your bridesmaids are there already."

"Doing what?"

He grinned. "As near as I can tell, learning how to be fashion models."

"James is having fun, isn't he?"

"Yeah, I think he is. It's hard, transitioning from a regular life into covert ops. Some, like your mother, do it naturally. Some, like me, learn it easily enough. Some, like you and Reader, do well with it but have a strong need to still feel like 'regular' people."

"You go through this a lot with your operatives?" We got out at the launch level.

"Yeah. Not everyone can be an operative, not everyone can last as an operative."

"You think I'll last?"

He shrugged as our gate was calibrated. "You have the genetics for me to say yes. On the other hand, your husband may not want you to."

"You think Jeff's going to make me stop being the head of Airborne?" Chuckie made the "you first" gesture. I groaned and stepped through the gate. Icky as always. The stall was really nice again and familiar, so I knew we were in the Mandalay complex. I stepped out, Chuckie right behind me. The several men in the place all stared. "Wow, that was great, stud," I said as I wrapped my arm around Chuckie's waist and headed us for the door. "The earth moved."

"For me too." We managed not to laugh until we were out. "I hope that's recorded somewhere so I can torture Martini with it."

"Uh-huh. So, my question?"

"Yes, I think he's going to ask you to stop being an active agent. I would." He steered us through the casino. Like Reader, he kept a firm hold on my shoulders so I couldn't detour to a craps table.

"Why?"

He rolled his eyes. "Well, I'd want to keep the mother of my children safe and protected and all that."

"I guess I'll cross that bridge when we get to it."

"Yeah, since I blew it by admitting I'd do the same thing, and so can't use that as leverage to get you to say yes and run into the Blue Velvet Chapel."

"See, now, that's the difference between you and Jeff."

"Gee, that's all? Maybe I still have a chance. How about it?"

"Lemme ponder."

"Take all the time you need."

We sauntered through the casino, and I felt comfortably dressed again. I had more on than the cocktail waitresses, after all. I felt someone watching us, so I did a casual scan of the room. No one seemed to be taking that much of an interest.

"What?" Chuckie asked quietly.

"See anyone watching us? Specifically, Mister Joel Oliver anywhere? Or more potential A-C spies?"

He did a similar scan. Well, his was a lot more casual, but still, a scan. "Nope, no one out of the ordinary. What's your spider-sense picking up?"

"No idea. I guess nothing. Probably just tired still."

"Maybe." Chuckie didn't seem to dismiss this, which was kind of flattering. Or would have been if I had any clear reason for feeling that we were being watched. I looked around again, but I couldn't spot anyone paying us undue attention, not even our personal paparazzo.

We were near the Sports Book, and Chuckie turned in. "Need to bet on the ponies before we catch up with everyone else?" For all I knew, that was another way he kept the millions rolling in.

"No." We went up to someone whose back was to us. All I could see was that the person wore a hat and trench coat. Chuckie tapped a shoulder. "Oliver from the *World Weekly News*, I presume?"

Sure enough. He turned around and heaved a sigh. "*Mister Joel* Oliver. Please. It's only polite to address someone in the manner of their choosing."

"If I were concerned about being polite to you, that could matter to me." Chuckie sounded calm but quite unfriendly. "What are you doing here?"

"Not taking pictures." This seemed true. I couldn't spot anything remotely cameralike on him.

"I'll bet." Chuckie looked around and waved down a security guard. "This man has a hidden camera on him."

The security guard looked at Oliver. "Oh. Him. We searched him before he came into the Sports Book, sir."

"Search him again," Chuckie said, patiently but with authority in his tone.

"Yes, sir, Mister Reynolds." The guard started to pat Oliver down.

"I note you have a good deal of influence," Oliver said to Chuckie. "Must be because you're C.I.A."

The security guard snorted. "No. It's because he's got more money than God, and all the staff's on alert to do whatever the hell he wants." The guard looked over his shoulder. "No offense meant, Mister Reynolds."

"None taken," Chuckie said amiably. "I appreciate the staff taking care of me and my friends and associates. It's why we're at this complex." I managed to keep my mouth shut, though it took an effort.

Sure enough, there was a hidden camera on Oliver. The security guard called in a couple of his associates to help escort Oliver for a more detailed and personal search. Chuckie gave each security guard a tip, for which they all thanked him as if he were the most important man in the world.

"How'd you know?" I asked quietly, as the guards hustled Oliver off.

He shrugged. "Some things are a given. A so-called photojournalist like Mister Joel Oliver always has more than one trick. Besides, I saw the flash when we were walking by."

"How did you make out a camera flash from all the other flashing going on?"

He grinned. "Advanced training techniques to enhance the observational skills I already had."

"Will you ever teach those to me?"

"Sure. Your mother taught me most of them." Always the way. Mom trained everyone *but* me, it sometimes seemed. Chuckie laughed at my expression. "But after your honeymoon."

We left the Sports Book and went to THEhotel and up to the top floor. Chuckie headed us toward his side of the floor. "Um, I'm in the other gigantic room."

"Yes, but Reader and your bridesmaids are not. So if you want to go cheat on Martini with me, your room is the right spot. If you want to hook up with the others and get the dresses straightened out, you have to go to my room. I'm sure you know my vote."

"Oh, fine. Your room."

"Step one of my master plan is achieved. She foolishly believed me." He opened the door and I saw—what looked like an entire wedding boutique.

"Um, Chuckie?"

He led me inside. "Have I mentioned that I'm really rich, the Martini family is really rich, and you're all still, technically, C.I.A. operatives? I mean, the aliens are still here, and until they safely leave or sign the 'we love the Earth' oath, you all, by Martini's agreement and the original 'we A-Cs love the Earth' agreement, still work for me."

I looked up at him. He was grinning. "You really are a great guy."

"Yeah. That and three bucks will get me a small latte I get to drink alone." He kissed my forehead. "I console myself with the fact that I get to watch the modeling session, seeing as I am representing the groom's interests and allowed final say."

"Wow. Money really does change everything."

CHAPTER 60

"KITTY!" MY NAME WAS SHRIEKED** by seven women in unison. This unison thing was getting out of hand. Maybe it was wedding related.

I looked around. They were all giggling and laughing. Each one of them was in a different formal dress, and they seemed to be having a great time. "You guys aren't drinking, are you?"

"Well, duh," Lorraine said. "Serene, Claudia, and I can't."

Queen Renata smiled. "The rest of us decided to err on the side of safety. But Charles ordered delicious sparkling apple cider."

"Oh, good."

"Cheapest party I've ever thrown," Chuckie said with a grin, as he filled up everyone's glasses and gave me one. Crystal champagne glasses. I felt like a real grown up teenybopper.

Reader came out from the bedroom. "Okay, the gals are in a variety of bridesmaid dresses. You can't really choose theirs until we have yours."

"Hi, James, good to see you."

"Yeah, on a schedule here. Chop-chop." He grabbed me and pulled me into the bedroom. I expected some questions about Chuckie. I saw a long, mobile clothing rack with a lot of white dresses hanging on it. "I have an assortment here. I want to see you in all of them, even if you fall in love with one immediately. Got it?"

"Um . . ."

"Don't worry about shoes or lingerie. Just go commando while trying them on; we'll get appropriate lingerie once we've picked the dress and, of course, same with shoes. No worries about fitting, your breasts are perky enough that you can get away with no bra in at least half of these dresses, and you'll be good enough to test in the rest."

"Um . . ."

"Oh, same with veil. I'm not sure I want you in one in the first place, but it'll depend on the dress."

"Um . . ."

He took my glass out of my hand. "Right. This is a no-no around these dresses. You can have some in between changes."

"Um . . ."

"Call me if you need to be zipped up. The girls are a little giddy, and I don't want any rips or tears. The rejects have to go back."

"Um . . ."

"What?"

"Where did these come from?"

He grinned. "I still have contacts, babe. Designers are really cutthroat and competitive. Just told them I had a friend marrying into a lot of money who needed to look beyond beautiful and who might, you know, have some paparazzi at her wedding. Amazing what showed up as options."

"We're having paparazzi?" I wasn't putting anything past Reader or Chuckie right now. And Mister Joel Oliver certainly seemed capable of getting out of the clutches of the law with ease.

I got the cover-boy grin. "You do understand the definition of 'might,' don't you? Now get out of that great outfit I picked for you and into the designer dresses I ordered for you."

He zipped out of the room, taking my cider, and shut the door behind him. I stared at the dresses. I stared some more. I contemplated where to start. Had no idea.

Heard some more squealing and shouting. They were all having a lot more fun than I was. I was, I realized, intimidated by the array of designer beauty in front of me.

There was a soft knock, and the door opened. "Ah, what a surprise." My mother came in and closed the door. "Charles called to let us know you were finally here."

"Who?"

"Me, your grandmothers, and Lucinda. I told the other girls they'd have to wait for later."

"Wait for what for later?"

"Your bachelorette party." She said it like it was obvious. Then she sighed. "Kitten, just one question."

"Yeah?"

"Do you love Jeff enough to live with him the rest of your life, deal with problems, worry about him, have his child or children, go through good times and bad, sickness and health, prosperity and poverty, times when you'll hate each other, be bored with each other, wonder if you should have married one of those other options, and yet still stay with him, happily, both over time and in the end?"

I thought about it, about everything I'd been through with him since I'd met him a year ago. The great sex. All the times I'd harpooned him or he'd caught me. The fights. The making up from the fights. What I'd learned from him, and about him, and about myself because of him. The great sex. The way he never treated me as less than his equal. How he could protect me without making me feel helpless. How I couldn't have any real secrets from him. How, when I got right down to it, I didn't want secrets, in fact, loved that he not only could but would adapt to make me happy, help me feel secure, calm my fears. And, of course, the great sex. It was great because he was a god in bed, but he was a god in bed because he loved me and went out of his way to make sure it was great, every time.

"Yes."

"Good. Then stop standing there panicking, get out of that Super Slut outfit all the men love, and start trying on dresses." She took my purse and put it on the bed along with hers. "James wants us to start with the cocktail length ones. I think because he has his favorites already picked out but doesn't want you guessing and being contrary."

"That's it? No hug? No atta girl? No other marriage talk?"

She grinned at me. "Awwww." She came back and gave me her breath-stopping bear hug. "Atta girl," she whispered. "That was my entire marriage talk. The rest is up to the two of you."

I hugged her back. "I love you, Mom."

She kissed my head. "Good. You know the saying—your son is your son until he takes a wife, but your daughter's your daughter for the rest of your life. Your father and I wouldn't have it any other way. And we love Jeff, too, just in case you were worried we were going to suggest you marry Charles or Christopher, like every other relative."

I laughed as we separated. "You mean you're finally off the 'check out your options' bandwagon?"

Mom shrugged as she went back to the clothing rack, and I started to get out of my clothes. "You checked, and your decision seems made. While we love Charles and Christopher and Brian, too, they aren't your choice. We'd love any decent man you were in love with, kitten, but your grandfather's right. You do need a big tomcat to take care of you and keep you in line—and Jeff seems to be the best there is at that job. Besides," she added as she tossed me a grin over her shoulder, "Jeff seems to want lots of children."

"Why is it always about the babies with our family?"

She shrugged as she brought Option 1 over. "It's natural. You always want to see your children get children they deserve."

"Thanks ever." Tried on the dress. It fit and looked really good. "Wow."

"James insists you show him everything, whether you like it or not."

"I like this a lot."

"Yes, I'm sure." She led me out.

Got a ton of squeals from the various females. Reader looked extremely critical, and Chuckie shrugged. "It's nice."

"Take it off. Next." Reader sounded like my Uncle Mort.

"Um, James? I like it. Chuckie likes it."

"He said it was nice. Nice is fine for dinner with the boss. Nice is not fine for your wedding. Back in the room, next dress." It was clear from his tone that there would be no arguing allowed.

Mom and I went back and did the whole thing over again. And over again. Mom got tired and called Lucinda in for assistance. So she helped me do the whole thing over again. And over again. The girls and my grandmothers squealed with joy at each appearance. Chuckie pronounced a few more nice, a couple as okay, several as gag-worthy—at least, I took him sticking his finger toward his open mouth and making gagging sounds to mean that he didn't think they were the best choice—and a couple as deathly dull, indicated by him leaning his head back and snoring loudly.

"I thought this was supposed to be fun."

Lucinda laughed. "I understand now why James told us concentrated and fast was the correct choice. Imagine doing this at dress shop after dress shop. For weeks on end. And not coming up with anything."

I thought about it. "Wow, let's try on the next dress that's right here!"

She nodded. "Jeffrey's always said you were smart."

CHAPTER 61

WE WERE DOWN TO THE LAST TWO DRESSES. I was clear that mermaid style was the way to go, since Chuckie had started perking up as soon as I tried the first one. But that had been several dresses ago, and nothing had made Reader happy.

Mom was on dress duty so Lucinda could sit and rest. The three of us needed a vacation already. But it was great for girl bonding. I'd heard a lot about Martini's youthful exploits and mishaps, so I had a good arsenal of stored blackmail. Same with Christopher. They had pretty much been inseparable, but I'd known that. I reminded myself that they'd both had a year to get used to me, and everything would be fine.

I realized I was worrying about things I never thought of normally as I slid into another dress. This one was simple but gorgeous. Mermaid style, sleeveless with straps, and a lot of fancy embroidery with silver thread on shiny satin.

"Wow, this one looks wonderful." Mom sounded impressed. "It'll take a while to get in and out of it with all the buttons in the back, but it's worth it."

Went out, got the requisite girl squeals—their enthusiasm, unlike mine, Mom's, and Lucinda's, hadn't waned—and Chuckie sat up. "Nice. Very nice." The way he said it made it sound better than nice.

Reader nodded slowly and made the twirly-finger move he'd been perfecting. I only twirled when Chuckie liked something, so I hadn't twirled all that often. "Good. Keep it as·an option. Let's see the next."

"James, there's only one next."

"Fine. Let's see it."

Sighed, went back into the room. "Chuckie likes it, James says we can keep it as an option." Mom and Lucinda both heaved sighs, and Mom started unbuttoning while Lucinda took the last dress down.

"It's very similar," she said, sounding thoughtful. "Less . . . showy than the other one."

It was similar. Sleeveless with thin spaghetti straps where the other had thicker ones, embroidery that was the same color as the main fabric so it was more subtle, silk instead of satin so softer and less shiny than the first. It hugged my body and flared out just above my knees. It had a short train that complemented my entire backside. Cut low enough in front and back that a bra was out of the question, but I didn't need one with the way the bodice was designed and fitted. The back cut straight across, under my shoulder blades, the front had a subtle dip instead of cutting straight across or plunging. Like the other, it buttoned all the way down the middle of my back to the end of the train.

Mom and Lucinda stared at me. "This is the dress." They said it unison. The unison thing was starting to really freak me out. It had to be wedding related.

I was heading out when Lucinda stopped me. "Take your hair out of the ponytail."

I did. I mean, why not. Mom dug my brush out of my purse, and I did a full brush and fluff. Noted that I could actually move in this dress, form-fitting though it was.

Went out, wondering what the male reaction was going to be. Interesting reaction from the girls: They all went quiet, as though they'd drawn their breath in. My grandmothers looked as if they were going to cry.

Okay, great. What about the male opinion? Looked over to Chuckie and Reader. Chuckie was sitting up like he'd been goosed, his eyes were wide, and he looked shocked and wistful at the same time.

Looked at Reader. Got the usual frowny-face of concentration and the finger twirl. Twirled. Reader indicated I should twirl again. "On your toes."

"Yes, sir." Twirled again on my toes. Once more for good measure. "Getting dizzy, James."

He grinned. "I knew Paula wouldn't let me down."

"Paula?"

"Paula Varsalona. Great designer. Great lady, too, love her." He waved his hand in front of Chuckie's face.

"Uh-huh." Chuckie was still staring at me.

"Perfect! That's the reaction we're looking for. Get out of that one carefully, please. I'll bag it and move it as soon as you're dressed."

"Um, does that mean I can sit down and have something to drink?"

"Yes. For a few minutes."

"Thank you, Sergeant Reader. Thanks for starting me on the exact opposite end than this dress was, too."

Got the cover-boy grin flashed at me. "You deserved to have the full experience. Just did it in a short amount of time. Thank me later." He turned to the other girls. "Okay, we're going to stick with the same designer for you. So, everyone but Lorraine I want changing into one of these other dresses. Should have all your sizes in here." He pulled a rack over and looked at me. "Go on, out of the dress."

I rolled my eyes and went back into the bedroom. "Well?" Mom asked. "What did Charles and James think?"

"This is the dress."

Mom and Lucinda high-fived each other. They got me out of the dress and hung it carefully while I put my clothes back on. Grabbed my purse—the Poofs were snoozing. They seemed to do that a lot. Lucky things. Then the three of us went out of the room.

"Now what?" I asked Reader.

"Sit." He put me in a chair next to Chuckie, who still seemed dazed.

"Dude, you okay?"

"Yeah." Chuckie shook himself. "That's a great dress. Have I mentioned that Martini's a total womanizer, has a major gambling habit, and secretly hates dogs and cats? And children, he hates children."

I laughed. "No, you actually said he was a great guy who didn't have a roving eye and was focused solely on my happiness."

"Did I? Man, am I a moron."

"Nah, but I love you for the honesty." I patted his hand.

"Yeah, great. Lucky bastard."

The girls were out and dressed now. Reader had them all

in the same thing. "James, the dresses are all black." Well, with a white flower at the hip. But still, black. Gorgeous, but black.

"Yes, your wedding colors are black and white." He looked at them with a critical eye and made the twirly-sign.

"James, I thought we were tired of black and white."

"We are. Your groom, however, is not. He loves black and white. Several of your bridesmaids love black and white. And half of your guests think black and white is da bomb in terms of color choices. We're on a limb by not going with Armani in the first place. Let's not push the luck."

"I was thinking blue."

"Yes, I know." He looked pained.

"I had a really pretty blue all picked out."

"Yes, I know. It was a great color and honestly would look wonderful."

"Then why not?"

"I refer you back to argument number one. Girls, really, how hard is it to remember to twirl? You're not even drinking alcohol."

They all sighed and twirled, and I looked closely at the dresses. Full-length satin, sleeveless with a plunging neckline, plunging back, gathered midriff from just under the breasts to the top of the hips, A-line skirt that went out pretty wide. Excellent for hiding tails and such.

"I like it. Not wild about the flower."

"Of course. Don't care; it makes the dress more dramatic. But have to be sure it's the right choice." Reader had the frowny-face on again. "Girls, go back, walk out one by one, twirl, go back."

They all sighed but did what he asked. While we watched the impromptu catwalk, I polled my mother, Lucinda, and my grandmothers. "So, what do you guys think?"

Nana Sadie was watching intently. "I don't want them to look better than you."

"Not my fault they're all gorgeous."

Nona Maria sighed. "True. But you were perfect in the dress. James is so good with fashion."

"That's why he's my partner, yeah."

Both grandmothers looked at me, gave me very innocent smiles, then turned back to watch the rest of the girls do their modeling thing.

Something about their expressions made me wonder. I

watched the girls more closely. The dresses were really great—
they looked good on all of them, even Jareen, and when you
considered that the dresses were looking good on Dazzlers as
well as Giant Lizards, you had to figure the designer was fabulous. No tails showed at all, no matter how the Animal Planet
girls moved. Awesome dresses. I'd live with the flower at the
waist, it *was* more dramatic.

My brain kicked. None of the girls were disguised as
human. I had seven aliens parading up and down in designer
wear, and no one was batting an eye.

I cleared my throat. "Ah, Nana? Nona? What do you see,
when you look at the girls?"

"I see seven lovely ladies," Nona Maria said. She sounded
like she was trying not to giggle.

"We're very proud of you for having such an interracial
wedding party," Nana Sadie added. Considering how upset
she and my Papa Abe had been when my parents got married, her attitude was impressive. Nona and Nono hadn't been
much more thrilled at the start. Now each set loved the other
like true family. My grandparents had come a long way on
religious tolerance over the ensuing decades. I got the feeling
they were coming along even quicker on species tolerance.

"Um, Chuckie?"

He sighed. "Ask your mother."

"Mom?"

She sighed. "Your grandparents had a difficult time believing your reasons for leaving the party in the first place. Then
when you and Michael came back and others started acting
like the end of the world was coming and so forth, they got
more suspicious."

"So, what, you just broke down and shared highest-level
government secrets with them to stop them from complaining?" How had this woman been working in covert ops for
most of her life?

Mom gave me a dirty look. "No."

"Did Dad crack?" He was the more easily guilted of the
two of them.

Dirtier look. "No."

"Who shared, then? Not Uncle Mort!" The high-up-there
career Marine? I would figure someone would have to be cutting off body parts to get Uncle Mort to share any secret, let
alone government ones.

Dirtiest look yet. "Hardly."

"Who then?"

Lucinda sighed. "We discussed it. They're all becoming family now. That means what we do affects them. Alfred, Stanley, Ericka, Richard, and I made the decision. Richard told them. Most of them took it very well."

"Most of them?" My voice was heading to the dog-only register. "You told my entire family tha—" Chuckie put his hand on my wrist and I stopped myself. Maybe they hadn't said what I thought.

"That you're marrying a space alien?" Nona Sadie finished for me. "Yes. You know, Kitty, a prince is a prince."

"Oh, my God." It hadn't occurred to me that this was what Martini's title was if he wasn't king. "Guess it's a good thing Jeff passed on the Alpha Four crown then." Whoops. My mouth was doing that speaking without thinking thing again. Hated that.

My grandmothers exchanged glances. "Pay up," Nana Sadie said.

Nona Maria sighed and nodded. "I always take the long shot." She dug into her purse and handed money to Nana Sadie.

"You two knew about that? And you were *betting*? On whether or not Jeff would choose the kingship over me? You were betting on it? And Nona picked that he *would*?" My family. The love was overwhelming.

Nona Maria shrugged. "I told you, I always bet long shots. Besides, he'd had to deal with Carla. I mean, lesser men have run screaming away because of her."

"Like three husbands," Mom muttered.

"Right," Nana Sadie said. "And he'd already dealt with our Ruth, too." She shook her head. "I almost felt daring, taking you over the kingship."

I looked at Reader. He was focused on the dresses. "Girls, bend, sit. Want to make sure no one's going to bust out." They groaned but followed his orders.

Looked to Chuckie. He shrugged. "It's a security breach, yeah. Considering Angela's technically my superior, though, nothing I could do about it. Besides, I wasn't there when it happened, and Richard, as the Sovereign Pontifex, has free rein to make these decisions."

"They were betting! On Jeff and me!"

He looked over at my grandmothers. "Did you give me any odds at all?"

"Oh, yes, Charles," Nona Maria said. "If Jeffrey took the kingship, you were the clear favorite to marry her."

"Christopher had longer odds because of his relationship to Jeffrey," Nana Sadie added.

"Thanks. Oh, I assume everyone did the spit swear and pinkie oath?"

"Yes, Charles. Carla had to have a special memory implanted. Everyone else, no issues. Most of us had our suspicions aroused last year, when all those handsome men came and took us to special bunkers for our protection. It was nice to know what was really going on. The children were all given the same lectures the A-C children get, apparently, and they seem clear on why secrecy is important and why you don't talk about your alien relatives or you go to the doctors for special tests." Nona Maria was laughing.

"So you were all busy while we were out saving the world?" I didn't know whether to be relieved or upset. Settled for a combination of the two. "And, Mom, everyone in the family knows, other than Aunt Carla? Even Aunt Ruth knows?"

"Your Aunt Ruth was relieved to find out that by A-C traditions you and Jeff had been engaged for six months. She was on board after that. Your Aunt Carla firmly believes you're marrying the Martini and Rossi scion and one of the top field-imageering teams is assigned to her. She'll see what we want her to see, just like all the hired help, and that will be fine."

"I can see so many ways this could end up not being fine. I can't even talk there are so many ways."

"Oh, Kitty, relax," Nana Sadie said. "James, what's your decision?"

"We'll keep them." He nodded. "Okay, girls, out of those. Make sure you bag your dress and mark it with the tag so there's no confusion about whose is whose." He pulled out his phone. "Need the pickup and returns I told you about. Right, very thankful, just didn't work with the bride's personal style. Right. Good, pronto."

Reader closed his phone and looked at me. "I have the mother and grandmother dresses already picked out."

"What's Jeff wearing?"

He grinned at me. "What I picked out."

"Is it a white jacket?" I asked hopefully.

Reader looked pained. "No, it's not. He looked smarmy in the white jacket. He's in something that looks great on him, and that's all you need to know until the wedding." He went into the bedroom, presumably to bag my wedding dress.

"I wanted a white jacket," I called after him.

"Don't care," he shouted back.

"Ten dollars says she loves it," Nana Sadie said quickly.

"Taken," Nona Maria said just as quickly.

It was like I was in the middle of the Old Ladies Bookie Club. And it was run by my grandmothers. I needed a drink, but that was out of the question.

Made do. Grabbed a bottle of sparkling cider and chugged it.

CHAPTER 62

SEVERAL A-CS SHOWED UP and took the vast array of dresses away. I discovered we had a shoe store and a lingerie department in Chuckie's suite, too. They'd just been hidden by the clothes.

Shoes and lingerie went a lot faster. Since I didn't need a bra, Reader put me into a white lace garter belt with thigh-high white hose. We had the commando versus thong argument. I won; in my experience, being dressed up meant I was at risk for my clothing being destroyed and my dress flying up in the air. We compromised, and my thong was white lace. Shoes matched the dress; they were high, but comfortable.

"I need something old, something new, something borrowed, and something blue."

"Dress is new and borrowed."

"James, that means I can't get it dirty. It's me, you know it's going to get dirty."

He sighed. "Fine. Jeff already told me to spend whatever on the dress you liked. Blue is handled." He pulled a light blue garter out of his pocket.

"Nice. So, blue and new handled, right?"

"Right." He looked at my grandmothers. "Who has a necklace or bracelet Kitty can borrow that will go with her dress? Older the better."

Mom raised her hand. "I do. It's what I wore at my wedding. Yes, it's with me," she added.

"What is it?"

"Diamond necklace, should work just fine with the dress, bracelet matches. It was your father's wedding present to me."

"Dad was a grad student when you got married."

Nana Sadie shook her head. "Your Uncle Jacob is a jeweler. You think he didn't give his brother a deal?"

"Right, sorry. Sort of dizzy and overwhelmed."

"That's the story of your life," Chuckie said with a grin.

Everyone's accessories covered, I was ready to collapse. Killing parasitic superbeings and dealing with psychos and megalomaniacs seemed so much easier than all of this. Everyone else also seemed to be having a great time. I wondered what was wrong with me.

"Okay, Four Seasons time," Reader announced.

Every other woman squealed. "Um, huh?"

"Spa treatments. Of course, we had to stagger because we had so many, but everyone should be done with plenty of time for the party."

"Party?"

"Your bachelorette party. Mentioned before? Let's keep with the program, shall we?" It was like Reader had channeled Martha Stewart.

"Is Jeff going to have a bachelor party?" I tried not to sound apprehensive about this and failed utterly.

"No." Reader was ushering. Chuckie already had the elevator, as near as I could tell.

"So, I get a party but Jeff doesn't?" The last thing I wanted was him around a stripper, and it wasn't like he could get drunk. But it didn't seem fair that I'd get a party and he wouldn't.

Reader sighed. "He'll be taken care of."

"How? This is Vegas. Define 'taken care of.'"

"Tell her," Chuckie said as Reader dragged me to the elevator. One car, with all my bridesmaids, had already gone down. "She'll just whine and badger it out of you."

"Fine. Jeff and the other guys will be 'crashing' your party. Okay? Happy the surprise is ruined?"

"Yes. 'Cause now I can enjoy it." We held the elevator; Chuckie locked up; we all went down. The girls were waiting for us, all looking human. Chuckie led the way. I hung back and grabbed Reader. "I want a word with James. Not Sergeant Reader."

He sighed dramatically. "Okay, girlfriend. What?"

"Do I get to plan anything?"

He gave me a long look. "Do you want to? Truly?"

I thought about it. "Honestly . . . no."

"Right. Can we go?"

I took his arm, then stopped dead. "Oh, my God. James, I don't have a ring for Jeff! I don't have anything for Jeff!"

Reader shook his head. "Oh, ye of little faith." He put his arm around my shoulders and started moving us along. "Do you really think I was going to let that slip?"

"You picked out the wedding ring I'm giving to him? I love you, and you have awesome taste, but, um, shouldn't I be doing that?"

"You wound me." He wouldn't say another word until we were at the Four Seasons.

Right before we went in I got the "being watched" feeling again. I looked around without any attempt to appear casual. Saw no one taking an undue interest. Looked for Mister Joel Oliver. Didn't see him or anyone in a trench coat. But I hadn't spotted him before, Chuckie had. "James, do you feel like we're being followed?"

"Feel like? No. Know we are? Yes."

I stopped walking. "Excuse me? You know we're being followed and you haven't mentioned it? Is it more A-C spies? And why doesn't Chuckie know?" I wasn't at the dog-only register yet, but it was only going to be a matter of a few seconds.

"Slow down, calm down, deep breaths. We're not being followed by A-C spies, at least not that I'm aware of. What we *are* being followed by are paparazzi."

"I thought you told the designers we might have paparazzi as a clever ruse to get free dresses."

"I did. The dresses arriving, however, ensured paparazzi. Sort of like a symbiotic relationship."

"Why can't I spot who they are?" I asked while looking around wildly.

Another sigh, this one heaved. "Girlfriend, the really good ones don't stand outside and scream at you to get a shot. The really good ones ensure you have no idea they're there."

"I know they're there. I just don't know where. And why doesn't this bother you?"

"Lived through it, it's better if you just ignore that they're there. Trust me."

"Mister Joel Oliver's found us every time. Is he watching us again?"

Reader grinned. "He's handled."

"Chuckie tell you about Security taking him away?"

"Yes. And we have an effective plan in place to circumvent his interference. That I'm not going to tell you about at this time."

"What about the other paparazzi?"

"The plan will circumvent them, when we need it to."

I figured we could stand outside the Four Seasons and argue about this some more, and thereby give the Invisible Spy Paparazzi more time to really get the lighting right for their shots, or I could do what the former top international male model said. I chose to go for the smarter option. "Fine. I'll pretend I don't feel eyes on me."

"That's my girl."

We went in, and Reader checked me into the spa but had me stay in the waiting room. Two burly men came in with a couple, both dressed in business suits, the man in brown, the woman in red. Clearly, they were humans. They gave Reader wide smiles.

The burly men were carrying large cases wrapped in velvet. The couple gave Reader air kisses. I tried not to gag. The burlies opened the cases up—and I was treated to an amazing array of men's wedding rings.

"James? I have no idea of Jeff's ring size." Wow, I sucked as a fiancée, big time.

He sighed. "I know. I, however, do. All the rings here are sized for Jeff. Pick one."

"Mademoiselle is assured of quality," the man said, in a fake French accent, oozing attempted charm.

"These have diamonds in them," the woman said, pointing to the rings that obviously had diamonds in them. "Perhaps mademoiselle would like to consider some of these for her lucky husband-to-be?"

"Mademoiselle has an uncle who's a jeweler. Please stop with the unctuous charm. I don't need a sales pitch, I need help."

"I did warn you," Reader said.

"Fine, you never know who's listening," the man said, sounding a lot more like he was from the Bronx than from France. "Look, honey, it's a symbol. Sure, he'll wear it every day for the rest of his life, or until you get divorced, but they're all good."

"His family mates for life."

The woman snorted. "Yeah, heard *that* before."

"James? Who are these people?"

"Among the best jewelers in Vegas."

"And his cousins," the woman said. "He visits when his friends are doing it up right, but during other times? Not so much."

I looked at Reader. He shrugged. "Family. You know."

"Yeah." 'Nuff said, really.

I started looking in earnest for the right ring. This was, of course, easier said than done. There were at least two hundred to choose from. My eyes started to cross. "Um . . ."

Reader sighed. "Cut down to the twenty I selected." I opened my mouth; he gave me the hairy eyeball. "The ones closest to her wedding set." I closed my mouth.

"I'd still like a look," the man said. I put my hand out before Reader could glare at me, and he slid the ring off and examined it. He whistled. "Know where he bought this. You're marrying well. Finest quality diamond. Small though."

"She has small hands," the woman said. "Looks better on her." I decided she might have taste.

"Yeah! It's like almost no one gets that."

She grinned. "If you weren't with family? I'd be discussing how we needed to trade you up, pronto, to a diamond of decent size. Since you are with family, I agree that anything too large on a smaller woman looks fake. Stick to your guns."

They both examined my engagement ring, then produced Reader's much smaller selection.

Now that I finally had time to examine it, my ring had an unusual and intricate design, and I realized it looked a very little bit like the design of the Unity Necklace. All I wanted to do was find Martini, cuddle up in his lap, and tell him how he was the most romantic man in the galaxy, and I knew I was the luckiest girl in the universe.

Not an option, so I looked carefully for a ring that might somehow manage to say the same thing to him every day. I was able to discard some right away because the designs were Celtic and while beautiful and intricate, they were too human.

I was down to ten and had to decide if I wanted a dia-

mond or not. What word had Chuckie used . . . unostentatious.
"James, are diamonds in a man's ring ostentatious?"

"Depends on the ring. If you're asking me if I think Jeff will
like a diamond in his ring, yes, if you give it to him, because it's
you giving it to him, but if he had a choice, no." He checked his
cell phone, sighed, and pointed to two rings. "This one or that
one. Take your pick; they're both 'him.' "

"I had two hundred and you just cut me down to two? Am
I off the schedule?"

"Yes, by a lot. Girlfriend, this is why you two couldn't settle
on anything."

"Jeff's picky, too."

"Yes. The prosecution rests."

I examined the two rings. They were both very unusual in
their design. One was thicker than the other, which allowed
for more design and also made it sturdier. I stared at them. The
thicker one seemed more manly. "Which do you like best?"

Both jewelers pointed to the thicker ring.

"James?"

He sighed. "Two things. Yes, the thicker one. And . . . it's the
one I would have told you to go with in the first place."

"We'll take it. Excuse me while I strangle your cousin."

"It's a common desire in the family," the woman said, while
the man cleaned the ring to perfection and put it into a nice
ring box. "It's worse because he's always right."

"Yeah, good point."

The man held the box out. Reader took it and put it in his
pocket. Money changed hands. He ensured I didn't see how
much.

Shook paws, the burlies loaded up the merchandise, and
Reader's cousins left. "You never introduced me."

"Nothing gets past you." His phone rang. "Hey, Christopher. Oh, good. Yeah, you're a little late, but, shocker alert,
no problem because things on this side took a while." He
laughed. "Of course, what else did you expect? The rest of the
guys are waiting in my room. Right. Tell him she's fine." He
snorted. "Well, yeah, but as fine as she's going to be. Tell him
that it's tomorrow, no matter how much he whines. Humans
have rituals. Yeah, more than A-Cs. Yeah. Great, see you in a
few minutes." He hung up.

"What's going on? Is everything okay?"

"Yep. Jeff's out of isolation, feeling fine. Christopher's riding herd on him."

"You know, I could pass on the spa thing and feed Jeff. He's always hungry when he gets out of isolation."

"No." Reader bent and kissed my cheek, then sat in the chair next to me and put his arm around me. "I know you're scared," he said softly. "He's scared, too. You two have been trying to make everything so perfect that nothing was happening. That's why I'm in charge of Operation About Time."

I started to laugh. "Yes, you totally are."

He smiled. "I've known Jeff for several years—he's always wanted to find the right girl and give her the wedding of her dreams. Only, his right girl didn't spend her time daydreaming about weddings and gowns—she spent it reading *Ms.* and the *Feminist Manifesto* and doing her best to not be shallow. None of her close girlfriends are girly-girls. One of her best friends is a guy, and not just any guy, but a brilliant nerd."

"And her other best friend is a gorgeous gay guy. Yeah, okay, sensing the trend."

"Now, for a little bit of a lecture."

"Oh, goody."

"All the ritual stuff? It's not for you and Jeff, so much. It's for everybody else. The actual ceremony? That's for your parents and grandparents. The reception, that's the wrap party. The honeymoon? Now that's only for you. But all the things leading up to it? Most of those are for your families and friends. For them to get this time with you before your life changes in a huge way. Now you're going to go into the spa and have a massage with Lorraine and Claudia, so they know they're still the more special of your friends."

"Okay." That sounded nice, actually.

"You're going to relax in the whirlpool with Felicia, Jareen, and Wahoa, who didn't want to try to explain to the masseuse why they look like humans but feel funny."

"Makes sense."

"Then you're going to have a facial with your mother, to have that private Mommy and Me time."

"What if it makes me break out?"

"Using stuff that won't—it's the freaking Four Seasons, babe. Next, you're going to have a manicure and pedicure with Lucinda, to have that bonding over the salon experience with your not-so-future mother-in-law."

Looked down at my fingernails. Fighting Moira and Bitch Leader hadn't done them any favors. "Okay, good plan."

"And, finally, you're going to join your grandmothers, Renata, and Serene in between each of these and have tea sandwiches and other girly things with them. Your grandmothers only wanted hand and foot rubs, and then they wanted to see everyone as they came through to tell them about their fun spa experiences. Renata's religion kind of forbids this sort of massive indulgence. But she enjoys your grandmothers very much, and she also took the hand and foot rub option."

"Why is Serene relegated to grandmother duty?"

He laughed. "It's not relegation, it's her choice. Serene is so happy to feel included that we can barely pry her away from them. She was up first of all of us and checking on your grandparents to see if they needed anything. When I was describing the spa plan, she begged, and I do mean begged, to stay with your grandmothers. So she gets the hand and foot option, too, and gets to feel like a part of a family."

"Works for me. What will you be doing while I'm spending the next hundred hours here?"

"It'll be the next, oh, five hours, give or take. And, what I'll be doing is riding herd on the male half of this extravaganza. We have tuxedo fittings that you've made me late for *but* it's okay because Jeff came out of isolation a little late."

"Is he—"

"He's fine. If he weren't fine, then, yes, we'd both be there, not here. But he's fine. Complaining that he knows you're stressed and need him."

"I am stressed, and I do need him."

"Right. The two of you are going to have to deal with the fact that for one more day, you aren't going to be making with the sexual Olympics. Think how much better it'll make the wedding night. Anticipation and all that."

"You're kidding me. Where am I sleeping tonight?"

"In the suite. With all the girls."

"Are you *kidding* me?"

"No. Jeff'll be with Christopher. Who's the best at keeping him under a semblance of control."

No sex with Martini until we were married? What was this, 1950? "When is my bachelorette party?"

"Around seven or eight, depending on when you're all done here. Guys will crash it a couple hours in. You can have some make-out time then. I'll be shutting the party down around midnight and riding herd on the ladies, particularly you."

"Jeff won't like me being on the same floor as Chuckie, you know."

"Nice try. See, the thing is, Renata is going to be with you. And Queen of the Amazons is clear on the 'no nookie with any man, even husband-to-be' rule for you tonight through wedding hour."

I gave up. "Okay. Are you getting us or is Chuckie?"

"Probably both of us. So there're two of us watching you."

"You make me sound like a criminal attempting to escape prison."

Reader kissed my cheek again. "I promise you, marriage isn't a prison. Just relax and enjoy the process." He stood up, helped me up, and ushered me into the main spa area, patted my bottom, then disappeared, off to do his Super Savior thing with the guys.

I considered my options. Decided that he and Chuckie had spent so much time and gone to so much trouble and expense, I should at least try to enjoy it.

Turns out, I did.

CHAPTER 63

TRUE TO HIS WORD, READER COLLECTED US around seven in the evening. None of us were overly hungry because we'd been grazing on all the girly food for hours. It was yummy girly food—the Four Seasons really did that up right—and I didn't have anyone stealing it off my plate, so I actually got enough to eat.

Chuckie was there, too, looking very amused. "Martini spent most of the time whining. You two are a fun couple when you're apart."

"We like being together, so sue us."

"No problem," he said as he took my arm. "I actually had a great time. Nothing like knowing something he doesn't to drive him insane."

"So he knows you helped choose my dress?"

"Knows, hates it, has to deal with the fact that he's going to be happy I helped." Chuckie sounded pretty happy about this. I tried not to worry about Martini's reactions to this, everything else Reader had going, and my dress. What if he didn't actually like it?

I was still relaxed enough from the spa experience that I only fretted about this a little bit. Besides, had a different fret to think about. "James says we have paparazzi. Other than Mister Joel Oliver, I mean."

"Yes, so he told me." He didn't seem fazed.

"This doesn't worry you?"

"I'm used to it."

"Excuse me?"

He shrugged. "One of Australia's most eligible bachelors, remember? Just ignore them and they'll go away."

"How are you doing . . . the job you do with paparazzi following you?"

"It's part of my cover." He sighed. "Your mother thinks it's great."

"I'll bet she does. Why are we worried about poor old Mister Joel Oliver, then?"

Chuckie gave me a long look. "Because he's actually right."

I considered this. "But no one believes him."

"Right." Chuckie's expression told me exactly what he was thinking.

"You kind of like him, don't you?"

He shrugged. "I'm not ready to go bowling with him, but I do understand what it's like to be in the position he's in."

"What's going to happen to him? James insinuated we didn't have to worry about MJO for a while."

"It's need to know, Kitty, and you don't."

I decided to give this up. Clearly only I was worried about strange people with stealth cameras following us around, and also clearly Chuckie wasn't going to tell me what was up with Oliver, either. I prayed it wasn't going to be something horrible like Oliver had been sent to Guantanamo, but I decided there was nothing I could do about it at this particular time. Besides, supposedly there was a party with my name on it in my near future. "So, where are we going?"

"Well, while Mix has a great view, I'm not sure it's your style. It's sort of hip, cool, and trendy."

"I think I should be insulted you know me this well."

"Right, so, we're going to House of Blues."

"Cool! Great food."

"Live band."

"House band?"

"Not exactly." He looked as though he was trying not to laugh.

"Who is it?"

"Well, we considered booking Aerosmith, but then we realized that would mean you would spend the evening offering yourself to Tyler and Perry, and that didn't seem like something Martini would appreciate in the short or long run."

Dang. They knew me far too well. "So you guys booked this

band specially? How in the world could you have done that on this kind of short notice?"

Chuckie shrugged. "As you said and Cyndi Lauper sang so well, money changes everything."

"Elton John?"

"Bank of Chuckie is not able to make that kind of loan."

"I thought you were rich."

"I still need to eat next week."

"Fine. Girl act or boy act?"

"Boy, because we also didn't think it was fair to you to put someone like Gwen Stefani up there so the guys both crashed the party early and spent the time offering themselves up to Gwen. We're going for 'fun party' here, not 'ending the relationship the night before the wedding.' I'd like to mention that this is a sacrifice on my part."

"You're both so thoughtful, and you're a prince. So, do I need to go through my entire iPod or are you going to tell me?"

"I'm going to make you wait until we're there."

"Humph."

Of course, it didn't take us long to get there. The "closed for private party" signs were kind of cool, since I was part of the private party. Got inside and wondered who all these people were. The place was packed. Realized it was packed with every female relative of mine, a great number of my female friends, every female relative of Martini's, and a lot of females who were also, technically, relatives of Martini's. The Dazzler quotient was as high as at the Science Center.

Chuckie kissed my cheek. "Have fun. Control yourself. At some point, the males will rejoin you. Make sure you're not doing something Martini will make you regret."

"Thanks for the warning, Voice of Doom."

He laughed. "I'm here for you should something go wrong."

Reader got the rest of the gals inside, then hugged me. "Behave."

"It's a bachelorette party, not tea with the Queen of England. Why are you and Chuckie telling me to be a good girl all of a sudden?"

Cover-boy grin flashed. "Because we know you, girlfriend. So does Jeff, so you'll probably be okay."

"Yeah, Chuckie said no Aerosmith or Sir Elton."

"True. Just think you'll like the alternative."

"Motorhead?"

"Considered it. Then realized that most of the guests don't want to hear the loudest rock and roll band in the world up close and personal." He looked really pleased with himself. "I got Emily and Melanie to promise to take pictures when the band hits the stage." He kissed me on my cheek, sauntered over to Chuckie and they both sauntered off.

Food and drink were all over the place. I was pretty full from the girly food, but House of Blues had some yummy stuff out. I managed to find the room to stuff in a good sampling.

Drinks were flowing. The bars were clearly marked as alcoholic and nonalcoholic. The room was about one-third alkies to two-thirds abstainers. A couple of my cousins, cousins supposedly in the know now, grabbed me and asked me if I was marrying into a Mormon family. Shared I wasn't, didn't share that I was marrying an alien—maybe Christopher had come to his and everybody else's senses and wiped all their memories.

I'd originally thought we only had the over-eighteen crowd, but I discovered all the little girls were here, too. They all seemed to know something I didn't, because they were already in the concert hall, practically vibrating with excitement.

There was a very pretty blonde in there with them. She was dressed nicely like the other guests, so I figured she wasn't an employee. "Hi, I'm Kitty." Put out the paw.

She stood up, took my hand, and smiled. Looked very athletic as well as gorgeous. "I'm Denise Lewis, Kevin's wife."

Figured. The gorgeous guy with bags of charisma had married the gorgeous gal with bags of charisma. I figured I'd be able to pick their kids out easily—look for the gorgeous ones with bags of charisma.

"Great to finally meet you. And thanks for coming."

"Happy to be invited. We really appreciate how the A-Cs have protected us."

"Did you know what Kevin did before last year?"

She laughed. She had great teeth, just like Kevin did. Wow, amazing. I wasn't gay, but if I'd been forced to go to the Free Women planet, this would be the mate I'd pick to take with me. "No, but when you're being kidnapped by a terrorist organization and a group of the most handsome men you've ever seen rescues you and your kids, you catch on really fast that your husband didn't stop being a running back because of a bad knee."

"So Kevin was a professional athlete before? I knew it!"

"Yeah, not too long, though. Your mother recruited him early in his career."

This was probably a story for another time, but I made a note to get said story later. "So, why are you on babysitting duty?"

"Oh, the kids are so excited about the band."

"It's not Hannah Montana or the kids from *High School Musical*, is it?" I could see Chuckie doing that, but not Reader.

"No." Denise laughed again. "And no one's going to tell you, so don't try to ask."

"So, again, you're riding herd on the rugrats why?"

"I don't really know anyone." She looked as though she hadn't meant that one to slip out. "I mean, I know Gladys and your mother, sort of."

I looked around. "Kids, Denise and I are going to the bar area for a little bit. Who's big enough to behave themselves without us?" All the hands went up. "That's why I love you all, you lie so well and quickly. Injure no one, including yourselves, break nothing, rip nothing, be good or I'll send in a lion to eat you all up."

Shrieks of laughter from the littler girls, rolled eyes from the bigger ones. I grabbed Denise's hand and dragged her out. "You don't get to hide in here while I have to see everyone and pretend this is fun."

She laughed. "Kevin said you were a fun girl."

"That's me, Miss Fun." Found the women I was looking for. "Emily, Melanie, Ericka, this is Denise Lewis, Kevin's wife. Denise, Ericka is Paul and Michael's mother, Melanie is Lorraine's, Emily is Claudia's. This may not help much. Denise doesn't know anyone. Let's change that, shall we?"

Ericka laughed. "From what my sons have told me, Kevin's an honorary member of the family, so that makes you family, too." She linked her arm through Denise's. "Let me take you around and force you to meet everyone. I'd do the same to Kitty, but she's supposed to be having fun."

Denise grinned. "Like your friends and family, Kitty." I would have replied, but Ericka was already moving her off.

"Nicely done," Melanie said.

"Even gorgeous people can be shy."

Emily hugged me. "I'm so glad you'll be a real part of the family soon."

"Oh, yeah, how are you guys related to Jeff?"

"Oh the usual several cousins several times removed." Melanie laughed. "Really, don't try to keep it straight."

"Wow, no worries there. So, who's the band? The kids are beyond excited."

"I'll give you one hint," Emily said, and it was clear she was trying not to grin. "Most of the men are going to be happy to miss them, and all of the women are going to love them."

"Everyone loves a mystery."

"Yep!" Lorraine and Claudia came up. "James told us to make sure you got a drink, even though it won't be alcoholic, and to get you into the seat of honor in time. Band starts in a few, so, stealing our girl now." She and Claudia each took an arm and dragged me off.

Since I had to relax and have fun, I forced myself to do it. Lorraine and Claudia were great at the Aunt Carla avoidance, also great at the moving me away from the nosy friends and relatives stuff.

Ran into a gaggle of my sorority sisters. After the shrieking, hugging, and recitation of the not-so-secret sorority pledge were over, and Lorraine and Claudia were introduced, I got a lot of hairy eyeballs from the girls. I tensed for what I knew was coming.

"So, Kit-Kat, Chuck's throwing this party for you but he's not the guy you're marrying?" Jeannine asked, semi-nicely. She was the only brunette in the group—our pledge class had run toward blondes, light browns, and redheads. Like all the rest of the girls, she was pretty and petite. We'd run to the short side, too.

"It's not like that, JellyBean—" I started.

"I'm more upset that Caro Syrup's not here," Tamara said quietly. "She was your bestie, Kit-Kat."

"She still is, Twix," I said quickly. "She just couldn't—"

"Get here in time," Cathy said. "Yeah, Chuck told us." She shook her head. "I can't believe you dumped Chuck." Well, at least they weren't discussing their concerns about me marrying a space alien. That was something, right?

"We weren't an item, Wonka. We're still friends. Same with Caro and me. She's out of the country right now." I was starting to get worried that this was going to turn into a nightmare fast.

"Chuck said Kit-Kat's marrying a great guy," Kay said, cheerfully, thank God. "Face it, this puts Chuck back on the market. I say hurray for that."

Oh? This was news. I knew my sorority sisters loved him, but I hadn't realized they'd considered Chuckie off the market. "Why so, Almond Joy? Not that I'm saying he isn't on the market and all."

Kay grinned. "Chuck was interested in one girl and one girl only, and that was you, Kit-Kat. He seems okay with you marrying someone else."

Christie snorted. "He's not okay with it. He's just faking it the way he always did when she was head over heels over some guy who wasn't good enough for her." Guilt came over, drink in hand, to enjoy the party. Stress was already here, having a blast, and made room for its buddy.

"Skittle, have I mentioned that my friends Lorraine and Claudia are my fiancé's cousins?" My voice was starting to head to dog-only levels. Not good.

Claudia shook her head. "I'm still sort of stuck on the nick-names. You're all named after candies?"

"Or sweet things, yeah." I felt my cheeks getting hot. It never seemed stupid until I was telling someone outside of the sorority about it. To a girl, my sorority sisters' eyes narrowed.

"How do you keep all the nicknames straight?" Claudia asked. She sounded like she did whenever she was discussing something scientific: interested and serious.

"Um, just do." I enjoyed winning the Lame Reply Award on a regular basis. Guilt and Stress both sniggered and got another drink.

Lorraine laughed. "I think it's cute."

Claudia grinned and nodded. "They do seem to fit you all. From everything Kitty's said, you're all very sweet, just like she is." My sorority sisters seemed to relax; at least they weren't glaring any more.

"And I think it's great your sisters are going to be around to keep Jeff on his toes." Lorraine nudged Jeannine. "Trust me, I'm with you. I think brains are the better option, too, but who can fight love?" I was tempted to ask Lorraine why none of the Dazzlers I knew were throwing themselves at Chuckie, but I had enough sense to know where that question would take this conversation, and things were already bad enough.

"Jeff's not stupid." The Dazzler brain-love was great, but not at the expense of Martini's feelings.

"Where are your girlfriends from high school?" Tamara asked. She looked the most upset of the girls, but in a quiet way. I wasn't sure why.

Claudia answered before I could. "They couldn't come out, either, because Jeff and Kitty had to move their wedding date up."

"Why?" Cathy asked. "Oh, my God, are you preggers already?"

"No!" This was devolving into that nightmare I'd hoped to miss. I scrambled for an acceptable reason for my wedding date and party being as they were and came up with nothing that was going to work.

A throat cleared behind me. "Nice to see you girls," my mother said. She sounded pleasant and, as always, in complete control of the situation. But I wasn't sure if I should relax or not.

The choruses of hellos and hugs took a while. When they were done, Mom went on without missing a beat. "We're not talking about it, but Jeff's family is quite politically connected. Religious issues meant they had to move the wedding up to ensure the head of Jeff's religion could officiate. And Kitty didn't have a lot of choice in her wedding party, either. She was hoping to have the five of you in, but we had to choose the wedding party based more on political expediency than the bonds of friendship."

Mom sounded totally believable, and she looked it, too. Amazingly enough, Lorraine and Claudia didn't give away that at least the latter half of this explanation was something of a whopper.

But it worked. My sorority sisters went from upset to commiserating instantly. It dawned on me that they were hurt they hadn't been asked to be in my wedding party, which should have dawned on me much sooner. Of course, I'd been distracted with that whole saving the world thing. Not that it would get me a free pass, because it never did.

"Jeff's a prince," Claudia said conspiratorially to Christie.

"Chuck said he was a great guy," Jeannine agreed.

"No, a *real* prince," Lorraine said. My sorority sisters looked impressed.

"Does that make you two princesses?" Kay asked.

"No," Claudia said with a laugh. "We're too far away from the main bloodline."

"Will that mean Kit-Kat's a princess, sort of like Grace Kelly?" Tamara asked, perking up. Apparently if I was marrying royalty, all was going to be forgiven.

"Um . . ." However, I had no idea and no answer. I also didn't think Mom wanted these details discussed, and I sure didn't. But I was saved from any further journey down the Excuses Rabbit Hole by what had been saving me from day one with Centaurion Division—rock 'n' roll.

CHAPTER 64

WE ALL HEARD A GUITAR BEING TUNED and wild shrieking from the little kids. "Gotta get our girl into her seat," Lorraine called to my mother and sorority sisters. Then she and Claudia zoomed us into the theater, and there I was, front row center. I stopped worrying about anything other than figuring out who the band was going to end up being.

Kimmie, one of Martini's many nieces, came running to me. "Kitty! Kitty! The band's going to start soon!"

I pulled her onto my lap. "Yeah, and I don't know who it is."

She grinned, and I saw the resemblance to Alfred and Martini. "Uncle Christopher said we couldn't tell you. And Uncle Jeff said he wanted me to make sure to watch your face. He said it should be funny."

"Your Uncle Jeff is going to get it when I see him again."

"He said you'd say that. I can't wait to see them—Uncle Jeff gave us all their CDs for Arrival Day."

"He did? Why?"

"He said they helped keep you and him and Uncle Christopher alive. My mommy loves them too. Grandma does, too. Everyone likes them." She looked very pleased. "I get to be your flower girl."

I hugged her. "I know!" I could lie better than anyone when I had to. "And I'm so glad, too!" I was. If anyone had asked me, or, more importantly, it had dawned on me to think of it, Kimmie was who I'd have wanted. I reminded myself that Reader was the best friend in the world. He was also on the stage. "Why is James on the stage?"

Lorraine laughed. "He's the emcee, silly."

"Is there anything he can't do?"

Claudia leaned over and whispered in my ear. "Turn straight. Otherwise, nothing."

"True . . . true." I looked around—the place was filled, at least the lower level. Looked up. Wow, we had Dazzlers up there, too. The entire A-C female population was in here. My sorority sisters were surrounded by Dazzlers. They seemed to be fitting in with no issues, and apparently they knew who the band was, because they looked as excited as everyone else.

I spotted Mom and the other mothers and grandmothers behind us a few rows. Chuckie's mother was there, too, and waved to me. I waved back, relieved she didn't look disappointed in my romantic decision. Mom didn't wave—she was scanning the crowd, and I had a feeling she was doing a last-minute security check. She caught my eye and gave me a smile and a nod. Okay, we were secure. "So, you and Lorraine excited about the band?"

"Can't wait, we love them." Claudia started to bounce in her seat. Lorraine already was.

Reader flashed the cover-boy grin. I heard a lot of squeals. Yep, even bald he was amazingly hot. "Ladies!" More squeals, a few shrieks. "I know you're all excited to be here. I'd make a big speech, but that's what the reception's for." Laughter from all the adults. "But before I get out of the way of tonight's entertainment, let me just congratulate our bride-to-be on her musical choices." Lots and lots of screams.

I heard music starting in the background. It was low, just the guitar riff, just the first few chords, played over and over, waiting for the intro. But they were opening chords I knew really, really well. I hugged Kimmie tight. It was a hypnotic beat, rocking, but soothing at the same time. I started bouncing. The rest of the crowd was going easily as wild as when the Beatles first hit America.

Reader grinned again. "Kitty, from me, Tim, and all the rest of Alpha and Airborne teams, thanks for loving this band. Now . . . ladies, all the way from Bath, England, please welcome our very special guests . . . Tears for Fears!"

Okay, I admit it. I screamed. Loudly. Hey, needed to let the band know I was with them, right? It was only polite. And I was beyond excited.

Reader got off the stage, and the curtain rose. I was already on my feet, holding Kimmie up. The band opened with "Cold," which meant Claudia, Lorraine, and I were already singing along at the top of our lungs. In between screaming.

I'd seen them before, and I had the T-shirts to prove it, but it was different seeing them here, and knowing they were here for, well, *me*. It was also a really neat surprise to discover that Martini had turned Dazzlers of all ages into TFF fans. I wouldn't have to worry about finding someone to go with on their next concert tour.

They did song after song, and not just all the hits, but all the ones I liked the best. I assumed Tim had had a lot to do with the song selections. After me, he knew the music I liked to listen to the best, both when and why.

They did a full ninety-minute set without anything other than a water break. They were awesome, charming, and funny. But even great concerts have to end. They closed with "Goodnight Song." The screams were deafening, and continued on.

I was shocked, but they came back out for an encore. "We had a special request for this encore, from the groom-to-be." The band went into a slow song that I recognized in a few lines: "I Choose You." There was a lot of sniffling in the audience. I did my best not to start bawling my head off.

The band let the end of the song hang on the air, then went into "Closest Thing to Heaven." I was still trying not to cry. I felt someone watching me and handed Kimmie to Lorraine. Looked around and spotted him. No idea how long he'd been in the room—like the rest of the guys, he was in the shadows. He was leaning against a wall at the end of the row, watching me. I ran past the rest of the front row and jumped into his arms.

Martini caught me and kissed me as the band rolled into "Secret World." He kissed me all through the song. I heard the band joke that the bride seemed happy with the encore, and I could tell from the way they were laughing and the audience reaction that everyone knew Martini and I were kissing. Didn't care.

The band said goodnight, screams and thunderous applause were heard, concert was over, and we were still kissing. Best concert of my life.

CHAPTER 65

THE REST OF THE NIGHT WAS A BLUR. Got to meet the band, with Martini keeping a firm hold on me, just in case. How the guys in the band didn't drop from exhaustion was beyond me—our crowd was pretty well-behaved, but I caught that the Dazzlers felt, particularly after this concert, that musical genius was almost as good as scientific genius, and we had to do some crowd control before we ended up with a mob scene.

Once the band was finally safe, we all went back to the main party. Martini was carrying me around on his hip, which earned us a lot of jokes, all of which he seemed to enjoy. I was just so happy to finally be with him that I didn't care.

He grinned. "Nice to know you pine for me every time I'm in isolation."

"Every single time, Jeff." Had to make out a bit after that, which earned us more ribbing from the various family members.

"So," I asked after we broke the latest lip-lock, "how long were you watching?"

"Oh, a while before you noticed. I didn't want you to know I was there until the encore started."

"And then you did?"

"Then I felt how much you liked it." He sounded so happy, had to make out again.

"Do you two *ever* stop?" Christopher was laughing.

"Nope," Martini said with a satisfied smile.

"Christopher, did you, um, have the wise idea to change viewpoints?"

"You're trying to be secretive. So not your forté."

I rolled my eyes. "I had cousins asking me if you guys were Mormons. My sorority sisters seemed clueless. I thought your father and Jeff and Paul's parents had spilled the beans, so to speak."

"Oh, you mean the total security breach that could cause untold ramifications?" He sounded as thrilled with it as I was. Thank God someone else saw this as a potentially bad thing. "It's handled."

"What did you do?" Martini asked, as he moved the three of us into a quiet corner.

Christopher shrugged. "It dawned on me a few months ago that Kitty was probably right."

"Wow, I may faint. Right about what?"

"Genetic mutations. Between us and humans."

"Serene *is* our poster girl."

"Right. But Paul's talents are normal, at least as far as we know. And Michael has no special talents." Christopher stared at me.

"Um . . . this is a test? You're testing me at my bachelorette party? Is it just 'cause I talked all smack about this and I'm right or is it because you like to torture?"

"Both."

Made the exasperation sound. "Fine." Thought about it. Thought about it some more. "Serene is more powerful . . . Paul and Michael are not . . . oh, wow, really?"

"Yeah."

"Feeling left out and stupid here," Martini said dryly.

"I'm guessing that Naomi and Abigail Gower have powers no one's told anyone else about. Right?"

"Right." Christopher looked around. I did, too. No one was paying us much attention. "Naomi has Paul's talent, but it's different, the way Serene's an imageer but with expanded powers. Naomi can read dreams and memories, but she can also alter them."

"Wow. That's a scary talent."

"If allowed to go uncontrolled, yes."

"Does Abigail have a . . . mutation?" Martini sounded worried.

"Jeff, we're not the X-Men."

"Starting to sound like it," Chuckie said as he joined us. "Not that I mind."

Christopher sighed. "Yeah, we know. This is a great day for the C.I.A."

"Abigail?" Martini asked, Commander voice on.

"She doesn't need an implant to affect the gasses. It's a combo dream-imageer talent, we think. She just moves them around without outside assistance. She can also pick up thoughts, but she feels them as emotions, sort of empathic but not quite. She can pick up if someone is thinking angry thoughts, because she feels angry when she's near that person, as an example." Christopher sounded only mildly worried.

"They must have been fun in puberty."

"They were controlled by then." Christopher sounded more worried.

"By whom?"

He shook his head. "They have no idea. They just know someone was helping them when they were little girls. They don't know who, they never met the person, both think it was a man but aren't sure." He sounded full-on worried.

"I'm going to bet that when we ask Serene, it'll be the same for her."

"Probably." Martini's voice was brisk. "So Abigail's altering what Kitty's family and friends are seeing and will see?"

Christopher shrugged. "In a way. If she spots people who are afraid, angry, and so on, Naomi will alter their memories. The girls work well together."

"How long have you been testing them without telling me?" Martini didn't sound happy.

Christopher shrugged. "A couple of months. Jeff, you were too distracted."

"With what?"

Christopher coughed. "Marrying Kitty."

"Oh."

"We're going to run some tests on them," Chuckie said. "Standard emotional and mental stability tests, long-term effects on both of them and those with altered memories."

"Wait, we don't know the results? So, what, you're going to use my family as part of an experiment?"

Chuckie rolled his eyes. "Yes and no. You have a choice: We can let the Gower girls do their thing, or you can allow the security breach the four of us and your mother are all unexcited about. From what White's told me, the tests they've already done are pretty comprehensive; we just want to be more sure."

"The C.I.A. does not have the right to test any of our people on anything." Martini sounded like he was heading toward angry with a potential stop at furious.

Chuckie raised his hand. "Look. This was being discussed before I had to assume control of Centaurion. Make a scene, start shouting up the channels? They'll make sure I keep control of Centaurion. Shut the hell up and let us do the tests of your personnel with your permission, and everyone's so pleased Centaurion is playing nicely with others that they won't notice control's returned back to you."

Martini shook his head. "We don't trust you."

"Jeff, has he lied to you about anything yet? Not trusting the C.I.A. I can agree with. Not trusting Chuckie seems more like kicking the one guy who hasn't done you wrong just because you can. Of course, if he's really that evil and my mother and I've just missed it for fifteen years, we could just not go on a honeymoon, and you could fight the C.I.A. about this."

Martini gave a martyred sigh. "I do have a job to do."

"Yeah, Jeff, you do. And, right now, your job is to marry Kitty and go on your honeymoon. *My* job is to cover your job when you're on vacation or out of commission, remember?" Christopher sounded somewhat annoyed, but not overly so.

"Oh, fine," Martini grumbled. "You could have shared this sometime other than right now."

"It was relevant right now," Christopher snapped. He looked at me. "So don't worry—the friends and family members who need to have a different memory will all have the same one, congratulations, you're marrying into the Martini and Rossi fortune. The others will have a suggestion implanted that makes them loath to talk about Jeff's side of the family except in nice, vague, very human terms."

"Hope it works. Claudia and Lorraine told my sorority sisters I was marrying royalty."

Christopher shrugged. "If they buy it and they're happy with that story, Naomi and Abigail will know. If not, Martini and Rossi."

"I hate being royalty," Martini grumbled.

"It's a better cover than being a space alien," Chuckie said. "Politically and just from a common sense standpoint."

Martini glared at him. I heaved my own sigh. "Chuckie's right. Jeff, you done sulking and stomping and attempting to wreck my cool coed bachelorette party?"

"Yeah, I suppose."

Christopher shook his head. "You get to go have a slumber party. I have to spend the night with him."

"I'll trade."

Christopher snorted. "As if James will allow that." He looked around. "Where is the drill sergeant, anyway?"

"Managing the photographer." Chuckie sounded like he was trying not to laugh.

"What photographer?" I hadn't seen any flashes.

"The one you were too into the concert and far too into making out with each other to notice," Chuckie said, now openly laughing. "Ah, to be a rock star of any age. Walk on stage with a guitar, watch the women swoon."

"Did the photographer take pictures of us making out?"

"Yeah," Christopher said with a grin. "Glad Jeff's been carrying you the whole time. You're showing a lot of leg."

"A lot of everything," Chuckie added with an exaggerated leer.

Martini shrugged. "My arm's covering anything you're not allowed to see."

"I hope."

"Truth'll come out in the darkroom." Chuckie winked. "I paid for the photographer."

"Oh, great." I looked hard at Chuckie's expression. He was definitely laughing at his own private joke. "Oh. No way. Is the photographer who I think it is?"

He grinned. "Yes. We wanted someone who was good at avoiding your notice while getting your picture at the same time."

"Are you and James both high?"

Chuckie laughed. "No. We gave the *World Weekly News* the exclusive on the party. White's team will alter anything necessary photographically, the rest of the paparazzi are shut out because the *WWN* people are keeping them out, and nothing's happening here that would give anyone a reason to believe the A-Cs are anything other than what we're saying they are."

"While I can appreciate the brilliance in having one set of paparazzi in place to keep all the others out, Mister Joel Oliver is supposedly a photojournalist. How are we going to ensure the journalistic portion doesn't get out of control?"

Christopher shrugged. "No one believes him, Kitty. And,

frankly, it's safer to keep him close so we can monitor what he's photographing and who he's talking to." He grimaced. "I'll take the risk Reynolds and James took with the photographer over the risk our parents took with telling everyone at this wedding who and what we really are."

"I'm with White. Oliver's thrilled to be getting the exclusive," Chuckie added. "Believe me, he has a team of C.I.A. operatives and two A-C field teams assigned to guard him. Every person assisting him is either from my team, your mother's team, or an A-C. His footage is being altered immediately, and the only conversations he's catching have more to do with your clothing, or lack thereof, than anything else." He flashed the exaggerated leer again. "From what Oliver's already told me, he's gotten some excellent shots."

"Let me know if there's anything really good," Christopher said. "I'll probably place a big order. Most of the guys want a shot of Kitty in her lingerie."

"It's an outfit. For clubbing. Like this is a club and I'm wearing it here, at a club. At a party at a club. Chuckie made me wear a jacket and everything."

"Right. So, Reynolds, remember, pull out the good ones, and don't let Kitty or Jeff see them. I figure we can charge, easy, ten to fifteen dollars a pop."

"Oh, the shots of her butt? Those're worth at least twenty-five per eight by ten." Chuckie and Christopher were really cracking each other up. Of course, I knew my skirt was tucked between my bottom and Martini's arm, and I hadn't seen Oliver or a camera flash once this entire time, so I wasn't overly concerned. If I'd really been showing that much, one of my relatives would have mentioned it.

Aunt Carla showed up, effectively breaking up our meeting. "So, Katherine, nice party. And, young man, you're fine with her displaying everything she owns all over?"

Then again, maybe they were all just waiting for Aunt Carla to mention it.

Martini grinned. "Yeah. I like showing off what no one else is ever going to get to touch." He walked us away, leaving Aunt Carla open-mouthed.

"Have I mentioned I love you?"

"More than the guys in Tears for Fears?"

"Yeah."

"More than the guys in Aerosmith?"

I had to ponder. "Yeah. Even more than Steven Tyler and Joe Perry. Put together."

"Wow. Guess I'd better marry you, then."

"Well, only if you want to."

Martini spent the next hour or so showing me that he really wanted to. It was a great party.

CHAPTER 66

OF COURSE, READER WAS TRUE to his word and dragged the wedding party off at midnight. I made some Cinderella jokes he didn't laugh at. I was allowed to stay with Martini all the way through the casino and up the elevator. Martini carried me through the casino—some I figured because he enjoyed it, some because I'd whined that we'd been here ages and I hadn't gotten to gamble once, and he wasn't taking any chances.

For once I didn't feel like I was being watched. Apparently the plan Chuckie and Reader had in place was working. Let the one paparazzo in, and the others were miraculously kept out. Worked for me.

Reader actually let us take our own elevator but left Christopher and Chuckie stationed at the top floor and himself at the lobby level.

"James, you're taking this whole Wedding Planner from Hell thing a little far, aren't you?"

"Uh-huh. The elevators send off major alarms if you stop them on the way up or down. I'll be paying attention, but if you try getting off on another floor and hyperspeeding somewhere, we'll know."

"It's the night before our wedding," Martini grumbled.

"Yeah. You know, in the olden days, I'd have her under lock and key because you still wouldn't have scored a tongue-kiss, let alone anything else."

"Thank God for modern times." Martini carried me into the elevator, waited for the door to close, then pushed every button at hyperspeed. "Let 'em worry." He put me up against the side of the car, and we proceeded to make out like mad.

The positive on stopping at every floor was that we got to make out a lot longer. The negative was that we couldn't do anything more because, well, we were stopping at every floor, and this was Vegas—people were up at any and all hours. We knew there were people on some of the floors because we heard them. All but one guy were nice and didn't try to join us in the elevator. The one guy came in, made a comment, Martini reached out, grabbed him, and threw him out, all while continuing to ravage my mouth and grind against me. I found this so awesome I almost ripped his clothes off.

We finally got to the top floor.

"You know, some of us have to sleep and get up tomorrow," Christopher snapped.

"I expected you to go up and down a few times," Chuckie said. "You're slipping, Martini."

"Good idea." Martini moved for the "door close" button, but Christopher was faster and got his body blocking the doors just in time.

"Out." We didn't move. "Now." Still didn't move. "Or I get Renata."

We moved.

Martini put me down and walked me to the door. I could hear the girls in there, shrieking with laughter. He leaned against the wall and stroked my face. "I don't want to sleep apart tonight."

"Me, either. But James has rules."

"Humans have silly rules."

"And aliens are weird. What's your point?" I'd unbuttoned his shirt while we were in the elevator. I ran my fingers over his chest.

"You really liked the concert?"

"You know I did. Especially the encore."

He smiled. "Then it's all worth it." He bent and kissed me. "I feel like we're on a date."

"And you're taking me back to my sorority. Yeah."

"What're you going to tell the girls when they ask you how the date went?"

"That I just went out with the guy I'm going to marry."

Martini grinned. "Then it was a good date."

I leaned up. "The best ever."

He kissed me again, then opened the door, handed me the key, and walked back to Christopher and the elevators. Chuckie was already in his room. I watched Martini walk away, turn around, and watch me until the elevator came and Christopher dragged him inside it.

Heaved a sigh, closed the door.

"So?" Lorraine shouted. "Did you two do it in the elevator?" All the girls were giggling—it *was* a slumber party.

"No, but we hit the buttons to stop it on every floor. And made out the whole way."

"Wow, total restraint," Claudia said. "I'm impressed." She looked at Lorraine. "Pay up."

Lorraine sighed and slapped a bill in Claudia's hand. My grandmothers had clearly rubbed off on everyone.

A lot more bantering, laughing, and joking went on while I worked my way to the bedroom. Everyone had loved the concert, even Jareen, Renata, Wahoa, and Felicia. Apparently Princess Victoria had been in the audience as well, though I'd missed her. Alexander was also on the premises.

"They left their world unattended? Just to show up for all our wedding stuff?"

Renata nodded. "This is an important diplomatic mission. Earth has shown its power, and our solar system must ensure we remain on friendly terms."

"Diplomacy and marketing have a lot in common. Both use a lot of fancy words to lie really impressively."

She laughed. "True. But the result is the same—this will solidify relationships. Victoria said they were most impressed that you asked representatives from each of the loyal worlds to be a part of the prince's wedding."

"I really don't think of him as a prince. I mean a royal prince. And I know Jeff doesn't think of himself that way." For which I was very thankful.

"No. But it is better for all of us if he is presented as such. I assure you, his reasons for refusing the throne will filter down to the idea that he rules here already, or soon will, and that he chose Earth over Alpha Four because Earth is stronger."

"But Alexander was just made king. Shouldn't he be there, reassuring his people he's on top of things and ready to rule?"

Renata shrugged. "Chief Councillor Leonidas is there. His presence is more vital right now than the royal family's."

"Seriously?"

"Yes. Charles said that, should you ask, to mention the Churchill and royal family of England relationship. He felt you would ask, I must add."

"He does know me well." Guilt tried to muscle in, but I kicked it to the curb. Fine, so Leonidas was the glue and the real leader and Alexander was the figurehead with power. I decided I'd ask Chuckie about the ramifications. Later. After honeymoon later. "Okay, well, good."

Renata chuckled. "You need to get some sleep." She mother-henned me into the bedroom and started shushing the other girls.

I didn't argue. I was wiped. Undressed and looked for nightclothes. No A-C Elves here, but what seemed like ages but was only a couple of days ago, I'd unpacked our stuff and put it somewhere. Couldn't remember where. Went to hang my clothes up and discovered a cute shortie nightgown hanging there. Wasn't mine, but I assumed Reader had left it for me. Didn't argue; put it on, and crawled into bed.

I was almost asleep when I heard some soft mewling. "Come on." I had Poofs on me immediately. Harlie and Poofikins, but there was a third one. "Are you Fluffy?" No reaction. "Fuzzball?" Again, nothing. "Gatita?" Nada. Called Christopher on the house phone. "Is your Poof with me?"

"Yeah. Jeff's got the jealousy thing, you might remember? Wanted it there just in case Reynolds tried to slip past seven women, including the Amazon Queen, in order to steal you away in the night."

I snorted. "Sweet. So, what's your Poof's name?"

Silence.

"Christopher, I know everyone else's, and I don't want to say, 'hey you,' to it."

More silence.

"How bad could it be? Chuckie's is named Fluffy, for God's sake."

"Fine. Toby." I heard Martini start laughing in the background. "Toby?"

"Yes, Toby." Christopher sounded really annoyed and I was worried Martini was going to die, he was laughing so hard.

"Why is Toby such a funny name to Jeff?" I heard some mumbling, but no answer. "What? Speak up."

He heaved a sigh. "It was the name of my stuffed toy when I was little, okay?"

"Awww, that's sweet."

"Yeah, thanks." He didn't sound thankful. Martini was still laughing.

"Did Jeff have a stuffed toy when he was little, too?"

"Yes, he did," Christopher shouted this. Didn't slow down Martini's laughter. "His was named Murphy."

"Also sweet. There's nothing embarrassing about naming your Poof Toby, you know. I think it's cute."

"Wonderful. Jeff's Poof came named. Have I mentioned that we look like idiots with those things?"

"Oh, no! Toby! Don't touch that!"

"What? Is it hurt? What happened?" He sounded totally freaked.

"Toby's fine. I think you can stop pretending you don't like it now."

"I hate you."

"Yeah, yeah, just stop trying to be all Mister Macho about them. They're adorable, and you know it."

"Fine. Can we hang up now?"

"Sure, I'm tired. See you in the morning."

"Doubt it. Our drill sergeant has views on when any of us will see you again."

I yawned. "Fine. Well, whenever. Night, Christopher. Love to Jeff."

"Goodnight, Kitty. Enjoy your last night as a single woman."

We hung up, and I snuggled into the bed. It seemed huge without Martini in it. The three Poofs cuddled up around my head and started purring quietly. Heard the girls out in the other room—they were still wide awake and having fun. Me, all I wanted was to be cuddled up next to Martini. I wondered if I should get up and work on the enjoying some more but realized I didn't want to. Maybe marriage wasn't going to be all that different, after all. Possibly Martini's jealousy might abate somewhat, that would be a good thing. Of course, maybe he'd want me to cook, too. Then again, maybe he would just want things the way they'd been. On the other hand, I knew he wanted kids, and as soon as possible, though he had said when I was ready. What if I was never ready? What if we couldn't get pregnant? What if he got bored with me?

My cell phone rang. My purse was by the side of the bed, so didn't take too long for me to dig it out. "Jeff, what's wrong?"

"I will not get bored with you. I am not going to force you

to cook. My jealousy is never going to go away, get used to it. Yes, I want kids, I'm sure we won't have a problem, and from what my father's said, you're never really ready to have them, you just think you are. Stop worrying or else I'll have to hurt James in order to get up there with you. I love you, go to sleep."

"I miss you."

"Me too. Last night like this, okay? I think that's James' sadistic point."

"Yeah. Would you have named your Poof Murphy if it hadn't been named Harlie?"

"No idea. Happy I don't have to worry about it. Go to sleep, baby. Tomorrow's a big day."

"Do you like your tux?"

He laughed. "Yes. I just hope you like it. Reynolds insinuated I'd love your dress."

"I hope so." I was starting to get sleepy, but I didn't want to get off the phone.

"You want me to talk you to sleep?" He sounded amused, not upset.

"Sort of. The Poofs aren't the same as being with you, you know."

"Thank God. You like the nightgown?"

"Oh, it's from you? I thought it was from James."

"There's nothing like your bride-to-be saying she thought the lingerie you bought her was from another man to make you feel all warm and secure."

"Oh, stop. He's been doing everything else. I'm afraid he's going to drop dead from the exertion."

"He's having a field day, I'll give you that. So, you don't like it?"

I laughed. "I do like it. I didn't spend a lot of time looking at it, because I didn't realize it was from you."

"Oh, that's fine, then." He sounded reasonably pleased.

"You want me to get up and look in the mirror or something?"

"Yeah," his voice dropped to a purr. "Then think about me."

"So you can see me?"

"Yeah."

"Mmmm . . . that sounds interesting."

"Yeah." His voice was still a purr. I heard Christopher in

the background and Martini sighed. "My nanny says we have to get off the phone. You could still look in the mirror," he added. I heard Christopher bark, "No." Martini sighed again. "Or not."

"Okay. I'm tired anyway." I was, but it had sounded kind of weird and fun at the same time.

"I love how you think."

"Then I'll go to sleep thinking of you."

"Sweet dreams, baby."

"They will be. I promise." Closed the phone, snuggled back up into the pillows and the Poofs, and went to sleep.

My last thought was that maybe, for once, nothing would go wrong with a big, important extravaganza. Our track record wasn't that good, but I optimistically hoped for a reprieve. Did kind of think I'd earned it.

CHAPTER 67

SOMEONE SHOOK ME AWAKE. It felt like a man's hand. "Jeff?"

"No. Time to get up, girlfriend."

I cracked an eye. "It's dark."

Reader sighed and walked away. I tried to go back to sleep. I heard a noise and there was bright light right in my face. "What is *that*?" Flung a pillow over my eyes.

"We call it sunlight on our planet. Get up. We are, as usual, running late."

"James what are you doing in here?"

"Getting you and the rest of the females moving."

"Get the guys up first." I rolled over.

Covers were pulled off. Poofs started grumbling. "Interesting, you sleep commando. Bummer, though . . . I'm still gay."

"Then go away."

He laughed. "You want me to give it a shot anyway?" He grabbed my ankles and pulled me to the edge of the bed.

"Oh, fine." I rolled over and sat up. "There, sitting up. What time is it, anyway?"

"Nine. You're supposed to be at the salon at nine-thirty." He dragged me to my feet and into the bathroom. "Shower. Quickly. Don't worry about your hair."

"*James*." I said this with as much whine in my voice as humanly possible.

He kissed my forehead. "Do it, or I'll tell Jeff I saw what he wants no other man, gay or straight, ever seeing."

"He'll pick it up if you enjoyed it."

Reader patted my butt as he shoved me into the bathroom. "Guess I'd better plan to say that I object to the wedding, then." He closed the door but I could tell he was waiting.

"I want to, you know, before I shower."

"Fine. I'll be back in five minutes. If you're not in the shower, I can't be held responsible for my actions."

"Nazi." I whispered it under my breath. Then felt guilty. "Okay, not a Nazi. Just suddenly a major anal retentive."

"Heard that, both thats. Get into the shower."

"Eavesdropper!"

"Laggard."

Decided he was more awake than me and so likely to win the war of wit right now. Started the water. Showering quickly wasn't an issue if Martini wasn't with me. Dried off, wrapped the towel around me. Checked to see if the coast was clear. It was, unless I counted Reader standing there with his arms crossed.

"That's the fastest you could shower?"

"I had to shave my legs."

"Fine, I'll accept that excuse." He checked my legs out. "Okay."

"What, you didn't believe me?"

He rolled his eyes. "Put on the white dress Jeff bought for you. It's a color match to your wedding dress."

"Well, how lucky." I looked at him. "Where are you going to be while I do this?"

"In here."

"James, we're about at that point where Jeff and Paul might have real reasons to question us."

"Yeah. However, there are seven other naked women out there and I've already seen everything you own. So I'm sticking with you. I'll turn my back."

I looked closely at his head. "Geez, you know, you already have stubble."

"Yeah, thank God."

"I didn't realize your hair grew so fast. That's really manly and virile." At least, in my opinion.

"Back to that part where Jeff and Paul start worrying, babe."

"Fine, fine." Went into the huge closet. "I put my wedding lingerie on before I get into the wedding dress, not now, right?"

"Right." He sounded distracted.

Peeked out to see him sitting on the edge of the bed. He had his back to me, and he was playing with the Poofs, the three with me and his own. It dawned on me that he wasn't an empath. I got dressed and sat down on the bed next to him. I hugged him from behind. "I'm sorry, James. You're doing everything I couldn't even think of doing or have planned for myself, let alone someone else. I'm sorry I sound like a whiney brat instead of grateful."

He chuckled, but I felt him relax. "It's okay, girlfriend. I know how it is. The person in charge always gets the complaints."

I leaned my head against his back. "I'll stop complaining. Because everything you're doing is beyond wonderful, and I appreciate it a lot more than I'm managing to let you know."

Reader shifted and hugged me back. "It's okay. I understand, don't mind, and love you, so even when you're being a pain in the butt, you're still my girl."

"I love you even when you're channeling Martha Stewart, Emily Post, and every fashion designer on the planet at the same time."

The Poofs crawled into our laps and started purring. "The love in the room is amazing. Let's move before Jeff or Paul come in and I have to turn straight, because we'll have to run off to the Free Women's planet in order to escape their wrath."

"Wise choice."

We got up, and I got the critical eye. "Not bad. If we'd had to, you could have gotten away with this as your wedding dress."

"Only if we wanted my side of the family to die of embarrassment. This is sort of revealing for a wedding gown."

"The lingerie helps." He rubbed his hands together. "Grab your purse, load up the Poofs, and let's get going."

Checked to make sure the other girls were ready—they were. Apparently Reader had woken me up last. He hustled us down to the salon, installed everyone other than me with a stylist, and took me to the back.

A slim, reasonably attractive man was waiting. "Jimmy, it's about time." He sounded huffy and like he was faking a French accent.

"We were delayed." Reader didn't sound apologetic. He put me into the chair. "Kitty, this is Pierre."

"Is Peter another cousin of yours?"

"Oh, she's a bright one, Jimmy," he said, fake accent gone. "But, no, darling, long ago ex-boyfriend. Still, how can one say no to those cheekbones?"

"No idea, I've never been able to."

"I see we agree. The start of a lovely relationship. Call me Pierre here, though, will you, darling? It's an image thing."

"No worries. James, what is Pierre doing to me?"

Pierre answered. "Darling, we're fluffing you up." Reader started to cough.

"I know what that term means."

Pierre gave me a wicked grin in the mirror. "I'm so impressed. No wonder our Jimmy adores you."

"James?"

Reader managed to recover himself. "Pierre? It's her wedding day, okay?"

"I imagine her intended can't wait to lock up the darling who knows how to fluff."

"He's all over it. He likes my hair the way it is."

Pierre snorted. "I'm sure, darling, I'm sure. Jimmy, the veil is, what? A piece of netting? This is all you could come up with?" He pointed to the veil which was hanging off a cabinet at his station. It didn't look like much, I had to admit.

"I don't even know if I want her *in* a veil." Reader sounded exasperated.

"She's in a mermaid I presume?"

"Yes."

"Wow, you're good." I was impressed.

"Darling, no one has a better eye for what to wear when than our Jimmy. But he's lost it with the veil." Reader started to argue and Pierre put up his hand. "Dearest. You're tired and look peaky. No one is accusing, no one is berating. Give me a moment." He pulled out a cell phone. "Dennis, darling! Yes, yes, no time, darling, no time. I have a blushing bride in my chair, and the veil someone foisted off on her is ghastly. It'll be death, *death*, to the whole ceremony. Hang on." He handed his phone to Reader. "Describe the ensemble to Dennis, Jimmy."

Reader rolled his eyes but took the phone. He wandered off to have this conversation in semiprivate.

Pierre turned back to me. "Now, darling, Dennis will get us something immediately. I know why Jimmy wasn't thinking veil, no reason to hide that pretty face. Speaking of which, makeup thoughts?"

I got the impression this was a test question. "I pretty much never wear makeup. I don't think I should today, because Jeff wouldn't know who I was."

"Jeff is our eager groom?"

"Yes." I was hoping Martini was picking up some of this. Pierre was a hoot and a half, and I was actually starting to enjoy being with him.

"Wise choice, darling, very wise. You have enough color in those lovely fair cheeks, your lips clearly haven't been drained of color by too much lipstick, and your eyes are, or, well, will be once you've had a latte, bright and sparkling." He looked over his shoulder. "Janice! I need a double latte." He looked back to me.

"Vanilla. Extra vanilla."

"A double vanilla latte with a triple shot of the vanilla in it, immediately."

I didn't see Janice, but I assumed she scampered off to fill my drink order. I was really enjoying this, and Chuckie's warning from the day before surfaced. I knew he was right—Martini would be open to me doing this all the time. As a thrilling indulgence on the big day, it was great. Every week and I'd feel like the Queen of Shallow.

Reader came back and tossed Pierre his phone. "Dennis says he'll get the right thing over immediately."

"Fabulous. Jimmy, dearest, I understand why you didn't want to cover up her face. But, truly, netting?"

"I had a lot of other things to take care of."

"James was running around like crazy."

"She is adorable. I'd wrap her up and take her home if I could. Fine, darlings, all is forgiven. We'll see what Dennis sends and go from there."

My latte arrived before Dennis. I shared it with Reader, who was starting to pace like a caged leopard. "James, you okay?" He nodded. "We're really behind schedule again, aren't we?"

"No, not so much." He sounded distracted. Pierre and I exchanged looks in the mirror.

"Darlings, going to step aside just for a moment, be right back." Pierre trotted off.

I got up out of the chair and grabbed Reader's arm. "James, what's wrong?"

"I think I've forgotten something."

"Like what?"

"Something important." His voice was tense.

I hugged him. "James, whatever it is, I'd have forgotten it, too."

He hugged me back, tightly. "No, I don't think so." He was quiet. "Run though the things you'd think you needed for your wedding. No pause, just rattle them off."

"Um, location, reception, dresses, tuxedos, rings, gifts for the bridal party—which I don't have. Shoes, gift for you and for Jeff—which I also don't have. Flowers, deejay, wedding cake—"

Reader cursed. "I knew it!"

"What? No cake? We can live without a cake."

"Possibly. However, not without flowers." His heart was pounding. I was used to this with Martini, but not Reader.

I dragged him to Pierre's chair and made him sit. "James, it's okay." I went behind him and started to massage his shoulders. "Really, it's okay. Breathe, deep breaths, deep breaths. It's Vegas, for God's sake. They have everything here. You seem to know everyone here, too."

"I'm from here." He said it like it was a confession.

"So? I'm from Pueblo Caliente. We're Southwesterners, desert dwellers. Makes us great under pressure. James, really, stop stressing." I hugged him. "James, you almost died, and you're miraculously here, doing everything for my wedding. It's more important to me that you're with me than if I'm carrying some dead plant life. Okay?"

He closed his eyes. "No, but I'll take it."

"So dramatic." Pierre was back. "As if, as our darling girl said, we don't have florists all over. We're a wedding capital, Jimmy." He shook his head. "He's such a doll, isn't he? I know he adores you, he only gets like this with people he cares about."

"The flowers have to be right." Reader sounded anal again.

"No, they don't. They just have to be there. James, I don't care. I mean, I do, but not this much. You found the most gorgeous dress for me, in a sea of gorgeous dresses. Same for all the other dresses. And I'm sure I'll love Jeff's tux. We'll love everything else, too."

My phone rang. Made the exasperation sound, let go of Reader, dug it out. Got it on the sixth ring. "Not such a great time."

"I know," Martini said. "That's why I called. Look, what's wrong with James? Your worry is off the scales, and it's centered around him. And the less said about what I'm picking up from him the better."

"Uhhh . . ."

He sighed. "He's right there, right?"

"Yeah."

"Me or Paul? Who's going to solve the problem best?"

"Option two. Fast. Like, really fast."

"Got it. Love you." He hung up.

"Who was that?" Reader asked me, sounding stressed.

"Uhhhh . . ." I didn't know how to answer.

Pierre rolled his eyes where Reader couldn't see. "She can have a call you're not privy to, Jimmy."

"No she can't."

"Sure she can, Jamie." Gower was with us. I tried to remember if I'd ever been this happy to see him before and came up short.

"Paul, what are you doing here?" Reader sounded upset.

Gower shook his head. "What happened?"

"Major screw-up," Reader snapped.

"We forgot about the flowers. It's not a problem, Paul."

Gower nodded. "Jamie, can I talk to you, privately?" Reader looked ready to argue. "Now, Jamie. I mean it."

"Tanning room, just over there, is quite free and very private." Pierre pointed and arched his eyebrow meaningfully. Gower nodded. Reader heaved a sigh, got up, and went with Gower into the room. "He's strung a little tight, isn't he?"

"Yeah. I think it's my fault, too. I think I've made him feel bad for complaining about him being sort of beyond anal-retentive about all he's been doing when I should have been saying thank you, only."

Pierre snorted and shoved me back into the chair. "Darling, please. I've known Jimmy a long time. Straightest gay man I've ever met. Other than that gorgeous hunk who, if I'm any judge, is who has Jimmy's heart these days?"

"Yeah, for a long time. They're really great together."

"Then our tall, dark, and fabulously handsome will solve the issue. Jimmy's got just enough straight man in him to demand everything be in his control at all times. But his beloved should be able deal with him. Sometimes it takes a talking to, sometimes a cuddle. He'll be fine in a bit." He looked at me critically. "Sleeveless with spaghetti straps?" I nodded. "I think we're going to do something simple yet effective. But before we start, must make another call."

"Florist?"

"You got it, sweetness." Pierre shook his head. "My darling drama king—face it, can't call Jimmy a queen, now, can we—needs to relax and let others handle the little details for a bit."

"I agree. And thank you for handling them."

Pierre waved his hand to indicate no big deal. "Rebecca! Darling, we're in a level-five emergency. Yes, for you, the usual. You know how they make the arrangements sound so large and lovely? Well, I have a darling girl from our nearest neighbor of any import, and they have trashed her flowers. Her family refused them, they were that awful. Yes! I know. And, of course, since she's in my chair, the wedding is today. I know! No, lips are sealed. If I told you who did this atrocity, you could never look at them again, and we're still a small town, aren't we?"

Pierre was good. I was impressed. Reader had this entire network of people he never talked about, and they were all interesting. I thought about it. I had interesting friends, too. And the only reason my A-C circle had met any of them was because Brian happened to have been an astronaut, Chuckie had become a C.I.A. bigwig, and some of my sorority sisters had made my bachelorette party. Otherwise, Martini had met Amy, no one had met Sheila or Caroline, and I almost never saw my other friends much because how did you lie to their faces about what you did and who you were in love with all the time?

I reminded myself that at least those friends had been invited to my wedding and, thanks to Chuckie, most were here. I hoped the big extravaganza would cover some of my total lack of good friend-ness for the past year, but I figured it wouldn't. My luck so rarely ran that way.

Pierre looked at me. "Colors, darling? Of the wedding."

"Black and white."

"Seriously?"

"Yes."

"Our Jimmy. Always so dramatic." Pierre went back to his

call. "Black and white. Yes." He looked at me. "Fair, excellent skin, no tanning booth for this one. Oooh, Rebecca, darling, that sounds divine." He looked at me again. "Darling, where are you at?" I looked at him with what I knew was a blank expression. "The wedding, darling, where is it to be? And the reception?"

I had no idea. "Uh, hold that question." Trotted to the tanning room and knocked softly. "Paul? Can I come in? I'm so sorry, but I have to ask James something." The door opened. I slipped inside. Gower had his arms around Reader and was rocking him. Reminded me a lot of Martini and me. "Is James okay?"

Gower kissed the top of his head. "Yes. Just overdoing it a bit."

"I'm fine," Reader said as he shifted to look at me. "Just sort of feel like you did when you called me the other night."

Gower reached out and pulled me into the group hug. "Now, before we tell Jeff we've decided to go bi and steal Kitty from him, you think you can calm down and remember that we all love you, and if you forget one, or even two, little things, it won't really matter to her?"

"It won't James, I promise." I hugged him harder.

The door opened. "Oh, my. A camera phone would mean I was a rich man, I'd guess. Darlings, Rebecca has to know the location, wedding and reception both, and the times. Can't save the day without those teensy details."

Reader took a deep breath and seemed to relax. He stepped away from Gower and me and put out his hand for the phone. He left the room, and Pierre closed the door behind them.

"He doesn't want me knowing anything, does he?"

"No. He wants this to be perfect for you and Jeff. He doesn't want you to regret anything about it."

"Because it's the only one we'll have, right?"

"Somewhat." Gower hugged me. "But mostly it's because he loves you." He kissed my forehead. "We both do. And we love Jeff, too. And," he added softly, "he almost died. Before he could take care of this. He's trying to make up for lost time that I know you don't care about, because we both are happier to have him still with us than anything else."

"Yeah." I leaned my head against Gower's chest. "I just want to get it all over with and go to Cabo. Nothing's worth getting James this upset."

He kissed my head. "I know. Jeff feels the same way. But you'll be glad you have the memories of all of this, trust me."

"Will do."

Pierre popped his head in again. "Darlings, while I think I'd adore hanging with you people after hours, Dennis is here with some options, and we need to get moving."

We separated and went out to see another nice-looking man who was carrying a selection of veils. Reader was back to channeling Karl Lagerfeld. He had me try on all of them, discussed the fabrics with Dennis and Pierre, and seemed back to normal. Gower stayed with us, which I thought was probably a really good idea.

Reader finally settled on a fine silk mesh with a solid silk border and white roses embroidered in it. "This reminds me of what my Nana Sadie told me she wore at her wedding."

Dennis nodded. "You going under the canopy?"

"Fairly nonsecular," Reader answered quickly. "Kitty's a Jewish-Gentile mix, Catholic on the mother's side, and her fiancé is Protestant." Well, that was technically true: They'd protested the world religion. The world religion of Alpha Four, but still, I could say that without feeling a total liar.

Dennis shrugged. "Half of your family will still appreciate the nod."

Reader paid for the veil, and Dennis shook hands all around.

Pierre sighed. "Lovely man." He looked at me. "Straight, more's the pity." He scrutinized the veil. "Darling, hoping not to sound sacrilegious here, but if we're going to drape it over your head, once the ceremony is over, it would make a lovely wrap."

Reader looked shocked, but in a good way. "Yeah, it would."

"My Nana would consider that a great way to get double out of it, so no worries. I think that's a good idea, too."

"Fabulous. Now, let's get started on making you look just as your Jeff's used to, only more so."

CHAPTER 68

PIERRE DID WONDERFUL THINGS WITH MY HAIR.
Bouncy curls that made it look thicker and would look
great with the dress. Reader had the veil safely wrapped up,
and Gower finally felt it was safe to go back to the other
men.

I insisted on giving Pierre a huge tip in addition to whatever Reader had given him. I still had a lot of Martini's cash
on me, and I didn't think he'd mind. Pierre said I was always
welcome. Then we gathered up the other gals, and Reader
hustled us to our next location.

It was just before noon now, and we were headed to the girl's
luncheon. I had no idea how Reader could be berating himself
for forgetting flowers when he'd managed to plan everything
else down to the smallest detail in a matter of hours.

This time I knew we had paparazzi because they were all
over the place. The fine dining area wasn't inside the casino,
in that sense, and there were cameras and men shoving themselves at us. It was weird and not at all pleasant. The only one
missing was Mister Joel Oliver.

My mother seemed unperturbed. "Why are you so okay
with all this?" I hissed to her as we walked quickly past a
clutch of them.

"It's amazing. You work for Centaurion Division and have
no idea of how this will play out?"

I thought about it. "Oh. Just like last night—Imageering
will handle it?"

"And the reports will show that there was a huge wedding

with a lot of money spread around. We call it a 'cover story' where I come from."

"You want them here, don't you?"

"I understand how to use and influence the weapons at my disposal, yes." She heaved a sigh. "Somehow they made you a Commander and yet barely tolerate Charles. I wonder about Centaurion Division's judgment sometimes, I really do."

"I'm wondering about your judgment, so that's fair. You really think it's okay that they're getting pics of you and Chuckie, too?"

She sighed. "An international playboy-millionaire being in attendance enhances the cover story. I'm your mother, where else should I be when my daughter's getting married?"

"Chuckie honestly has a playboy rep?" He'd told me so, but I was still having trouble seeing it in my mind. I loved him, but I didn't see Chuckie as Batman. Then again, maybe Iron Man—Tony Stark was brilliant, after all. I didn't figure Mom would appreciate discussing which comics character Chuckie would most align with, so I kept these thoughts to myself.

"In the circles we need him to, yes, particularly internationally. It covers why he travels so much, has a home in D.C. as well as Sydney, and so forth. Why is this even remotely surprising to you?"

It was surprising mostly because I still wasn't sold on the paparazzi being useful to covert ops in any way, but I decided not to argue this any longer. "I'm distracted."

"Good line. Stick with it. Doesn't work on me, but maybe someone else will fall for it." My mother—the love was overwhelming.

We shoved through the men with cameras, and Reader deposited us at Shanghai Lily, then left to meet up with the other men, who were having their lunch across the way at Lupo. Strict instructions were left that I wasn't to go to the bathroom alone, since I might manage to meet up with Martini and have sex in the middle of the casino or something.

Casino Security showed up and moved the paparazzi away just as our food arrived. I was impressed and was finally able to relax. I didn't know how the celebs handled it on a regular basis, but I was fine with never seeing another camera again.

All the female guests were here with us, though my wedding party, complete with mothers and grandmothers, was in its own section. I tried not to think about the costs of this.

I knew there was no way Chuckie or the C.I.A. was footing these bills, and, during the second course, I started to really wonder if Martini had any idea of how much money we were spending like it was water.

My phone rang. "How's Lupo?"

"Food's great. Is your theme for today ultra worrying?"

"Jeff, it's just . . ." I didn't want to say what it was in front of everyone, his mother in particular. My mother in the other particular.

He sighed. "James explained a little of why you might be worried. In our culture, the groom's side pays for everything."

"You're just saying that."

"No, I'm not. If you can't afford to pay for everything, then you can't afford to marry the girl. It's an A-C thing. Ask Victoria, for God's sake. Alexander just confirmed it's still the same on the home world."

"Okay, but still."

"But still nothing. Baby, this is how we do things. I realize we added in some human customs, but marriages are a huge deal for us. Mate for life, remember? We do them big, we do them expansively, and we do them with gusto. Huh?" I heard him talking to someone else in the background. Martini started to laugh. "To reassure you and your father, no, this wedding is not going to cause me or my family to go bankrupt. Is that what you're worried about?"

"A little." A lot.

"Been saving for it for years. Now, stop worrying, and enjoy yourself. Because if you don't, then *that's* a waste of the money."

He was good, and he was right. We hung up, and I decided to be a good girl and enjoy the heck out of this. Wasn't too hard, I liked food, and this was good food. The luncheon lasted around three hours, which was nice because it was three hours I didn't have to run to do something else. But, finally, it was time to head back and start getting ready for the actual wedding itself.

It was a blur of activity. Had to get the dresses and everything else. People had to run back for all the things forgotten the first time. And the second time. The paparazzi had to be removed again. And again.

The Mandalay Bay had a nice set up, and we were all installed into the various locations within it—women's dressing room, men's dressing room, and foyer for those involved but not intimately. The majority of our guests were being routed to the actual room where we were getting married. I caught a glimpse of Martini, but Serene dragged me around a corner so no unauthorized sightings were committed.

The A-C side of my wedding party had spent most of lunch explaining the ceremony to me. I'd already researched it and gone over issues with Richard, but we hadn't had time to rehearse what, in fact, I was supposed to do once things started.

By A-C custom, if both parents were living, both parents gave you to your intended. I thought this was a nice custom. I wasn't clear on the giving, but Mom assured me that Lucinda had given her the skinny on what to do, so I stopped worrying.

Denise Lewis ran in. "We have a ring-bearer emergency."

"What happened?" twelve women asked in unison. Yes, the unison thing was definitely wedding-related.

"Jeff's nephew, George, has come down with some typical childhood ailment. None of the other Martini boys are old enough or young enough, at least according to James."

Much consternation ensued. By A-C tradition, the ring bearer kept the rings secure and hidden until they were requested, usually in a suit pocket somewhere, so no pillow or ring basket or whatever was required, making it a fairly simple job. As far as the A-Cs were concerned, anyone could bear the rings and anyone could toss the flower petals, with no age restrictions.

Of course, Reader was representing the human view that said ring bearers and flower girls needed to be adorable moppets. I was fine with this, but whatever George had, I didn't want, nor did I want him sharing the contents of his stomach with us, right moppet age or not.

"Could Kimmie carry the rings, too?" This was met with dead silence. "Or another girl?" More dead silence. "Okeydokey. That's a big no." I looked back to Denise. "You have two, right?"

"One boy, one girl."

"Is your son the right age?"

"Well, yes, but, we're not family."

Lucinda and Mom both snorted. "Yes, you are." The unison thing again. It never stopped being creepy.

"I think he's elected. Stress James out, get him into a tux."

"Raymond should fit into George's. Do you want me to send him in so you can recognize him?"

My turn to snort. "He'll be the incredibly gorgeous kid with perfect teeth and bags of charisma, right?"

Denise smiled. "Just like his father."

"And mother. So, yeah, I think I'll be able to spot him, even with all the A-C gorgeous around. So, let him stay with the men and be all manly like. Besides, Kevin's a groomsman, so it's all good."

Denise hugged me, then raced out to share the problem solve. Jeff's sister Marianne brought Kimmie in now. She looked gorgeous in a little girl version of what the bridesmaids were wearing, but with the colors reversed.

The florist arrived, Reader in tow, and more bedlam ensued. The flowers were gorgeous—my bouquet was all red roses with two white roses in the center. The girls were each carrying smaller versions, and Kimmie had a basket with red and white rose petals to scatter. The men's boutonnières were white roses, but I caught a glimpse of one red one, which I assumed was for Martini. The women's corsages were red with white.

It was simple, but because we had so much black and white going on, the red roses looked dramatic and beautiful. Reader seemed pleased, which, by now, was all that I was looking for. If he was happy, things were going as planned.

Reader had to go change, and my father came in, apparently to ensure that no one let me see Martini or vice versa. Dad was in the same tuxedo as the groomsmen, so I got to finally see something from the male side.

Tuxes were black, of course, double-breasted with a notch lapel. The main part of the lapel was wide and black satin. White shirts with the black things whose name I could never remember over the buttons, black bowties, no vests. It looked great on my dad, so I figured it would look great on everyone else, including Martini, and I said as much.

"Oh, Jeff's in something different," Dad said with a twinkle.

"What would that be?"

"You'll find out soon enough." He was clearly enjoying being in on the big secret.

"Sol, stop torturing Kitty." Mom sounded mildly annoyed.

Dad gave her a peck. "Only chance I'll have to do it. I only get room duty until James comes back. Most of the men are ready. It was nice—this is the only group of young men whom I didn't have to teach how to tie their ties, not even the bowties."

"They tied their own bowties?"

"Yes. It's a lost art." Dad sounded impressed. I looked closely at his tie. Darned if he wasn't telling the truth.

Reader came back, and I got a better idea of how the tuxes were going to look on the guys in the wedding party. Drool-worthy about covered it. He grabbed Jareen for some instructions, and Dad went off with them.

Mom put her necklace on me. I'd seen it before, of course, but she only wore it for special occasions, so not that often. A thin band of tiny diamonds curved down to a diamond-encrusted Star of David. The pendant hung just at the start of my cleavage. The bracelet was another thin band of diamonds. Mom had me wear it on my right wrist.

Jareen was back, and it was time for me to get into my dress. Managed to score some privacy but not a lot, since I couldn't button the dress myself. Jareen, as matron of honor, got the thrill of being alone with me while I put on my lingerie.

"Naked Apes really go through a lot of ritual."

"This Naked Ape was fine with just racing off to some sleazy chapel in town and doing the quickie wedding."

"Everyone is happy you didn't."

"I know. Do I look totally slutty?" I was still in my lingerie.

"Yes. Jeff will love it." She handed me the blue garter. "James says to wear this and not lose it."

I put it on my right leg, ensured it was secure, then shimmied into the dress. "This is really a great dress."

"Yes, but it's the one because of how it makes you look in it."

"Geez, James is rubbing off on you."

"Perhaps. Hmmm . . . I think we need human fingers." She called Serene in. "Need help with the buttons."

"Okay." Serene sounded nervous.

"Serene, they're buttons. You button them."

"I know . . . but I don't want to ruin your dress."

"Button them slowly."

"James said to hurry up."

"Button them slowly, and we'll lie to James."

She did as requested. "You look so beautiful."

"Thanks."

"Richard's really happy you and Jeff met the deadline."

I heard the words. I reran them in my mind. They made no sense to me. "Uh, what deadline?"

"The one for you and Jeff to get married."

"I thought we had six weeks more, minimum. I mean, that's when we were telling everyone we were going to get married."

"Oh, yes, for you two, it wouldn't have mattered." She was buttoning carefully and concentrating on doing it well, I could tell. So I didn't want to throw her, but I did want to find out what in the world she was talking about.

"Then who was the deadline for?"

"The rest of us. You know, in order for Richard to approve any other marriages this year, he had to agree that you two would marry by May first. Some of the older A-Cs forced him into that."

Jareen and I exchanged a look. "So, since I'm not from around here, what would the ramifications have been if Kitty and Jeff had, say, gotten married as they'd planned, six weeks from now?"

"No one else could be married for a year after, because it would mean the process was too complex. Also, they wanted to see how Jeff and Kitty did for a year before allowing any others to marry. Richard got the deadline as a compromise."

And he'd never mentioned it once, to either me or Martini.

"Huh. That seems odd to me, as a Giant Lizard. They gave a deadline of May first, and if Jeff and Kitty met that, then everyone can get married?"

"Yes," Serene said, still concentrating on the buttons.

"But if they got married on, say, May second, then everyone else would have to wait until May of the next year before they could consider marriage? And it would be dependent upon how Jeff and Kitty were doing?"

"Yes. There, all done. Jareen, can you check and make sure it looks right?"

Jareen moved around behind me. "Perfect." Serene beamed.

"Thanks, Serene. So, pretty much, we have until midnight to get married or else no one else gets hitched to a human?"

She nodded. "But we're fine. I think the ceremony's scheduled for six." She left the room.

Jareen and I looked at each other. "Twenty of your dollars says someone tries to stop this wedding."

"Unlike my Nona Maria, I don't take sucker bets. This is why James is so frantic. He knows about it—but I don't think anyone else we're close to does. I mean, why would Christopher have let us dawdle along if there was this kind of restriction on us?"

Jareen shook her head. "No idea."

"James must have discovered this when he was in the hospital wing. He would have told me if he'd known before all the invasion stuff started. I mean, he was going to help me get a dress before Moira attacked him, but there wasn't any urgency, not like he's had since he made his miraculous recovery."

"Then why hasn't he told you?"

"Maybe he can't. Or else he's protecting someone." Neither answer seemed totally right. I had no idea what was going on. Conveniently, I knew someone who could always figure out what was going on. "No one's going to like this, James and Jeff least of all, but I need to talk to Chuckie, right now and in person."

CHAPTER 69

JAREEN NODDED. **"I KNOW HOW** to get him in here. Just sit, well, stand tight."

She hypersped out of the room and was back in a flash with Chuckie. "Oooh, dude, nice tux." It was nice. Of course, I'd seen it before, at our ten-year reunion. When he'd proposed. Worked very hard on being emotionally cool and calm.

"What's up? Jareen said 'emergency,' grabbed me, and I'm here." I brought him up to speed. He looked thoughtful. "Get Serene, Lorraine, and Claudia, only, in here."

Jareen went off and got them. "What's up?" Lorraine looked perfectly calm.

"Serene, could you tell everyone in the room what you told me and Jareen? About the deadline, I mean?"

She looked confused but told the others what Jareen and I had already heard. There was dead silence when she was done. Claudia and Lorraine looked beyond shocked. "You didn't know?" Chuckie asked them.

"Hell no," Lorraine said. "We're in the next group to get married. So's Serene."

A thought occurred. "Serene? How did you find out about the deadline?" She looked really embarrassed and more than a little scared. "Honey, you're in Airborne now. That means if you were doing some sort of, ah, intelligence work, that's okay."

She looked a little less scared. "Well, when the invasion stuff started, after James was hurt, everyone was running around and doing a million things, and you'd brought me out, but I didn't have anything to do. So I figured maybe I should make sure I was watching Richard—you know, he said I could call him Richard—just to make sure nothing happened to him."

"Yes, he's fine with you calling him Richard. And that was really good thinking on your part, Serene."

"Really? Great!" I gave her a meaningful look. "Oh. Okay. So, at one point, he was talking to a group of people—it was right when you guys brought me out, so James was still in the hospital—and since I couldn't see them in my mind I . . . spied on them." She looked ready to run.

"Good job," I said quickly. Relief washed over Serene's face. "What did you see and hear?"

"The people were really upset with him, saying he was destroying the race. Lots of arguments went on, and they made him agree to a new deadline."

"There was always a deadline?" Chuckie asked.

"Yes, I think so. At least from what they said, it seemed that the issue wasn't the deadline itself but the new date for it."

"I don't understand why Richard would cave to anyone."

"Serene, were these people you knew?" Chuckie had his eyes closed.

"No. From where I was hiding I couldn't really see anyone other than Richard, and I didn't recognize their voices. But I don't know everyone."

He opened his eyes. "You don't know all your relatives?"

"No." She looked down. "I spend most of my time with the NASA team."

"So it wasn't anyone from the Space Center." I looked at Chuckie. "What are you thinking? I mean besides that this is just freaking typical for my luck."

He shook his head. "I'm trying to figure out who has the most to lose, or gain, by humans not being allowed to marry A-Cs. The American government wouldn't be the answer—what we talked about last night is hugely exciting, and we will, of course, want to maintain a lot of interaction and such, but prevention wouldn't be the idea."

The girls all looked at me. "Top secret, Commander-level clearance only, sorry." I got four disgusted expressions staring at me. "Really. Bug Chuckie and Christopher later, okay? I think we have more urgent issues."

Chuckie nodded. "We do. This is beyond bizarre."

A scary thought occurred. "Serene? Where's Richard?"

She concentrated. "He's with Christopher and all the other men." She blushed bright red. "Jeff only has his pants on." I refrained from mentioning she'd seen Martini with his pants off when we were in Florida. He and I spent a lot of time not mentioning that we'd unknowingly given Serene a personal how-to class in sexual athleticism.

"So Richard's fine?" She nodded. "Who could have the influence to cause him to change his decision?"

"No one from our generation would," Claudia said. "Even the ones who do want to marry A-Cs think it's right for the rest of us to marry who we want."

"None of our human operatives are against it, either," Lorraine added. "I mean, Jerry, Matt, and Chip are playing the field, but with intent to find the right girl and settle down. They're hotly contested items, so I can't imagine they or any of our other human males would be causing this problem."

I shook my head. "No human working with A-Cs would be talking about purity of the race, at least not since Brian had his wake-up call."

"I agree." Chuckie's tone was thoughtful. "Humans who can work and live with aliens like your operatives do aren't normally loaded with xenophobia." He shook his head. "I can't believe I'm going to say this, but you want to bring Brian in for his perspective?"

"Maybe." It was there, tickling the back of my mind.

A knock came on the door, and Mom stuck her head in. "Hello, Charles. I'm not going to ask. I assume it's something horrible. Kitten, what do we do about the feuding families?"

"Pardon?"

Mom sighed. "Doreen's parents, the entire A-C Diplomatic Corps, a few of the other parents of A-Cs dating humans? You know, the people who really don't want to accept change?"

Chuckie and I looked at each other. "Oh. Duh." Said in unison.

I looked back to my mother. "Can you please get Lucinda in here?" She rolled her eyes, but went off, presumably to comply. "Lorraine, please get Doreen."

"On it." Lorraine zipped off.

Lorraine, Mom, and Lucinda all joined us. Doreen came in right after them. We were now officially in Marx Brothers territory. However, it was better than where the Diplomatic Corps wanted us headed.

"My parents are doing something awful, aren't they?" Doreen asked without any preamble.

"Shockingly, yes." I brought everyone up to speed on what we'd gotten from Serene. No one seemed overly surprised by the information. Meaning everyone else had a clearer view of what was going on than I did. How unusual. "Mom? What's your honest, brutal assessment of the A-C Diplomatic Corps?"

"That they're not actually diplomats. It's a pretty title for this side of the house. But what they actually function as are lobbyists."

"Lobbying for what?"

"Protecting our interests," Lucinda answered. "They deal the most efficiently of all our people with those in political power."

Meaning they were the A-Cs most likely to be capable of lying. That some A-Cs could indeed lie had been proven at least somewhat by the fact that the late and unlamented Adolphus had had spies on Earth for a long while. "Do you trust them, Mom?"

She glanced at Doreen. Who grimaced. "Tell the truth, Missus Katt, I don't know how anybody could trust my parents."

Mom shrugged. "No, I don't either. But, then, I don't trust most lobbyists. What do you think they're going to attempt?"

"My guess is that they aren't going to go for violence," Chuckie said, "which is one small favor. However, if they can cause chaos and disruption long enough . . ."

Lucinda looked ill. "I had to invite them. It would be very bad for Richard and the boys if I hadn't."

"They'd have shown up even if you hadn't," Doreen spat out.

"Things still tense between you and your parents?" I asked her.

She nodded. "We haven't spoken, not really, since I moved to Caliente Base. The only messages I get from them say I have to leave Irving if I want their forgiveness. I don't want anything from them, not any more. Not now, not ever."

Lucinda put her arm around Doreen. "It'll work out, dear." Doreen didn't look as though she believed this. I couldn't blame her—I didn't either.

Mom shook her head. "We need to stop them, but it has to be done in a politically correct manner, or we'll all feel a lot of heat I'd like to avoid."

"How long has Robert Coleman been in charge? Maybe we can use inexperience as an excuse."

"Hardly. He replaced Theresa White after her death." Lucinda looked uncomfortable. "He wasn't who Richard would have chosen. But he was in no condition to help make a selection."

"The Pontifex normally chooses the Diplomatic Corps?"

"Yes, he makes the recommendations. They have to be approved by the majority of our people over the age of forty, though."

"Who assigned the Diplomatic Corps when you all first arrived?" Chuckie asked.

"Richard and Theresa did. But once she died and Ronald came on in her place, most of the original Diplomatic Corps resigned."

"Coleman moved the Pontifex's supporters out and his own supporters in," Chuckie said. The way he said it, I knew he had no doubts, meaning I had no doubts.

"I suppose so." Lucinda sounded as though she had some doubts. "None of us were in any condition to worry about it. Losing Theresa the way we did . . . the boys and Richard consumed all of our attention. Besides, the Diplomatic Corps perform a hugely important function for us. Robert is the person who ensures any issues we create get smoothed over and smiled away, if you will. He's done a good job, honestly, they all have. We don't get along with every government agency as well as we do with NASA, Angela, or Mister Reynolds."

"And Jeff would never say he and Chuckie get along."

"Neither would I," Chuckie said. "So the people with the most influence in both the A-C community and with all the governmental agencies, outside of those in the actual wedding party, want to stop this marriage. And we have to stop them in a way that won't cause repercussions in the A-C community."

"Nicely summed up, dude."

"Great. Have you any idea of how we're going to manage this?"

"Give me a minute." I closed my eyes. ACE, I have to talk to Richard White. Can you help me do that?

Yes, Kitty, ACE can help. There was a pause.

Yes, Miss Katt? You never fail to surprise in your ability to communicate at any time and via any source possible.

Robert and Barbara Coleman and their cronies forced you to make a bad deal, right?

Yes. Long story I shared with the only person capable of doing anything about it.

You told James because you knew I'd do what he said?

And because he would do it with haste, discretion, and accuracy so to speak. How did you find out?

Serene has a daddy-crush on you. She spent her time when we weren't fighting for our lives watching over you, so she saw the 'let's attack Richard when he's got a lot more important things going on' meeting.

Ah, intriguing. However, you and Jeffrey are racing along, so I foresee no issues.

This is why you have Alpha and Airborne. We have identified major issues. My question to you—if I have the Colemans and their gang detained and removed from the premises, what kind of problems does that create for you?

What would your reasons be?

Suspicion of terrorist activities.

Sounds nasty.

Sounds like a trip to wherever the C.I.A. likes to take people.

We can't have these people disgraced, harmed, and so forth. The Colemans may be unpleasant, but they are quite vital to our race's well-being.

So I keep hearing. And I know only someone you saw as important would have gotten away with this dirty trick.

And we are speaking in this amazing manner so we can both say you never asked me for permission?

I have always respected your ability to see through the marketing-speak.

Then as long as I can be upset and outraged once you and Jeffrey are on your honeymoon, and Mister Reynolds will release the offending parties without problems the moment I request it, go to town Miss Katt.

No scuff marks on the merchandise. Other than Barbara. I can't promise there, but I'll make sure she's still somewhat presentable.

Your restraint is admirable. Jeffrey is picking up your distress, by the way. I think we'd best break off so I can keep him under control.

Tell him I'm handling it.

He knows Mister Reynolds is with you.

Tell him Chuckie saw everything I own years ago, and if I

weren't interested in marrying Jeff, I would let the Colemans do their thing. But diplomatically.

Anything I could come up with would be more diplomatic than that. Best of luck, Miss Katt. I'll keep the boys in here with me.

Wise man always does the smart thing.

Let us hope.

I sent a thank you to ACE, then looked at Chuckie. "I think we have suspected terrorists, Chuckie. They could be altering themselves to look like people we'd trust."

"I could spot tha—" Serene was shut up by Lorraine's hand slamming over her mouth.

Chuckie nodded. "Missus Martini, I'm sure they'd disguise themselves as your Diplomatic Corps, who would normally be above suspicion. But since all of Centaurion Division reports in to me at the moment, I'm going to override diplomatic immunity. Could you come with me and point out whom we should be concerned about?"

Lucinda nodded. "Absolutely. I wouldn't want to help terrorists disguised as important people in our community."

"How many, do we think?" Chuckie asked as he pulled out his phone.

Lucinda thought about it. "A dozen. If I were going to attempt some sort of terrorist overthrow, I'd only need to imitate the Diplomatic Corps. If they were taken away, anyone following them would likely lose their will to fight."

He nodded and dialed. "I need a low-key pickup of about a dozen or so suspected terrorists. They could be impersonating high-level A-Cs, could be mentally controlling them. I don't want any of the subjects injured, just detained safely far away from where we are. Good. Yes, at least double the A-C operatives. Yes, right away. Yes, I'm very aware it's your wedding day. I'm also aware you're the one who knows which of your Field agents are available and which aren't."

Chuckie glanced at me. "Yes, she looks great. A little upset that you're arguing with me instead of taking care of this so you two can get married, but, you know, otherwise, great." He rolled his eyes. "Because I need the big, nasty guys, and the imageers usually aren't. Yes, great plan. Have her call in my human team as well; they need to appear to be in charge. Right. Hate you as well."

He hung up and shook his head. "Are you marrying the

most contrary man in the universe, or is that merely my impression?"

"What's Jeff doing and why did you call him?"

"He's contacting Gladys, who is still running all Security operations. She's sending personnel over right now."

There was a knock at the door. An A-C I'd seen around stuck his head in. "Mister Reynolds? Commander Martini said you needed us."

"Back in a bit. I recommend you all stay here, other than Lucinda who, regretfully, has to risk herself by identifying those potential terrorists."

"I'll go, too," Mom said. "Might help in the long run."

They all left, and Lorraine took her hand off Serene's mouth. "While Kitty's on her honeymoon, Claudia and I are going to teach you two things. When to tell Kitty something the moment you learn it, and when to keep your mouth shut."

Jareen chuckled. "Naked Apes really make things exciting. When Neeraj and I were joined, we just went to the head Iguanodon, made a couple of promises, hugged and kissed, and that was it."

"I want to get married on your planet."

"You don't have time. The wait list for joinings is ten years. Our little wrinkle is that only the head Iguanodon can join anybody. See? Each planet has its stupidities."

"I'll bet you twenty of my dollars my planet's winning."

Jareen grinned. "I don't take sucker bets, either."

CHAPTER 70

DOREEN CALLED IRVING, then went off to perform crowd control of the younger A-Cs. We heard a lot of ruckus start. My phone rang.

"Girlfriend, what did you just start?"

"You know, you didn't have to carry the weight of the world by yourself, James."

He sighed. "Yeah, I did. It was a specific, personal request."

"You are the best, and I love you, you know that, right?"

"Right. So, what's happening? Richard won't allow any of the wedding party to leave the groom's room."

"Good. Keep Jeff and Christopher in there, in particular. That mean Mister Reynolds got a tip there were terrorists disguised as the A-C Diplomatic Corps trying to kill off all the high-ranking A-Cs as well as the head of the P.T.C.U. and the head of the C.I.A.'s ET division. We are very worried about where the real Diplomatic Corps is, of course, and will have to ensure these people tell us what they did with the real A-Cs."

He laughed. "I like it."

"So you can slow us down a bit."

"No. They can hold to the timeline. But I'm guessing you just stopped something I would have no control over."

"Yeah. Why is Jeff only in his pants?"

"I'm not going to ask how you knew that. No nefarious reason. All the rest of his tux is here, and I'm looking at it. He's just nervous, and I don't want him sweating in it."

"He's an A-C. They don't sweat."

Reader chuckled. "He's sweating. Just a little." I could hear someone in the background say something, then roars of male laughter. "Jeff said I should tell you he's not nervous at all."

"Yeah, the laughter isn't a giveaway. Anyway, I'd imagine Chuckie will tell you when it's all clear. The only ones who know are my female Airborne members, Mom, Lucinda, and Jareen. Oh, and Doreen, but she won't give anything away. She might try to kill her parents, though."

"I'm sure Reynolds can handle it. Okay, you dressed?" The drill sergeant was back.

"Yes. And unlike Jeff, I'm not sweating. It's well air-conditioned in here. Not in my shoes or veil yet, but I'm wearing everything else."

"Your dad has the veil. He's in here with us, of course, but it's safe."

"I wasn't worried."

"How's your hair?"

"Holding without feeling like it's plastered. Pierre is amazing."

"Yeah, and well-connected, thankfully."

"Not as much as you."

"I suppose." I heard more voices in the background. Reader sighed. "Jeff's doing his jealousy thing where he's wondering why you seem so much happier talking to me than to him."

"We'll get off. Tell him it's because I don't sleep with you."

"I don't know if that'll help or not."

"You get to find out. Enjoy."

We left the dressing room and got a lot of excited comments from the other women in the larger women's changing room. We waited for what seemed like forever but Claudia insisted was only thirty minutes, and then Doreen came in. "All clear. The situation was unpleasant but handled."

I pulled her into the private room. "What's the plan?"

She shrugged. "Their children will identify them."

"When?"

"Later. Like, after you're on your honeymoon later."

"Works for me."

Went back out and waited some more. My dad came in and sent any females not in the wedding party out, which included my grandmothers. I started to feel a couple of butterflies in my stomach. Dad said Reader wanted me in the shoes and veil now, so he went into the private room to help me.

"Is Jeff dressed yet, Dad?"

"He was starting when I left." Dad was humming softly. The Wedding March, I realized, as I listened closely.

"You happy I'm getting married?"

"What? Oh, yes. You have a wonderful world ahead of you, kitten."

I waited. Nothing. "Um, Dad? Isn't this the time for the father-daughter talk?"

"Huh? Oh, the veil." Dad pulled the veil out. Undid the tissue paper, spent a little time draping it just right. My hair stayed in place. I had to find out what brand of hairspray Pierre used; it was the best.

"I kind of meant the father-daughter talk where you give me those bits of fatherly wisdom that will make my marriage work." Mom's had been pretty darned brief, but I'd been expecting more from my father.

"Oh." He looked a little blank, as though he'd never considered the idea. "Never go to bed angry with each other."

"Yes? That's sort of a bumper sticker by now, Dad. I meant something I couldn't learn from a quick browse through *Cosmo* or *Maxim*."

"Oh. Well. Huh." Dad was clearly out on the high diving board over an empty pool.

"You know, things you did and do to make sure you and Mom have such a great marriage."

"Oh! I gave that advice to Jeff already. Applies to him more than to you."

"Share with me anyway."

Dad shrugged. "I told him that he just needed to remember three things. First, he doesn't run your life, and after today, he won't run his life, either. Second, in any argument, there is your wife's side and then there is enemy camp; never choose enemy camp in an attempt to be reasonable, because it never works. And third, to remember that a happy wife is a happy life."

"Can't argue with the genius." I waited. Nothing. "So, any little genius stuff for me? Just asking because Mom was about as hot with the help as you are."

Dad laughed. "Kitten, you're a big girl. You've chosen a wonderful man." He cocked his head at me. "I can suggest one thing." I nodded. About time. "You had several wonderful men to choose from, and you picked Jeff. When you fight, as I know you do and will, don't bring up your options, either out loud, in your mind, or in your emotions. Marriage is a lifelong commitment, through good and bad. If you don't believe you can make that commitment with Jeff, now is the time to run. On the other hand, if you do believe you can, then whatever compatibility you have with the others doesn't matter, now or in the future."

I hugged him. "Thanks, Dad."

He patted my back. "Happy to help, if that was a help."

"It was." I was about to say more when there was a knock at the door and Jareen poked her head in. "It's time."

CHAPTER 71

DUE TO THE SHEER SIZE OF OUR WEDDING, we couldn't actually get married in the wedding chapel. We'd been able to use the dressing rooms and such, but we had to move to the convention area for everything else. So we'd get married in the Islander Ballroom, shout hurray, and walk through the door to the South Pacific Ballroom, where the tables and dance floor were already set up.

The men left first and led the rest of the guests to the ultimate location. Then Chuckie, not Reader, came to escort the women, a contingent of A-Cs following him to perform cleanup.

On the plus side, there were no paparazzi. I thought about it. "Who's doing our wedding pictures and video?"

"Exactly who you think."

"You and James did another exclusive?"

"Yes. Reader felt we needed the A-C manpower used elsewhere, and I had to agree. The *World Weekly News* folks do a great job keeping the rest of the vultures away."

This seemed true enough. "Are we doing all the standard kinds of photos?"

"Doubt it. Reader insinuated we didn't have the time, and after our little fun with the Diplomatic Corps, I'm sure he's right. Trust me, Oliver will get all the shots you'll want and more, I'm sure. He's got a full video team on hand. And we have our own teams working with and watching each of them."

"Great." I didn't think it was great, and my voice clearly showed so.

Chuckie sighed. "Reader insisted. I do know when not to pull rank, you know."

"Where *is* James?"

"He's in the wedding party, remember? I'm not, so I have this portion of Wedding Control to manage."

"You don't mind?"

He squeezed my hand. "Not at all. I even have an official title. Bridal Majordomo."

I laughed. "Right."

"He *is* right," Claudia said. "It's a huge position in the wedding, always assigned to someone close to the bride."

Lorraine coughed. "We told you about this. A lot."

I vaguely remembered someone mentioning this and thinking then it had been a joke. Ah, well, what a shocker, I was wrong. "Well, then they picked right."

Chuckie squeezed my hand again. "Glad you think so. Martini even agreed."

"Wow."

"The Majordomo cannot be considered as an alternate to the groom," he said dryly. "That's also in the rules. The job usually goes to an uncle, sometimes a grandfather, occasionally a brother who somehow isn't in the wedding party. Your Uncle Mort was gracious enough to say that he felt I was better qualified for it."

Yeah, Uncle Mort loved Chuckie. Pushed back the twinges of guilt. Uncle Mort loved Martini, too.

"No need to rush," Chuckie added, slowing me down a little. "Believe me, from what White told me, we've got an easy thirty more minutes to kill."

Conveniently, most of the wedding ceremony took place without the wedding party, which was one of the many little quirks that made marrying an A-C fun to explain to the human relatives.

Once Dad had sent my grandmothers off, they and the rest of the guests had done some weird ritualistic seating rigmarole that involved a lot of walking in between a variety of blessings. I hadn't been able to see this in my mind's eye no matter how many different ways it had been explained to me. I was going to remain in the dark, since it had been over for at least fifteen minutes.

Now they were on to the Statements of Fidelity, which a human would think should come from the two people about to be married, from the clergy officiating, or even from someone in the bridal party, but, instead, came from random people sitting in the audience. Per the little I'd gleaned, this was to ensure the entire community would be focused on the couple's lifelong happiness. Per what I'd guessed from reading between the lines, it was a great way to make the less beloved relatives and those friends who hadn't scored a place up at the head table a chance to feel deeply involved.

Bizarrely but happily, only the groom and his parents had the "privilege" of hearing these little speeches. Again, no guess as to why, but I had to assume it was because everyone knew the bride was going to take longer to get ready. Or they wanted to give the groom plenty of time to run screaming into the street. Pushed back the little twinge of panic. Martini wasn't going to run off. Right?

It was quite a hike, and while we got some looks, not the kind we could have. All the Animal Planet attendees had been wearing and continued to wear their cloaking jewelry. Chuckie had requested it, but no one had objected, if only to make the pictures easier to explain. Considering who our official photographer was and that there were undoubtedly other random paparazzi lurking somewhere, it was a brilliant order.

We finally arrived outside Islander and laid eyes on all the guys. They looked wonderful. Bored, but wonderful. Everyone paired off, and then we waited while the Statements of Fidelity droned on. Chuckie had the unenviable task of being the only one allowed to listen—he had the door cracked and was stuck to it.

"Glad I have the right career for this," he muttered while the rest of us fidgeted and my father quietly went over what Kimmie and Raymond were supposed to do. "I think they're winding down. White, what's the most likely word cue from your father?"

"We ask you now to join hands for the final preblessing," Christopher replied.

Chuckie sighed. "Haven't heard that yet." We waited another ten minutes then he nodded. "Finally. Okay, everyone ready?"

There were assents from my wedding party. We lined up, and Chuckie opened the door. Alexander and Serene were first, followed by Queen Renata and Kevin, Felicia and Tim, Wahoa and Jerry, Gower and Claudia, Reader and Lorraine, with Christopher and Jareen going last.

Mom and Dad were on either side of me, but I was clutching Kimmie, who was holding a basket almost bigger than she was loaded with rose petals. She was also so excited she was ready to run down the aisle. I had a sudden death grip on her, though, so she wasn't going anywhere.

Mom was holding onto Raymond for the same reason, well, to keep him from racing off. Unlike me, Mom was cool as an igloo. Raymond looked just as I'd imagined a child of Kevin and Denise's would, though his skin was more of a creamy brown, versus the dark chocolate of his father or fair of his mother. He was five and was already more charming than men twenty years his senior. He also took the guarding of the rings as a serious duty and had his hand in one pocket, where the rings were, I assumed, to ensure they weren't lost.

Dad spent some more time going over their duties with them, though, and they seemed clear. He had time—both ballrooms were beautiful, and while Islander was about three-quarters the size of South Pacific they were both huge. A-C tradition required the wedding party walk down the aisle, the men going to the left and the women to the right, walk around the crowd, join up again at the back of the room, then walk back up the aisle to the altar set up at the head of the room. Then they'd do the same thing again, only with the men going to the right and the women to the left.

This meant the wedding party was doing a *lot* of walking. It probably seemed like less when you were moving at hyper-speed. At human speeds, it was long and drawn out. I wasn't sure we'd make the marriage deadline at this rate, but everyone else seemed really calm and unworried.

"When do I see Jeff?" My voice sounded squeaky, and half our wedding party hadn't made it inside the room yet. Chuckie was busying giving the "wait" and "go next" signals. I heard a lot of oohs and ahhs from inside, over the strains of wedding-type music coming from somewhere in there.

"The groom is already inside," Jareen said, sounding like she was reciting from memory. "He waits on one side, for his bride to enter . . . and, that's all I can remember, other than what I'm supposed to do later. Christopher?"

He laughed. "She really is just like you. Jeff and his parents are waiting for you at the left side of the altar or, in this case, front of the ballroom. Once you walk in, you don't go down the aisle and neither does he. You both circle the attendees—

Jeff going clockwise, you going counterclockwise. You pass once, near the altar, then keep going. You meet back up pretty much in front of the door we're going through. Then the parents give you to each other, and Jeff walks you down the aisle."

"White! Move it!" Chuckie hissed.

"You'll be fine," Christopher tossed over his shoulder. "Just do what you always do. You know, fake it until it works."

Mom sighed. "He knows you well."

"Last chance to tell me why I shouldn't marry Jeff, Mom."

She kissed my cheek. "Can't think of one reason. You look so beautiful, kitten," she added in a whisper. "Jeff's going to be so happy."

My throat was tight, and I was having trouble focusing. "Uh-huh."

Chuckie looked over and grinned. "We've all spent too much money. Too late now, no matter what the movies want to tell you. Bachelor Number Three," he nodded his head toward Christopher's back, "and Bachelor Number Two here are both going to be big boys and tell you to marry the guy you're in love with." He looked down at the kids. "You guys ready?"

"Yes!" they chorused together, sounding totally excited. Wow, the only unison thing that didn't freak me out.

"Okay, remember, dignified, don't run, and if you do run, don't get in front of Christopher and Jareen, okay?" They nodded. "Oh, and Kimmie, those petals are mostly for the main aisle, so do most of the dropping there, when you're with Raymond, okay?"

"Okay, Chuckie!"

He looked shocked, then started to laugh. "Okay, you, and only you, can call me Chuckie like Kitty does. But I draw the line there."

Raymond nodded, and he looked very serious. "I understand, Mister Reynolds. And I'll make sure we don't go too fast."

"Good man. You're up." Chuckie ushered the kids in. Then he came back to us. "I'm going inside. Per A-C regulations, the last person to walk through this doorway has to be the bride. Angela, watch the door, you know when to enter." My stomach clenched. I didn't want him to leave.

Mom nodded. "Once all the hiking is over."

"Right." Chuckie examined my expression, took my hand, and led me a few steps away. "You alright?"

I swallowed. I didn't really know how to put it into words. But they came anyway. "You'll always be my friend?"

Chuckie smiled. "Always. And I'm not deserting you—I'll be right up front in the Majordomo seat, ready to take care of whatever you need."

I relaxed a little. "Then I'm good to go." He turned, but I grabbed his arm. A thought had occurred. "Chuckie?"

"Yes?"

"Do you have any advice?"

He was quiet for a long moment. "Actually, I do."

"And?"

"Be yourself."

"That's it?"

Chuckie nodded. "That's it. Because the reason we love you, Martini and myself particularly, is because of who you are." He leaned down and kissed my cheek through the veil. "I know you're scared, but it's no bigger step than any other you've taken. Now do me proud and go show everyone out there how the comics geek-girl who made good gets married."

CHAPTER 72

CHUCKIE WENT BACK TO THE DOOR, took a look, and nodded. "Almost showtime. See you on the other side." He winked at me, went in, and left us out there. Alone. Just me and my parents.

Mom went to the door. "You know, am I the only one of the three of us who thinks this parading all over the place is more like being at a beauty pageant than a wedding?"

Dad and I stood there in shock for a moment, then we both started laughing. "Yeah. What's the bet on our side for how many times I trip?"

"Nana Sadie called ten," Mom replied. "Nona Maria called twenty. I was too busy to catch the rest. But the A-C side's betting, too. And all your friends."

"Viva Las Vegas."

Dad moved up next to Mom and took a look. "Ready, kitten?"

I took the requisite deep breath and waited for ninja or alien attack. Remarkably, there was none. "Yes."

Unlike an Earth wedding, neither Dad nor Mom was holding onto me. I'd thought they would be on either side, but they linked arms and went in front of me. Right, last one through had to be the bride. That had seemed almost logical when Chuckie had explained it. Now? Not so much. "I have to close the freaking door?" I muttered, as I closed the door. Managed not to catch my train. Wondered why I'd said yes to this all of a sudden.

Delayed by door closing, so now had to somehow catch

up to my parents, who, once inside, started sauntering along, waving to guests, as if they were freaking Hollywood types at a premier. Got a glimpse of the wedding party standing far, far away. Couldn't spot Mister Joel Oliver or his camera crew anywhere. Good lord, this place was humongous.

Couldn't run, of course. May have looked great, but nothing says "you will walk slowly" like a tight mermaid gown. Felt the veil slip and wondered why I'd ever questioned Reader about not wearing one. Tweaked it back into place, not as surreptitiously as I'd hoped, if the grins were any indication. Maybe this was the A-C version of the gauntlet or gladiator fighting.

Gave up on catching my parents. They were what seemed like miles ahead of me now. Seriously considered the benefits of turning and running. Remembered I couldn't run in this dress. Tripped, recovered, tripped, recovered, started to crack up, maintained decorum, tripped, recovered, gave up. Paused, took off my shoes, held them in my right hand and my bouquet in my left. That way, the shoes were, at least, on the side facing away from my audience.

I was a hit, if I was going for comedy. I realized as I looked around that A-Cs didn't seat groom side and bride side, because I saw my friends and relatives scattered in there with A-Cs. Apparently the seating ritual was in part to get the families jumbled up, because no one was where I'd have expected them to be. Not that it mattered. Everyone near me was trying hard not to laugh. Most were failing. Utterly.

Fine, whatever. Moved the veil to the wrap position. I'd fix that later. I hoped. Got up onto my toes and did the girly run I detested. The one where the girl is pretending not to run, so doesn't move her arms, doesn't move her thighs, but somehow bounces as though she's on a trampoline? Yeah, that one. I felt like an idiot, but my parents had rounded the corner, and that meant I had miles to make up. For all I knew, the Martinis were already behind me. No, couldn't be, they were going the other direction. And I was supposed to do that lover's crossing thing in front of the world. Operative word being front. I was on the side. Not so good.

Girly run sort of worked. The dress was great—didn't rip, didn't allow my breasts to fly out, didn't unbutton. One thing in the win column.

Rounded the corner to see my entire wedding party looking my way. The men, to a guy, were standing there open-mouthed. I chose not to make eye contact with Reader—I just hoped he wasn't having a heart attack. The girls, on the other hand, were all, to a one, laughing. Lorraine and Claudia were leaning on each other, they were laughing so hard. Same with Felicia and Wahoa. The others were no more reserved. Serene had her hand over her mouth, Jareen was doubled over she was laughing so hard, and Queen Renata, by benefit of being royalty, was merely doing that whole body shake thing where the laughter's inside but could come out any moment. My friends, there for me when I needed them.

Richard White was up there, between Christopher and Jareen, Kimmie and Raymond in front of him. Thankfully, he was really good with the poker face.

My parents had finally picked up that they'd lost me. Martini's parents had picked this up a while earlier. All four of them were standing there, chatting, while waiting for me. I risked a look at the audience. Chuckie and Brian were sitting next to each other, right there in the front. I was worried they were both going to die they were laughing so hard. My grandparents were next to them. Money was changing hands so fast it was almost impossible to keep up with, at least in the quick glance I allowed myself.

The seating was as wide as it was long. I decided I'd had it with the girly run and slowed to a walk. Close enough to see tears of laughter running down Serene's face. At least the Diplomatic Corps had missed this. Another check in the win column.

I took a deep breath, put my shoes down and back on. Back to mincing. Head held high. Remembered the stupid veil. Flipped it on. Accidentally looked at Reader, saw him wince. Realized the veil was upside down. Well, who the hell could tell? I'd fix it after my next wind sprint.

In all the excitement, the one thing I hadn't done was try to figure out where Martini was. Looked around and found out. He'd stepped out of line with our parents, and I was erratically weaving in and out of line with them, so he was now right in front of me, though about a hundred feet away. I forgot everything else looking at him because he looked so incredibly, totally, drool-worthily hot.

He was in a longer, four-button, peaked-lapel tuxedo jacket that hung down to just above his knees. It emphasized his size in a really sexy way. Unlike everyone else, he was in a white, buttoned vest over a white shirt. Long black tie, done four-in-hand, red rose on his lapel. He looked incredibly gorgeous and masculine, and I stopped dead.

Martini was staring at me. He wasn't laughing, thank God, and he didn't look horrified, also thank God. He looked as though someone had kicked him in the stomach. I started to worry about how I looked, not to mention how I'd pretty much destroyed whatever beauty this ceremony had.

He shook his head a little bit, and my whole body went tight. I'd blown it, and he was going to turn around and run. My eyes filled with tears, and I tried to swallow but I couldn't. My breathing got fast and shallow, and I realized I was about ten seconds away from hysterics.

All of a sudden he wasn't a hundred feet away, he was right in front of me. "Shhh, baby," he said softly, and I could see he was smiling. "It's okay. I'm here."

I took one of those gasping breaths where it's a tossup whether you're going to get it under control or burst into tears. Martini took my right hand and wrapped it through his left arm.

"No one leaves the sexiest girl in the galaxy at the altar just because she had a little mishap on her way to catch up to you. Especially when seeing you makes her stop in her tracks, for all the right reasons." He stroked my hand. "I was trying to tell you not to worry about the ceremonial parade, baby, not that I didn't want you any more."

"I've embarrassed your family, haven't I?" Mine, clearly from all the betting going on, were neither shocked nor embarrassed. At least, the winners weren't embarrassed.

He shrugged. "Doubt it. Don't care."

"But I've embarrassed you." I could barely get the words out.

"Is that what you think?" He laughed softly. "Baby, this is why I love you."

"Because I'm a dork?"

"No. Because nothing you do comes out like you plan it, but it still always works out." He grinned. "Put the veil back on as a wrap and take your shoes off." He looked around. "Kids, c'mere."

Raymond looked confused, but Kimmie grabbed his hand and raced them over. At hyperspeed. "Yes, Uncle Jeff?" Fortunately, it was a short enough distance that Raymond didn't look as though he was going to be sick.

"Kitty and I have to get around the room one more time. She used to be a track star, and I'm a lot bigger, but she can't go as fast in her dress. So, it's fair."

"What's fair?" Raymond asked, sounding as confused as I was.

Martini grinned. "We're going to race. No hyperspeed, though," he said to Kimmie. "Has to be running Raymond and Kitty can do. Winning couple gets twenty dollars each."

"I don't have any money," Raymond said, sounding uncertain.

"Then you'd better hurry up. Go!"

Kimmie squealed with laughter and dragged Raymond off. He didn't argue. Martini unhooked my hand from his arm, grabbed my shoes in his free hand, and grinned at me. "They're ahead, and you can't run fast in that dress."

I flipped the veil to the wrap position. "I'm still a sprinter." I grabbed his hand, and he started us running after the kids. "We'll be back," I shouted to our parents as we ran by them. "We're racing for money."

"I love how you have to run in this dress," Martini said as we moved around the room. The kids were little, but they were money-motivated, because they were far ahead. Kimmie looked back, Martini made a lunge forward, she shrieked a laugh, and they kept on going. "Is asking you to wear it once a week too much, you think?"

"Probably, but we can discuss it. Jeff, is anyone going to speak to us ever again?"

"Don't care," he said cheerfully. "Boy, are you slow in this. I have a great idea for our honeymoon. You try to run away from me in this, and I'll chase you."

I started laughing. "I do love how you think."

"Yeah? Tell me so in another minute." He stopped, flipped me gently over his shoulder, then took off at a better trot.

I was laughing too hard to protest. Got a glimpse of Aunt Carla's face. The Gower girls were by her, but they were laughing so hard I was pretty sure they weren't using their A-C talents for anything right now, and Aunt Carla's expression seemed to confirm that. I wasn't sure if she was going to have a conniption fit, a heart attack, or merely storm out, but the horror on her face was worth the whole experience. She shook her finger at me, and I shrieked with laughter.

"Are we catching them?"

"Yeah, but Kimmie's not clear on the concept. We're taking a full lap."

"You up to it?"

He snorted. "Baby, I could do this all day. I plan on doing this all day, too." We rounded another corner, and I saw people I'd seen before. Martini put on another burst of speed. "Kimmie, go up and down the aisle next, okay? From Uncle Christopher to the back and then back to Uncle Christopher, okay? Then stop."

"Okay, Uncle Jeff," she called out at the top of her lungs, giggling like mad.

"Come on," Raymond said. "They're catching us!"

Martini slowed down a little. "You okay back there?"

"Yeah, view of your butt's great. I love this tuxedo, by the way. I can't wait to rip it off you." I heard a couple of gasps and a lot of laughter. "Whoops."

Martini just laughed. "Yeah, it sucks to be me."

Rounded another corner. Waved to the people in the front row. The ones who weren't rolling with laughter or shocked out of their minds managed to wave back. Rounded another corner, got to see our wedding party. The guys had given up and were laughing, too.

Kimmie and Raymond must have reached the back, because they passed us. "We're beating you," Kimmie shrieked joyfully.

"We can still catch you," I called back. They ran faster.

We reached the back, and Martini flipped me gently back onto my feet. "Your shoes." He handed them to me with an almost wistful look on his face.

"Wow, just like our first date."

"Yeah." He smiled, and I realized he'd wondered if I remembered.

"I could never forget the first time I met you, Jeff," I said softly, as I put my shoes back on.

"No one ever forgets their first superbeing."

"No. No girl ever forgets the first time she meets the man of her dreams."

His expression was so loving and tender, I couldn't help it. The tears started to roll down my face. But they weren't tears of shame or fear or hurt.

Martini took my face in his hands and gently wiped the tears away with his thumbs. "I love you. Now, let's go finish getting married." He pulled the veil on, right side up, adjusted it carefully, then wrapped my right arm in his left again.

We walked up the aisle. There were a lot of people watching us, but we only looked at each other. It was the most romantic thing I'd ever experienced.

Reached the front. "We beat you," Kimmie said.

"You did. Fair and square." Martini reached into his tux and pulled out his wallet, extracted two twenties, squatted down and handed one to each of them. "Well done. Raymond, you still have the rings?"

"Yes, sir, Mister Martini." He held out his fist.

"Good man. Keep hold of them for a bit longer." Martini stood up. "We're ready."

Our parents looked at each other. "We're supposed to do the big exchange," Alfred said.

Martini shrugged. "I know. Already took her."

"Works for me," Mom said. "Let's sit, for God's sake." I started laughing again.

"Alfred, Lucinda? After you," Dad said, doing the ushering into seats move. "Trust me, in the end, it doesn't matter what kind of ceremony you have, just that you have one." Martini's parents shrugged, and all four of them took their seats.

Martini moved us up in front of White. "I hear we're on a schedule."

White made a display of checking his watch. "I believe we have time to actually perform the ceremony."

"Great. Let's roll."

I caught Reader's eye. "He sounds so street when he says that."

He cracked up. "Yeah, girlfriend, we're all keepin' it gangsta."

White cleared his throat. "Children, if I may?"

"Sure, sure, sorry." Martini sounded relaxed and happy. I stopped worrying about anything other than what I was supposed to do. He leaned down. "Richard tells you what to do. It's simple."

"I'm the girl for the job then."

White rolled his eyes and moved into the ceremony. He had a lavaliere mike on, so he was easily heard through the huge room. The beginning was fairly standard and about the only thing similar to Earth ceremonies—gathered here to join, discussions of why we were worthy to marry, deep love for each other, commitment and fidelity, any objections. I was a little tense during that part, but no one said Martini was crazy to marry me, so all was well.

As we moved into the official vows, things changed a bit. Christopher and Jareen each held one end of a long, shiny rope made out of some kind of metal. I'd never seen one like it before, but it was familiar, so I assumed it was the same metal as the Unity Necklace. As the vows began, they wrapped it around us. Each vow agreed to meant the rope was pulled a little tighter, until we were very close to each other.

"Jeffrey, do you take Katherine as your wife, to hold her to you until death, only, parts you?"

Martini looked right into my eyes. "I do."

My throat was tight again.

"Katherine, do you take Jeffrey as your husband, to hold him to you until death, only, parts you?"

I swallowed. I didn't want my voice in dog-only register. "I do." Martini gave me a long, slow smile.

Raymond came over and handed us our rings. Martini took my hand, slid my engagement ring off, hooked it into the entwined wedding band, and slid it back onto my finger.

"It's beautiful, Jeff," I whispered.

I took his hand, he pulled it away. I looked up at him, wondering if he was upset with me. "Wrong hand," he whispered, with a small grin. He offered his left hand, and I slid his ring on. He stared at it. "You picked this for me?" I nodded, as worry raised another fin. "It's perfect." He looked at me again, and his expression said the ring was telling him exactly what I wanted it to—how much I loved him.

"These rings are symbols of your love and your union—unbroken, never ending, precious, never tarnishing, enduring and beautiful. And with the rings willingly given and happily received, as Sovereign Pontifex, I pronounce you married. What has been joined will never be broken, in this world or the next."

I heard a lot of quiet sobbing. But I was looking only at Martini. Who it dawned on me I should start thinking of as Jeff. Since my last name was now Martini, too.

He grinned. "I don't care how you think of me, as long as it's as the man you love."

"Always, Jeff."

White cleared his throat. "Jeffrey, you may kiss your bride. Remember there are children present." This got a good chuckle.

Martini removed the veil and wrapped it around my shoulders. Then he took my face in his hands. "You're mine, you know." His eyes held mine and I knew the truth—I'd been his since the moment he'd told me his name.

"Yes, Jeff. Only and always yours."

He bent and kissed me deeply. I'd been wrong before. This was the best kiss ever.

CHAPTER 73

THE KISS WAS WONDERFUL, but not too long. By our standards, anyway.

Christopher and Jareen untied the rope, and White came to us. He hugged Martini, who I was going to start thinking of as Jeff any minute now, then hugged me. "My dear Miss Katt," he whispered, "let me be the first to call you by your married name, and know I do it with great joy and pride."

He let me go and turned to the audience. "Beloved guests, please welcome Jeffrey and Katherine Martini."

We got a standing-O, led by Chuckie and Brian who were still working at not cracking up. I was kind of impressed, though.

Martini grinned. "First act as a married man is to tell you all to get over to the other ballroom right next door. All that running worked up an appetite."

This was met with cheers and laughter, as everyone did what he said. "You're so good with the Commander thing."

"I command you to wear that dress every day on our honeymoon."

"Nice try. But no."

He sighed. "Your father warned me about this." He scooped me up into his arms. "Can't hold you the way I like in this dress. So, I guess it's okay if you don't want to wear it all the time."

I kissed him. "You're so good to me."

He put me back down. "True, true."

Christopher shook his head. "Only the two of you would have ended up turning your wedding into a track meet."

"It could have been worse."

"Yeah, we might have had a superbeing formation." Christopher looked around, as if he were waiting for something. "Well, small favors, I guess."

"Yeah, that's how I feel about it."

"I see why we paraded all over the room," Jareen said. "Sort of just ends and everyone wanders off."

"Not normally," Jerry told her. "Only when Kitty's involved."

Reader came over and pulled me away from Martini. Jeff. Guy I was now married to. Reader hugged me tightly. "You looked great. Even upside down."

"Yeah, the twins stayed inside."

"For the most part." He laughed. "Next wedding I run, I'm not going to be in the wedding party."

"Don't count on it. You're the guy everyone wants with them, James."

He kissed my cheek. "Tell me that later." He let go, and there was a twinkle in his eyes.

"What are you planning now?"

Reader just grinned at me. He put his arm around Gower, and they headed to the ballroom.

Martini made sure no guests or members of the wedding party were straggling. Once we were alone, he stroked my face. "So, wedding of your dreams?"

I thought about it. "Married the most gorgeous, wonderful man in the galaxy, so yeah, pretty much." He took my hand and led me back down the aisle. "We running away already?"

Martini laughed. "No. I just wanted to walk down the aisle with you this way, as a married couple." We looked at each other the whole way. It was romantic and sexy. We reached the end, and I flung myself at him. He gathered me up and kissed me, deeply, passionately, and for a long time.

I heard someone tap a microphone. "Jeff, if you and Kitty can stop making out for a minute, the rest of us are starving." Christopher sounded as though he was trying not to laugh.

Martini ended our kiss, sighed, and let me slide back to the floor. "No problem. I sleep with you tonight, not him." He swept me up into his arms and strode through the now empty ballroom into the bigger, very full ballroom. "They'll be pretending to faint from hunger if I let you walk it."

"Humph."

He grinned. "Really. Wear this on our honeymoon."

I rolled my eyes. "We can play Chase Me, Chase Me or Pretend Attacker tonight, you know. The suite's big enough."

"Mmmm." His eyelids dropped and he purred. "I love how you think."

We got to the head table, and things started to blur again. Lots of great food. Lots of long speeches, some funny, some touching, some dull. Reader cut off the dull ones, earning himself yet another gold star in drill sergeanting.

"Only known Kitty and Jeff a short time," Jareen said for her toast. "But once you find your soul sister, she's yours for life. So, take good care of her, Jeff—you don't want to find out how we avenge our sisters out my way. We make Renata's girls look like babies. Oh, and Kitty? Way to go on landing His Royal Hotness." The girls in my wedding party were howling by the time she was done, Wahoa almost literally.

Christopher got the mike. "I've had no choice but to know Jeff all my life." Lots of A-C chuckles for this. "But if I'd been able to pick the person who I'd go through everything with, risk my life every day with, and even fight with, I couldn't have found anybody better than Jeff, even if I'd searched through two solar systems." I heard sniffles from the audience. He closed his eyes for a moment. I took a fast look—Martini was trying not to lose it.

Christopher opened his eyes. "Jeff, I've told this to Kitty, but I don't think I've ever been man enough to say it to you. You're more than my cousin, more than a brother, even. You're the best friend I've ever had and many times a better friend than I deserved, and . . . I love you."

People were sobbing. I was teary. Martini was really trying not to lose it. So was Christopher. He took a deep breath. "She's the greatest girl, Jeff, and you're perfect with her and for her. You make each other better, and you make other people better, me especially, because of how you are together. And if anyone was going to come along and force me to share you, I thank God every day it was Kitty."

I joined the rest of the audience and started sobbing. Martini got up and hugged Christopher. I knew they were both shedding the manly tears while I was busy wiping my eyes on the tablecloth. They separated, and Martini pulled me up and we did the group hug thing that was so popular among the A-Cs. I heard more sobs.

"You two are just a couple of softies, you know that."

They both laughed and kissed my cheeks, at the same time. More unison stuff. I didn't mind this kind of unison at all, though.

No one wanted to follow Christopher's act, so we were mercifully done with the toasts. Next up was the cake, which we did have. I had no idea if Reader had already ordered it or if Pierre had come through again, but either way, it was great—chocolate with white buttercream frosting. No figurines on it, just the symbol for eternity on top. It was a real piece of artwork, not food. Apparently an A-C custom—we would keep it somewhere in our home at all times. I thought it was romantic. I was getting big on the romantic feelings.

Cut the cake, Jeff (ha!) did not do the smash it in the face thing, further proof I'd picked the right guy. Then it was time for the first dance.

We had a deejay and a karaoke machine. I had reservations about the karaoke but decided not to worry until I had to. The deejay looked familiar. I got closer. "Pierre?"

"MC Peterman here, darling. Oooh, is this our lucky groom? It was hard to get a clear view while you two were practicing for the Boston Marathon."

"Yes. Jeff, this is Pierre, uh, Peter, uh, the Peterman. My hairdresser from today. And the guy who found the people to do my veil and get the flowers and probably other things James needed."

"Like a decent deejay, darling."

Martini—Jeff—stuck out his hand. "Nice to meet you."

"Kitty, darling, I understand why you're hanging your hat with this one. Charmed, Jeff. I'd shake, but I must keep the tunes going. Darlings, did we have a special 'our song' for the first dance?"

We looked at each other. "Uh, no."

"Leaving that one to Jimmy too, were we?"

"No, just didn't think about it. It's been kind of whirlwind."

Martini got a funny look on his face. He let go of my hand and walked around the equipment to whisper something in Pierre's ear. "Oooh, darling, are you sure?" Martini whispered again. "Ahhh . . . no, darling, no more explanations needed. I'm sure our darling girl will swoon."

Martini led me to the dance floor. Reader had the mike and was doing the usual emcee stuff to get everyone around to watch us dance. The music started, and it was a song I knew well also—"Angel" by Aerosmith.

Martini pulled me into his arms and led me in a slow dance that worked well with the song's rhythm. I didn't know the dance, but it didn't matter—I had no problem following his lead, and all I wanted was to be in his arms, anyway. My throat was tight again. "You are my angel," he whispered to me. "I promise I'll never let my jealousy keep us unhappy and apart, even for an hour. And I want you to know—every word of this song is how I feel about you." Pierre called that right—I did almost swoon.

All things end, and awesome rock songs sooner than you want them to. The music died away.

Reader was back on the mike. "Normally we'd do the parents' dance right now, but we like to mess it up around here. So I thought we'd play our team's official song." I looked at him, hoping he caught my WTF expression. Then "Keepin' it Gangsta" by Fabolous and a bunch of other rappers came on. I started to howl.

"I don't get this song," Martini said within three chords.

"You're so street, Jeff, and you don't get it? Let me show you how we roll downtown." I stepped back from him a bit and went into some hip-hop moves I could do in my dress. Tim and Reader joined me on either side. A-Cs might have it over us in speed, but we could out hip their hop without any problem.

Christopher and Gower joined us and stood next to Martini. "This is half of Alpha Team, you realize that?" Christopher asked.

"Yeah, and we're gonna teach the three of you how to dance like this, too."

Christopher and Gower shook their heads. Martini grinned. "Move on over, Tim." He moved next to me and started doing the same hip-hop moves we were.

"You really can dance to anything, Jeff." I found this ability a major turn-on.

He grinned. "Anything I can do to keep you happy."

Song ended, we got a round of applause. Now it was time for the parents to come on and dance with us. Dad and I danced to "Thank Heaven for Little Girls" by good old Maurice Chevalier, Martini and his mother danced to "The Perfect Fan" by the Backstreet Boys, then I danced with Alfred while Martini danced with my mother to "What a Wonderful

World" by Louis Armstrong. Then the parents danced with their spouses, and I was back with Martini, dancing to Sting's "Fields of Gold."

The rest of the guests started to join in, wedding party first, then the couples split up and started dancing with their real mates. Reader and Gower pulled Queen Renata in to dance with them.

Pierre moved the song into Sting's "When We Dance." Martini pulled me closer, and I leaned my head on his chest. "You really don't regret marrying an alien?"

I nuzzled closer. "Nope. Have a hard time sleeping without a double-heartbeat right next to me."

The music ended and Reader had the mike again. "We have a little thing we'd like to do for the bride . . . and to remind the groom to never get complacent." He was grinning, and I got a little nervous.

They put chairs for us at the end of the dance floor farthest from the deejay. Then the karaoke machine was fired up. Reader jerked his head, and he wasn't alone up there any more—Christopher, Chuckie, Gower, Brian, all my flyboys, Tim, and Tito were there with him.

"Hit it," Reader said, and the song started—Elton John's "Kiss the Bride." I started the laughing that so easily turns into hysterics.

Reader had a great voice, and he could really move, too. I found myself wondering why he hadn't gone for a musical career. The rest of the guys were joining in, all on the chorus, some on more of the song. Hearing all of them sing out, "I wanna kiss the bride" was pretty funny and darned flattering and also kind of embarrassing. I risked a look at Martini. He appeared to be vacillating between shock and amusement, but he didn't look upset. The rest of the guests were enjoying it, if the cheers were any indication.

During the musical solo portion of the music, Reader pulled me out of my chair and handed me off to Christopher. Got a peck on the lips, passed to Gower, same thing. Next to Tim, then to Brian, Jerry, Joe, Randy, Walker, Hughes, and Tito, who handed me off to Chuckie. Got the requisite peck on the lips and a wink. Then I was spun back to Reader for the last part of the song. He twirled me up next to him, arm tight around my waist. Dipped me at the end of the song and gave me the final peck on the lips.

Thunderous applause as he brought me up. I hugged him around his neck. "James, that was awesome. Everyone was great, but you were fabulous."

He grinned. "Glad you liked it. Think Jeff's gonna kill me?"

"Nah," Martini said from behind me. "You all got your last kisses from her." He looked over at Pierre. "MC Peterman, you have a tango in there anywhere?"

"Of course, darling, I have everything."

The beat started up, and Martini moved me into the alien tango. Since the first time he'd danced with me like this I'd loved it. The dance was wild, sexy, and enthralling. And, as always, by the time the dance was over and my chest was pressed against his, my body curved back, with one of his arms on my upper back and the other pressing my pelvis against his, I was ready to go over the edge.

"Now *I* get to kiss the bride," he said, his voice dropped down to a purr. He pulled me up and covered my mouth with his. Everyone was still there, I could sort of hear them, heard the music change to "Your Body is a Wonderland" by John Mayer, but the only thing I was aware of was Martini's kiss.

We finally had to break apart to do the bouquet and garter stuff. Kimmie ran a new bouquet to me, a little safer for throwing over my head, while I discussed things with the photographer, also known as Mister Joel Oliver. It was the first time I'd actually seen him, but he insisted he'd caught pretty much everything.

"Pictures are going to be amazing," he said cheerfully. "The video should be particularly good."

"I don't think I want to know. But glad you're enjoying yourself."

He grinned. "Scoop of the year, at least this half of it. Royalty, huh?"

"That's the rumor."

"I'll take it. It flies better than the truth."

"It is the truth."

Oliver winked at me. "Sure it is. Now, let's keep the events moving."

The single gals were all behind me, so I decided to get back to having fun. Pierre played Madonna's "Material Girl" while we got ready, and I did a couple of fake tosses for Oliver and also because hearing the shrieking behind me never got old. Did a mighty fling back there and spun around to see who would come up with it. Tim's girlfriend, Alicia, was the lucky winner. She blushed bright red, and he grinned, while the other guys did the ribbing thing.

Next it was garter time. Back in a chair on the dance floor, Pierre spinning the stripper music. Martini went down on one knee and slowly slid my dress up to a ton of hooting, cheering, and catcalls. He gave me a wicked grin, then ran his tongue up my leg and pulled the garter off with his teeth. I managed not to have a screaming orgasm from this, but it required more self-control than I was normally able to exert. He knew it, too, and looked extremely pleased with himself.

Martini's turn to do the fake tossing a few times, then for real. Since the guy who caught the garter would put it on the bouquet winner's leg, Tim was doing his best to catch it. However, going into outer space apparently gave you the edge, and being an A-C meant he could really jump, and Michael Gower came down with the garter in hand.

He enjoyed putting it on Alicia, but then he had the whole "you're getting married next" thing explained to him. Offered to do the toss over again. Entire crowd said no in unison. Tim explained that Michael wasn't marrying his girl, and much more hilarity that's only funny when you're there ensued.

More dancing, mostly slow songs, and Martini and I made out through most of them. It truly was the best reception ever.

CHAPTER 74

SOMEWHERE ALONG IN THE NIGHT the dance floor got crowded enough that no one was paying attention to us any more, and Martini took my hand and led me off to the side.

Reader joined us, carrying my veil. "I have the gate scheduled for noon tomorrow."

Martini nodded. "Sounds good."

"Girlfriend, unless you want to take it with you, I'll get your bouquet preserved."

"Anything you're not taking care of for me?"

He grinned. "Only the wedding night and honeymoon. You two are on your own for those."

"I think we can handle it." Martini hugged Reader. "Thanks, James. For everything." They patted each other's backs in that man way, then Martini put his arm around my waist.

"James . . ." I moved away from Martini and hugged Reader tightly. "I don't have any gift for you." That wasn't everything I wanted to say to him, but all the things I wanted to say I didn't want to share with anyone else, not even Martini.

He hugged me back. "It's okay. This working out is the best present." He kissed the side of my head and whispered in my ear, "Now Paul and I can get married, too, you know. I do have some skin in this game."

"You'd have done it if you hadn't."

"Sure, but I'm not completely altruistic. Bring me back something nice from Cabo. It'll give you two a reason to get out of the bedroom—shop for your wedding party while you're on your honeymoon."

I laughed. "Will do." I kissed his cheek and whispered in his ear. "I love you, James. Thank you for always being there for me."

We finally broke apart, Martini put his arm back around my waist, and Reader hustled us off in the middle of a particularly popular song, "Pennsylvania 6-5000" by Glenn Miller. Why this song had brought all the guests to their feet I couldn't say, but they all, young and old, seemed to be loving it.

We got out into the foyer, and Martini cocked his head at me. "So, you want to hit the tables before we hit the room?"

I was kind of surprised at the offer. "Erm . . . well . . ."

He grinned. "That's a yes, isn't it?"

"You don't mind? You're not hurt?"

"Nope. You've wanted to gamble since we got here. And dressed like this, you should be Lady Luck personified." He scooped me up and carried me off. We got a lot of looks, lots of comments, all of them funny or nice. We continued on into the casino, where we got more looks, several rounds of applause, and a lot of positive catcalls.

Martini spotted a somewhat empty craps table and set me down there.

"Lady shooter!" the stickman called. "Just married lady shooter!" He slid the dice to me, as the table started to fill up. Martini tossed some cash down, but he stood behind me.

Did the thing my Nana had taught me, moved the dice to show seven, tapped them against the table three times, and rolled.

"Seven! Winner!" A lot of chips were shoved toward me. Whoops. I'd had all of Martini's money on the pass line. Thank God I'd rolled decently.

"Jeff, can you handle the betting? As in, get most of that money off the table?"

He laughed and reached down and put a more reasonable number of chips on the pass line.

Did the dice thing again, got another seven. Table started to get excited and loud, more people shoved over and in. Rolled another five sevens in a row. Started to wonder if Martini was using hyperspeed on the dice but decided not to care. I was winning back a small portion of the vast sums he'd spent on our wedding and felt pretty darned good about it.

"Go shooter!" The voice was familiar. I looked at the other end of the table. My grandparents, all four of them, were there.

Nana Sadie laughed at my expression. "Taught her everything she knows about the dice, folks. Roll 'em, kitten!"

Shrugged, did the dice thing, got an eleven this time. "Winner! Lady Luck at the table tonight," the stickman called out.

Rolled again, finally rolled a number. "Eight, the number is eight. Place your bets, ladies and gentlemen."

I avoided looking at the money on the table, particularly the money Martini was putting on and around. I wanted to stay in the zone. Dice slid over to me, the stickman turned them to double fours for me. Did the tap, tossed the dice. Got the hard eight. The table went nuts.

I ended up rolling for over forty-five minutes. Finally crapped out and apologized. Had chips tossed to me from most of the table. Nana Sadie got the dice next, held onto them for fifteen minutes. The gambling force was strong in my family. Interestingly, Martini had pulled most of our money off the table both for my last roll and Nana's. "Table's cold," he said in my ear.

I didn't argue, just gathered up our chips, gave the dealers each a nice tip, then we left the table. My grandparents followed our lead. "Where to next?" Nono Dom asked.

I looked around. We were near a roulette table. I never played roulette unless I wanted to sit down. "Go ahead," Martini said.

I shrugged and put some chips down on double zero. It was the longest shot around, but I didn't care. Nana Sadie and Nona Maria followed suit.

I watched the wheel spin with no expectations of winning. I realized I'd dropped more money down than I'd planned. Martini stroked my neck. The ball stopped. Double zero. The screaming was loud, especially from my grandmothers. I stood there in shock. Martini nudged me. "Get your chips, baby."

I did, and they had to exchange them for the pretty black chips because I couldn't carry what I had. I looked up at Martini. "I want to cash out now."

He grinned. "You sure?"

"I'm all over the stopping while we're ahead thing."

My grandparents were all for keeping us around, as were several other folks. But I'd had a great time for a little over an hour, made the most money gambling in my life, and wanted to get up to the room and rip Martini's clothes off. I kissed and hugged the grandparents good-bye, and then we cashed out.

I'd won several thousand dollars. Tried not to squeal and jump up and down. Failed.

I handed the money to Martini. He pushed it back. We did this for a bit. "Jeff, I have nowhere to put it unless I stuff it in my chest."

He got the jungle cat smile. "I'll put it there for you."

I snuggled up to him. "Later. In about five minutes later. Put the money away in your wallet. Please?"

He did as asked. "Well, it's all yours now anyway." He took my hand, and we walked through the casino back to our elevator.

"Jeff? Did you . . . do anything . . . to help me win?"

He laughed. "No, baby, I didn't use hyperspeed or anything else. Gambling is luck, but at the tables, craps in particular, much of it's how the person with the dice feels. Too scared, nervous, or overconfident usually means they'll crap out. I could tell when you and your grandmother felt the stress, and that meant you'd crap out the next roll. Everyone else at the table was worried they'd break the streak, meaning they would."

"What about the roulette wheel?

He grinned. "Again, I didn't do a thing. Nerves have nothing to do with roulette, either. You just picked wisely for that spin of the wheel." He nuzzled my ear. "I told you—you're personifying Lady Luck right now."

We got into the elevator and made out the whole way up. Martini kissed me tenderly and stroked my bare skin with his fingertips until I was a puddle. We walked hand-in-hand to the room. He opened our door, then picked me up and carried me inside.

I gasped when I saw the room. It was loaded with flowers.

"You like them?"

"Oh my God, Jeff. Are these all from you?"

"Yeah. Just wanted to make our wedding night special."

I grabbed his face and kissed him. "Just being with you makes it special, Jeff."

He nuzzled my neck. "Always like to be sure." His tongue traced my skin, right where my shoulder met my neck, and I started to moan. He smiled against my skin. "How long is it going to take to get you unbuttoned?"

"Probably longer than we want," I managed to gasp out.

He set me down. "Guess I can't chase you, then."

"Maybe later. You'll like what's under the dress, anyway."

"Mmmm, I love what's under the dress." He turned me around and started unbuttoning. "Wow, called this one right. Good thing I'm doing this now." He slid his thumbs down my spine and I gasped. It took him a little while, but he got the dress unbuttoned to about the middle of my bottom. Then he slid his hands around my waist, up my stomach, and cupped my breasts. I leaned back against him, my breathing heavy. He toyed with me for a bit. Once I was a puddle again, he picked me up and carried me into the bedroom.

He took his wallet out of the tuxedo jacket. I took off his boutonnière. "Don't take the tux off yet." He started the low growl that always sounded like a purr. I backed away and shimmied out of my dress. His purr got louder.

I turned around and hung my dress up. Turned back and he was right there, jungle cat look on his face. He picked me up by my waist and slammed our pelvises together. I wrapped my legs around his waist, and his mouth ravaged mine.

I was already moaning by the time we fell on the bed. He grabbed my wrists and held my hands captive up over my head. Then he proceeded to do one of the many things he did best—bring me to screaming orgasm at second base.

Martini let go of my wrists and slid my thong and shoes off. He left the garter belt and hose on. His hands slid up my legs. By the time he was at the middle of my thighs I was moaning and when his tongue followed I was back to my typical cat-in-heat yowl.

Lost count of the number of climaxes, couldn't think much or form coherent words to beg him to make love to me. He finally moved back up my body, and I managed to get his pants undone and him in my hands while he made sure my breasts didn't feel unloved or slighted in any way.

I was moaning and writhing under him. "What do you want, baby?" he whispered in my ear.

I'd been practicing for this moment. Had to get a whole sentence out, when one word was difficult because I was so far gone over the edge. "I want . . . my husband to make love to me."

He smiled and kissed me. "Can't refuse my wife's first official request." He slid into me—my head went back, my back arched, and I clutched at him. It was intense—wild and tender at the same time, and I was gone in a matter of moments.

"That's what I want," he purred against my neck. "Over and over again."

I obliged. I had no choice—everything he did made me want him more, and I was screaming and sobbing and begging him to stop and keep going all at the same time. We were slamming into each other, fast and furious, then he threw his head back and roared as he erupted inside me, and I flipped so far over the edge I almost passed out.

The feelings lasted for a long time, but finally our bodies quieted. Once my body stopped shuddering enough so I could walk, I undressed him and hung his clothes up. Then he took the garter belt and hose off me, so we were both fully naked. He slid us under the covers and made love to me again, for hours.

Just before dawn we wrapped around each other. "I never got time to buy you a wedding present," I murmured against his chest.

He kissed the top of my head. "You are my present. I got to unwrap you, too."

"Cabo tomorrow?"

"In a few hours."

"Goody."

Martini laughed softly. "Can't wait for it, myself. Go to sleep, baby. Tomorrow's the first day of our married life, and I want you rested so I can exhaust you."

I heaved a happy sigh. "I love being married to the alien sex god."

CHAPTER 75

"IT'S SO BEAUTIFUL HERE."

"Yeah. Glad we could get the same cabana as our first time, especially since we were six weeks earlier than I'd reserved."

"You passing the desk clerk an extra hundred probably didn't hurt."

Jeff laughed. I was managing to think of him as Jeff about fifty percent of the time on our honeymoon and was immensely proud of myself for it, too. "You weren't supposed to see that." I shrugged, and he purred. "Do that again." He buried his face in my breasts for a bit.

Finished that round of lovemaking. I was on my back and he was on his side, head leaning on his hand, while he stroked my skin lightly with his fingers. He had a funny look on his face.

"Jeff, are you okay?"

"Yeah. Just thinking."

"About what?"

"You. When we're going to have kids. That sort of stuff."

"You want them right away, don't you?"

He nodded. "Always have. Once I met you . . . I've always known I wanted you to be the mother of my children."

My throat felt tight. "Same here." I thought about it. Everything I'd done since I'd met him a year ago had been a step into the scary unknown. And, scary or not, everything had worked out all right in the end. "We can start trying right away if you want."

He didn't get the excited expression I expected. He still looked kind of funny. "I don't want you to feel rushed or frightened."

"I'm twenty-eight and you're thirty-one. We have to start sometime. Might as well have them while we're young enough to handle them. Besides, you're going to be the best daddy in the universe, so I'm not as afraid as I could be."

Mar- . . . Jeff smiled at me. "I hope so. You'll be a wonderful mother."

"Hope so." I wondered if he was worried about how the drugs that had enhanced his powers could affect our getting pregnant. "I'm sure we won't have any trouble."

"No. We won't." He sounded both sure and unconcerned, not breezy, but definite. He also seemed to be struggling with something.

"Jeff . . . is there something you need to tell me?" I tried not to get worried, and failed, as always.

He kissed me tenderly. "Yes. But it's not bad. At least, I don't think it's bad."

"Okay, so tell me." He took a deep breath. Opened his mouth, shut it, tried again, didn't work again. "Jeff, we're not making any progress here on the telling."

"I don't know how to tell you." He looked nervous and worried all of the sudden.

"Just blurt it out. Before I start freaking out."

"Yeah, don't want you getting upset." His fingers were running over my stomach. Normally he drew circles around my navel, but this time I could feel he was drawing the infinity sign. "Getting upset's not good for you. Especially . . ."

"Especially . . . what? Do I have some dread disease you're trying to tell me about?"

"No, not a disease." He kissed my forehead. "I just . . . I need to take care of you, baby, that's all."

"Why? Not that I'm arguing, but you always sort of take care of me. I take care of you, too. That's why we got married, remember?"

"Yeah. I'm glad we had to speed it up."

"Well, it might have been nice to have had a few more weeks to adjust, but it was all great, so I'm glad, too."

He shook his head. "No, I think we'll be happy for the extra adjustment time now."

"Back to totally cryptic. Would another girl get what's

going on and I'm just dense, or is it that you're not telling me anything that resembles a fact?"

He shrugged. "If I hadn't been drugged and had my powers altered, you'd probably be telling me, so maybe that's why it's confusing."

He was still tracing infinity on my stomach, and a stray bit of conversation I'd had with Reader months previously floated through my mind—something about me saying that Jeff would probably know I was pregnant before I would.

"Oh, uh, wow. When?" I wasn't excited or upset, I was in shock.

"Sometime when we were in Vegas, but before our wedding night."

"How do you know?"

"Since being drugged . . . I can sense the changes in your body. It's a big change."

I thought about it. We hadn't made love between him giving up the Alpha Four throne and our wedding night. Which meant . . . "You knew when we were fighting the invasion?"

"Yeah. I wasn't thrilled with how you got into the middle of the fight, I have to mention."

My throat felt tight again. "Is that why you gave up the throne?"

He snorted. "I gave it up because I love you, and there is no way in the world I'm living anywhere without you. You being pregnant with my child was added incentive." He kissed my forehead. "You know, I was sort of surprised you didn't realize it when the late and unlamented Adolphus said you'd failed the tests."

"I did fail."

He snorted again. "Uh, how, exactly, do you think conquering all the warriors sent to destroy us would be failure? The tests were to prove ability to lead and rule. You passed those better than I did."

"So what test did I fail?"

Jeff grinned at me. "Chastity."

"Oh." Duh.

"Believe me, I don't object at all. I knew whose baby you were carrying, though Adolphus might not have."

"I'm like a week and a half pregnant, does that count as carrying?"

"Does to me."

"Is that why you were and have been carrying me everywhere?"

"I love carrying you, but yeah."

"You're so sneaky with the taking care of."

"It's a gift." He kissed me, and we made love again. He was gentle and tender and loving. He murmured how he was going to take care of me and keep me safe against my skin, while I clung to him and let him carry me along to a mutual climax that was both soft and special, just for being when it was in our lives.

"You want to swim before dinner?" Jeff asked as he kissed my forehead.

"I'm still allowed to exercise?"

He laughed. "Yes. You already do all the good mommy-to-be things, other than your soda addiction, but we'll work on that slowly." I dreaded that but figured now wasn't the time to whine about how I didn't want to do without Coca-Cola products in my system.

"Okay, then, a swim sounds great." He pulled his trunks on, helped me into my bikini, then slathered the sunscreen on me. "Guess I shouldn't suggest racing you to the water this time."

Jeff stood up and lifted me into his arms. I wrapped my legs around him just like always. "No. Like everything else for the rest of our lives, we go together."

He kissed me, and I forgot about everything else . . . everything other than what we'd created together. We didn't make it to the water. We had other things to do, and I loved every moment of them.

Nothing in my life ever goes according to plan but, as my husband says, things always work out perfectly in the end.

Coming in December 2011
The fourth novel in the Alien series
from Gini Koch

ALIEN PROLIFERATION

Read on for a sneak preview

JEFF GLARED AT CHUCKIE AS HE WALKED IN. "Why are you still here?"

"Because we have a problem," Chuckie said. He wasn't looking at Jeff, or me, and he was still pacing.

Jeff somehow reined in the jealousy all on his own. Either he wanted to impress me or Chuckie's stress levels were particularly high. I figured on the latter. He shot a worried glance at Chuckie then looked at me. "With the C.I.A.?"

"In a way. More with what you were doing in Paris."

Jeff nodded. "Whatever we were fighting, they weren't superbeings."

I felt all proud. "See, Chuckie? Someone other than us was monitoring the weird."

Chuckie heaved a sigh. "And that makes it better how?"

"Pardon me, Mister Glass Half Empty."

"It doesn't," Jeff agreed. "We have nothing left to study."

"You weren't able to contain them any other way?" Chuckie asked.

"No. We weren't the ones who destroyed them."

Chuckie spun so fast I was worried he'd fall over. "Explain that, please."

Jeff sighed. "It looked like normal clustered activity, only there were no emotional warnings whatsoever. There were a dozen of them. We were barely able to contain them, but they destroyed no significant property and, as far as we can tell, no one was killed."

"That's not normal at all." Every superbeing was a destruction machine and their overriding desire was to kill any humanity in their vicinity.

"Right, baby, it's not. We herded them to the Seine—we were going to use self-contained nukes to destroy them. Right before I could give the order, they all blew up. At the same time."

"I monitor for super-soldier projects all the time," Chuckie said. "So does your mother. Nothing like this has come up on either of our radars."

"If the lie is good enough, and the support is high enough…"

"Yeah, that's what's really worrying me."

"How trustworthy are your superiors?"

He chuckled. "They're top in the C.I.A. How trustworthy do you think that would make them?"

Jeff snorted. "Not at all." Chuckie shrugged and managed a grin.

"I meant for you, for us, for the safety of the U.S. and the world. That kind of thing?"

"They seem reliable. Your mother doesn't trust them overly much, but she trusts them more than some." He looked thoughtful. "There was a shake-up right before I became head of the ET division."

"Any of our four friends involved in that?"

He nodded. "Cooper and Cantu for certain. Cooper wasn't promoted, Cantu was." He shook his head. "I'll need to discuss this with your mother."

"She's on alert, just waiting for the baby. You should be able to get a hold of her easily enough. But I'm kind of curious why and how the people we met with today, who shouldn't have known anything about this, knew all about the attack, when none of us did."

Jeff's eyes narrowed. "Who shouldn't have known?"

"A senator, a Pentagon liaison, the head of one of our terrorist units, and John Cooper," Chuckie replied. "Cooper's angling for my job."

"He's a prick," I added. "Not that I liked any of them much."

Chuckie nodded. "I'd really hoped to have both of you at this meeting, and White, too, if possible. I need these people read."

"Sorry, busy trying to stop an international incident. Christopher's still there—the imageering alterations necessary are unreal."

"Why are you back already?" I asked. "Normally you'd be taking care of the cleanup portions.

Jeff shot me a "duh" look. "I knew who you were with."

Chuckie rolled his eyes. "Just the two of us and four people we can't trust at all."

"Am I right that all four hate you and want Centaurion turned into the War Division?" It was such a safe bet—most people were intimidated by Chuckie's brains, drive, and success and channeled that into hating on him. And there was a much longer list of those who wanted us to be the War Division than those who didn't. Every day it seemed like the ones who didn't got fewer and fewer.

"In a nutshell." Chuckie sounded like he always did when talking about people who didn't like him—resigned. I knew there was hurt under there, too, but he hid it well.

Jeff looked like he was going to say something nasty to Chuckie, but I glared at him and he stopped himself. Possibly he'd picked up the hurt, too, but I wasn't sure if he cared about it. "But are they in any position to be in on whatever the hell is going on?" he asked instead.

Chuckie nodded slowly. "It's possible. I wouldn't put anything past Cooper. He wants my job, and every job above mine, too. Cantu's a slippery bastard. And Anderson's your typical politician on the rise. Cartwright I'm not sure of, but she works closely with the three of them."

There was a knock at the door and Wayne and William came in. "We have what you wanted, Mister Reynolds," William said, handing him a file. Wayne handed one to Jeff.

"That was fast."

The brothers grinned at me as Jeff and Chuckie both sighed at me and shook their heads. "Hyperspeed," Wayne said.

"Oh." Okay, had to give Jeff and Chuckie the "duh" on that one. I chalked it up to another Space Cadet moment and called the Poofs over to make myself feel better. I petted the cuteness bundles while Chuckie and Jeff both read through the files.

"Good work," Chuckie said finally. "I wish I could get field reports from my operatives this well-detailed."

Wayne and William looked pleased, but then they both looked at Jeff. He nodded. "Lots of good information here, thank you." Both brothers visibly relaxed. "I appreciate the notes from the C.I.A. meeting, too."

"We recorded it as well, Commander," William said, "per Mister Reynolds' request."

Jeff raised his eyebrow at Chuckie. "You tape everyone?"

"Just everyone I don't trust. I'd like a copy of the recording." Jeff nodded and William pulled out his phone.

"Coming down to you now, sir," he said, hanging up.

Chuckie heaved a sigh. "I don't think we have enough to go on definitively yet, but I'll work on it."

"It's the holidays. You're allowed time off. The rest of your agency's taking their two weeks, why not you?"

Chuckie shook his head. "You know the saying—evil never sleeps."

"Yeah, too true." I yawned. Wow. Nap time already. In addition to the other joys, I got tired out much more quickly these days.

Jeff opened his mouth but Chuckie beat him to it. "I'm going to get back to my office. I'll be in touch on this, and I expect the same from you if you hit on anything. You get some rest, Kitty. Gentlemen, Martini," he said with a nod. He whistled softly and Fluffy jumped up onto my shoulder, purred, rubbed, and then leaped onto Chuckie's shoulder, did the purr and rub thing, then snuggled into his pocket. I managed to refrain from saying how adorable this was, but it took real effort.

Before Chuckie could leave, William's phone rang. He put up his hand. "Yes, got it." He hung up. "Commander Martini, we have an issue with the recorded copy Mister Reynolds requested."

"And that is?" Jeff asked.

William looked grim. "All the recordings have been destroyed."

That sat on the air for a moment. "How?" I asked finally.

He shook his head. "We don't know. All recordings for the past week have been corrupted, the ones from today are completely gone."

"Internal sabotage," Chuckie said, and from his tone, he was certain. "Not good. Any clues as to who did it?"

"No, sir," William said. "Commander White's ordered a full investigation."

"It'll have to do." Chuckie didn't look happy, and I couldn't blame him. I also couldn't control another yawn. "I'll add this to the pile of things we need to know about. Please guard those reports—you two are the only proof we have now that something was wrong with those superbeings."

"Yes, sir," Wayne said with a small smile. "We'll guard them with our lives."

Chuckie managed a short laugh. "Good job."

Jeff seemed to be struggling with something. "I'll walk you out," he said finally. "You two, take down the equipment."

They left while William and Wayne did as instructed. "You didn't give me a file," I mentioned.

Wayne laughed. "We're already clear you wouldn't read it." He grinned and put a folder into my nightstand. "Here's a copy for later, though. You know, when you get around to it. In about a year."

"Wow, you *are* good. So, what's the CliffsNotes version?"

They both looked at me blankly for a moment. A-Cs were capable of reading at hyperspeed, too, so why read an abbreviated version? William recovered first. "You want the highlights, Commander?"

"Please and thank you."

"We think they're genetically engineered," Wayne said. "But there's no human in there."

"That we can tell," William added. "Didn't feel like there's parasite in there, either."

"That we can tell," Wayne said. "They didn't feel…right."

"Robotic?"

"Could be," Wayne allowed. "But if so, it's a more natural robot."

"Like an android?"

William shrugged. "Could be. We don't really work with this side of things. Kill 'em, get the folks to safety, that's our normal assignment."

"Why are you doing live at the exciting scene of my bedroom, then?"

They exchanged a quick glance. "Ah, special assignment," William said.

That meant either they were being punished or they were hand-selected. "Assigned by whom?"

"Commander White," William answered.

So, handpicked. Unless Christopher was really interested in seeing how my space cadet ways messed with their minds. I voted for the former. "Why you two?"

Wayne's turn to shrug. "We're really good. Commander White doesn't trust the C.I.A. any more than any of the rest of us do."

"So, what did he have you read on Chuckie?"

They both busied themselves with the screens. I doubted these two were going to fall into the "able to lie to us" category.

"Dudes, don't make me pull rank. What were you monitoring Chuckie for?"

"Whatever he might be hiding," Wayne said.

"Chuckie's not hiding something from us."

"Everybody's hiding something, Commander," Wayne said as Jeff came back in, accompanied by several other A-Cs who were clearly along to help with clearing out the video stuff. "Everybody. But not always for the same reasons."

Gini Koch lives in the American Southwest, works her butt off (sadly, not literally) by day, and writes by night with the rest of the beautiful people. She lives with her husband and daughter, three dogs (aka The Canine Death Squad), and four cats (aka The Killer Kitties). When she's not writing, Gini spends her time going to rock concerts with her daughter, teaching her pets to "bring it," and driving her husband insane asking, "Have I told you about this story idea yet?" You can reach her via her website (www.ginikoch.com), email (gini@ginikoch.com), Twitter (@GiniKoch), or Facebook (facebook.com/Gini.Koch).

Gini Koch

The Alien *Novels*

"This delightful romp has many interesting twists and
turns as it glances at racism, politics, and religion en route.
Darned amusing." —*Booklist* (starred review)

"Kitty's evolution from marketing manager to member of
a secret government unit is amusing and interesting
...a hilarious romp in the vein of 'Men in Black' or
'Ghostbusters'." —*Voya*

TOUCHED BY AN ALIEN
978-0-7564-0600-4

ALIEN TANGO
978-0-7564-0632-5

To Order Call: 1-800-788-6262
www.dawbooks.com

Seanan McGuire

The October Daye Novels

"...will surely appeal to readers who enjoy my books, or those of Patrica Briggs." —*Charlaine Harris*

"Well researched, sharply told, highly atmospheric and as brutal as any pulp detective tale, this promising start to a new urban fantasy series is sure to appeal to fans of Jim Butcher or Kim Harrison."—*Publishers Weekly*

ROSEMARY AND RUE
978-0-7564-0571-7
A LOCAL HABITATION
978-0-7564-0596-0
AN ARTIFICIAL NIGHT
978-0-7564-0626-4
LATE ECLIPSES
978-0-7564-0666-0

To Order Call: 1-800-788-6262
www.dawbooks.com

DAW 142

Tanya Huff

The Confederation Novels

"As a heroine, Kerr shines. She is cut from the same mold
as Ellen Ripley of the *Aliens* films. Like her heroine,
Huff delivers the goods." —*SF Weekly*

A CONFEDERATION OF VALOR
Omnibus Edition
(Valor's Choice, The Better Part of Valor)
978-0-7564-0399-7

THE HEART OF VALOR
978-0-7564-0481-9

VALOR'S TRIAL
978-0-7564-0557-1

THE TRUTH OF VALOR
978-0-7564-0620-2

To Order Call: 1-800-788-6262
www.dawbooks.com

Jim Hines

The Jig the Goblin series

"Clever satire… Reminiscent of Terry Pratchett and
Robert Asprin at their best."
—*Romantic Times*

"If you've always kinda rooted for the little guy, even
maybe had a bit of a place in your heart for Gollum,
rather than the Boromirs and Gandalfs of the world,
pick up Goblin Quest."
—*The SF Site*

"This exciting adult fairy tale is filled with adventure
and action, but the keys to the fantasy are Jig and the
belief that the mythological creatures are real in the
realm of Jim C. Hines."
—*Midwest Book Review*

"A rollicking ride, enjoyable from beginning to end…
Jim Hines has just become one of my must-read
authors." —Julie E. Czerneda

GOBLIN QUEST   978-07564-0400-0
GOBLIN HERO   978-07564-0442-0
GOBLIN WAR   978-07564-0493-2

To Order Call: 1-800-788-6262
www.dawbooks.com

DAW 100

Once upon a time...

Cinderella, whose real name is Danielle
Whiteshore, did marry Prince Armand.
And their wedding was a dream come true.

But not long after the "happily ever after,"
Danielle is attacked by her stepsister Charlotte,
who suddenly has all sorts of magic to call upon.
And though Talia the martial arts master—
otherwise known as Sleeping Beauty—
comes to the rescue, Charlotte gets away.

That's when Danielle discovers a number of disturbing facts: Armand has been kidnapped; Danielle is
pregnant; and the Queen has her own Secret Service
that consists of Talia and Snow (White, of course).
Snow is an expert at mirror magic and heavy-duty
flirting. Can the princesses track down Armand and
rescue him from the clutches of some of
Fantasyland's most nefarious villains?

The Stepsister Scheme
by Jim C. Hines
978-0-7564-0532-8

"Do we look like we need to be rescued?"

DAW 130